Alexander grinned.
Ah, life is sweet!

He hadn't had a pretty woman to look at in a mighty long time. Having her around was definitely better than being alone.

But he didn't like those newfangled contraptions like this one was wearing that showed every curve and too much skin. He preferred those ruffled and lacy things that women wore back in his day. Made a man long to peel away the layers to find the sweetness beneath.

Just the thought of it made him slink down to the floor and bury his head in his hands. If he could shed a tear, he would. Damn, he missed being alive. He hadn't touched a woman in a hundred very, very long years.

Amanda. He silently whispered his lover's name. *Oh, darlin'. Do you think this is the one? Do you think this woman can get me out of this place and back into your arms where I belong?*

Other Avon Contemporary Romances by
Patti Berg

WISHES COME TRUE

Patti Berg

TILL THE END OF TIME

AVON BOOKS NEW YORK

This is a work of fiction. Names, characters, places, and incidents either are the product of the author's imagination or are used fictitiously. Any resemblance to actual events, locales, organizations, or persons, living or dead, is entirely coincidental and beyond the intent of either the author or the publisher.

AVON BOOKS
A division of
The Hearst Corporation
1350 Avenue of the Americas
New York, New York 10019

Published by arrangement with the author
Visit our website at **http://AvonBooks.com**
Library of Congress Catalog Card Number: 96-95165
ISBN: 0-380-78339-8

First Avon Books Printing: June 1997

Printed in the U.S.A.

RAI 10 9 8 7 6 5 4 3 2 1

For Bob and Melanie—
the magic in my life.

And to Jenny and Luann for their laughter,
encouragement, and friendship.

Chapter 1

An icy wind snaked its way along the main street of Sapphire, Montana, a swirl of powdered snow following in its wake. It slithered uneasily around the old, abandoned hotel, past the ornamental hitching posts in front of the First National Bank, slowly meandering across the road and up the steps, circling about the boots of the man standing in the doorway of the Tin Cup Cafe.

Jonathan Winchester shivered in the cold, turning up the collar of his rawhide and lamb's wool coat to ward off the bitter January chill. He tucked his chin into the fleece hugging his neck and let the brim of his Stetson shield his face from a sudden blast of frosty air. But his eyes didn't turn away from the cold; instead, they stayed focused on the snow-and-mud-crusted red Jeep Cherokee sliding to a stop in front of the Sapphire Hotel.

The new owner had finally arrived. Crazy woman! For the life of him, Jon couldn't imagine why anyone would buy that old hotel unless they'd been sold a damn fine bill of goods by that cousin of his. Wouldn't be the first time Matt had sold a worthless piece of property; wouldn't be the last.

But the Sapphire Hotel? Hell, it was nothing more than a hundred-and-ten-year-old relic of the town's better days. It hadn't been fit for human occupancy in half a century and would be better off torn down, or left empty and uninhabited—at least, by anything human. Jon laughed at his thought, and a cloud formed in front of his face from the warmth of his breath. He'd dispensed with thinking the house might be haunted when he was a kid. He didn't believe in ghosts. And he never would—not again.

But a movement in the hotel's third-story window drew his attention, bringing all the old memories back to the surface, and he gave in to those thoughts for just a brief moment. He looked upward, to the top of the weatherbeaten building. The remnants of a tattered pair of curtains swayed gently behind the broken glass. Only the wind, he decided. He hadn't expected anything else—not a phantom, not a spirit, not a lost soul haunting the upstairs rooms. Only the wind. Yet that one small movement made him wonder anew if what had happened all those years ago might have been real.

Again he laughed, pushing the thoughts away, and turned his attention to the movement inside the Jeep. Through the fog-coated driver's side window he could just barely make out the woman's form, could see her struggling into a parka and pulling a hood over her head.

Leaning a shoulder against the jamb, he watched as the car door cracked open, then whipped out of the woman's hands in the force of another burst of wind. She quickly reached out and grabbed the handle, stopping the door before it broke from its hinges, but the force of the gale yanked her body halfway out of the vehicle, and she held on tightly to the handle for balance. A knee-high red leather boot swung from the car, then another, both heels digging into the ice-and-snow-crusted ground before the warmly bundled driver climbed out.

Jon grinned as he watched her struggling against the wind and snow and the heavy door. Somehow she shoved it closed, slipping on the ice, catching hold of the handle again to keep from falling to the ground. She labored to stand up straight, and Jon gave a moment's thought to offering her help. It seemed wrong to stand and stare, to laugh at her expense. But, hell! She was wearing hooker boots in the middle of winter. What was she thinking? They might be practical on some sleazy big-city street corner, but they had no business on the icy roads of Sapphire.

No, Jon would rather stand back and watch, laughing softly to himself.

The humor disappeared, though, the moment the hood she wore blew away from her face, revealing a woman Jon thought he'd seen before—in his dreams. He'd seen her in books, too, in oil paintings by the Old Masters, in marble statues—a goddess with ebony hair; high, noble cheekbones; sensuous red lips. Damn! Even a blind man could caress the planes of her face and see her beauty.

Jon didn't believe in love at first sight any more than he believed in ghosts, but he knew instinctively he'd been waiting for this woman all his life. She was the woman he'd wanted to sculpt, the woman whose curves he'd wanted to study and mold. The woman whose beauty he'd longed to have stretched out, naked, on a chaise in his studio.

Slowly, methodically, he moved away from the cafe's door to the edge of the snow-dusted boardwalk. He watched her even more closely as she rounded the car, one hand on the hood for support to keep from sliding on the treacherous pavement.

Tall. Very tall, especially in those heels. She had great legs, too, encased in black knit pants that hugged her right up to her thighs. Then, unfortunately, the body he could picture just in his mind disappeared under that furry red parka.

Only a greenhorn would wear a get-up like that in the harsh Montana winter. She should be wearing heavily treaded boots, at least until she could learn how to walk on the frozen ground. On second thought, he was beginning to like those three-inch spiked heels. Again he thought about that imaginary woman on the chaise in his studio, but this time she wasn't completely naked. No, that red leather hugged her ankles and calves and stopped just at her knees. The rest of her porcelain-skinned body radiated in the natural light that beamed from all corners of his solitary turret.

It didn't seem possible that a stranger could mesmerize him so, but she had. Much, much more than any woman he'd ever known.

Jon sucked in a deep breath of icy air, letting it out slowly as he studied her movements, just as he would study any other being he planned to sketch and mold. He'd sculpted eagles and mountain men, grizzlies and buffalo, but he'd never created a woman in bronze.

But he would.

Soon.

* * *

Elizabeth Fitzgerald ground her spiked heels into the snow and ice at the base of the hotel's steps and tilted her head upward, using her hand to block the wind from her eyes as she inspected the ancient structure. Gingerbread dripped from the overhangs on all three levels, and scallops of wood rimmed the windows and embellished the facade of the once proud Victorian. Salmon paint had flaked off the walls, forest green stiles were missing from the porch railing that wrapped around the building, and where the roof wasn't covered with six inches of snow, loose shingles hung haphazardly on the steepled slopes.

So, this is the hotel that brother of mine talked me into buying. Elizabeth shook her head and sighed deeply, wondering what kind of mess Eric had gotten her into this time. She took another quick look and smiled. At least the old place was standing—something she couldn't say about the house she'd left behind in Los Angeles.

She put a hand on the wobbly banister and inched her way up the stairs of her new home. It was far from the picture of perfection her brother had painted of a Victorian masterpiece. "You'll love it, Ellie," he'd told her. "It's the perfect place for those antiques you love to buy. We'll turn it into a country inn and you can test your gourmet food out on someone other than me."

Eric's excitement had rung out loud and clear. She'd heard his words, gotten caught up in his enthusiasm, and given him the money to buy the place without checking it out herself.

In other words, she'd been irresponsible—just

like her brother. "Don't worry, Ellie," Eric had said. "Matt Winchester told me once the place was refurbished, he'd keep the rooms filled with paying guests. It won't take much to get it into shape. A little paint. Some cleaning. We can have it up and running in no time."

Elizabeth looked around her again, taking note of all the obvious things that needed repair or replacement. Without a doubt, she knew she'd definitely made a mistake. And the biggest mistake of all was believing Eric would really join her in Sapphire, Montana, population 372.

The words Eric had uttered to her months after she'd bought the hotel and weeks after she'd closed her photography business rang out strong in her mind, too. "Sorry, Ellie. I can't go with you. I'm getting married." A week ago she'd smiled and thrown rice, and tried to feel good about starting a new life in a new town. It was one of the promises she'd made the year before; it was one of the promises she wouldn't forget. Eric had a new life now, and she, apparently, had one, too.

Only, Elizabeth hadn't planned on being alone.

In the cold.

In the middle of nowhere.

She took a deep breath of the frigid air and climbed ten creaking stairsteps that led to the expansive covered porch surrounding the Victorian. She ran a gloved hand over the railing and pictured a fresh coat of forest green paint glistening in the summer sunlight. Maybe Eric was right; maybe all it needed was a little cleaning, some paint and polish. A lot of work. And a lot of love.

Her home in Los Angeles had looked like a

dump in the beginning, but she'd turned it into a showplace. It wouldn't be difficult to do that all over again. Maybe, just maybe, this was what she needed to take her mind off what had happened a year ago. Heaven knows the psychiatrist hadn't been much help. Work had always been her salvation, and from the looks of her new home, she'd be stress and worry free for the rest of her life.

She studied her surroundings, picturing the place as it might look when summer arrived. She'd fill planter boxes and Grecian urns with red, pink, and white geraniums and scatter hanging baskets of English ivy and Boston fern along the beams. She'd serve iced tea and lemonade to her guests in cut glass tumblers and cheesecake and petit fours on antique china. Men and women would sit in wicker rockers on the porch and talk about the latest good book they'd read, about music, and their travels, or maybe debate politics.

It all sounded so wonderful, so dreamlike. She'd have a home again, a garden. She'd be in a town where clean, fresh air was the rule rather than the exception. Where people walked by slowly and smiled and maybe even stopped for a moment to chat. Sapphire, Montana, sounded so perfect.

Except for the cold.

She pulled the collar of her coat more tightly around her neck and attempted to get a view of the town through the blowing snow. She hadn't seen much while she'd driven; most of the time she'd kept her eyes glued on what little road she could see and fought the storm to keep the Jeep on the highway. Now, only the brick bank building on one side of the hotel and the Tin Cup Cafe, which sat directly across the street, were in sight. And out in front of the rustic restaurant was a man standing at the edge of the boardwalk—staring directly into her eyes.

A shiver ran down her spine and she couldn't tell if it was from the cold or from the eyes boring into hers. The man reached up and tipped his hat, welcoming her, she imagined, in typical cowboy fashion. But he made no other move to approach, he just continued to stare.

Elizabeth's heart began to race. She felt it thumping under the thick layers of her coat and sweater. What was it about the man's eyes that mesmerized her? She'd been stared at before, but never so intensely, so thoroughly. She was flattered, yet frightened.

She forced herself to turn away and quickly retrieved an old brass skeleton key from her pocket. She slid it into the lock of the grimy beveled glass and oak-framed door, anxious to get inside, away from the heat of the man's eyes, which she could still feel beating against her back. For some strange reason, she felt she had to get away from him. She attempted to turn the key, but it stuck.

She tried again. Nothing.

She looked back across the street. The man was still standing there, still watching.

Ignore him, Elizabeth. Just ignore him and maybe he'll go away, she told herself.

But he didn't go away. Instead, he walked down the stairs and into the street. He was moving toward her. Still staring. With those eyes.

She turned away and tried the key again, imploring it to turn, but it wouldn't budge. She gripped the old brass knob with her leather glove and attempted to twist it, wishing she could push open the door and escape from the stranger.

She heard his boots on the walk. Coming closer. Closer. She gave the knob one more try. The leather of her glove slipped from the handle; it was as if she were trying to twist a ball of melting ice. The soles of her boots slid on the icy doorstep and she grabbed at the handle again, trying to keep herself from falling. But her efforts were in vain, and she landed loud and hard.

And absolutely mortified.

"Need a hand?"

She looked up at the giant of a man looming over her. He didn't look threatening any longer—even from this position. He just looked big and powerful, and those eyes of his blazed down on her from under his snow-dusted black Stetson. He was staring, from the top of her head to the tips of her boots and back again. She hated to be stared at. She hated to be laughed at, too, but those bright blue sapphire eyes of his were doing just that.

He reached toward her with a rawhide-gloved hand. "You're going to get awfully cold if you lie on the front porch the rest of the day," he said, and instead of watching his eyes, she looked at the grin on his face, at the lopsided way his lips cocked up on the right and not on the left.

The easy thing to do would be to accept the help he offered, but she'd been doing things for herself most of her life. She wasn't about to accept help now, especially from a stranger. "Thanks," she finally said, "but I got down here by myself; I'm sure I can get up on my own."

"Suit yourself." He leaned against the porch railing, folded his arms across his chest, and glared.

Her jaw tightened. Her eyes narrowed in determination. She pushed up with her elbows and hands until she was sitting upright. That hadn't been too difficult. She hadn't slipped even once. Proud of herself, she looked at him again to see his reaction to the feat she'd accomplished.

He just glared. Even that lopsided grin was gone.

She smiled sweetly, and with great effort.

She drew up her knees, ground her boots into the thin sheet of ice on the porch, wrapped a hand around each knee for leverage, and pulled upward.

Whoosh! Her boots lost their grip and slid right out from under her again. Her bottom landed with a thud on the wooden planks and she didn't know which hurt more, her backside or her pride. She looked at the man out of the corner of her eyes. His grin had returned.

Slowly his arms unfolded from in front of his chest, and she heard each of his bootsteps as he moved toward her. "As much as I'm enjoying the floor show, I think it's about time I stepped in to help."

He didn't wait for her to accept, didn't wait for her to reach out, he just leaned over, slid his big hands under her arms, and lifted her easily, like a tiny child.

Which she wasn't.

"Thanks for your help," she said, pulling quickly out of his arms and latching onto one of the porch rails. Hard wood seemed a much safer thing to hold onto than one of his arms. This man, this stranger, might not look intimidating up close, but when she felt herself in his arms, breathing became much too difficult. And she had to breathe, for heaven's sake!

"Need help with anything else while I'm here?" he asked, folding his arms once more across his chest. "Or do you have everything under control?"

She could answer yes, but the problem with the lock on the door hadn't been resolved, nor had the problem of how she could get up off the ground if she fell again. "I can't seem to get the door unlocked," she answered. Oh, how she hated to ask for help, but she swallowed a bit of her pride. "Do you think you could give it a try?"

His grin widened. She knew he sensed her discomfort in asking for assistance and that he was bound and determined to make her wallow in forced acquiescence. Slowly he unfolded his arms, took two steps to the door, pounded the side of his fist on the wood just below the lock, and turned the key.

Elizabeth heard the click. Why did it have to be so easy for him? Why couldn't *he* have trouble, too?

"Anything else?"

She looked away from his eyes, over his shoulder, at the facade of the Victorian she'd purchased. "You could replace the roof, fix the banister, and apply a coat or two of paint to this place."

He smiled finally. It wasn't just a grin cocking one side of his mouth, but a wide, white-toothed smile. Even those sapphire eyes of his smiled, filling with glints of sparkling light. "It's not exactly what you expected, is it?"

"No," Elizabeth said, shaking her head. "I

thought I was going to have a little work to do, not a major overhaul."

"This place was boarded up for a good sixty, seventy years. A few months back, someone came in and did a little work, but not much."

"My brother," Elizabeth divulged, feeling an uncommon need to explain. "Buying it was his idea. He put in new wiring and got the lights working. He said he put in a stove and refrigerator, too, but that's about it. He was going to come here with me." She shrugged slightly. "He got married instead."

"So it's all up to you now?"

"It's all mine. Every creaking board, every broken window." She laughed for the first time in weeks, maybe even months. "I don't mind hard work."

With her left hand still wrapped around the railing for support, she stuck out her other. "I'm Elizabeth Fitzgerald."

He moved easily from the door to stand right in front of her. He took her gloved hand in his and she liked the way it felt—not too tight, not too loose. That hand was just as powerful as the rest of him. "Jonathan Winchester," he said, and for the first time she noticed the deep baritone of his voice. She also realized that in spite of the freezing temperatures, in spite of the chill that had run through her body earlier, she now felt warm: her toes, her fingers, the tip of her nose.

He was still holding her hand in that just right way and the warmth began to spread. "Do you go by Jonathan, or John?" she asked, prolonging the introduction, prolonging the way his gloved thumb absently circled the back of her leather-covered hand.

"Jon, without the H. And Jonathan when I'm being chewed out, but no one's dared do that since I was a kid."

Elizabeth laughed again. No, she couldn't imagine anyone daring to confront the man who stood in front of her. He had a strong chin and a broad, cleanly shaved jaw, tanned a rather nice bronze from many days in the sun. She couldn't see his shoulders and chest through the coat he wore, but from sheer size alone she figured he was a cross between Paul Bunyan and Arnold Schwarzenegger. And she had to look up at him, something she rarely did with a man because she stood just over six feet in heels. But looking up at him now, she assumed Jon Winchester must stand at least six-foot-six, and that didn't include the inch or two added by the heels of his boots.

If she hadn't sworn off photographing men, especially the emaciated-looking types, she might have grabbed her camera out of the car and asked him to pose.

"Is it the coat you find interesting?" he asked, his voice interrupting her thoughts and drawing her attention from his chest back to his face. "Or maybe you're wondering just how many sheepskins it takes to make a coat this big?"

He was laughing, and she felt heat rush up her neck and come close to flowing into her cheeks. Blushing was something entirely new. She'd photographed nude men and women alone, in pairs, even in triples, and in all sorts of compromising positions. Yet she'd never blushed. She'd never even felt uncomfortable, because it was all part of the business, all part of the game.

But Jon Winchester, with his hot, mesmerizing sapphire eyes, made her cold body turn warm and her face feel as if it had been hit with a blowtorch.

She pulled her hand out of his and wrapped it around the rail right next to the other. "In my former life I was a fashion photographer," she told him, trying to redeem herself and make up for her unconscionable stare. "A lot of underfed people paraded in front of my camera. There weren't many like you."

The lopsided grin returned. "Do you have a preference in size?"

"No," she lied, and realized if this conversation continued, she'd dig herself into a hole she'd never climb out of, so she sought a topic that would change the conversation completely, and Jon's last name came to mind.

"I bought this place from Matt Winchester. Are you related?" she asked.

"Cousins." Short. Clipped, as if uttering that word bothered him. She didn't know Jonathan Winchester well enough to ask him if there was a problem between him and his cousin, but she planned to ask anyway.

"It doesn't sound like you and Matt are the best of friends."

He laughed, just as short and clipped as when he'd said the word "cousins." "We live in the same town. We run into each other occasionally. That's enough."

"Then I suppose he hasn't told you we've formed a type of partnership?"

A slow frown crossed his face. His answer came even slower. "No. I hadn't heard." He backed against the peeling paint on the side of the house and folded his arms over his chest—again. But this time he didn't have a grin on his face, nor a smile, and his eyes didn't twinkle with laughter. "What kind of partnership?"

"My brother and I send would-be hunters in his direction; he lodges his clients here as part of his outfitting packages. I've been exploring other ways to entice guests to this place once I get it up and running, but Matt's idea intrigued me."

"I take it you don't have a problem with hunters staying here?"

What a crazy question. They were in Montana; everybody hunted in this part of the country. "My brother's a hunter so, no, I don't have a problem. I might even get some venison or elk as partial payment."

"Is that what you plan to feed your guests?" Jon asked.

"Maybe on occasion. Not bear though. I tried it once, and that was more than enough. Matt plans to take me hunting in the spring. He's got some wild game recipes he wants me to try out."

Jon pushed away from the wall and paced across the porch. He stood right next to Elizabeth and gripped the banister, staring off in the distance where wind picked the snow up from the ground and tossed it around and around. Finally he turned, looking her straight in the eye. He was close, much too close for comfort, and she leaned back into the post behind her. "What are you going to hunt in the spring?" he asked, as if he were an attorney and she the witness he was grilling.

"I don't know. Deer. Antelope. Does it really matter?"

"Of course it matters," he exploded. "The only things you can hunt legally in the spring are turkey and black bear. Is that what you want? Do you plan on putting bearskin rugs on your floors? Are you going to stuff a turkey to stare at and show off to your friends?"

"I don't plan to do any of those things," she fired back, confused yet angered by his words and tone. "And I don't plan to do anything illegal."

"Then I suggest you find another outfitter to be partners with." His coat brushed hers as he moved away and stalked down the stairs.

"Why?" Elizabeth called after him.

He turned when he reached the street, tilting his Stetson low on his forehead. "Because," he said, his blue eyes pools of cold, hard anger, "if you stick with Matt, one of these days you're going to find yourself in a whole hell of a lot of trouble."

Chapter 2

Elizabeth could almost hear the earth quivering as Jon stomped away. If his boots came down any harder, she thought for sure the resultant pressure would put dents in the earth's core.

She laughed softly. How many times had she been accused of having an easily combustible temper? How many times had she exploded over the years? Too many to count, in both instances, although she'd made a promise a year ago to try and curb her fiery emotions. She'd done a pretty good job of it, too, but she had the feeling if she spent much time around Jon Winchester, a man whose passions appeared to match her own, she might have to forget all about that promise.

She laughed again, crossed her arms over her chest, and tried to rub some warmth back into her body. Funny, how she'd turned cold the moment Jon had stormed away.

Without giving it another thought, she eased her way to the door, pulled out the key, and easily turned the knob. The door pushed opened with a soft, wailing groan.

A strong, musty odor smacked Elizabeth in the

face, and she quickly covered her nose and mouth with one gloved hand, inhaling leather instead of decay. The entrance was dark and oppressive, dusty, and strewn with spiderwebs, what she imagined it might be like if she'd stepped inside a crypt. She pulled a heavy, tarnished brass hat rack across the entryway floor and propped it in front of the door to let in clean air. She didn't care if drifts of snow and icy wind accompanied the freshness, because the stale air inside made it nearly impossible to breathe.

Stepping out of the doorway, she searched for a light switch to brighten the room, finally finding it hidden behind a long strip of wallpaper that had peeled away from the top of the wall and now lay haphazardly over the wall plate. She muttered a silent prayer for the room to fill with light when she switched it on, crossed her fingers, and flicked the lever.

Above her, dim light beamed from the few unbroken bulbs in a chandelier draped with strings of crystal teardrops and dusty cobwebs. The immense fixture hung lifelessly from the high stucco ceiling, sculpted in intricate patterns of swirling leaves and vines. The plaster had yellowed, but as with the chandelier, she could see the beauty beneath the thick coat of grime, and she knew if the rest of the hotel was just one-tenth as spectacular as this room, Eric's decision to purchase the old place hadn't been such a bad one.

Slowly she moved from the entry to the parlor, surveying the grandeur and formulating a plan of attack. The room needed a good scrubbing from floor to ceiling. The drapes were in tatters and would have to be replaced, but the many Aubusson and Turkish carpets of deep gold with kaleidoscope patterns of red, green, and blue could be salvaged with a thorough cleaning. She'd have to strip away all the wallpaper, and sand and refinish the woodwork, but it would be a labor she'd love. She'd carefully wash and dry thousands of cut-glass teardrops and icicles to make all the chandeliers shine. So far she'd counted three—one in the entryway, one in the parlor, and one in the library, and when she had them sparkling clean, she'd turn on every one and fill the rooms with as much light as possible to show off the beauty within.

And she imagined the hotel—the Sapphire Inn, she'd call it—constantly filled with guests—more than just hunters. Honeymooners would come from far away, looking for a memorable setting for their first days together. Long-married couples would renew their love in one of the bedrooms upstairs. And others would come just seeking a quiet, beautiful setting for a romantic tryst. No, the rooms of her inn would never be empty.

Nor would her life. Not again.

After she quickly assessed the downstairs, she marched from one room to another, ripping rotten fabric from the windows and dusty covers from tables and chairs. The place was a veritable treasure trove of antiques: French art nouveau tables and chairs in mahogany and walnut and fruitwood, carved cherrywood armoires, side cabinets, and secretaries, just waiting to be stripped, sanded, stained, and polished—something she'd loved doing in her spare moments. Scattered about were porcelain and ceramic figurines and vases and plates, nearly all in mint condition except for the layers of grime.

She couldn't understand why so many valuable pieces littered the hotel, why the place had been unoccupied for over sixty years and no one had taken these treasures. They were worth a small fortune—she knew because she'd filled her place in L.A. with dozens of similar priceless pieces. They'd looked ugly and forlorn when she'd found them in thrift stores and out-of-the-way antique shops. She'd haggled and bargained and gotten her finds for a steal. And she'd lost them all in a matter of seconds.

Well, now she had the chance to turn another place into a living, breathing museum of beautiful antiquity.

Oh, it felt so good to be in Sapphire, Montana, population 372. Her life had been spared a year ago and she had the chance to start all over again. This town and this hotel seemed the perfect place for new beginnings.

She began to hum as she uncovered sofas and chairs upholstered in worn purple velvet and faded tapestry patterned in multicolored roses and ferns. She smacked one of the cushions and dust billowed out of the fabric. She couldn't help but laugh. It would take an army and endless amounts of time to get this place fit for paying guests. Fortunately, she had the time, and the money; unfortunately, from the looks of Sapphire, Montana, she doubted she'd find the army.

When all but one dust cover had been heaped in a pile in the middle of the room, she grabbed the edge of the last one that hugged the high back and arms of a soft, comfortable-looking chesterfield. She pulled, but the dust cover wouldn't budge. She pulled again and frowned. If she didn't know better, she'd swear someone was sitting smack in the middle of that sofa, laughing at her predicament.

Casually, she moved around the couch, inspecting the sheet, looking for pins or tacks or something that could be holding it in place, but she found nothing. She could lift the corners, the edges, but one strip about two feet wide stuck to the back and the seat; as if Crazy Glue had been applied, or as if, she laughed to herself, someone invisible sat there, refusing to move.

Alexander Stewart slouched in the dusty chesterfield and twiddled his thumbs. Haunting a hotel without any guests had been a miserable way to kill time, and boredom was a pain in the rump. Finally, someone had invaded his turf, but he hadn't yet worked up the energy or desire to kick up a ruckus. He wanted to wait, to give this person time to settle in, and then . . .

Thunder and tarnation! What was he thinking? He'd been waiting too long already, and this woman looked like the perfect foil for his games.

Alex let loose a laugh that shook the walls and made the crystals in the cobweb-coated chandelier clink. What a hoot, the way the woman dropped the edge of the sheet and rolled her eyes, looking from one wall to the other, then to the swaying light fixture overhead. He'd frightened her, and all he'd done was laugh. What an easy target! This one was bound to be a whole lot more fun than the last occupant, that dandified young man with a ponytail down to his waist and a ring in his ear who wouldn't stick around at night and had hightailed it out of town after only thirteen days.

But that had been a long time ago. Seven months, to be exact. Seven months of roaming the halls and rooms aimlessly, looking for something to occupy his time. It had been a hell of a long time—maybe he shouldn't get all fired up to get rid of this newcomer.

He stopped laughing.

He waited in silence.

His timing had to be perfect for his next move.

Alex watched the woman roam around the room, staring again and again at the sofa, at the sheet, at the precise spot where he sat—invisible to human eyes.

She seemed to have regained her nerve, her drive. The woman grabbed two corners of the sheet into tightened fists. She was going to try it again.

"One."

Ah, she was counting down. A grin crossed Alexander's face.

"Two."

Alex got ready. Three had always been his favorite number.

"Three."

Alex swooped from the couch to the mantel, stretched out on the cold slab of marble, and watched the woman yank as if she was pulling out an old man's stubborn and rotten tooth.

The sheet pulled away. The woman lost her balance, and those highfalutin boots of hers slipped out from under her bundled-up body. She flew backward across the room and landed with a thud on her rump, her legs spread-eagled, right there in the middle of the pile of decomposing sheets.

Alexander grinned. Ah, life was sweet!

He watched the woman push up from the floor, dust off her behind, and unbutton her parka. She was going to get down to work. Alex liked that idea. Just what his old place needed—someone to liven it up a bit, put a broom to the floor, a swat to the carpets, and maybe some water and good old lye soap to the windows. Hell! They were so crusted over with dust and dirt and grime, he couldn't see out. And he liked looking out at the town. It was the only connection he had to the outside world because no matter how many times or how hard he tried, he just couldn't bust through the doors, the windows, or the walls.

Of course, maybe staying inside wasn't all *that* bad. At least it seemed a little better, now that this woman had come into his home. She sure was fun to watch, especially when she was falling down.

Having her around was definitely better than being alone.

He watched her close the front door and finally shrug out of that big furry coat. She tossed it over a hook on the rack and slowly walked into the parlor. She started to grab an old broom someone had left standing against a wall. She touched it gingerly with the tips of her fingers, peeling away cobwebs wrapped around the handle. Alex came darn close to bursting into laughter at the grimace on her face. Watching the way her body moved when she finally swung the thing was no laughing matter, though. He hadn't had anyone to haunt and he hadn't had a pretty woman to look at in a mighty long time.

But he didn't like those newfangled contraptions like this one was wearing that showed every curve and too much skin. He wasn't a prude, but he preferred those ruffled and lacy things women wore back in his day, clothes that covered their necks, their wrists, their ankles, and their legs. Made a man wonder what was hidden under all that fabric. Made a man long to peel away the layers to find the sweetness beneath.

And oh, how he missed that sweetness, every fold and curve, every soft, mysterious spot that reacted so nicely to his touch.

Just the thought of it made him slink down to the floor and bury his head in his hands. If he could shed a tear, he would. Damn, he missed being alive. He hadn't touched a woman in a hundred years—a hundred very, very *long* years. Not since Amanda.

Amanda. He silently whispered his lover's name and a deep sadness encompassed his face. *Oh, darlin'. Do you think this is the one? Do you think this woman can get me out of this place and back into your arms, where I belong?*

He wrapped his hands around the post of a bentwood lamp and pulled himself up. He didn't need the support, not physically. He could swoop from the entryway to the top of the attic and back in five seconds flat. But when he was sad, it felt good to grab hold of something real and tangible. At times he hugged the posts on the big oak bed upstairs, just to remember how good it felt to hold onto something more than air. A hundred years was a long time to hold onto things that couldn't hold you back.

He looked again at the woman who'd invaded his domain, the woman he might be able to talk with, who might make his blasted home somewhat less boring. She was staring at the swaying lamp, a frown on her face. In fact, Alex realized, she was looking straight at him, studying the spot where he stood. Could she sense his presence? Could she see him? Neither seemed possible—he hadn't allowed her or anyone else that privilege.

Not yet, anyway.

Size-fourteen double-E cowboy boots left their deep, heavy imprint in the snow-dusted street as Jon walked toward the end of town, his head tilted, his face protected from the chill behind the brim of his hat. He'd spent the past hour drinking coffee at the Tin Cup, waiting for his temper to cool, and spent another fifteen minutes standing on the boardwalk outside, contemplating whether or not he should apologize to the new woman in town. He thought he'd overreacted, thought he might have exploded without giving her a chance to explain her partnership with Matt. But she hadn't even tried. Instead, she'd feigned ignorance about what was really going on. In the end, he'd decided he'd ignore her and forget the fact that he wanted to sculpt her, forget the fact that he liked the sound of her voice, the openness of her laughter, and those red hooker boots that molded over her ankles and calves like a coat of red paint.

She wasn't the type of woman he was usually attracted to, anyway. He liked them blond, petite, and classy. No, Elizabeth wasn't classy. Not at all—and that observation had nothing to do with the clothes she wore. It rested solely on the fact that she was in partnership with Matt Winchester.

She didn't have a clue about hunting seasons, and more than likely, didn't know the difference between elk and antelope. She probably didn't know one end of a gun from another, or how to aim to kill so an animal wouldn't suffer. Chances were she probably didn't care, either.

Of course, she could have been putting on an act. His cousin had done a good job fooling the wardens and anyone else who'd ever questioned him about his outfitting activities. Maybe Elizabeth was smart in that way, too.

Hell! Why did she have to be involved with Matt?

At the end of town where the narrow road swerved to the right and looped back toward the highway, Jon pushed through the arched black wrought-iron gates leading to his home. At least ten feet tall and fifteen feet wide, they had elaborate scrollwork that became a mass of entwining leaves at the top, with an ornate D forged at the center of each gate. Jon's great-great-grandfather Jedediah Dalton had founded the town of Sapphire in 1880 and had built an empire that now stood in the center of nowhere. Jon liked it that way. He liked the solitude, the quiet. The town rarely attracted anyone but hunters and fishermen, sightseers and hikers, people just passing through because there was nowhere in town to stay. But Elizabeth planned to change all that, and Jon didn't like it one bit.

He climbed the cobbled drive and mounted the walk that wound its way up the gentle rise where Dalton House stood guard over the town. Three stories of limestone block with massive round towers at each corner, it might have looked like a fortress if it weren't for the elegance of its arched windows and sloped roofs of black tile. Jedediah Dalton had covered the spires in copper, one of the area's natural elements, and one of the things that had made Mr. Dalton a very rich man. Opulent and majestic, the Dalton mansion had stood a hundred years and was designed to stand a thousand more.

Pushing through a side door, Jon tossed his Stetson on a butcher-block table and draped his coat over the back of an oak captain's chair. As he crossed the room, his boots left dirty wet imprints on the black-and-white tile floor, but he gave little thought to the mess. He wanted to get upstairs. He needed clay in his fingers, something tangible to bear the brunt of his anger and frustration.

He opened the refrigerator, grabbed a can of Budweiser, and mounted the narrow circular stairs that led to his studio.

On a good day, blue sky and sunshine would have radiated through the two-by-six windows that circled the room, but today only filtered light broke through the stormy gray sky. Jon preferred working by natural light, but he flipped one of the switches and filled the room with the best lighting money could buy.

He took a mound of clay from the refrigerator where he stored his supply and circled the room like a caged animal, digging his fingers into the cold, pliable clay, squeezing it, twisting it, until he'd created nothing more than a grotesque, two-faced abstract of a woman, sweet on one side, cunning on the other. He stopped at his workbench and slammed the clay into the wood. Damn! Picturing the woman that way didn't make him feel better at all.

He grabbed a charcoal pencil and a sketch pad. He thumbed through the pages until he found a clean sheet, dragged a wooden stool over to the window on the west side of the tower, and straddled the seat.

He looked down on the town, at the old hotel, at the windows filled with light. And he began to sketch what he'd seen, and what he imagined had been hidden behind that furry parka. Charcoal curves instantly appeared. Breasts full and round, a tapered waist, and hips made the way any man in his right mind would have made them—padded for comfort. Blue-black hair, shiny as a raven in the sunlight, trailed over one shoulder, the braid heavy and thick and curled at the end, where it grazed her waist. He penciled in high cheekbones, large, dark eyes, and thick, sensual lashes he knew would lie gently on her fair skin when she slept. And plump red lips that . . .

The blaring ring of the phone snapped him away from the sketch, away from the beauty he couldn't get out of his head. Stalking across the hard oak floor, he dropped the pad on his drafting table and grabbed the phone. "Hello." Annoyance rang loud and clear in his voice.

"Sorry to disturb you, Jon."

Andy Andrews never imposed or disturbed anyone unless it was important. "What is it?" Jon asked.

"Harry found a bear and her cub yesterday," Andy said slowly. "Their paws and gallbladders were gone."

Jon closed his eyes and silently counted to ten. "Where?"

Only a slight static sounded through the phone. Andy was hesitating for some reason, but finally he answered. "Schoolmarm Gulch."

"Damn!" The charcoal pencil snapped in half from the pressure of Jon's fingers. "Any sign of the other cub?"

"No. Harry checked the den, but nothing. Sorry I had to tell you, Jon, but I knew you'd been watching them last fall."

"Spring and summer, too." Jon sifted through a pile of sketches lying on his drafting table. He stopped when he reached the ones he'd done of the black bear and her cubs shortly before they'd gone into hiding in early winter. It wasn't the first time a slaughter like this had happened, and he knew it wouldn't be the last. But it didn't make their deaths any easier to accept.

"I suppose Harry's going to look for the other cub?" Jon asked.

"Guess so. I'm having dinner with him at the Tin Cup tonight. Want to join us?"

"Yeah. Might as well see if I can help him in the search."

Jon heard Andy clear his throat. The man was a rancher and had done his fair share of killing to protect his livestock and hunting to stock his freezer. But senseless murder didn't set any better with Andy than it did with Jon. "See you around seven," Andy said.

Jon heard the click and dial tone and hung up, but he stared at the phone for several more moments, then lifted it again and punched in a number he knew as well as his own.

He listened to the continuous ring and finally the voice on the other end, but he said nothing—just hung up again and took a long swallow of beer. He'd wanted to ask his cousin if he'd had a successful hunting trip yesterday, if he'd made a bundle. But he had no proof against Matt. Over the years, Jon had searched again and again for evidence to prove his cousin's outfitting business, like his real estate practice, had produced more ill-gotten gain than legitimate profit. But Jon had continually failed. He didn't want to fail again.

He picked up his beer, downed the remainder, crushed the aluminum in his fist, and easily tossed it into the trash across the room.

He looked through the stack of sketches again, his eyes resting finally on the one he'd just done of Elizabeth. He ripped it out of the tablet, crumpled the thick paper, and tossed it just as he had the crushed and empty can.

He couldn't allow himself to think about her, not as a friend, not as the woman he wanted to sculpt. No, he had more important things to deal with now.

Plowing his fingers through his hair, he went to his desk, flipping through the Rolodex till he found the number he wanted. He stabbed the buttons on the phone, listened to the ring and the voice answering on the other end.

"It's Jon Winchester," he said. "I have a plan."

Chapter 3

Dust permeated not only the chesterfield's worn fabric, but Elizabeth's clothing, her nose, and her lungs. Every pore in her body felt as if it had been invaded by dirt. She knew she should climb into the tub and wash away some of the grime, but she couldn't work up the energy to test the water in the bathroom. Three long days of sitting in the car and one long day of fighting spiders had sapped her strength. Now it felt good just sitting on the comfortable old sofa, not moving a muscle.

For the first time in hours she relaxed and took stock of things that needed repair or replacement other than the cracked paint and peeling flowered wallpaper. The red, blue, and green fleur-de-lis that had been stenciled over the doorways and windows had faded with time. It would take patience and a steady hand to restore them to their original beauty. Heavy velvet drapes with fringed edges no longer swagged in the wide windows and doorways, but she had easily seen the richness of the fabric and wanted to duplicate them exactly. Now, though, they lay with all the other tattered and torn items in a heaping pile.

It might have appeared dismal if Elizabeth hadn't seen the charm deeply hidden away.

Gilt mirrors and framed landscapes and portraits hung on the walls and made her smile. They'd look good as new, once they were cleaned, and they'd add a wonderful touch of authenticity to the room when the walls were repainted and papered and new drapes were hung. And the pink marble fireplace—she'd never seen such beauty, carved with rosebuds and twisting vines.

The only down side to the whole place was that she couldn't get used to the cold.

She hadn't ventured to the basement to check out the furnace. She had no wood to burn, and that pile of ragged drapes was looking like the perfect thing to toss on the hearth. She longed for a blazing fire, something to warm her insides. She hadn't been this cold since . . . since she'd been trapped beneath the stucco and plaster and wooden beams of her former house in Los Angeles.

A lone tear puddled at the corner of her eye, and she wiped it away with the back of her hand. She refused to cry. She'd cried too many times for all the things she'd lost when the earthquake had hit and her house had slid from its cliffside setting, slid away from its view of the city lights, from the gardens she'd lovingly planted and nurtured for years.

There was nothing in this room that brought back memories of the ten years she'd collected Tiffany lamps to brighten the rooms of her home, or the pieces of Wedgwood she'd found while haunting thrift stores and estate sales. Those things had been shoved into a pile by a bulldozer and hauled off to the dump, along with her china, her Waterford crystal, her Lladro, and the one-of-a-kind pottery she'd purchased from starving artists.

Only her jewelry and some of her clothing had been salvaged, along with the cameras she kept in well-insulated and cushioned cases, and a few odds and ends that had survived the crush. The earthquake had been devastating enough. Why had the relentless rains hit, too, sending mud flowing down the hill right along with her house?

At least she hadn't lost loved ones, like so many others. All she'd lost were three days of her life as she lay pinned between the center beam of her house and her mattress. That mattress. Her brother had laughed when she'd spent a fortune on bedding. But the feathers had been soft, comfortable, and it was the only thing that had kept her from being crushed when the roof had crashed down and shoved her deep into the cushion of goosedown. How often had she thought during those seventy-two hours that at least she would die in a cradle of luxury, cuddled up snug and close with a pillow and blankets, even if they were permeated with dirt and mud and shards of glass?

She'd suffered a fractured arm, two broken ribs, a slight concussion, multiple cuts and abrasions, a case of dehydration, and the sorest throat she'd ever had. She'd screamed for twelve hours straight, hoping someone would find and rescue her. That strong, deep voice of hers had given up long before help had arrived. And while she'd screamed, she'd prayed, and that was when she'd begun making promises. She'd be a nice person. She'd make friends. She'd help others. She wouldn't swear.

She'd even promised to keep her promises, no matter how difficult they might be.

He'd listened. He'd kept her company. And He'd sent that good-looking fireman, the poor, unfortunate soul who'd had the misfortune of locating her would-be grave. She'd wrapped her one good arm around his neck and kissed him like they were long-lost lovers, kissed him with bad breath, a blood-crusted face, and a runny nose. And some lousy photographer had chosen that pathetic moment to snap her rescue and been lucky enough to have it plastered across the front of the *L.A. Times* and most of the newspapers in the country.

She'd always joked about winning a Pulitzer for her photography. She hadn't wanted to be the pitiful object captured in someone else's winning entry.

Finally she laughed, and the memory of that kiss made her smile. That miserable seventy-two hours of being buried alive had had at least one reward. Her rescuer might not have enjoyed the kiss, but it was the nicest one she could remember in thirty-one years of living.

Alexander rested his elbows on the back of the chesterfield and watched the lady laugh, and smile, and shed a tear. He wondered what strange thoughts were going through her head.

Why did women have to be so perplexing? Why did they laugh and cry at the same time? Amanda had done the same thing, especially during those days right before their wedding. He'd never been able to figure her out, either. But he'd loved her—the crazy emotions didn't matter at all.

Tarnation! He didn't want to get sentimental. He had a guest, and he wanted to have fun. He'd befriended an intruder in his house once upon a time, and what had it gotten him? Just another person to miss. He'd thought the little boy was his friend, but friends don't tell secrets, and that one had. Alex had told the boy what might happen if he told people he'd been talking to a ghost, but the boy didn't listen. He'd brought the men into Alexander's home, and he'd begged Alex to talk, or to show himself. But Alex hadn't made a noise. They'd laughed at the boy, and the kid had gotten mad.

The boy'd yelled at Alex when the others had gone. He'd said he didn't believe in ghosts, that he didn't want to be friends any longer, and he'd run out the door, crying. And he'd never come back again.

Hell! Alex refused to get sappy over something that had happened twenty-five years ago. Nosirree. Next time someone ran out of this house, it would be because *he* had scared the bejeebers out of them.

In fact, he just might scare the bejeebers out of the woman sitting on his couch.

He stalked around the sofa, checking out those big old puddles of water in the corners of her eyes. Perfect timing. The lady was ripe for scaring.

She laughed again in that strange, reflective way, and Alex wondered what she'd do if he laughed, too, and continued to laugh. He'd scared away a helluva lot of people in the last hundred years with his laugh. But did he really want to scare this woman away? He didn't know for sure. She might be the one who could help him get out of this place. He thought his instincts were good, thought he knew who could help him and who couldn't. He'd thought the boy might have been the one, but the kid had been too young. He'd never even let the boy see him. All they'd done was talk about crazy, unimportant things. No, Alex figured the person who could help him had to be someone strong, someone brave, someone who wouldn't frighten easily and could stand up to anything—even the odd, eerie laughter of a ghost.

Might as well put her to the test right now, he thought. If she wasn't fearless, if she caved in to his antics, she wasn't cunning enough to help him get out of his hell on earth.

A strange, unearthly laughter thundered through the room, and Elizabeth shivered. Wrapping her hands around her arms, she attempted to massage some warmth into her body while her eyes scanned the open spaces of the parlor and the cobweb-strewn stairway. Could the plumbing be acting up? she wondered. The house needed so much work, the noises she'd been hearing could easily be from rickety pipes, wind whipping through broken windows, or possibly bats or some other unwanted creatures stirring around in the attic.

That's how Matt Winchester had explained the noises. Even Eric had told her that the funny sounds were nothing more than the old hotel stretching and groaning with age.

No, the noises she'd heard definitely hadn't been laughter, but she could clearly understand why no one had wanted to stay in this place or buy it. It was probably the reason no one had run off with the antiques . . . they'd been too afraid to set foot in the place.

Well, it would take a whole lot more than eerie noises to make her run away. Montana didn't have earthquakes—at least, not the house-leveling kind they had in southern California. This place was standing on solid ground. Its walls were upright. Those were good enough reasons to keep her from going back to L.A. Sapphire, Montana, and this rickety old hotel were home—and she planned to make the best of both of them.

Right after she took a bath.

Right after she found the army she needed to help her turn the hotel into a showplace.

Bathing had proved rather difficult. Reddish-brown water that looked like strained minestrone didn't appear too appealing to Elizabeth. She'd run out to her car, dragged in the ice chest, and taken a sponge bath with ice she'd melted on top of the stove. Her efforts took care of one layer of dust, enough to make her presentable. If she didn't find a plumber soon, she'd have to melt snow in order to bathe.

She'd halfway tackled her first task of the evening. Now came the time to work on the second.

The army.

She'd called Matt Winchester to ask if he knew anyone looking for work. All he'd said was ask the mayor, that he himself didn't have time to help her out now. "Maybe when I return from visiting my folks in Florida," he'd said, and rushed her off the phone. His evasion speech was perfect. Just the right amount of laughter, the right amount of sincerity. She'd done the same thing a time or two. Yet it didn't feel so good being on the receiving end.

But that was in the past. The hotel needed refurbishing, she needed help and had to locate the mayor, and she was hungry—now.

She slipped into her coat and gloves and thought about how she would navigate the icy steps and road to get across the street to the Tin Cup Cafe. She'd already fallen three times since her arrival, and twice she'd been seen. Adding a fourth fall to an already eventful day didn't sound promising.

She was just about to open the door when she heard heavy footfalls on the stairs and porch, and an even heavier knock against the door. The steps sounded familiar. She'd heard them stomping away earlier in the day, and the thought of facing Jon Winchester again didn't sound any more promising than falling on her rump. What could she do, though? She had to open the door.

He stood on the porch with his arms laden with firewood—no smile; no lopsided grin. Snow dusted his Stetson and the shoulders of his coat that three normal-sized men could probably squeeze into.

She didn't smile, either. Instead, she waited for an apology.

Which didn't come.

"I didn't see any smoke rising from the chimney and figured you might need some wood," he said, brushing past her and walking straight to the parlor and the pink marble fireplace as if he knew his way around . . . as if he had every right to just walk into her home.

"I'd prefer heating the rooms with the furnace," she said, ignoring her earlier thoughts about a cozy fire. If he couldn't apologize for the fight he'd tried to start this morning, she didn't have to thank him for the wood. "Wood fires aren't nearly as efficient," she said.

He ignored her comment, of course, and proceeded to dump the wood into the hearth and strategically place each piece. He stuffed kindling here and there, building the framework for a fire that would probably blaze and warm the room within seconds.

And probably be very efficient.

Slowly he rose from his crouched position and scanned the room for a moment, his gaze settling on the slight sway of the chandelier.

"It's the drafts," Elizabeth told him. "All the chandeliers swing just a bit when I enter the room."

The lopsided grin touched his face. "I used to sneak into this place when I was a kid. The chandeliers shook back then, too." He walked toward the center of the room and steadied the swaying fixture with the casual, easy reach of his arm. "I thought there was a ghost sitting up there, watching me." His grin widened. "Did Matt tell you about the rumors?"

"Yes, I've heard the rumors. No, I don't believe they're true." Ghosts! Personally, she thought it was a lot of nonsense.

He went back to the fireplace, leaned against the marble mantel, and folded his arms over his chest, a mannerism that was beginning to infuriate her. "Have you heard the laughter?" he asked.

"Creaking floorboards," she threw back. "Look, Jonathan—" She waited for his eyes to narrow when she called him that instead of Jon. He'd said no one dared to call him Jonathan, but he didn't flinch. Not one muscle. "I don't believe in ghosts," she continued, "and if there was one living here I'd welcome the companionship. I'm sure it would be preferable to keeping company with some of the other residents of this town."

He laughed, and a few glints of light bounced from his eyes. "I'm starved," he said, ignoring her once more. "I'm meeting a few friends for dinner. They might not be the company you prefer, but I thought you might consider joining us anyway?"

What? No *I'd love to have you join me*? No *Would you care to go out with me*? The man was absolutely insufferable, but she could dish it out, too. "You thought wrong."

"Suit yourself," he tossed back, then tipped his hat and walked across the parlor, through the entry, and out the front door.

It wasn't supposed to happen that way, Elizabeth thought. He was supposed to argue; he was supposed to convince her, ask her to change her mind. Heavens! She could have at least held his arm and let him help her across the road.

She rushed after him, threw open the door, and planned to holler at him before he went inside the cafe. But he had the nerve to be leaning against one of the pillars on her porch, arms folded, with that Stetson tilted low over his eyes. "Change your mind?" he asked.

"Not really. I was on my way to the cafe when you barged in. I do have to eat, you know."

"Well, maybe you'll at least let me help you get across the street. If you'd like, you can sit on the opposite side of the room from me once we get there."

She couldn't help but laugh. He said it so seriously, yet she could see the twinkle in his eyes and just the beginnings of a grin. "Thanks for the offer," she said, closing the door behind her and taking hold of his arm. "If you're sure I wouldn't be imposing, I would like to join you and your friends, too."

"If you were an imposition, I'd tell you. I don't mince words."

"I've noticed. Of course, you don't talk a lot, either."

"Always believed if you don't have anything important to say, you shouldn't say it."

"Then I imagine the two of us will have a rather quiet dinner."

He looked down at her and winked. "Don't forget, we're joining some of my friends. I'm sure they can keep the conversation going if we can't."

They headed down the stairs and into the street. She squeezed her hand tightly around his arm when she felt the slippery pavement under her shoes and smiled up at him when he reached across his chest with his other arm and slipped his gloved fingers over hers for a little additional support. The road didn't seem nearly so treacherous when she walked at his side.

He stopped right in the middle of the street and she had the horrible fear he planned to let go of her arm and walk away. Instead, he started pointing out landmarks. It seemed a crazy thing to do at twilight, with the snow falling down. But it was quiet out, the street wasn't exactly bustling with traffic, and it was the first time the storm had let up enough for her to see the town.

Besides all that, it felt rather nice being held in such strong arms. If he kept it up, she just might find herself liking him.

"All but one of the buildings in town are well over a hundred years old," he told her. "Used to be a thriving community when copper was mined here. Not much left anymore." He pointed to a narrow, two-story white clapboard structure west of the cafe. "That was the newspaper office once; now it's the grocery store and post office. You won't find everything you need there, but it beats driving fifty miles for milk or beer. That's Matt's real estate office next door, and if you haven't seen it by now, that place at the far end of town, past the gas station, is Winchester Place—Matt's home."

Through the lightly falling snow she saw an immense white mansion with columns out front. It looked like it belonged in the deep South rather than in cattle country.

"My great-grandfather considered himself a southern gentleman. Actually, he'd been a riverboat gambler before he came west, and when he struck it rich, he built a place that reminded him of home."

Jon turned slightly, drawing Elizabeth's attention to the other end of town. "We have only one church in Sapphire and most everyone shares it," he said, pointing to the end of a tree-lined walk just east of the cafe. The church was white clapboard, like the grocery store, and had half a dozen stairs leading to its double doors and a tall steeple with a cross on the top. It looked exactly like every church she'd ever seen in black-and-white westerns on TV. So did the entire town, only Sapphire wasn't quite as big as Dodge or Tombstone, and there weren't nearly as many people.

"That big stone place up on the hill," he said, a smile of pride on his face, "that's where I live."

Elizabeth looked beyond the wrought-iron gates, past the high granite barrier that tapered down to a lower wall and eventually became a wooden fence that seemed to trail on forever.

High on an incline she saw the white stone fortress, its black tile roof and copper spires looming over the town. At each end were towers with tall arched windows, and stained glass panels framed the massive front doors on both sides. "It's beautiful."

"Most people find it intimidating."

"Not much intimidates me." She looked at Jon and grinned. "Not even you."

He only laughed and continued on across the street.

When he pushed open the cafe door, Elizabeth was amazed by what she saw. It was like looking back in time into a gay nineties saloon with red glass chandeliers and a highly polished bar. She expected to see a burly man with a handlebar mustache tending to customers and saloon girls sashaying around, serving drinks. But the place was nearly empty except for a few tables scattered about. It wasn't brimming with patrons, either, just two men sitting at a center table.

She stepped inside and turned around, smiling her pleasure to Jon.

"I take it you like our cafe," he said as he entered, his broad shoulders barely squeezing between the jambs. He even had to tilt his head down to keep the top of his hat from brushing the dried mistletoe hanging overhead. He looked powerful and intimidating, just like the mansion he lived in, but she sensed that buried deep, deep beneath that ominous exterior there might be a touch of warmth.

"The atmosphere's wonderful," she said, slipping off her gloves as she studied the room once more.

She was just unbuttoning her coat when she felt Jon's hands on her shoulders, felt the leather of his gloves lightly touch the hair at the nape of her neck. He was standing very close, peeling her coat away as she released the last of the buttons, and she felt uncommonly warm all over. In fact, she realized, she'd felt warm ever since she'd opened her front door and seen him on the doorstep with firewood in his arms.

Their gazes met when she turned around, his sapphire eyes shining brightly from under his hat. He reached somewhere to his right and got rid of her coat. And he didn't look away. Not once.

He swept his black felt Stetson from his head. A lock of wavy blond hair fell across his forehead as he smacked the brim against his Levi's to shake off the snow. It was the first time she'd seen him without his hat. Oh, she'd seen the neatly trimmed sideburns, but she hadn't noticed the way his thick blond hair waved around his ears and just barely brushed the collar of his coat. She liked what she saw, and she liked the way that errant strand fell right back over his forehead after he combed his fingers through the top.

With their gazes locked, she was finding breathing difficult. Somehow she tore her eyes away and watched him shrug out of his jacket, getting her first good look at his body. Not an ounce of fat anywhere, and she'd been right when she'd made her earlier observation about his build. He was definitely a combination of every he-man on record. Through his blue denim shirt she could make out the play of muscles in his arms and his chest, even the flat planes of his stomach. She couldn't picture him standing on stage with his body oiled and glistening. No, Jon would never stand around flexing and posing. He didn't have to prove himself that way.

He took her arm, drawing her attention from his chest to the smoothness of his cheek as he leaned over to whisper in her ear. "My friends have been staring at you since we walked into the room. Promise you won't ogle them like you've been ogling me."

His words stung, and she tried to pull away, but he kept her close, that insufferable grin spreading across his face before he whispered to her again. "They've got wives at home who might not approve. I don't have a wife—"

She gritted her teeth and started to throw back a retort, something like *An arrogant son of a gun like you will probably never have a wife,* but he ushered her across the room before she had the chance.

"Elizabeth Fitzgerald," Jon said, as they reached

the only occupied table, "I'd like you to meet Andy Andrews and Harry Dodge."

"Nice to meet you," she said, shaking Andy's hand.

"You, too." He was short and rotund, with gray hair styled in a crewcut. He stood and reached a red flannel–covered arm across the table, taking her hand in his and pumping it up and down. "I own the spread just south of town. You probably drove through a few miles of it on your way here. Couldn't miss it."

"You mean the place covered with snow?" Elizabeth laughed. "Of course I remember it."

"I like this one, Jon," Andy said, pumping Jon's hand just as he'd done Elizabeth's.

Harry had stood, too, extending a thick, callused hand which seemed the perfect match for his darkly tanned weatherbeaten face. He had near black hair salted with white, a broad chest, and an even broader stomach that pushed at the buttons on his green plaid shirt. "I'm the warden for fish and wildlife," he said rather quietly. "It's nice you could join us."

"Thank you," she said, taking the chair Jon pulled out for her.

A petite, white-haired waitress with a pencil stuck above her ear bustled over to the table and slid white ceramic mugs in front of both Jon and Elizabeth. She poured coffee and placed the black and bronze thermal pitcher in the center of the table. "You must be the new owner of the hotel. We heard you were coming. Elizabeth Fitzgerald, right?"

Elizabeth had no time to answer. The woman

talked so fast she could hardly keep up.

"I'm Libby. I own this place, along with my husband, Jack." She nodded to the bald man sliding a steaming plate onto the stainless steel counter between the kitchen and the dining room.

"Nice to meet you," Elizabeth said.

"You, too, honey." Libby whipped a menu out from under her arm and held it out to Elizabeth. "You can order just about anything you want, but the special tonight's pork chops. Same special every Monday night. That's what Harry and Andy are having, and I highly recommend it—right, Mayor?" She looked straight at Jon.

"Right, Lib. Best in Montana."

Mayor? Jon Winchester was the mayor of Sapphire? He didn't look like a mayor; he looked more like a rancher just in from the range.

"So, would you like the pork chops, hon?" Libby asked.

"If that's what the mayor recommends, guess I'll give them a try."

"Make that two, Lib," Jon said.

"Double order?"

Jon grinned. "You know me too well."

"Been feeding you since you were a baby," she said, pouring out more coffee. "Orders will be up in just a few minutes. I've got fresh huckleberry pie in the back, too. Make sure you save room."

As Libby tucked the menus back under her arm and bustled away, Elizabeth picked up the steaming mug of coffee and turned her attention to Jon. "You didn't mention anything about being mayor."

"No, guess I didn't." He dumped two heaping

spoons of sugar into his coffee and stirred it slow and easy. "Harry and Andy are the town council," he said with a laugh. "The sign at the edge of town says three-seventy-two, but it's more like one-hundred-and-one, give or take a few. Not too much to govern, and not much to make a big deal over."

"Most of us aren't big on politics," Andy chimed in. "Just want to keep things running right around town."

"Would that include helping me find a contractor to do some hotel renovation?" She started to relate Matt's comment about the mayor helping her out but remembered Jon's reaction the last time Matt's name had come up and decided it might be better left unmentioned.

Jon tilted his cup toward his mouth and watched Elizabeth through the steam. "We don't have any contractors in town. No builders, no plumbers, no electricians, and no handymen."

"What do you do when you need something fixed?"

"Do it ourselves."

"Is everyone in town that self-sufficient?"

"Have to be when you live out here," Harry told her.

"Well," Elizabeth said, "I can do a lot on my own. Nothing ever stopped me before. Of course, I'll need help with the heavy stuff. Maybe you know some high-schoolers looking for spending money."

"Kids are in school and have chores and sports after. Sorry, Elizabeth," Andy said, "there just aren't too many people in Sapphire looking for jobs. They're either retired, working out of town, or too busy."

"Andy's right," Harry said. "This town's too small, and anyone who'd be able to give you a hand is probably already busy at something else. You could try calling someone in Anaconda. Maybe Butte or Helena, but I've never seen anyone want to come this far out to work."

"I'd have thought the city council would be eager to assist me. Once I get the hotel opened, there might be a few more people frequenting Sapphire businesses. That means more money in town."

All three men laughed. "I ran on a platform of no growth for Sapphire," Jon said. "I don't think any of us would mind having at least the outside of the hotel fixed up, but having it open for business is another matter entirely."

"You can't be serious!"

"Forty-eight people voted for mayor. I won forty-seven to one. Matt Winchester—my opponent—wanted to bring more business into town. He wanted to restore all the buildings and make this a historical tourist trap full of souvenir stores, antique shops, and cheap museums." Jon smiled slowly. "He lost."

"Doesn't seem like anyone in town looked at the positive side of his ideas. Business never hurt anyone. If I'd been living here, you probably would have won forty-six to two."

"Yeah, you'll probably vote for him next time there's an election, too. He *is* your partner, after all."

Harry came close to choking on his coffee. "You're partners with Matt Winchester?" he asked.

Libby shoved plates in front of everyone and added her two cents to the conversation. "I'd have thought someone like you would have more sense."

Elizabeth sighed. "It's not a true partnership." She wished the subject could just go away. The pleasant dinner with new friends she'd envisioned as she'd walked across the street was turning out to be anything but. Throwing her association with Matt into the mix was bound to send the conversation spiraling downward.

Jon sliced into a pork chop, but his glare was fixed on Elizabeth. "Okay, so maybe it's not a real partnership. It's more like he scratches your back, you scratch his." He moved the fork toward his mouth and hesitated. "Isn't that right?"

Elizabeth stabbed at her mashed potatoes. "It's a business arrangement, as I already explained."

Jon laughed. "So you did." He bit into the pork chop, but his eyes stayed fixed on hers.

Harry and Andy were eating in silence, eyes tilted toward their plates. Libby was leaning her elbows on the counter, watching the table. And Elizabeth wanted to get up and walk out the door.

She felt a whole lot more comfortable when Jon turned away.

"Heard what you found out at Schoolmarm yesterday," he said, directing his words to Harry. Elizabeth could see the noticeable thumping of a vein at his temple. She'd noticed it there before—when Matt's name was mentioned. "Any sign of the cub?" he asked.

"No. Snow covered up any tracks there might have been. Didn't see any blood except right outside the den, where we found the other cub and the sow."

Elizabeth's eyes narrowed. "What happened?" she asked.

Jon faced her, his eyes dark blue and angry. "Poaching. That's what we call it when so-called hunters go after game out of season. The bears are hibernating now. They're easy prey."

"Is bear meat that popular?" she asked, feeling oddly naive and not wanting to mention again that she'd disliked it the one time she'd given it a try.

"It isn't the meat," Harry said.

"It's the gallbladders. The paws," Jon interrupted. "That's all they take. The poachers aren't interested in the meat or the skins, so they take what they want and leave the rest to rot or as easy pickings for scavengers."

Elizabeth pushed her plate away, her hunger diminishing with the talk. "Why?" she asked again.

"Greed. Bear paws and gallbladders supposedly have some kind of medicinal value. It's easy money. Big money, if you've got the right connections. But it's not just bears these guys are after. Anything illegal, anything endangered, is a target. A few months back I found the headless carcasses of two bighorn dumped on a pile of rocks. And this," he said, pulling a short, dark brown–and-white feather from his shirt pocket, "is what's left of a bald eagle. It happens way too often, and there doesn't seem to be a damn thing we can do about it."

Andy leaned forward. "I heard they finally convicted that outfitter out of Billings," he said. "Guy got off with a twenty-one-thousand-dollar fine and three years in jail."

"Probably won't be there more than six months," Harry added. "Then he'll be right back doing the same thing all over again."

"Do you have any idea who's doing it here?" Elizabeth asked.

All three men looked at her, then Harry and Andy looked at Jon. "Yeah, we have an idea," Jon said, "but the hell of it is, we've never found any evidence."

Suddenly Elizabeth knew who they were talking about. "You think Matt's responsible, don't you?"

Jon's gaze beat into hers, deep and intense. "Like I said, we don't have any evidence, and I'm not pointing any fingers till we do."

Jon dived into the meal before him, discussing other matters with Harry and Andy, like repairing potholes in the road through town when springtime arrived, and organizing a workday late in March to get the townspeople together to paint the community church.

Elizabeth pulled her plate back toward her when she regained her appetite and ate in silence. She listened to the men's discussion, wanting only to finish her meal and leave. She'd felt a glimmer of friendship when she'd entered the cafe—at least from Harry, Andy, and Libby. But it had seemed to disappear the moment moneymaking and her offhanded association with Matt Winchester had come into the conversation. She'd wanted so much to be part of this community—to make friends, something she hadn't had a lot of. Apparently she wasn't going to have them in Sapphire, either.

With the food thoroughly cleaned from their plates, Harry and Andy pushed away from the table, and both reached out to Elizabeth, shaking her hand. "It was nice meeting you," she said quietly. They smiled, said they looked forward to seeing her again—which she doubted—donned their coats and hats, and left the cafe.

"I'd better be going, too," Elizabeth said, but before she could leave the table, Jon captured her hand.

"Stay awhile longer," he said. "Keep me company, at least while I eat some of Libby's pie."

"Why?" she asked, pulling her hand from his. "I didn't think my presence was all that desirable."

"Your presence isn't a problem, Elizabeth. Not at all." His lopsided grin returned. "Stay. Please," he said, and when she leaned back and folded her arms across her chest, his grin softened into a smile, one she was sure wouldn't last long. It seemed they were destined to fight about one thing or another.

Libby had disappeared into the kitchen, leaving them completely on their own. It wasn't a comfortable feeling, Elizabeth realized. They were too alone, and the room was too quiet—for now.

Jon grabbed an extra fork from the table beside them and placed it in front of Elizabeth. He pushed the huge portion of huckleberry pie to the center of the table. "Care to help me with this?" he asked, digging into the pastry. He took a bite and pulled the fork slowly from his lips. It was the first time Elizabeth had noticed them. They weren't particularly remarkable, except when they cocked up on one side in that crazy grin. But below those unremarkable lips he had a slight cleft in his chin with a half-inch scar off to the left.

"How'd you get the scar?" Elizabeth asked, ignoring the offer of pie.

"A well-swung two-by-four."

"I imagine you deserved it," she said.

"More than likely. Of course, I knocked Matt out cold with my bare fist right after. *He* deserved it, too."

Jon pushed the pie a little closer. "You really ought to give this a try. Libby makes the best huckleberry pie in Montana."

"I make the best cheesecake west of New York," Elizabeth tossed back, getting ready to open a sore subject again. "Of course, I can't treat you or anyone else to my culinary masterpieces until I get the hotel refurbished."

"I'm sure someone would let you use their stove."

"I have a stove, thank you. What I don't have is a decent place to cook, and it looks like I won't unless I do all the work myself."

"That's probably true."

"Nothing I say is going to make you help me, is it?"

"I'm a busy man."

"Yes, you're the mayor. I'd almost forgotten."

"I have one hundred and one people to keep happy," he said.

"One hundred and two. You forgot about me."

"I didn't forget you at all. You've been on my mind since your car slid into town and I helped you get up off the porch."

Elizabeth sighed deeply. Turning her eyes from

his, she finally cut into the pie. Their bantering was getting her nowhere; it was only making her confused. One moment he badgered, the next moment his voice would soften and he'd say something nice, sometimes suggestive. She didn't know what to make of it.

"Y'know, Jon, every once in a while I get the feeling you'd like me to get back into my car and drive out of town."

He laughed. "Even if that's what I wanted, I can't see you running off. You're not going to let me or the fact that you can't get help interfere with your plans. Something tells me you're too stubborn and too resourceful."

"I've never roofed a house before," she stated. "I don't know anything about plumbing, either."

"Minor details." A slow smile tilted his lips. "I'm sure you can handle just about anything."

He scooped up the last piece of pie, holding the fork close to his mouth. "Why did you come to Sapphire?" he asked, changing the tone of their conversation once again.

"Do you want an honest answer?" she asked.

"It beats a dishonest one."

"Well—" she began, then hesitated. She scraped her fork over the few remaining huckleberry seeds and the thin coating of purple filling on the plate in front of her. Jon already assumed the worst of her. He thought she'd come to Sapphire strictly as Matt's partner. It wasn't true, but did he have any right to hear the real reason? And if she gave him a straight answer, would he even believe it?

She set the fork down on the plate and looked into his eyes. He might be one of the most insufferable men she'd met in a long time, but he stirred something inside her that hadn't been touched in a long time—every one of her emotions. Maybe an attempt at friendship was needed. Maybe she had to make the first move.

"I got tired of L.A.," she told him. "I got tired of the business I was in and the people I was working with day in and day out. I wanted a change, something completely new and different."

He didn't speak for a moment. Instead, he folded his arms on the table and looked into her eyes. "Do you think you'll be happy here?" he asked.

"I hope so. Right now, I'm not totally sure."

"I've lived here 'most all my life. I've never gone looking for something new. I don't imagine it's an easy thing to do."

"It's not. I gave up a lot to come here. I had a successful business." She drew in a deep breath, thinking of what she'd left behind, what she'd found today. "I thought I'd come here and everything would be perfect. I hate the cold. The hotel's a disaster. I can't get help. But I won't give up."

"You may find help eventually," Jon told her. "You may even get that hotel up and running. But there's not a damn thing you can do about the cold. It's that way eight months out of twelve. As for paying customers, you're not going to get anyone except Matt's clientele. I'm afraid they might be few and far between, and they might not even be the kind of people you want to cater to."

Oh, he was so self-righteous, so . . . so . . . "With the right advertising—"

"Wrong," he interrupted. "Do you think you're the first person who thought they could start a business here and make a go of it?" He laughed. "Two years ago it was a couple from Arizona who thought they could capitalize on the town's name and sell custom sapphire jewelry. They failed. Before that it was a 'Made in Montana' gift shop that failed."

"Nothing you say will convince me to give up or leave."

"You don't have to leave, just give up your crazy idea about bringing tourists and hunters to town."

"Are you finished?"

"I could go on."

"Don't." Elizabeth pushed away from the table, drew a ten-dollar bill from her pants pocket, and slapped it on the table. "That should cover my dinner and two bites of your pie."

Jon grabbed her hand again. "I invited you. I'll pay."

She pulled her hand away. "I don't particularly like you, Mr. Winchester. I don't like your superior, condescending attitude. I don't care for your opinions, and I don't want you buying my dinner—tonight, or any night. You might be mayor, but you don't own this town . . . or me. So do me a very big favor and stay out of my business and out of my life."

Jon folded his arms across his chest, but she didn't give him the opportunity to utter words she didn't want to hear, like *Suit yourself.*

She walked away from the table and pulled on her coat and gloves. She stuck her head through the kitchen door, said a quick thank-you and goodnight to Libby and Jack, and left the cafe, knowing Jon watched every step of her retreat. Just like earlier in the day, she could feel the intense heat of his eyes against her back.

She crossed the boardwalk and gave little thought to being cautious as she went down the stairs and onto the road.

Behind her she heard the door open and close.

She heard Jon's distinct bootsteps on the wooden planks. "Slow down, Elizabeth," she heard him call out. "You're going to fall."

She wasn't about to slow down. She wouldn't dare fall.

But she did. One boot slid and the other followed.

She struggled to get up, struggled to keep tears out of her eyes. This wasn't the way her new life was supposed to begin. Where were the friends she was going to make? Where were the people wanting to help?

"Give me your hand, Elizabeth," she heard Jon say.

He was standing over her again, looking big and ominous, and oh so superior.

"I don't need your help. I don't need anyone's help." She attempted to get up only to slip again.

She felt Jon's hands slide around her arms, but she shook him off. "I don't care *what* you think of me. I don't even care what you think of Matt. But trust me, I have every intention of fixing up that hotel and renting rooms to anyone willing to pay my price. As I said before, I don't mind hard work. I don't mind getting dirty."

"Just let me help you up, Ellie."

"My name's not Ellie." She glared up into his

eyes. "And if I have to crawl the rest of the way home, I will."

Jon shook his head. "Suit yourself," he said, as he walked away.

And Elizabeth's tears began to fall.

Chapter 4

"It didn't work," Jon said into the phone. "I badgered, I intimidated, I made a fool of myself in front of my friends. Hell, they must have thought I was on drugs, the way I launched into her."

He listened to the voice on the other end.

"Look, I'm not a cop. I tried, but I don't know how to question people to get them to tell their deepest secrets. That's your job."

He paced across the studio floor, the cordless phone stuck to his ear, and stared out the window at the hotel in the distance. "What do I think?" He laughed. "I think she doesn't have a clue what Matt's up to."

Again he listened, the person at the other end of the phone attempting to convince him that this was their opportunity to catch Matt and others. But damn, he didn't want to be involved. Not any longer.

"Look, she's a nice lady. Maybe her brother's involved. I don't know." He fingered the scar on his chin, remembering the curious way she studied his lips, his chin. He thought of the mixture of hurt and anger in her eyes when she told him, basically, to get out of her life. "Even if I wanted to find out more, I blew it tonight," he continued. "I was rude and arrogant. I made her cry. There's no way in hell she's going to let me get close to her again."

The voice on the other end was calm—too, too cool.

"I know it was my idea, but I'm not going to get involved with her just so you can catch Matt."

The voice was louder now.

"Yeah, I want him, too. But it's not right. It's not fair to her." He took a deep breath. "It's not fair to me, either."

Calm again.

"I'll think about it," Jon said, hanging up before the conversation could continue, before he agreed to get further involved.

An entire week went by. Jon was out of town half the time on business, preparing for a show in Denver. People would come from all over the world to see his latest pieces of bronze. The wealthy would scribble out checks or plunk down credit cards to claim a sculpture. Half of them bought because they liked the work, half because of the intrigue. For seven years now, Jon had displayed his work, selling at exorbitant prices—and giving all proceeds to wildlife organizations. Of course, no one knew the artist's identity. He'd insisted on remaining anonymous, and that added to the attraction of his work. Write-ups had been done in magazines, in newspapers. The more publicity, the higher the prices and the more that was donated.

Jon didn't need the money; he didn't want the

fame. He'd found his niche in life. He loved to sculpt, but he also liked his privacy. The world might share his finished pieces, but his work and his art were something he shared with no one but his closest friends, and they'd long ago learned that his secret was just as valuable as the pieces he sold.

But in spite of his trip to Denver, the impending show wasn't foremost on his mind. Elizabeth Fitzgerald was.

As he drove through town one day, he saw her hauling a five-gallon bottle of water out of the store and down the street toward the hotel. He'd thought about stopping to offer his help; instead, he tipped his hat and kept on driving. She wouldn't have wanted his help anyway.

But the vision of what he saw remained in his mind as he drove into Helena for supplies. Elizabeth had on a furry parka and black knit pants that hugged her legs rather nicely. God, she had great legs! And she'd come up with some kind of black combat boots that laced all the way up to her calves and looked like they had two inches of tread on the soles.

He didn't see her slip once, not when he drove toward her, not when he tipped his hat, not when he watched her through his rearview mirror. She was just as self-sufficient as she'd said.

And damn if he didn't admire her.

Alex wrapped his legs around the brass arms of the crystal chandelier hanging in the middle of the parlor, leaned against the glass beads suspended at its center, and watched the lady work.

For seven days he'd spied on her. For seven days

he'd done a fairly good job buttoning his mouth. Somehow, he'd kept his hands to himself, too. Oh, he'd played a trick or two, but keeping an eye on her was much more fun than haunting had ever been.

She moved kind of nice and graceful around every room, polishing mirrors and wood, sweeping away dirt and cobwebs. She'd even cleaned his favorite chandelier. It sparkled like new, and he knew if he could smell, the scent would remind him of the lemon cleaner Amanda had often used, the sweet scent that had lingered long into the evenings and was often on her hand when he had kissed it goodnight.

Oh, Amanda. Alex sighed deeply and remembered the way his pretty lady had floated from one room to another, polishing this, dusting that. She'd had servants, of course—a dozen or more. But Amanda was never one to sit back and let others do all the work.

She could cook, too. And bake. And he thought back to that church social when Mr. Dalton had auctioned off cakes and pastries the ladies had made. Amanda had tried out a new recipe for berry pie, crimped the edges to look like ruffled lace, and cut two entwined A's—her first initial and his—into the flaky crust. Alex had doubled every bid, captured his prize, and enjoyed every morsel of pie while Amanda had talked of plans for their future.

They'd have had a great future, too.

If his life hadn't come to such an abrupt end.

He felt tears forming in his eyes—tears he knew didn't really exist. But the heartache was real. And the loneliness.

He didn't want to watch the lady in his house anymore. Not right now. He swooped out of the chandelier and up the stairs to the attic room, to the window where he liked to stand and look out at the house that should have been his.

The home he should have shared all his life—with Amanda.

Jon couldn't remember a longer week. When he was gone, he thought about what he should or shouldn't do as far as catching Matt was concerned. Thinking of that made him think of Elizabeth, and what he should or shouldn't do about her, too. He'd damned himself again and again for his actions her first night in town.

He'd been hot about the poaching, and the thought of Sapphire growing and prospering hadn't set well, either. But he didn't have any proof she was involved with the first, and as to the second, if she was able to attract a few visitors to Sapphire, what did it matter? They wouldn't stay long; there was nothing to do in town. On top of that, that old hotel would creak and moan, and if there was a ghost, it would send her guests packing—fast.

But Elizabeth had been there a week and nothing had made her leave. Not his arrogance; not a phantom.

Which proved she was strong enough to stand up to anything—which he liked—and that a ghost didn't exist, just as the psychiatrist had told him all those years ago.

That meant there was nothing but the animosity he'd built up between himself and Elizabeth to keep him from going back to the hotel and helping her out.

She'd asked for help. She'd need it, too. That place was too big, too old, too run-down for her to do everything on her own. And no one else was going to assist.

He should have told her the truth about why she couldn't get help. He should have told her that the rumors about a ghost might be just crazy old stories, but they'd long kept the place uninhabited and long kept anyone from venturing into the hotel. He might be the only one with guts enough to go inside—since he'd been there so many times before. But she'd told him to stay away; she didn't want his help.

That's why he kept his distance, and when he wasn't out of town, he sat in his studio and remembered the pretty lady he'd hurt so badly.

The Rubenesque beauty he longed to know.

It was three A.M. Pressing his fingers into clay, he shaped, molded, and smoothed out the facial contours until they matched the vision he'd committed to memory. Her nose was sleek and straight and as regal as her high cheekbones. And her eyes . . . he'd captured them just as they'd looked when she'd sat next to him in the cafe, before the arguments had begun. She'd listened to Harry and Andy, yet lowered her eyelids occasionally and given him a sideways glance, as if she didn't want him to know she was looking. But he knew, and he'd caught her a time or two. That was when the gold flecks in her amber eyes sparkled. He couldn't capture the brightness of her eyes in clay, but he could re-create that sidelong, secretive glance.

He'd molded her lips earlier, the slight, innocent smile embedded deeply in his mind. Now he traced his fingers over the full lower lip and wondered if the luscious red ones he remembered would be as soft and sweet as he'd imagined. Memories of her lips and her eyes had kept him awake long into the night. When fatigue made it difficult for him to keep his eyes open, he slept fitfully on the chaise in his studio, his legs and shoulders dangling over the edges. The antique satin lounge had been designed for a graceful beauty, not a giant of a man, and each time Jon tossed and turned, he nearly fell to the floor. When he did catch a few winks, Elizabeth Fitzgerald haunted his dreams.

Finally, he gave up his halfhearted attempt at slumber and paced his studio floor, back and forth, back and forth. He thought about her lips and those big amber eyes, envisioned her stretched out on his chaise in those red hooker boots and nothing else, and he watched the lights in the hotel windows, wondering if she was able to sleep peacefully in that empty hotel. And when pacing and thinking wore away at his nerves, he did the thing that had always given him peace—he turned a lifeless mound of clay into a thing of beauty.

Sitting down on a stool, he took a good look at the bust he'd spent the night creating. Wisps of hair softened the woman's forehead, and he'd swirled her long, heavy braid over one shoulder, draping it across the slight hint of her breasts, the place where his sculpting had stopped. He hadn't dared go any further. That he'd save for later, when he had a clearer image to commit to memory.

He drew up his shoulders, stretching out the kinks and tension from hours of painstaking work. Tomorrow he'd make the mold, and later he'd pour the bronze. And when the time was right, he'd break open the cast and polish the roughened figure until it glimmered, just the way he imagined Elizabeth's skin would glow when caught in the firelight, or after a night of making love.

Damn! He was obsessing about a woman who might never again give him the time of day. Long hours awake, too many hours wrapped up in his work, and a strange, overpowering desire to be with Elizabeth Fitzgerald again were taking their toll on his mind.

Maybe he needed a kick in the head.

He opted for coffee instead.

Elizabeth opened the kitchen screen door, shivering at the annoying squeak of the hinges, and threw out a bucket of dirty water onto the once pristine snow. She'd already discovered she couldn't dump anything down an inside drain. If she tried, the water wouldn't disappear; instead, it bubbled and glugged.

She needed to crawl under the sink or get a plumber. The first she didn't want to do because she hated tight, closed-in spots—a fear she hadn't rid herself of after the quake. As for the plumber, she'd called everywhere, but no one wanted to drive all the way to Sapphire. That answer didn't end with plumbers, either. Carpenters, handymen, housekeepers—no one wanted a job. Not with her. Not in her hotel. Not in the middle of nowhere.

Hauling water had become a necessity. Thank

God the stove and refrigerator worked, along with the toilet downstairs.

Closing the door, she latched it securely, wondering if it had been partly responsible for some of the thumps she'd heard during the night, thumps that had interrupted her slumber. Those disturbing thuds hadn't been the only noises to keep her drifting in and out of sleep. The creaking floorboards and wind howling through the windows had pierced through her subconscious over and over, long before the chandelier lights began to flicker and that horribly sour note pinged again and again on the old upright piano in the parlor.

Thank goodness her brother had warned her about the sounds. If he hadn't told her the truth about the old hotel, she just might have believed the place was haunted.

Which was impossible.

She set the bucket in the kitchen sink and dropped into a kitchen chair. Her body ached from a week of hard work. She'd mopped the floors downstairs, swept away all the cobwebs, dusted each piece of furniture, and moved every antique knickknack to the kitchen so they could be cleaned and polished.

She hadn't tackled the upstairs yet, except for hauling out a few old mattresses that had become home to critters too numerous to mention and ridding the rooms of spiders and their webs.

She'd dozed in a sleeping bag for seven nights. The old chesterfield was soft and big, and she found she could curl up nice and comfortable amid its high back and arms.

The storekeeper's son had been kind enough to

drop a cord of wood at her back door. She'd bought an ax and filled a box with kindling, and she'd managed to keep a fire going almost every night. She'd long ago given up hope of the furnace keeping her warm. The temperature control knob seemed to have a mind of its own. Every time she turned it up, it would slowly wind its way back down.

A week ago she'd halfway considered giving up on the place. The work was more extensive than she'd imagined, she had no help, and she had no friends.

But Jon Winchester's arrogant attitude had fired her resolve. Every time she thought of quitting, she remembered his words, that insufferable lopsided grin, those crossed arms. No way would she give up.

She had cried, of course. In the loneliness of these rooms her tears had fallen easily. And then she'd reflected on the good things. She had a home, a future; she was alive. A year ago at this time she'd thought she was going to lose all those things. Better off alive and lonely, she thought. Dead didn't seem such a great alternative.

The grandfather clock just inside the entry—still running in spite of its age and the filth she'd cleaned from it—gonged eight times to announce the hour, and with each gong she heard a thud. Those noises were going to drive her insane.

It wasn't until she picked up a cloth to polish a silver candlestick that she realized the thud was a knock. Going to the entry, she saw the shadow of a man—a big man.

Oh, heavens! She could think of much more appropriate words, but she'd promised not to swear. It didn't matter if the occasion warranted it.

She tapped her foot and counted to ten before opening the door and facing the titan.

" 'Mornin', Elizabeth." Jon tipped his hat. One side of his mouth tilted into a poor excuse for a smile, his sapphire eyes sparkled, and her feet and toes had the nerve to grow warm. She didn't like the effect he had on her. He was abusive and rude. How dare she let his looks interfere with the way she loathed the man!

"You didn't leave anything behind when you left here a week ago," she said flatly. "Is there some other reason you've dropped by?"

"City council's not too busy at the moment. You need help, and I aim to do the work."

"I don't need your help. I think I made that clear before."

"You made it clear, but I decided this morning that you hadn't meant a word of it." He knelt down, picked up the biggest toolbox she'd ever seen, and grabbed a ladder he must have propped up next to the door.

"I meant every word."

The grin touched his face. He laughed and would have walked right over her if she hadn't moved out of his way. She was sure he could do it, too. In fact, she had the feeling Jon Winchester could leap tall buildings in a single bound, swing a sledgehammer with his little finger, and drive a nail with just one blow.

He leaned the ladder against a wall in the parlor and turned around. "I've watched you hauling water all week. I take it the plumbing's not working too well."

"Oh, there's water, all right. It looks like sludge, and I imagine that's what's stopped up the drains."

He set the toolbox on the floor and walked toward her. Too close . . . way too close. She took a step back. He moved another step closer, reached out an ungloved hand, and gently brushed a thumb across the tip of her nose. "Y'know, Elizabeth, you're just as pretty with dirt on your nose as you are without."

Her eyes widened.

Red crept up her neck, and she hoped it had stopped before reaching her cheeks.

"If you want to work, fine. But please save the flattery for someone else."

He shrugged and she turned away, but his words stuck in her mind. *You're pretty* and *You're gorgeous* were such commonplace words thrown at the models she'd worked with that they meant little or nothing. They were part of the business, the hype. But *You're just as pretty* had sounded so much nicer, so much more sincere, coming from Jon. She liked it—but he didn't need to know.

She walked to the kitchen, coming to a sudden halt when Jon cupped his hand around her arm. "I owe you an apology."

His words surprised her, but she didn't turn around. She waited for more.

"I was rude the other day."

"Overbearing and judgmental, too," she added.

"You're probably right." His hand slid up her arm and rested on her shoulder. "I've got faults, Elizabeth. You're bound to find even more flaws in my character—if you're willing to get to know me better."

She stepped forward, away from the grip of his hand. She thought about turning around, she thought about giving him some kind of response, but instead she continued into the kitchen. Behind her she could hear Jon's boots on the hardwood floor. "You could start with the plumbing," she said.

"I could," he said, circling Elizabeth until he stood right in front of her. He leaned against the counter, and slowly she looked into his eyes. "Am I going to be just the hired help," he asked, "or will you give me a chance to make up for an unfortunate case of bad manners?"

Her smile came too easily. She wanted to hold it back, but she couldn't.

"Does that smile mean I'm forgiven?" he asked.

She shook her head. "Fix the plumbing for free and I'll consider it."

He laughed. "Ever the businesswoman, right?"

"*Successful* businesswoman," she corrected him. "I learned a long time ago how to deal with stubborn, egotistical men. That helped me succeed."

"That's part of why I like you."

"Because I'm successful?"

"No, because you think you know how to deal with me."

"You've already informed me that a two-by-four doesn't work. Guess I'll just have to stick with words." She turned away from his grin and ran a hand over the old and cracked linoleum countertop.

"This needs to be replaced," she said, effectively

changing the subject, "and the wallpaper needs to be stripped in every room. My first priority, though, is the plumbing. I'd like it to be *your* first priority, too."

He laughed. "Are you always this dictatorial with your hired help?"

She tilted her head and smiled. "It didn't endear me to anyone, but it got the job done."

"Good thing I decided I liked you long before I decided to be your slave."

And he did like her. He liked her spunk, he liked her drive. He liked the dirt on her nose and the wisps of ebony hair that had fallen out of her braid and encircled her face like a halo. But she was no angel. Hell, no! He'd dated angels, even been in love with an angel once—and he'd been bored to tears.

There was nothing the least bit dull about Elizabeth Fitzgerald.

"Before I shove my head under the sink, why don't you give me a tour of this place?" he said. "Haven't been in here since I was a kid."

"I doubt it's changed."

"A little boy's memories aren't always the same as a man's. Things seemed immense back then . . . of course, I've grown a bit since I was a kid."

Slowly her eyes traced the length of his six-foot-six frame from head to toe, and he just stood there and let her peruse him. A hint of a smile touched her face, tinting her cheeks a pale shade of pink against her porcelain skin. He thought she might comment on his size. Instead, she returned to talk of the hotel. "I guess there's time to show you around. The upstairs, at least. Once you finish the plumbing down here, maybe you can figure out how to add a few bathrooms."

"You have high hopes for my plumbing skills, don't you?"

"I would imagine a man like you thinks he can do anything," she fired back, and he liked the pretty grin that accompanied the words.

"I imagine I could, with the right incentive."

She laughed, and he sensed some of her animosity draining away. "Come on," she said, opening a narrow kitchen door that led to a small landing with steps going up and another flight leading to the basement. "The furnace is downstairs. Maybe you can check it out in the next few days. The fire's nice, but it doesn't warm the entire place."

She led the way to the rooms above and Jon followed closely behind. "There are two floors above us and the attic, with four bedrooms on each floor," she said, "far more than I'll need. What I'd like to do is put in four suites, two on each floor. One for me, the others for guests."

Jon listened to her talk as he followed her up the stairs, so similar to the spiral stairway leading from his kitchen to his studio. It was close, quiet, and dark. He could smell dust mixed with the light scent of Elizabeth's perfume. And then an odd sensation he remembered from his childhood caught hold of him: he felt as though they were being followed, that each step he took was matched by another step—*that wasn't Elizabeth's.*

He turned around suddenly, but saw nothing except darkness.

He placed a boot on the next stair and a strange light breeze blew against the hair that waved slightly over his collar. He gripped the iron railing. He didn't like what he felt. He didn't like feeling that something was mimicking his moves and breathing down his neck. He'd spent years in and out of a psychiatrist's office being convinced that ghosts didn't exist—except in his mind.

But, dammit, it had seemed real back then.

It felt real now.

The door at the top of the stairs creaked when Elizabeth opened it, and they stepped into the dimly lit hallway. "I turned all the lights on this morning to brighten up the place. Didn't do much good, though," she said. "When you have a chance, maybe you could put new bulbs in."

He quit thinking about ghosts and things he hadn't worried about in over twenty years and took a good look at his surroundings. Yard after yard of wainscoting needed to be stripped and refinished. Creaking floors needed the same thing. Yellowed wallpaper hung in strips, their edges curled and turning brown. There were waterspots on the ceilings, and the light fixtures were so dingy that putting in new bulbs wouldn't brighten the hall. "From the looks of this place, I think you'd be better off just tearing it down and starting over again."

The smile he'd seen on her face when they'd stepped into the hall faded away. "My last house fell down—with me under it—and this is the first permanent home I've had since then," she said. "If you think the job's too big, tell me now. I don't mind working hard . . . and I don't mind working alone."

He'd meant it as a joke, although he really believed it would cost far more than the place was worth to fix it up. He hadn't meant to hurt her—again. Her words about her last house falling down, and the almost tearful way she'd uttered them, touched him deep inside. It was an uncommon feeling, but he thought he could easily get accustomed to it.

She was tugging at a piece of wallpaper, and he pulled her hand away and drew her close. He tilted her chin and held it there so she would look at him. "I'm sorry." They were two words he hadn't said very often, but he meant them completely.

Her amber eyes looked into his, and they were filled with tears. Slowly she smiled. "Are you sorry about my house falling down, or about your insensitive remark about this place?"

"Both." He smoothed away a smudge of dirt from her cheek. "If you think this place is worth fixing, I'll help you out. If you want to talk about the other, I don't mind listening."

"I've talked too much about the other. It's not something I want to discuss anymore." She moved away from him and went through a door on her right. He followed behind and leaned against the doorjamb, watching her walk around the room, touching the old dusty furniture, grasping a bedpost and holding it tightly.

"This place may look like a dump to you, but it doesn't to me," she said. "There's so much I want to do around here."

"Tell me your plans."

"Are you humoring me?" she asked, "or do you really want to know?"

"I want to know."

She sat on the wooden bed frame and looked around the room, her amber eyes glittering as she spoke. "I want to restore it, make it look just as it did a hundred years ago. This is going to be my room," she said. "I've ordered wallpaper samples from a place in New York that specializes in Victorian reproductions. I've counted three layers of paper on these walls. I hope when I get down to the bottom, that I can match what was originally in the house. And this bed—" She ran her fingers over the footboard, then looked to the top of the tall, spiraling bedposts. "I've got fabric samples coming, too. I'll have yards and yards of Venetian lace draping the bed and the windows."

She smiled at him then. "It's going to be beautiful."

He folded his arms across his chest and nodded.

"This, of course," she said, moving across the room to a pink-and-white variegated marble statue of entwined lovers, "has got to go."

Jon grinned. "Oh, I don't know." He left his place in the doorway and crossed the room. He stood on the other side of the statue, studying it, studying Elizabeth. "It's got a certain charm, don't you think?"

"Obviously you don't know the first thing about sculpture."

He laughed. "Obviously."

"Well," she added, "I don't know much about it, either, but this piece seems a little crude. The marble's rough, and the sculptor must have had a very warped sense of lovemaking, the way he entwined their arms and legs."

Actually, Jon rather liked the way their arms and

legs were tangled together. He looked at Elizabeth's long, long legs encased in red knit pants that hugged every curve. God, she had great legs. And he thought about them wrapped around his.

It was a hell of a thought!

He touched the marble, slowly running his fingers over the woman's shoulder, the length of her arm. Elizabeth was right. The piece was rough, inexpensive. It was plaster, not marble. Poured, not sculpted.

"I could take it to the dump," Jon said, "or haul it up to the attic."

No!

The voice startled him. It came with a gust of air. Close to his ear, so close he knew Elizabeth hadn't heard.

"I'm not sure what I want done with it yet," she said, and he knew she hadn't heard the voice. "It's really funny, you know. I can't believe any good Victorian woman would have kept something like that in her bedroom."

He looked around the room. He saw nothing out of the ordinary, but he'd seen nothing all those years ago, either. It was only a voice he'd heard back then. It was only a voice he heard now.

And it was all in his imagination.

"Jon?" Elizabeth's hand was on his arm, a look of concern on her face. "Are you all right?"

He laughed. "I'm fine. I was just thinking about good Victorian women. They weren't all that way, you know."

"No?" She looked up at him through the longest, thickest black lashes he'd ever seen.

"No. In fact, the woman who owned this place

had a reputation that, well, didn't exactly fit the standard of an uptight Victorian lady."

"Tell me about her," she said, as she moved away from the statue.

"Would you like to know the history of the hotel, too?"

"Only if it has a less than pristine reputation. A good story or two might help attract visitors," she said, keeping her eyes turned from him as she walked about the room, inspecting the insides of drawers, the tops of tables, and the condition of a ceramic pitcher and basin set before a mirror on a more than dusty chest.

He leaned against the fireplace, thinking for a moment about some of the stories his grandfather had told, then forgetting them completely as he watched her move about the room. He studied her form, her voluptuous curves hugged tight by the red shirt and pants she wore. Botticelli had long ago painted curves like hers, but Jon wanted to sculpt them, and for a moment he wasn't sure if he wanted to do them in clay, then bronze, or sculpt the woman herself, molding her flesh in the depths of his palms.

He picked up a dusty glass vase that looked as though it had perched on the mantel forever and turned it around and around in his fingers, trying not to think about her body, trying to think of the stories. "It wasn't always a hotel," he said. "Actually, the first banker in town, Horace Carruthers, built it for his wife, Phoebe. I've seen a picture or two. She was a little too prim and proper to suit my tastes, but Horace must have loved her."

A trace of air blew against his cheek, the distinct

yet faint sound of a man's voice whispering a disdainful *Hah!* into his ear. Jon's senses went on alert. Had he really heard something? Or had he imagined the retort and the sound of someone speaking? He rolled his eyes slightly, tilting his head just a bit, but all he saw were the tattered drapes, hanging limp and lifeless, and a pretty woman across the room staring at him, waiting for him to go on.

"So, she was prim and proper. What else?"

Elizabeth hadn't heard or felt a thing, he realized. It was just like all those years ago. Maybe he was a bit crazy.

He ran his fingers through his hair and continued the story. "Phoebe was the epitome of high society, or so she thought. Back then, being part of the right circle was important in Sapphire. She liked the status of being the bank owner's wife, but when her husband passed away and the citizens learned he'd fooled around a time or two, squandered a lot of the bank's assets, and left Phoebe in debt up to her ears, she was scorned by most of the ladies in town."

"That doesn't seem fair."

"Fair or not, it didn't put a damper on Phoebe. What the ladies thought didn't seem to matter nearly so much as enjoying the finer things in life, and left on her own, Phoebe became a fairly enterprising woman. She turned her home into the Sapphire Hotel, and the more affluent men of the region stayed here when they came to town on business. She provided the finest food and drink, and she probably provided a few other services as well."

Jon stopped twisting and turning the vase and

set it back on the mantel. Crossing the room, he gripped one of the bedposts. "Do you think that's sinister enough to tell your guests?"

"It's a start." Elizabeth laughed. "Do you think that statue might have belonged to Phoebe? Maybe this room I've picked for myself was the place where she held midnight trysts?"

This is the place, all right!

The voice whispered in his ear again. Pretend it didn't happen, he told himself. Pretend you didn't hear a thing.

"It all happened a hundred years ago," he said, trying to ignore his fear that they weren't alone in the room. "I imagine you could make up any stories you wanted. No one would know unless they'd done some research."

"I have the strangest feeling the truth would be so much better than any stories I could dream up. Of course, I don't think I'll ever know the truth behind that statue or why it's in this room. I doubt any research I could do would tell what actually happened in the Sapphire Hotel."

"Are you really that curious?"

"I've fallen in love with this place, with the atmosphere and everything about it. I want to know all there is to know."

"Me, too," he said slowly, walking across the room toward Elizabeth. He wanted to know all about her lips, about the way they'd taste if he kissed her. He wanted to know about the feel of her body, and if her breasts were as soft as they looked.

God, she was breathtaking.

She must have sensed what was going on in his

mind. She backed away, right into a wall.

He stopped in front of her, nearly an arm's length away. "I've agreed to work for you," he said, "but we haven't discussed my price."

"No, we haven't," she said, turning her head away rather than looking into his eyes. "I'm not rich, but maybe you could give me an estimate—materials, labor. I always pay on time."

He watched the way her breasts rose and fell. He could hear the deepness of her breathing.

He wanted to kiss her.

Moving a hand close to her face, he wrapped his finger around a tendril of ebony hair. "I don't need your money, Elizabeth. Just consider it the mayor's job to help you out." He touched her cheek with his thumb, caressing the softness. "Maybe you'd consider thinking of me as something other than an employee, though."

"I think I could do that."

"And you'll forget what happened a week ago . . . you'll forget all about me being an arrogant, insufferable male."

She smiled.

He moved a little closer.

"I don't think I can forget, and I don't think you can easily change what you are. But I might be able to forgive."

Jon slid his fingers under her chin and tilted her face. God, she had beautiful lips!

He lowered his head.

He felt her rise up on tiptoe.

Hell and tarnation!

Thwack!

Chapter 5

Jon's head jolted up when the voice thundered through the room, when the picture frame slid from the wall and crashed, spraying shattered glass across the floor.

Dust and dirt swirled like a tornado over the floorboards, and the tattered drapes flew out at the windows.

Elizabeth ducked under Jon's arm—the one he'd almost wrapped around her to pull her into a tight embrace—and went to the window. It was opened just a crack, and she pushed hard to seal it shut.

She leaned against the wall and laughed. "It gets a little drafty in here at times. I thought I had all the windows closed, but I must have missed that one."

"You didn't hear anything?" he asked.

"No," she said, shaking her head.

Well, he'd heard it, very distinctly. That voice had interrupted everything; it had spoiled the moment, and no way in hell was a ghost or some crazy voice in his head going to get in the way the next time he came close to trying out those perfect lips that belonged to Elizabeth Fitzgerald.

* * *

Alex sat on the mantel, his elbows shoved into his knees, his chin into his fists, and stewed. How dare she bring a man upstairs, and to this room, of all places? A den of iniquity, that's what it was . . . a place for midnight trysts and secret, scandalous alliances. He'd watched it all when Phoebe had lived, watched it from this very same spot on top of the mantel.

Sweet, innocent Widow Carruthers, she'd been called. Hah! If the townspeople—no, if the town's *womenfolk*—had known what went on in the wee hours of night in this room in the Widow Carruthers' boardinghouse, they would have tarred and feathered the old biddy and strung their husbands up by their unmentionables. But tarnation, the goings-on had sure been a sight to watch. 'Tweren't much else to do on lonely nights, Alex thought, especially when one was dead.

He had no intention of watching this new woman do the things Phoebe had done, especially with that big galoot who was making moony eyes at her. The man was a Winchester, and Winchesters were low down, good-for-nothing, flesh-eating buzzards . . . murdering cheats who'd more than likely rip the gold right out of their grandmothers' teeth and spit on them as they lay in their coffins. It didn't matter at all, Alex thought, that this man had been his friend, once upon a time. Maybe he'd been only a kid when he'd stomped on their friendship, but that was no excuse. Alex had tossed aside his vow of revenge to help the kid, and what had he gotten for his efforts? He'd been betrayed.

The boy, just like the man, was a Winchester—

Alex should have expected to be treated like dirt.

But Alex wasn't about to let that Winchester fellow treat the new lady in his house that way. Alex had watched that dolt ogling her. He probably imagined the woman would give herself to him like a brazen hussy. The man was a Winchester, after all, and Winchesters were all alike.

Even this one.

Blast it all! He didn't have time to get maudlin and think about the recent past, and how much he'd enjoyed this man when he was a kid. He needed to think about getting back to Amanda. He didn't know how he was going to escape this mausoleum he'd been entombed in for a century, but he'd had a sixth sense for a very long time that someone good and kind and generous would come along and show him the way.

It had to be this new woman. And he wasn't about to let anyone or anything get between them, especially that overgrown oaf she'd invited to this room.

With that thought in mind, he knocked another picture frame off a wall.

Jon single-handedly carried the box springs and mattress up the stairs and positioned them on the bed frame. Elizabeth had slept in a sleeping bag for too many nights, and he wasn't going to let her do it again. He had a monstrous house filled with unoccupied rooms and unoccupied furniture; finding new bedding wasn't a problem.

Elizabeth had protested, of course. She wanted the plumbing fixed; he said he'd take care of that all in good time. She'd gritted her teeth and finally given in, and somehow they'd managed to laugh as they'd tugged and fitted sheets and blankets onto the bed.

Lord, how he loved her laugh!

He'd gone down to the basement and checked the furnace, and hauled mops and buckets and bottled water upstairs to clean the room where Elizabeth planned to sleep. He had to do something to exert some energy. He didn't have clay to pound his fist into. No, the only way he could relieve some of his frustration over that near-miss kiss was to work . . . *hard.*

Maybe work would push that voice out of his mind, too.

Not many things frightened him, but the thought of being crazy did.

He hauled a lamp upstairs and a few other pieces of furniture Elizabeth thought she'd like in the room, then stripped away the worst of the peeling wallpaper while Elizabeth dusted and polished mahogany and cherry and oak.

She was standing on his ladder, just beginning to clean a window, when he slid down on the floor to take a break. He leaned back against the wall, folded his arms over his chest and crossed his ankles, then watched her for a good, long minute.

She had no idea he was looking; if she did, she didn't let on. With her arms extended over her head and her hands making circular motions with a sponge on the glass, he could see the soft curve of her breasts. They were very full and very round, and they swayed just slightly as she moved. Absently, he looked down at his big hands and thought they might be the perfect fit for Elizabeth

Fitzgerald. Then he laughed to himself. It was a crazy thought. They had too much going against them—for a one-nighter, or something even longer.

He'd always liked his women petite. Redheads and blondes. He'd never been with a tall woman before, and never with a woman who enjoyed good food and didn't hesitate to eat gravy or pie. He'd sure missed out on a lot of awfully fine things. He liked looking at Elizabeth's long, long legs, at the roundness of her hips that tapered nicely toward a trim waist, and at that seemingly endless black braid that swayed when she moved. She was definitely a woman who'd stepped into his world from a different century, or from an Old Masters painting.

He very much liked what he saw.

"Elizabeth," he said, catching her attention. She turned slowly, one hand resting on the window frame for support.

"Are you comfortable down there?" she asked lightly, her cheeks flushed from exercise, her smile bright with laughter.

"Just enjoying the view." He laughed when she rolled her eyes. She said she didn't care much for compliments, but he had no intention of stopping. "As much as I like watching you work, I think you ought to take a break."

"Maybe a short one," she said, stepping down from the ladder. She pulled the Latex gloves from her hands, draped them over a rung, and crossed the room, sitting in a bentwood rocker Jon had brought upstairs earlier.

"Y'know," he began, "I've told you all about

Phoebe Carruthers; it seems only fair you should tell me a little about you."

"I don't like talking about myself."

"Then what about your work? What possessed you to give up photography to become an innkeeper?"

She leaned back in the rocker, resting her head against the high back. She closed her eyes and he thought for sure she might fall asleep rather than answer his question. But he waited, and finally she spoke.

"My parents were photographers. They traveled everywhere; they were caught up in social issues and wars. They took horrible pictures of starving families and bombing victims—and I wanted to work with them."

"Why?"

She opened her eyes again and looked into his. "Not out of some desire to help the world," she said. "I was a kid. I wanted to have a good time and what was going on in the world didn't interest me much. But being with my parents did. I saw too little of them, so I picked up a camera and learned everything I could."

"Did you get to travel with them?"

"No. They went to Northern Ireland and died in a bombing. I never had a chance to go anywhere with them."

"I'm sorry."

"It was a long time ago."

But it still bothered her. He could see the tears in the corners of her eyes. "What made you choose fashion photography?"

"My parents had friends in Los Angeles, and it

seemed like a logical place to go when I graduated from high school. I'd been cooped up in all-girl boarding schools most of my life; Eric—my brother—was a few years younger, and he hadn't had much excitement at school, either. So the moment I graduated, I exercised my newfound parental authority, pulled him out of school, and headed for L.A."

She closed her eyes again, rocking slowly in the chair. "I met a fashion photographer with a great reputation and asked him for a job. Of course, we had opposite things in mind. He wanted me to model," she said. The smile was gone from her face when she looked at Jon again. "Does that surprise you?"

"No. You're tall . . . you're beautiful."

"That's what he said, too. Of course, just like now, I preferred rich foods to carrots and celery, and I definitely didn't have a model's figure. But he changed all that—put me on a starvation diet and trained me how to walk, how to sit, and how to smile. He even wanted to change the way I talked. I lost nearly thirty pounds in less than two months. I had hollow cheeks. I even had protruding hipbones."

"You weren't happy though, were you?"

She shook her head. "I made the mistake of falling in love. I would have done *anything* for him at the time." She got up from the rocker and fidgeted with the covers on the bed, straightening wrinkles that weren't really there. "He started using me in a lot of his photo shoots," she continued, "but I didn't like the work. I wasn't happy, and I guess it showed. I couldn't be what he wanted, even though I tried. A year later I got sick. I was tired all the time—and he got tired of me and moved on to another pretty face."

She'd changed a lot since then, Jon realized. The Elizabeth sitting in this room would never bend to some man's will; she had too much drive and spirit. They were two of the things he liked so much about her.

"Did you quit modeling then?" he asked.

She nodded. "I was mad at myself for letting him take advantage of me; and I was mad at him for walking out after all I'd done to please him. I made up my mind I wouldn't let anyone do that to me again. Lucky for me, I'd always been more interested in what was going on *behind* the camera than in front, and a lot of people knew it. I took the money I'd made from modeling, bought more camera equipment, and started snapping pictures of some of the people I knew. I shoved my photos in front of every talent scout, every agency. Wasn't long before I was getting more assignments than my former friend." She laughed. "He wasn't happy, but I was."

"Were you?" Jon asked.

"I made good money. I sent Eric to college. I bought a home that I loved."

"But were you happy?" Jon prodded.

"I didn't care much for the people I worked with, and they knew it. I preferred staying at home when I wasn't working. I collected antiques; I baked and took cooking classes; I even liked to pull weeds and plant flowers."

He remembered what she'd said about her house collapsing. She hadn't wanted to talk about it before, maybe she would now. "What happened to your home?"

"An earthquake," she said flatly, then moved suddenly away from the bed and went back to the window. "Have I told you enough about me?" she asked, pulling the gloves back onto her hands.

"For now."

She climbed up a few steps on the ladder and looked at him as he rose from his spot on the floor and picked up the mop. "I don't talk about my life very much," she said. "I don't know why I did just now."

"Because I asked?"

She laughed. "The reason would have to be more compelling than that."

"Maybe deep down inside you like me and realize I'm a very understanding person?"

She smiled softly. "Maybe," she answered, then took the sponge out of the bucket and turned back to the window she'd been washing.

There were no maybes in *his* mind. He liked her—very, very much.

It must have taken nearly another fifteen minutes of swishing the mop around the floor before he had the parquet cleaned. He was rinsing the mop out when he heard the loud, clanking *thud* and the splash against the floor. He spun around and caught the sweet sound of Elizabeth's laughter. She was sopped from shoulder to waist, and the bucket of dirty water that had been sitting on top of the ladder now lay on its side with its contents spilled across the floor he'd just mopped. He laughed at the surprised expression on Elizabeth's face, but his body tensed the second he caught sight of that red thermal shirt she was wearing. Soaked right through, it clung like a second skin, and he could see every detail of her full, round breasts. And he liked what he saw.

"It's freezing," she said, her teeth chattering, her body shivering. There was no doubt at all in Jon's mind that she was cold, especially with his eyes aimed right at her shirt.

Slowly she crossed her arms over her chest. "I'm going downstairs to change," she said. "Hope you don't mind cleaning up the mess I just made."

He shook his head. "I take it you're not going to keep me company any longer?"

"I don't think so. I feel like I've worked nonstop for one solid week. I don't tire easily, but all I want to do right now is get out of these wet clothes, build a fire, and kick back."

"Have dinner with me instead," he said, and when she didn't answer immediately, he tried to think of a more compelling reason for her to say yes. "It's Monday. Libby's serving up pork chops again."

"I don't know, Jon. I really am tired. Could I give you an answer after I've cleaned up?"

Hell, women didn't normally turn down his invitations, but he rather liked the challenge he was facing with Elizabeth. He crossed his hands over the top of the mop handle. "Suit yourself," he said, and grinned when she rolled her eyes. He wasn't about to leave the invitation open; he wasn't about to close it, either. The next move was hers.

He could hear those combat boots of hers all the way down the hall and running down the stairs. He could picture that braid of hers swaying to and fro as she moved. He'd watched it off and on all day, just as he'd watched her hips.

God, she was everything a woman ought to be!

Leave her alone.

He heard it this time. It was real; it was close.

Anger spilled from the depths of Jon's eyes. He'd been a child the last time he'd let that voice intimidate him. He wouldn't let it happen again.

"Why don't you leave *me* alone instead? And that goes for Elizabeth, too."

Laughter pealed through the room, bouncing off the walls, echoing through Jon's ears.

The only fun in this existence is making you miserable. I have no intention of leaving you alone.

"What about Elizabeth? Do you speak to her? Have you shown yourself?"

Elizabeth doesn't know about me because . . . because her presence makes me happy. I'll let her know about me in my own good time. Until then, I'll annoy you.

"Just make sure you leave her alone. If you hurt her in any way, if you frighten her, I'll get even."

That's impossible.

"I'll find a way."

No answer.

"Did you hear me?"

Not a sound came from anywhere in the room. Not a creaking floorboard, not a moan or a groan or a laugh.

Jon felt the tightness in his shoulders, his jaw. He wasn't afraid now; he was angry.

A loud ring startled him, and he twisted around to the place where the noise came from.

It was only his cellular phone. Why did he habitually cart that thing with him wherever he went?

It was just as intrusive and just as annoying as that infernal ghost.

"Hello."

It wasn't a voice he wanted to hear.

"Yeah, I suppose I can. What time?"

He listened again and hung up the phone.

He definitely wouldn't be spending the evening the way he'd planned.

Logs crackled on the hearth when Elizabeth walked into the parlor dressed and ready for dinner. She'd made the decision to go just as she was lacing her boots. While she'd bathed, while she'd decided what to wear, she'd tried convincing herself she didn't enjoy Jon's company, but she did.

Getting to know him better probably wouldn't lead anywhere. They were both too strong-willed ever to get along. But she was determined to give it a try if he was.

Dinner tonight had sounded like a good place to begin, so it surprised her to see Jon kneeling before the fireplace, stabbing a long-handled poker at the wood, his face lit by the intensity of the flames.

"Does the fire mean you don't want a yes answer to your dinner invitation?" she asked.

Slowly he turned toward her, that lopsided grin on his face. "Sorry, Elizabeth. Something else has come up."

She wasn't about to let him see her frustration or her annoyance. She definitely wasn't going to let him see her disappointment.

She put her fingers to her mouth and attempted to stifle an exaggerated yawn. "I was too tired to go out, anyway. I'm glad you've got other plans, after all."

"Yeah, me too," he said, rising from the fire. He crossed to the entry, put on his coat and gloves, and pulled his Stetson tight on his head.

"Thanks for helping out today," she said, opening the door. She didn't want him to leave, but she didn't want him to know just how much she wished he could stay.

"Tomorrow I'll get to the plumbing."

"You plan to come back?" she asked.

She actually saw a touch of warmth fill his eyes. "I'll be back," he said. He reached toward her, cupping her cheek with one gloved hand. "Bright and early tomorrow."

"Okay," she somehow managed to utter. She hated the way his hand on her cheek and the closeness of his body were making speech so difficult. If he kissed her, she knew for sure her legs would collapse.

He gently smoothed his gloved fingers over her cheek, just barely touching her earlobe, the hollow beneath her ear. She felt the rough cowhide slide beneath her hair, around her neck. She couldn't help but move closer, closer, until her breasts pushed against his coat.

She needed no help at all tilting her face toward his. It went there naturally. The warmth in his eyes was flaming now. So were her toes and fingers. She stood on tiptoe; he lowered his head.

And a gust of wind blew through the open door and knocked over the coat rack.

"Hell!" Jon's temper flared and his head snapped up when the rack hit the floor.

Elizabeth laughed, just as she had the last time they'd attempted a kiss. Maybe it just wasn't destined. Maybe it was a sign that none of what was happening between them was right.

"You find it funny?" he asked.

"Very. You're awfully cute when you get frustrated."

His voice raised. His brows furrowed. "Cute?"

"Cute," she said flatly. "I suppose no one's ever called you that before?"

"Not anyone who's lived to tell about it."

She crossed her arms over her chest and grinned, mimicking the stance he'd used so often with her when she was frustrated. "I thought you had somewhere to go."

"Yeah, guess I do." He tilted his hat against the cold wind blowing outside and closed the door a bit too hard behind him.

Elizabeth laughed again.

And something in the house laughed right along with her.

It's only the floorboards, she told herself. Only the stretching and groaning of old wood. It wasn't real laughter. Besides, she was the only one in the house, and she refused to believe in ghosts.

Twice he'd tried to kiss her; twice he'd failed. Jon's frustration was outwardly apparent; Elizabeth kept hers bottled up inside, walked into the parlor and flopped onto the chesterfield. She'd missed out on two kisses, and now she was missing out on dinner, too. If she hadn't been so hesitant about going out, if she hadn't been so tired, maybe she'd be walking across the street to the Tin Cup Cafe right this very minute.

It seemed to be the story of her life. She'd been hesitant in most relationships. That's why she remained unmarried at thirty-one. Unmarried and pretty much untouched for over ten years.

She rested her head against the back of the sofa and watched a spider crawl slowly across the ceiling. That poor thing didn't seem to mind being all alone in this big old place. Maybe she shouldn't mind, either. But she did.

The loud rapping at the door startled her.

Jon? Had he returned? Had he changed his mind about that engagement that had crept up so unexpectedly? She felt good all of a sudden. She wasn't going to be alone. Not tonight . . . not tomorrow, either.

She rushed to the door and threw it open.

"Good evening." The joyous feeling disappeared with a thud. A black-haired stranger stood before her, looking just as striking as some of the models she'd photographed. He wore black-and-white ostrich-skin boots and a black wool coat tapered perfectly over a tall, slim frame. Pearly white teeth flashed from a perfect smile, and obsidian eyes stared at her through long, thick black lashes.

"Can I help you?" she asked.

"I'm Matt Winchester." He said, brushing flakes of snow from his shoulders. "Sorry I couldn't stick around when you arrived last week, but my business dealings keep me on the go most of the time."

"It's nice to meet you, finally. Eric's told me so much about you." She stepped to one side of the doorway. "Would you like to come in?"

"Actually, I thought it was about time we got to know each other. I was on my way to dinner. Care to join me?"

Why not? She was hungry. She didn't have any other plans, since Jon Winchester had chosen to come up with something else to do at the last minute. And Matt Winchester was gorgeous. It wouldn't be the first time she'd accepted a date for just those reasons. "I'd love to."

"I thought we'd drive into Helena. Shouldn't take much more than an hour to get there."

Matt's eyes slowly perused her attire—the combat boots with thick gray socks rolled over the tops, charcoal wool trousers with suspenders that raced over her breasts, and a red cashmere sweater with a cowl collar that nearly swallowed her chin.

She didn't exactly like the way he stared. His face showed a little distaste. Jon had stared, too, but Jon looked intrigued; he seemed to admire what she wore. Matt seemed appalled.

She came close to changing her mind about dinner. Of course, doing that would leave her alone and lonely again.

She ignored Matt's perusal, ignored her thoughts, and slipped into her fake-fur parka and red leather gloves, preparing for the blasted cold. She was just about to step out the door when she heard the voice behind her.

Don't go.

Elizabeth frowned. That didn't sound like floorboards or window frames. This time, she'd distinctly heard someone speak. She turned around but saw absolutely no one. She looked down at the floor and watched a hint of dust swirl at her feet.

"Something wrong?" Matt asked.

Elizabeth looked at him and smiled. "No. It's just the floorboards again. You were right when you told Eric they make strange noises."

He laughed, and she took hold of his arm, prepared to have a good time tonight in spite of Jon Winchester.

The drive to Helena took less than an hour as they whizzed along the icy roads. Elizabeth gripped the armrests in Matt's Explorer while he talked about his real estate and outfitting businesses, about his connections with senators and congressmen and other high-level officials who spent time with him hunting mountain lion, antelope, elk, and bear. In that hour Elizabeth rarely spoke except to ask questions, and never to answer any of his. Matt Winchester was, unfortunately, interested only in Matt Winchester.

The four-by-four jolted to a stop in front of a rustic log restaurant with Michelob, Coors, and Budweiser neon signs hanging in the windows and at least a dozen other four-by-fours parked outside. "This place has the best steak in the West. Great dancing, too. You *do* know how to dance, don't you?"

She just smiled, and wondered how she could get herself involved with arrogant men over and over. As for dancing, a good, slow waltz sounded more her style than some kind of country line dancing, although after Matt Winchester's comment, she was ready to give anything a whirl. But would she know what to do when her feet hit the dance floor?

They were ushered to a table near the center of the room by a cute young thing with long blond hair and a short gingham skirt, and the way Matt was checking out the girl, Elizabeth thought for sure he was going to pat the blond's butt and whisper sweet nothings in her ear.

Would Jon have looked at the waitress in the same way? Would he have made some condescending remark about her dancing?

Oh, heavens! She wished she could just put Jon out of her mind and concentrate on his cousin. Matt wasn't all bad, just conceited and arrogant—in the extreme. Jon's arrogance was a little more subtle; a little more likable.

Elizabeth drank three-fourths of a beer before a monstrous plate arrived bearing a sizzling steak half the size of Montana and a spud as big as Idaho. It might take her a good hour to clean her plate, but she had nothing else to do while Matt related more stories about himself. Even the men she'd known at home weren't quite this self-centered.

She found herself concentrating on the men playing pool at the far end of the room, at wooden beer steins lined up over the bar with names burned into them like Buck and Jake and Tom. And she watched the entrance, wondering if she could somehow sneak away and manage to find her way back home—alone.

She was staring good and hard at that entry door when it opened and Jon Winchester walked in, all six feet six inches of him, one big hand square on the shoulder of a petite, sophisticated redhead.

"Well, look what just walked in," Matt said, sliding an arm possessively around Elizabeth's back. "Think we should invite them to join us?"

"They don't exactly look like they're interested in anyone else's company," Elizabeth stated, wishing she could just crawl under the table or out the door and not have to see Jon again tonight . . . especially now that she knew what had suddenly come up that was better than having dinner with her.

"Oh, I don't know," Matt answered. "This could be fun."

In less than a heavy heartbeat, Jon and the woman neared their table, but Elizabeth doubted Jon had even seen her sitting there. The big oaf was too busy talking to the lady on his arm. But what could he possibly see in her? She had on a conservative navy business suit and plain old navy pumps. It didn't matter that she had the most gorgeously elegant red hair Elizabeth had ever seen, or big blue eyes and plump pink lips.

Elizabeth grabbed hold of her beer and took a long swallow. In thirty-one years of living she didn't think she'd ever been struck by jealousy, but tonight it was blazing as bright as one of the green neon signs in the window.

" 'Evening, Jon," Matt said. "Didn't expect to see you here."

"I hadn't planned on running into you, either." Jon's voice was hard, his demeanor less than friendly. His frown turned from Matt to Elizabeth, and that look that normally warmed her toes and fingers turned them to ice.

"Hello, Elizabeth." Jon tipped his hat in greeting.

"Hello."

Jon drew the redhead a little closer to him. "Elizabeth Fitzgerald, Matt Winchester, this is a friend of mine—Francesca Lyon."

The woman's handshake was firm and friendly. She had a nice smile, a lovely voice. And Elizabeth despised her.

"Care to join us?" Matt asked.

Jon looked down at his companion, then back at Matt. "Not tonight. Hope the two of you enjoy your dinner," he said, and without any further words, led Francesca to the far side of the room where the hostess was waiting to seat them.

"Jon's always had a penchant for picking pretty ladies," Matt said. "Wonder where he found this one?"

"Does it really matter?" Elizabeth snapped, instantly regretting her tone of voice.

Eyes narrowing, Matt studied Elizabeth's expression and grinned. "Jealous, huh?" He sliced off a hunk of steak and held it to his mouth. "Not a wise thing where that cousin of mine's concerned. Love 'em and leave 'em, that's the story I've heard."

Elizabeth managed to laugh. "Isn't that typical for most men? You, for instance?"

"Possibly. One big difference with me: I don't pretend to be anything other than what I am. I have no intention of ever hooking up permanently with a woman. I like having a good time, with no strings attached."

That statement didn't surprise her a bit.

Matt talked, and somehow they laughed the evening away. They danced, too, and Elizabeth managed to enjoy herself, except on those occasions when she caught sight of Jon and the redhead: the two of them talked incessantly, arms on the table, leaning intimately close, sharing confidences.

As if they enjoyed each other's company.

A dark, bearded man in army fatigues stopped by and chatted with Matt. No one bothered to introduce her, but Elizabeth didn't care; she was much too busy spying on the table across the room. She knew she shouldn't, and she wondered why she should even care what Jon did tonight—with Francesca or without.

The man with the beard was more than annoying. The few times she pretended to be interested in the conversation the man was having with Matt, he was stuffing another wad of chew in his cheek and swigging a beer. Their discussion was just as uninteresting as the man was disgusting. She could care less about the alligator skin boots Matt had picked up in Florida, but the two men seemed to find it rather funny.

When Matt's friend finally left the table, Matt spun Elizabeth around the dance floor one more time. She never once saw Jon and Francesca in the midst of the dancers; instead, they stayed together at their table and talked. She would have liked seeing him dance. Could that titan's body move as well as Matt's? she wondered. Would his hand at her waist make her tingle and wish he would pull her close? Matt's hadn't.

In the midst of her staring, Francesca got up from the table and headed toward the ladies' room. Jon was alone now, and his gaze darted across the room to her table. He frowned, then searched the room. His eyes found hers and stayed there—very intense, very cold.

Matt twirled her around, but she could still feel Jon's gaze on her back, a feeling she'd known again and again since that day she drove into town. That look still took her breath; still haunted her lonely evenings.

The music slowed, the dancing stopped for now, and Matt held her close as they returned to their table. She was laughing; she was having a good time in spite of her partner, until she saw Jon leaning back in one of their empty seats, his arms folded across his chest.

"Where's your girlfriend, Jon?" Matt asked. "Lose her so soon?"

"Not exactly." Jon sipped on a mug of beer. "Are you doing business with Floyd Jones again?"

Matt shrugged his shoulders, his ever-present grin not leaving his face in spite of the fact that sheer contempt was flying from Jon's eyes. "We're friends . . . old friends."

"He just got out of jail for poaching."

"Yeah, I heard that. Poor guy's looking for a new job now. Not too many people want to hire felons, I'm afraid."

"What about you?"

"He knows Montana better than most hunters, and that's the kind of man I need to lead my expeditions. You think I should hire an amateur? Put a bunch of greenhorns in the hands of someone who doesn't know how to stop a grizzly if it comes charging?"

Jon laughed. "Always have the perfect explanation, don't you?"

"I work hard at it."

Elizabeth could almost see the friction bouncing from Jon's eyes to Matt's.

"I suppose you heard about the latest poaching incident out at Schoolmarm."

"Yeah," Matt said, taking a sip of beer and appearing totally disinterested in the subject. "Heard they missed one of the cubs."

"I heard that, too. How much do you think the poacher missed out on? Another gallbladder, four more paws? Worth a pretty penny, huh?"

Matt laughed. "How would I know? My business is on the up-and-up, and this asinine suspicion you have is wearing on my nerves. I've been investigated ad nauseam, and no one's found a thing."

"That's something that's always bothered me," Jon said, shaking his head.

"Don't lose any sleep over it, cousin. There are more important things to worry about in this world than a few dead animals. But I'll tell you what. I'll keep my eyes out for poachers and for little lost bear cubs, and if I find anything, I'll make sure you're the first to know."

"Keeping your eyes open would be a wise decision, Matt. You never know who might be watching."

Elizabeth hadn't taken her eyes off Jon, wondering when his calm would ignite, but he seemed totally in control. She found herself breathing hard, caught as she was in the middle of the fray, and the cold look Jon bore when he looked into her eyes did little for her composure. Was he angry, disappointed, or what? It was impossible to tell, but her insides quivered and a lump formed in her throat.

This definitely hadn't been a good night for him to catch her with Matt.

It hadn't been a good night for her to see him with Francesca, either.

"Sorry to interrupt your evening. I'm sure you two have plenty to talk about," Jon said, as Francesca walked up to the table. He tipped his hat. "See you in the morning, Elizabeth."

"Nice meeting you, Francesca," she said. It was a lie, but a polite one. "Goodnight, Jon."

"So now you know a little bit more about my cousin," Matt said, after Jon and Francesca left the restaurant. "Lover of animals. Protector of the environment. That kind of nonsense doesn't set too well with most folks around here."

Matt's sense of humor was disappearing rapidly. He gave his watch a quick glance, then shoved out of his chair. "It's late, Liz," he said, grabbing his coat and tossing her parka into her hands. "Let's get out of here."

Elizabeth shivered when she stepped outside into the below freezing temperature, and Matt's arm around her shoulders did nothing to alleviate the icy chill that permeated her body. Even adjusting the temperature in the Explorer to "hot" appeared useless. She just couldn't warm up, not the way she could when Jon came near.

"Why is there so much animosity between you and Jon?" she asked, as Matt maneuvered the turns at breakneck speed.

"Animosity? I think you're reading something into our disagreement."

"There's a lot of sarcasm in those words you just uttered. Tell me the truth, Matt."

He laughed. "What can I say? There's been a feud going on between Jon's side of the family and mine since the turn of the century, and Jon just won't let it rest." Matt grasped the wheel with his left hand and stretched his right arm across the back of her seat to play with the wispy hairs that had slipped out of her braid. She felt no warmth in his touch, nothing tender or gentle, not like she had with Jon. He did it by rote, mechanically without much thought. If there'd been more room in the car, she might have moved away. She was trapped, though, and she hated the feeling.

"Only two Winchesters left now—Jon and me," Matt continued, "and he's bound and determined to make me regret we're related. The guy doesn't have much tolerance for outfitters or hunters, and he's going out of his way to prove I've been part of the poaching." Matt laughed. "It seems as if I did something wrong in my past and he's sworn to get revenge."

"That's a little melodramatic, don't you think?"

Matt shrugged. "He doesn't care too much for my real estate practices, either. But what the hell?"

It was the longest, most uncomfortable drive she could remember. Matt drove even faster than he had on the way to dinner. They hit ice a time or two, and one time came close to sliding into a ditch. Matt didn't seem to care. Elizabeth did, and she swore she'd never get into a car with him again.

The vehicle slid to a stop in front of the hotel, and Elizabeth gave a quick prayer of thanks for having gotten home safely. "Thanks for dinner,

Matt," she said, wishing she could get out of the car and inside the hotel before he made a move, but she wasn't that lucky. He'd rounded the Explorer and had hold of her arm before she closed the door.

She could feel the tight possessiveness of his grip through the sleeve of her coat, and when they reached the door he pressed his cold, leather-gloved hands to her cheeks and kissed her, hard and swift, and his lips were just as cold as the cowhide. "It was a nice evening, Liz. We'll have to do it again sometime."

All she did was smile and put her key in the door. "Thank you again, Matt," she said, praying he wouldn't ask to come inside.

And her prayer was answered in an instant. Matt blew her a kiss and walked away.

She twisted the key and stepped inside. Solitude had never been so welcome.

The foyer chandelier was swinging full force, and Elizabeth wondered if the firm Montana ground had decided to shimmy and shake like southern California dirt.

And then she heard it.

Spitooey!

She didn't want to hear it, though.

She closed the door gently, leaned against it, and listened.

And listened some more.

Impossible, she decided, and tried to convince herself that she'd heard nothing more than the tinkle of swaying crystals. She'd imagined the noise, but heavens, it *had* sounded as if someone had spit something nasty off their tongue. She imagined it was the same thing Jon would have done if he'd been peeking through the glass in the door and caught sight of Matt kissing her goodnight.

There was nothing to worry about, though. Matt's kiss had been as dry and tasteless as recycled cardboard, and she hadn't felt anything but a lump of foreboding in her stomach.

Quite similar to the foreboding she felt right now, thinking about that sound, and watching the chandelier sway when she'd felt no draft at all.

Chapter 6

Sometime in the middle of the night the storm subsided. The shrill screams of wind that had blown through the loosened windows quieted, and the long, bony fingers of the naked poplar outside the hotel ceased their incessant scratching on the glass and shingles. Yet the soft moaning in the attic continued, and Elizabeth lay awake, listening to what sounded like a sad, tearful man.

It's only the house, she told herself again and again. The floorboards. The windows. The ancient furnace.

Amanda . . .

Elizabeth's muscles tensed as stark, cold fear raced through her body. She shivered, pulling the blankets tightly under her chin for warmth and what little protection they could provide from the unknown. She focused her eyes on the darkened ceiling, waiting for another sound, for movement, for something that would explain that noise.

She listened more intently, slowing her own breathing so she wouldn't miss a sound, a heartbeat, a misplaced step across the floor.

Amanda . . .

No, floorboards and windows didn't resonate at all like that. They didn't echo through the rooms, or make the tiniest hairs on her arms prickle. She'd listened to floorboards and windows before. She'd listened to rafters and wall studs. She'd lain beneath them and listened to them groan and whine, stretch and crackle, but they hadn't cried, and they'd never sounded like a tormented phantom, or a lonely, sorrow-filled man.

Amanda . . .

And her house had never called out the name of a woman. Not once had anyone called *Elizabeth.*

She'd known loneliness. And that's what she heard now. As much as she wanted to deny the fact, at the back of her mind she couldn't help but wonder—could it be a ghost, some troubled spirit haunting this forlorn and desolate hotel? She continued to listen, but the lamenting had stopped just as the storm had ceased, and she found the quiet even more disturbing.

And even more lonely.

She rolled over in bed and hugged the fluffy down pillow, pretending for just one moment a lover rested beside her, someone with strong, caring arms. Someone to ease her loneliness and fears. She looked at the pillow and envisioned a face with a lopsided grin and sapphire eyes, and a slow, tender smile tilted her lips. She hugged the pillow tightly and sighed. Jon had such a unique way of warming her insides, making her tremble when he touched her.

But how could she think about him now? He'd ditched her tonight for some pretty, petite redhead.

She punched her fist into the pillow and twisted over in bed.

A lonely cry broke through her frustration and reverie, pushing thoughts of Jonathan completely from her mind. The desolate weeping was louder this time, stronger . . . an echo of her own inner thoughts. She needed to seek out the sound, needed to know why it came in the night. Was it only the wind howling through windows, or a lost, hopeless soul?

She climbed out of bed and crept up the stairs. The crying deepened as she neared the attic, but she added no sound of her own, her sock-covered feet quiet on the hard, dusty oak floorboards.

A thin stream of light sneaked under the partially open door and around the edge. Elizabeth rested her fingers on the dingy white wood and pushed gently. The moon shone through a far window, and just as she entered, the curtains dropped and fluttered as if someone had been holding them back to peer out. Listening intently, she heard no sound of footsteps. Searching the room, she saw nothing moving, no one hiding in a darkened corner. Nothing inhabited the room; not a soul occupied the large, empty space. And then she realized—the crying had ceased.

Slowly she crossed the room, stopped before the window, and pulled back the curtains and looked out. A deep blanket of snow covered the ground and settled thickly on tree branches and roofs. A lone set of tire tracks marred the road, and at the end of town, picture perfect with the big, fat moon shining overhead, sat the illuminated mansion of Jonathan Winchester.

It didn't look imposing or frightening. It looked immense and strong, a stone fortress that could withstand earth, wind, and fire—and probably earthquakes.

A trail of smoke rose from a chimney, and yellow light gleamed through the long, narrow windows that circled the top of one rounded turret. Did Jonathan sleep behind those windows? she wondered. Did he read in bed till all hours of the night? Could that be the reason for the lights? Did he find it difficult sleeping? Did strange noises keep him awake? Or did he hold a pillow tightly, just as she did, and pretend he was holding someone in his arms?

Folly. Pure, simple folly.

Heavens! Francesca was probably behind those windows, too. And more than likely, Jonathan Winchester was holding something much more substantial than goosedown.

Something soft, like a whisper of air, brushed against her cheek. She drew in a quick, ragged breath. Someone stood beside her. She jerked around but saw nothing. Not a soul was there, yet she sensed someone close, someone staring through the window just as she had done.

Again she felt the air stir, watched the curtains flutter.

Again she looked out across the snow-covered town to the mansion in the distance.

"It's a beautiful home," she whispered, half to herself, half to the unseen, unknown something that might inhabit her home and might be standing beside her. She moved slightly, offering her housemate a better vantage point, should someone really be there at her side. "Is that better?" she asked, feeling a trifle odd speaking to thin air.

She sighed and a ring of fog formed on the window in front of her face.

Another sigh sounded. Another ring of fog formed, a little higher on the window, a little to her left.

Oh, God! Elizabeth's fingers flew to her mouth to cover her quivering lips. Her shoulders drew up tight, tense, her panic nearly overwhelming.

Calm down, she told herself.

Just calm down.

Her breathing slowed.

No one had harmed her. If a ghost really did inhabit the house, it had made no attempt to hurt her. She'd felt no fear until tonight. Maybe that second sigh had been her own. Maybe she'd tilted her head to the left. Maybe she'd caused that second ring of fog.

And then again, maybe someone was in the house with her, someone just as lonely as she. Someone who needed her.

Her breathing steadied.

"Do you look out this window often?" she whispered.

No one answered.

"Are you lonely?" Still no answer. "Well, I've never admitted this to anyone before, but I am. I've been lonely most of my life." Reaching out, she lightly touched the ice-cold window, as if that would bring her closer to the house down the road. "I wonder if Jonathan Winchester's lonely, too?"

She sensed an abrupt movement, a turbulence in the room. She turned around. Dust motes swirled about, captured in a beam of moonlight. Suddenly everything was still, and all she heard was the erratic beat of her heart.

Once more she shivered. The room had become unbearably cold, and she wrapped her arms tightly around her body.

Finally she laughed, remembering the fear she'd lived through, lying amid the ruins of her house. She'd imagined people coming to rescue her. She'd imagined arms tightening around her, pulling her to safety. Maybe she had imagined everything that had happened tonight, too. Maybe she was so starved for companionship she'd dreamed up an invisible friend, someone to talk to, someone to listen to and comfort. The fantasy she'd conjured had seemed so real that it made this room and her new home seem less empty.

But if it was only her imagination, why, she wondered, did she suddenly feel alone?

Jonathan, Jonathan, Jonathan, Alex muttered, plinking the hanging crystals on a crimson Victorian lamp with his index finger and thumb. He'd been sitting on the nightstand staring at Elizabeth since she'd dropped off to sleep, and for the first time since she'd barged into his home, he was miffed. For good reason, he told himself. Not only had the woman mooned over that big lug as she'd stared out Alex's personal, private window, in his personal, private attic, but she'd had the gall darn nerve to croon that man's name as she slept.

Oh, Jonathan!

Dang it all, anyway. This was his home; she was his guest. If she was going to be friendly with anyone, Alex had every intention of claiming her attention all for himself. He didn't care a fig if Jonathan Winchester was lonely. It didn't matter at all. Alex knew all about loneliness, knew all about dealing with it, and if anyone deserved sympathy and concern, it was he. He had a hundred years of misery and loneliness stored up, and if Elizabeth Fitzgerald was going to ease anyone's desolation, he planned to take top honors.

Jon knocked half a dozen times, but even his hard, incessant pounding brought no one to the hotel's front door.

He knocked again, looked at his watch, and wondered if Elizabeth was ever going to answer. It wasn't quite eight in the morning, but the sun was inching its way over the mountains to shine down on the town. The sky was the color of blue Wedgwood slashed with tangerine, and after a week of minus thirty degrees with a wind chill that came darn close to freezing the hooves off cattle, it had turned out to be a damn fine day.

The only thing marring it was the fact that Jon had had a hell of a wretched night.

What on earth did Elizabeth see in Matt Winchester? They'd danced, they'd laughed. He'd held her close and whispered in her ear. He'd drug Floyd Jones to their table and proved her association with Matt went far beyond a somewhat insignificant partnership.

Hell, Jon had almost begun to trust her; but all that was blown last night.

It didn't matter if she caused his pulse to tremble, didn't matter that no woman had ever looked as good, smelled as nice, or sounded so damn sexy.

The only reason he was here now was because he'd promised to help her out, and by helping her out, he just might find out what Matt was up to.

He knocked again.

If she didn't answer soon, he planned to break down the door. Maybe he'd catch her with Matt. Wouldn't that be a pretty picture? No, he had to give her more credit than that. Elizabeth might be success driven enough to fall for Matt's business schemes, but she was too smart to fall for a man with a pretty face and a head filled with nothing more substantial than sludge.

Even though it looked last night like she was enjoying Matt's hands pawing her body.

If anyone could hear his thoughts right now, they'd think for sure he was jealous. But that was impossible; he'd never known a jealous moment in his life.

The creaking hinges and opening door startled him from his thoughts. The sight of Elizabeth's amber eyes almost made him forget his anger.

But not quite.

"It's about time you answered the door."

"Good morning to you, too," she said. She had a smile on her face, but it didn't look very sincere.

He wasn't even going to bother smiling in return. "I'm here to fix the plumbing."

"I gathered it wasn't a social visit," she tossed back, moving out of the doorway so he could barge through.

He shoved his hat onto the rack, yanked off his coat, and threw it over a rung. "Did you have a good time last night?" he asked, as he walked toward the kitchen and listened to the sound of her heavily-treaded boots right behind him.

She just might need those combat boots before the morning was over. He was mad and ready for a fight.

"Of course I had a good time. Why wouldn't I?"

"I can think of one very big reason."

She laughed. "You're jealous."

Those words put a stop to his steps. He turned around, his arms folded over his chest. "Jealous? Why *should* I be? You were with a man you obviously enjoy, a man you're business partners with, and I was with a woman who makes me completely happy."

"Then why are you angry?"

"Are you really that blind? I've told you before about Matt's unscrupulous tendencies, yet it doesn't seem to bother you."

Elizabeth sat down at the table, picked up a cotton cloth, and went to work polishing a piece of silver. "I'm condemned without a trial, aren't I?" She didn't look at him when she spoke, but there was something in her tone that made him relax, made some of the anger fade away.

"Do you care for him? Do you want to be with him?"

"No."

"Do you know anything about the poaching?"

"No."

"What about your brother? Is he involved?"

She looked into his eyes. "I don't know. I hope not."

"Okay." Jon unlatched his toolbox, pulled out a

wrench, and opened the cabinet door beneath the sink.

"Does that okay mean you believe me, or does it just mean we'll work in silence from now on?" she asked.

"I guess it means I'll give you the benefit of the doubt."

"Until something new comes up and gives you another reason to suspect me?"

"Maybe you should do something to make me believe you're innocent."

She slammed the piece of silver down on the table and shoved out of the chair. "Look, I don't know what your problem is this morning, but I'm not going to let you take it out on me. I was with Matt last night for one reason and one reason only. He asked me out and didn't have something more important come up. You, on the other hand, decided Francesca's company was much more exciting than mine."

She threw the cloth on the table. "I'm going to have coffee with Libby. If you think you can handle it, I would like that plumbing fixed this morning." She stormed out of the kitchen and a moment later he heard the front door slam.

He felt like a fool—again. His anger had nothing at all to do with the poaching; it was solely the fact that she'd been with another man last night—laughing, dancing, touching. It could have been any man and he'd be furious. Problem was, the man was Matt, and that doubled his anger.

He squeezed his head and shoulders under the sink, figuring he might as well take some of his anger out on the plumbing. He hadn't been there more than five minutes when he heard the faint sound of footsteps. "Returned so soon?" he asked, trying to sound civil, which she deserved.

She didn't speak. She didn't move again, either.

He continued working on the pipes, twisting nuts, tightening fittings, replacing rotten gaskets and tubing. What was she thinking as she stood quietly beside the counter? Was she wondering how long he'd stay mad? Was she wondering about his relationship with Francesca?

Maybe he should tell her the truth about Ms. Lyon. No, that wasn't a wise idea; not now. Maybe never.

He could hear Elizabeth rustling through his toolbox. He could hear the clanking of metal against metal and jars of nails and screws being shaken. "If you're looking for something in particular . . ."

Thud!

Jon's head jolted up when something heavy and hard dropped on his stomach. His temple smacked against a cold copper elbow, and he winced in pain. "What was that for?" he called out, but still she didn't answer. Maybe he deserved it for the attitude he'd assumed when he walked into her house.

He gritted his teeth, grabbed the pipe wrench that had landed on his belly, and massaged the aching spot on his head. No blood. No lump. It hurt like hell, but he'd suffered through worse.

An apology from Elizabeth would have been nice. Any word at all would have been appreciated. Instead, he got dead silence. Furiously, he continued tightening joint after joint. Damn! He might have lashed out at her, but he hadn't attacked with lethal weapons.

"I'm back."

Her voice startled him and he jolted up again, his head smacking the pipe once more. "Dammit!"

Elizabeth peeked under the cabinet and he could see her smiling face, sweet, innocent, as if she'd done nothing wrong. "Are you okay?"

"No!" he fired back.

"Libby was all out of the doughnuts she said you like, so I brought you one of her cinnamon rolls. Maybe it'll help calm your anger. It helped mine."

He slid out from under the sink and glared at Elizabeth.

Her brow furrowed in concern. "You *are* hurt," she said, putting icy fingers on his forehead. The pain instantly disappeared, replaced by a totally new sensation, something deep down in his stomach that gnawed at him.

Elizabeth hadn't been anywhere near the kitchen when that wrench had bombed him. She still wore her coat. Her fingers felt like she'd just walked in from the cold. He smelled the strong scent of cinnamon and sugar, the aroma filling the room along with her perfume—and he hadn't smelled either a few minutes before.

Someone else had definitely been in the room.

Or something.

"I'm fine," he answered finally. But he wasn't fine. Because he knew, without a doubt, that he hadn't been alone.

Jon watched Elizabeth take off her coat, drape it over a kitchen chair, and pour a cup of coffee. "Care for some?" she asked, warming her hands on the blue pottery mug. The coffee smelled good and strong, and through the steam he could see her dark amber eyes. They were actually smiling, in spite of what had happened earlier.

He leaned against the counter and took the coffee she offered. "I'm sorry."

"You should be." She handed him a cinnamon roll, then went to the kitchen door and looked out its window. "Does Francesca really make you happy?" she asked.

"She's a friend, that's all. She's having boyfriend problems," he lied, "and needed someone to talk to."

"Do you always help females in distress?"

"I'm here with you, aren't I?"

They were back to their banter, but Jon had the feeling it would be a long time before they returned to that stage where he was on the verge of giving her a kiss.

Elizabeth went back to work polishing the silver, and Jon tinkered with the plumbing. They must have been silent for nearly half an hour when Elizabeth spoke to him again.

"Libby told me your grandfather passed away recently. I'm sorry."

"He was ninety-nine years old," Jon said, fitting the faucet with new washers. "He'd been ill for quite some time."

"She told me he'd raised you."

"Since I was four." He wiped his hands on a towel, twisted a chair around, and straddled the seat. "My folks left me with my grandfather while they took a vacation. They went to Africa on some sort of wildlife safari. My dad inherited his love of nature from my grandfather; I guess I followed in their footsteps, too."

He picked up a piece of cloth from the table and dipped it into the silver polish Elizabeth was using, then slowly rubbed it across a tarnished oval tray. "The bus they were in had a blowout and rolled into a ravine. My mom was dead when help arrived. My dad had a broken back and they managed to get him to a hospital, but there wasn't much they could do. I remember my grandfather telling me what happened, but I didn't really understand."

"Do you remember them?" she asked, leaning forward as she polished, listening closely to each word.

"Not much, but I remember everything about my grandfather."

"Was he a good parent?"

Jon smiled. "He gave me every minute he had. He taught me to fish and whittle, he did homework with me, and he went to the principal's office every time I got in trouble. He told me his dad hadn't given him the time of day, and no son or grandson of his was going to be treated the same way."

"What about his mother?"

"Are you sure you want to hear about all this? It's history."

"I told you my story. Seems only fair I know something more about you."

"I'm an open book."

She shook her head. "I know how you stand on a few issues, especially those that differ from mine. I know where you live. But I don't know anything about you."

"Libby hasn't filled you in?"

"Not about you. She says you like your privacy and everyone in town—with the exception of Matt, she pointed out—respects it. Since I couldn't get anything out of her, would you mind continuing the story?"

"You'll have to remind me where we left off."

Elizabeth laughed and pushed an errant strand of hair away from her face. "Your grandfather's mother. Did she care for him?"

"She died when he was fairly young, but you'd have thought she walked on water, the way he talked about her. She sang and read him stories when he was little. She played the piano, even sat on the floor doing battle with him and a bunch of toy soldiers."

"She sounds wonderful."

"She loved her son, but I guess she didn't care all that much for her husband. He was the riverboat gambler, the one who built the house Matt lives in. According to the stories, he had a fondness for women. Probably not the most sterling character ever to live in Sapphire."

"Then why'd she marry him?"

"That's the best story my grandfather ever told—and he told a lot. Seems the man she'd been engaged to had left her standing at the altar. Let's see . . . what was his name?" Jon had to think a moment, trying to remember some of the tales his grandfather had related. "Alexander Stewart. That was it."

Jon felt a gush of warm air blow past his ear. He thought for sure someone stood right beside him, listening over his shoulder. But it was all in his mind; it had to be.

"I like the name," Elizabeth said.

"I doubt you would have have liked him. While everyone was at the church, he robbed the bank and killed the teller. They never found him or the money, and my great-grandmother ended up marrying Luke Winchester just a few weeks later."

"She wasn't brokenhearted?"

Jon laughed. "The man who dumped her was a thief and a murderer. Would you be brokenhearted?"

"I don't know. I guess I'd have to know the circumstances."

"Well, if you find anything out, make sure you let me know. He stole every town record, too, and, even today we still have property disputes that could be solved if only the paperwork showed up."

"I don't think I can solve some hundred-year-old crime, but I like the story. It might be fun telling my guests about it late at night. When I get a chance, maybe I'll do some research. What did you say the fiancé's name was?"

"Alexander Stewart."

"And your great-grandmother's?"

Jon smiled and shook his head. Elizabeth was going to be just like his grandfather—telling tall tales to anyone who would listen.

"Her name was Amanda," he told her. "Amanda Dalton."

Chapter 7

Amanda.

Alex whispered his lover's name once again. Oh, how he missed her. And oh, how she must have suffered at the hands of the man he hated, a man who would kill for money and ignore his own son.

But she must have hated Alex, too—for professing his love, then leaving her, for being branded with those horrible names.

Thief!

Murderer!

Anger swept through him as he swooped out of the kitchen and up the stairs to his attic room, sending dirt and dust motes flying helter-skelter through the air. Jonathan Winchester's words had angered him as no other words had. *Alexander Stewart, a thief and murderer? Never!* He wouldn't stand for such language, such balderdash, not in his house.

Jonathan Winchester would pay for his words and pay handsomely.

For one long week Jon tinkered with plumbing and electrical wiring. He patched holes in walls, stripped wallpaper, sanded oak windowsills and banisters, hauled trash to the snow-filled dump, and ran errands for Elizabeth. There was still a good month's worth of work to do just to make the place habitable, but the kitchen glistened after hours of scrubbing, they'd laid tile on the countertops, and clean, fresh water flowed through the pipes and down the drains.

Things might have been perfect, except he'd also spent the entire week suffering the pranks of a mysterious unseen entity. One day his hammer disappeared and he found it embedded in the chocolate soufflé Elizabeth had made. The hell of that was, he had to pretend to an outraged woman that he'd gotten hungry and dug into the thing while she was at the cafe trading baking secrets with Libby. A bucket of nails had been dumped in Elizabeth's lingerie drawer, and once again he'd been caught in the act of retrieving his things. Explaining why he was fingering a lacy red bra hadn't been easy. He'd gotten tongue-tied and felt like he was having hot flashes as he'd told her he'd been looking for rags to wipe down the woodwork in her room. She hadn't believed a word, and he didn't blame her a bit.

Whoever was haunting the hotel was making Jon's life a virtual hell.

The other hell he was living through was his relationship with Elizabeth. They hadn't shared a close moment since they'd talked of his grandfather. Of course, there wasn't much time for conversation. He'd never known a woman to dream up so many chores, or a woman to work from sunup till sundown without growing tired.

She had a fresh pot of coffee brewing each morning when he arrived. Sometimes there'd be muffins or cookies, and always a big bowl of fresh fruit. Every afternoon she'd go across the street for coffee and lunch with Libby, and she always insisted he leave by three because she was sure that as mayor he had other, more pressing matters to deal with.

Just when he thought she didn't like his company, didn't want him around, he'd see her standing in a doorway, watching him. He'd smile, and she'd smile back and usually walk away.

Jon wondered if this was the way it was between married people, spending too many hours together and rarely talking.

On the eighth day he had business of his own to attend to and she actually seemed disappointed when he told her he'd be in Denver the next two days.

"What's in Denver?" she asked.

"An art show."

She looked surprised at his words.

"It's what I do when I'm not playing mayor or attempting to be a handyman."

"You're an artist?" she asked.

He wanted to tell her. He wanted to share, but still he held back. That employee-employer relationship had settled between them, and they weren't the best of friends. He wished he had faith in her, and he wanted to get close; unfortunately, he'd seen her with Matt Winchester one too many times to trust her completely with his secrets.

"I'm a dealer," he finally answered. It wasn't a total lie.

"I never would have guessed," she said. "Of

course, we haven't talked about what you do when you're not here or being mayor. I figured you must be independently wealthy—or a crook."

Jon laughed. "Some people might think I'm a crook, considering the prices I charge for artwork. But I'm not."

"Do you enjoy what you do?"

"Most of the time."

She smiled. "I haven't been to an art show in ages. I used to go whenever I had a chance."

"You could go with me," Jon said, and wondered why. It didn't seem right to encourage a relationship that had no chance of going anywhere. But for some reason, none of that mattered. He liked being with her, whether he trusted her or not, whether they talked or yelled or spent a day together saying absolutely nothing.

"Thanks for the invitation," she said, "but I'd better pass. This time, anyway."

He was suddenly disappointed, and his days in Denver were more than lonely. He missed her smiles, her frowns, her laugh. He missed her amber eyes and her ebony braid, and he couldn't wait to get back home.

When he returned, he drove into town and saw Elizabeth standing on the porch, talking to Matt. Floyd Jones was with him, too.

He gunned the engine of his pickup and headed for home without bothering to stop. He slammed the truck door behind him when he got out of the vehicle, slammed through the kitchen door, stomped up the back stairs, slammed through his studio door, and spent that night pounding his fist into clay. The next day he spent at Schoolmarm

Gulch, sketching anything and everything that crossed his path.

Why had she been with Matt? She didn't like him, or so she'd said. She said she wasn't involved in his business, either. He'd tried to convince himself of those two things; unfortunately, she'd been with Matt—again.

Elizabeth stood at the front window, watching the snowfall. That's what she convinced herself she was watching when in reality she was waiting for Jon, wondering if he'd ever come again.

It was nearly seven P.M. He should have been there at eight that morning, but after seeing him race down the street yesterday afternoon when Matt had stopped by to ask her a few questions about her plans for the hotel, she sensed Jon might not return.

When the snow fell harder and the wind picked up, she turned away from the window and walked toward the parlor, stopping when she heard boot-steps on the porch. She listened closely. They didn't sound familiar. They didn't sound like Jon's, nor did the knock.

But she hoped.

She opened the door and disappointment ripped through her body at the sight of Matt.

"'Evenin', Liz. I had some advertising copy drawn up. Thought you might like to see what I've put together."

"Why don't I drop by your office tomorrow and take a look?" She didn't want him around, not when there was a possibility Jon might come by.

Actually, she didn't want Matt around at all—at any time.

"There's a chance I won't be in town for a few days," Matt said. "I need you to look at this tonight." He brushed past her and hesitantly looked about the room as he unbuttoned his black wool coat. "You need wallpaper in here. I hope you realize that."

Elizabeth rolled her eyes as she closed the door. "Thanks for the suggestion."

"I'm sure I could make others." He stuck his head through the doorway into the parlor. "You've got a hell of a long way to go, Liz. Are you sure you want to tackle this place?"

"We've already tackled the worst of it."

"*We?*"

"Jon and I. He's done most of the hard stuff."

"Yeah, he's a man of many talents." Matt handed his coat to Elizabeth without a word of thanks. Typical!

She heard bootsteps again out front. She heard the heavy knock. She closed her eyes and sighed, right before she opened the door.

"Sorry I wasn't here this morning," Jon said, looking straight into her eyes. "I—" He must have seen Matt standing near the parlor. He must have seen Matt's coat in her arms. "I guess I picked the wrong time to come by." He pivoted on his boot heels and started for the stairs.

Elizabeth stepped into the cold and slammed the door behind her. "Don't go, Jon. Please."

He stopped, but he didn't turn around. "I thought you didn't like him."

"I don't."

"Then why's he here?" He gripped the railing on the porch and faced her.

"Business. That's all."

"What about yesterday? Floyd Jones was here, too. Has he become part of this partnership?"

Elizabeth sighed and leaned against the door. "They wanted to know how things were going with the hotel. They wanted to know when they could start lodging people here—that's all."

Jon only glared.

"I don't want Matt here now. Please. Don't go."

The door opened and Matt stepped onto the porch, draping his arm around her shoulders. "Is he bothering you, Liz?"

Elizabeth watched Jon's right hand double into a fist, his arm draw back, then hesitate.

"Ah, hell!" Jon exploded, and shoved his fist into his pocket. "Go inside, Elizabeth. It's cold out here. In fact, I think it's the coldest it's ever been."

Jon didn't even bother tipping his hat goodbye; he just walked away.

Matt drew her back inside, but she shrugged away from his arm as soon as he closed the door. "I really don't want you here, Matt. We can talk about the advertising some other time."

"I'm here now, Liz. I can't see any reason to leave."

She didn't have the energy to argue. She threw his coat over the rack and walked into the parlor.

"Do you have some wine?" he asked.

She didn't answer right away. Instead, she went to the window and looked out at the snow once more. Jon's reaction at seeing Matt inside the hotel didn't surprise her, but the fact that he wouldn't listen, wouldn't stay when she asked, did. It hurt, too.

Obviously, he didn't care. Not enough, anyway. Maybe it was time to just give up on him. Maybe she should settle for Matt. He didn't care about anything but himself, so she'd never have to worry about offending him.

When she turned from the window, he was walking around the room, inspecting the furniture, the ancient crystal, ceramics, and silver. He was absolutely gorgeous; he was also insufferable.

Maybe he was just what she needed—tonight.

"I've got a '79 Cabernet that should be pretty good," she said, going to the table where she'd set it earlier, along with two glasses, when she thought—hoped—Jon might come by.

"French or Californian?" he asked.

"Does it matter?"

He shrugged, paying her very little attention as he walked to the chesterfield and ran his hands over the cushions. He carefully inspected his fingers, apparently for dust, then sat down and stretched an arm along the back. "I sensed a little tension between you and my cousin. I take it things aren't going well between the two of you."

Ah, he wasn't totally oblivious to everyone but himself. Elizabeth popped the cork on the bottle and poured wine into the glasses. "He works for me, that's all," she lied. "We seem to have rather frequent disagreements." She handed Matt the glass and sat in a chair across from him.

"I'm glad to hear that." Matt swirled the wine about and sniffed the bouquet before taking his first sip. "I suppose that leaves the field wide open for me."

Elizabeth laughed. "Only if I wanted you, Matt."

He toasted her with his glass. "You'll want me, Liz."

"You're a bit sure of yourself, aren't you?"

"Always."

He looked about the room again, at the stripped walls, the sanded wood paneling that needed to be stained and varnished, the curtainless windows. "From the looks of this place, it could be summer before you have rooms to rent. Of course, if that's going to hurt you financially, we might be able to work something out."

"What? Do you want me to help you out in one of your poaching expeditions?"

She couldn't believe she'd said those words. She expected Matt to fire something equally vile at her, but all he did was smile.

"You wound me, Liz. You're becoming as vindictive as Jon. Surely I don't deserve that from you."

Maybe he didn't. "I'm sorry. That was rude." She drank a long sip of wine and curled up in the overstuffed chair, thinking seriously about getting rip-roaring drunk.

Directly across from her, she could see, again, the snow falling. Didn't it ever let up? She was so cold right now. She'd been cold ever since Jon had gone to Denver, and she had the horrible feeling she might not be warm again until June.

"I don't know how anyone survives during the winter," she said, facing Matt again. "Isn't your income hampered by the weather?"

"I let very little hamper me, Liz, especially the weather. My outfitting business takes up most of my time in late summer and fall. In between times, I purchase and sell a lot of property. You'd be surprised how many greenhorns come here in the summer to buy up hundreds of acres of land under the 'Big Sky.' They get these grand notions of settling down in God's country and being gentlemen ranchers. Then the first snow hits and they hightail it for much warmer climes." He laughed. "They buy high, they sell low."

"And I take it you're there for the killing?"

Matt swirled the deep burgundy liquid around in his glass. "I've been known to make a shrewd investment or two."

He downed the rest of his wine and set the glass on the table in front of him. Slowly, he rose from the sofa and walked behind Elizabeth's chair. "You seem a little tense tonight, Liz." She felt his fingers on her arms, felt them move over her shoulders and along the base of her neck. "I could relieve some of that tension for you."

Elizabeth pulled away. It was Jon she wanted to touch her. It was Jon she wanted to kiss. Not Matt, in spite of her earlier insane thoughts. "I'm not the least bit tense, Matt." She rose and poured more wine into her glass. "Would you like some more?" she asked, but Matt shook his head. Why on earth hadn't she kicked him out? Why had she given him wine? Why had she offered him more when she just wanted to be left alone?

Matt leaned against the doorframe between the parlor and dining room, his arms folded across his chest, and watched her sip her wine. "Y'know, Liz, if you're interested in real estate, I could find you a good deal or two."

"But I already got a good deal from you. This hotel was a steal at the price I paid."

"I take it the noises haven't bothered you?"

"You mean the floorboards, the windows, the things you warned Eric about?"

He nodded.

"I've heard lots of noises, Matt. But it's not the house."

"No?" His eyes narrowed.

"No." She could see his shoulders tense, and she knew without a doubt that Matt Winchester thought the place was haunted. He might have told her brother that it was just floorboards and windows, but deep down inside Matt Winchester believed a spirit roamed the rooms.

She finally felt a little better about Jon's abrupt desertion. He was angry, but there was always tomorrow. As for Matt, he was a pretentious fool. He thought he'd sold her a piece of goods—he was wrong, of course, but that didn't matter.

He was obnoxious and rude, and she wanted to get even for him putting his arm around her and making Jon mad.

Maybe it was time for him to be a bit tense, too.

"I'm convinced there's a ghost here somewhere," she teased. "If you stick around long enough, it might appear."

"You've seen it?"

"Not exactly. It's more a feeling I get when I'm alone at night."

The crystals on the chandelier tinkled. It swayed slightly. She watched for any other motion, but the only thing that moved was Matt's gaze, drifting to the hanging lights.

She smiled. "Things like that happen all the time for no apparent reason. This could be a great advertising gimmick."

Matt faced her again and grinned, but she couldn't miss his deep, difficult swallow. "Like I said, Liz, it's only the house making noises. But if you're afraid—" He walked toward her, slowly, quietly, as if he were stalking his prey. He pinched her chin between cold, hard fingers.

Elizabeth wrenched away, but his hand swiftly wound around the back of her neck and he lowered his mouth. She felt the pressure of wet lips against hers as she struggled.

Spitooey!

Matt jerked away. "What was that?"

Elizabeth used the moment to back out of his grasp. She wiped her fingers across her mouth, removing remnants of Matt's kiss from her lips. "What was what?"

"That sound." He looked about the room, his face scrunched into a frown. "Like someone spitting."

"Oh, that." Elizabeth shook her head, brushing off the comment as if the noise was of no import. "It's the blasted pipes. They're filled with air and make noises day and night." She shrugged. "You get used to them after a while."

"Maybe you should get them fixed."

"All in good time, Matt."

Maybe he'll leave now, Elizabeth hoped.

"Why don't we get some dinner?" he asked, obviously not ready to dispense with her presence.

"I'll take you into Helena again tonight."

She didn't want his company, but quite obviously, she'd never mastered the fine art of bluntly getting rid of a man. At least one like Matt. "Thanks. Not tonight. I might just stop by the cafe later and get something quick."

"I'll take you there."

Couldn't he catch the drift of her subtle hint? "I'd rather kick off my shoes and eat here. It's been a long day."

"I'm sure Libby can dish up a gourmet meal, something drenched in gravy and grease. I'll pick up two evening specials and bring them back."

"Well . . ."

"It's no imposition, Liz."

Following Matt to the door, Elizabeth hoped against hope that he'd slip and fall in the snow, get his pretty clothes all wet, and be forced to go home for the evening. Unfortunately, she didn't think she'd be quite that lucky.

"Get comfortable, Liz, I'll be back shortly."

Closing the door, Elizabeth leaned against it for a moment. Get comfortable, huh? How? A slinky negligée? A chastity belt suddenly came to mind. She'd never thought wearing one would be comfortable, but if she had one, it might suit the occasion.

Laughing at herself and her thoughts, she sauntered into the parlor, remembering the distaste of Matt's kiss and its precipitous end. *Spitooey!* She'd heard it twice now, or at least, she *thought* she'd heard it, both times in that same cantankerous voice.

Both times when Matt was near.

Standing in the middle of the room, she stared at one of the hotel's many chandeliers. It wasn't swaying now; the crystals weren't tinkling, but that didn't mean her housemate, if she really had one, wasn't nearby. All of a sudden she was beginning to believe there might really be someone in the hotel with her. A restless spirit. A ghost.

She faced the ceiling and spoke to thin air. "There's no need to stay quiet any longer. I know you're in here."

As before, nothing and no one answered. All Elizabeth heard were the growing gale outside and the scrape of the poplar against the exterior walls. "Go ahead. Be silent. See if I care." She circled the room. "This is crazy. I shouldn't even believe you exist." She stopped again, dead still, and stared at the chandelier that hung slightly off-kilter, as if someone perched on one of the curving brass rungs. "Look, all I want to do is thank you for interrupting that kiss. Well, that's not all, really. I want you to know that I'm capable of handling things on my own—"

Like hell!

That time she did hear it, loud and clear, and she stood frozen in place, afraid to move. What on earth had possessed her to stay in this place? My God, it was really and truly haunted. But by what? Or who?

The crystals on the chandelier shimmied, clinking against each other, as the heavy fixture swung back and forth, back and forth.

A heavy thud sounded on the parquet beneath the chandelier. Had someone or something jumped or fallen to the floor?

Gradually, the chandelier ceased its movement. Elizabeth swallowed hard. So many noises. So many strange occurrences. She took one tentative step away from the craziness.

Keep him out of my house.

The voice was deep and loud and menacing. Her chest rose and fell heavily with each frightened breath she took. Her shoulders tensed. Something was circling her, she could sense the movement, could feel the rush of air, cold one moment, hot the next, against her cheeks. She took an even deeper breath and willed herself to be calm. "If you're trying to frighten me, you're doing a pretty lousy job." It wasn't the truth, but she refused to let the intruder see or hear her fear.

Get rid of him, or I will.

"Is that a warning?" she threw right back, making her voice sound just as low and just as menacing.

No response.

"Did you hear me?" she repeated. "Is that a warning?"

The front door creaked and Elizabeth spun around, half relieved, half disappointed to see Matt walk into the house with his arms laden with Styrofoam containers. "I was right. Gourmet pot roast, straight from the finest chef in Sapphire, Montana."

Elizabeth wished she had the bottle of wine in hand so she could down a healthy swig. Had her companion departed? she wondered. Had the phantom given up so easily? She doubted it, but she didn't sense it anywhere nearby, not at the moment.

"I got a little sidetracked while you were gone,

Matt. It won't take me a moment to get the table set."

With shaking fingers, she took red linen and white lace tablecloths from an armoire and draped them over the table.

"These ought to look nice, too," Matt said, picking up a set of silver candlesticks with long white tapers.

They look romantic, Elizabeth thought, and she didn't find anything the least romantic about what was going on in her home. She just wanted to eat and get Matt out.

"Nice table you're setting." Matt placed his hands on her shoulders and kissed her neck. A shiver ran down her spine.

The table looked too intimate. How could she expect Matt to keep his hands off her when she was setting a cozy table for two? In front of a fire. With wine.

And pot roast. Nobody ate pot roast intimately.

She felt a tiny prick on her earlobe, felt Matt's warm breath on her ear, his fingers lightly caressing her throat. She wrenched away from his touch, halfway wishing the spirit, or phantom, or ghost, would smack the guy upside the head for being such a pain.

She set out the food, the paper plates, and the plastic utensils Libby hadn't forgotten, all the while keeping one eye trained on Matt. He was leaning against the door again with his arms crossed, letting her do all the work herself. She started to light the candles, only because they looked so lifeless without flickering flames, but changed her mind and set the matches on the table.

She took her seat when Matt pulled out her chair, ever the gentleman, if only in the most superficial sense of the word. He leaned over, swept up the matchbook, and lit the tapers. She nearly groaned in frustration. "I like a more intimate touch when I dine," he said, and took his chair.

Casually, Elizabeth lifted a wedge of potato with her fork, holding it before her mouth. She smiled weakly at Matt, wondering how to hold a conversation with a man who wanted only to talk about himself, or make sexual innuendos. Business-related talk seemed safe. "So," she began, "tell me about the advertising copy."

"That can wait."

"Then tell me about the hotel. Why hasn't it sold before?" He ignored the pot roast, opting for more wine instead. "No one wanted it, plain and simple. Phoebe Carruthers, the original owner, left it to family members back east. She must have died in nineteen-ten or so, and it sat empty until about ten years ago, when the last of her nephews decided to dump the place. I bought it, but until your brother came along, I couldn't find anyone I felt deserved a place like this."

"Well, I'm glad we bought it. As I said before, it's proved to be a good investment."

Matt leaned his elbows on the table. "You look very beautiful in the candlelight," he whispered.

A cold blast of air rushed past Elizabeth's ear and the candle flames sputtered out, leaving only a thin stream of smoke.

Matt sat up straight, his eyes wide with fear. "Did you blow out the candles?"

Elizabeth shook her head and put another piece

of potato in her mouth. She chewed lightly and swallowed slowly. "This place not only moans and groans, but it's got a terrible problem with drafts. I really do have to get the weatherstripping installed."

Matt picked up his freshly filled glass of wine and drank the contents. "I don't have any drafts at all in my place. No air-filled plumbing, either. Maybe you'll consider coming to my house for dinner next time."

Elizabeth took another bite, enjoying his discomfort. She didn't intend for there to be a next time, and she hoped by the time dinner was over, Matt would feel the same way, too. But she couldn't help giving him a more hopeful answer. "Perhaps."

Like hell!

She'd expected that response and paid it no attention at all. Her nerves were getting accustomed to the strange goings-on, but not Matt's. His hand shook so badly his wine sloshed over the edge of his glass and down his shirt. "Did you hear it?" His voice quavered.

"Oh, Matt, you've ruined your shirt."

"The hell with my shirt. Did you hear that voice?"

Shaking her head, she got up from her chair and dabbed her napkin at the stain. "I don't think this is going to come out, Matt. I'm really sorry."

In one quick gulp, Matt downed the rest of his wine and filled the glass to the brim. "I suppose what I heard was the pipes again?"

"Honestly, Matt, I didn't hear a thing." Again she took her seat and took a healthy bite of the Tin

Cup Cafe's daily special. "Pot roast's delicious to-night."

"Yeah. I figured you'd like it." With his hand still shaking, Matt took a bite and Elizabeth watched him struggle to swallow. "So, do you know anything at all about this place you own?" He was trying to carry on a somewhat normal conversation, but she could sense that discomfort raged in his nerves.

"Only the few things Jon's told me. I know about Phoebe Carruthers, and why she turned the place into a boardinghouse."

"And you want to know more?"

Balancing her elbows on the table, and holding her wineglass in front of her face, she studied Matt's eyes. Did he know more than Jon? It seemed there was something he knew about this place, something he wanted to keep to himself.

"The story of Alexander Stewart sounds rather fascinating. Did he really rob the bank and leave Amanda Dalton standing at the altar?"

"He did all those things and more."

She heard a deep sigh, almost a moan, but saw no sign that Matt had heard it, too. She felt someone or something gripping the back of her chair, felt a presence close—very, very close. "Tell me about him."

"There's nothing documented, I'm afraid, and there weren't any witnesses. None who lived, that is. Seems everyone in town was at the church for Amanda's wedding. Must have been two hundred people crowded inside the place. Everyone but Alexander Stewart. No one knows for sure what happened, but as far as anyone can tell, he went into the bank, forced the clerk to open the safe, then shot him." Matt pointed his index finger at Elizabeth's head and pretended to pull a trigger. "Bang!" His face lit up. "Right between the eyes."

Elizabeth's chair shook, and her elbows slid. The tablecloth bunched up as if someone had grabbed hold, as if someone needed something to strangle in anger. The bottle of wine fell, its contents spilling over the red cloth and white lace, heading straight for Matt's lap, along with the piece of huckleberry pie Elizabeth had been eager to taste.

Matt jumped, but not quickly enough. "What the hell are you doing?" he yelled, looking straight at Elizabeth as if she were the culprit who'd caused the catastrophe.

"You scared me, that's all. My elbows slipped on the tablecloth."

"Scared you? With what?" Matt grabbed a hunk of pie from his lap with his napkin and flung it on the table.

"With that story!"

Slowly, Elizabeth watched Matt regain his composure, his regal and snobbish bearing returning. He took a deep breath and laughed as if nothing at all had happened. "I apologize. It was an accident. But like I said, next time we'll dine out, or we'll dine at my house."

"*If* we dine out again."

Matt moved closer, smoothing his fingers over her cheek. "There *will* be a next time, Liz. Rest assured." She tried to draw back, but his fingers wrapped around her neck and pulled her closer, his lips coming down on hers again. She attempted to struggle, but to no avail.

And then he stopped. "What was that for?"

"What?"

"Slapping me on the back of the head?"

"I didn't, but I should have."

Matt's lips pursed and he stalked toward the door. Elizabeth followed close behind, anxious to be rid of the man and knowing she wasn't the only one with that desire. She felt a strange upheaval in the room. Matt was close to the door when his body jerked. He stopped abruptly and twisted around, his eyes hot with anger. "Kicking doesn't become you, Liz. I'll try to forget you did that."

Kicking? She had no desire to touch the man. "Go home, Matt."

He opened the door, then appeared to change his mind about leaving. Again she watched his composure return. Never in her life had she seen anyone switch so quickly from hot to cold. "Maybe we're being too hasty, Liz. Let's try this again."

Stretching his hand toward her, she was afraid he was going to touch her again, afraid she would feel his cold, clammy hand on her cheek. She backed away, but it didn't matter. Matt's coat flew off the rack and out the door. His composure disappeared completely as unseen fingers twisted around his collar and propelled him toward the door. His body jerked again at the threshold, his collar instantly loosening, and he stumbled onto the doorstep.

And don't come back!

The door slammed shut.

Elizabeth's eyes widened in fear, then narrowed in anger. She didn't know in which direction to voice her fury, but voice it she did, calmly, coolly, and only mildly loud. "I don't know who you are, I don't know where you are, and personally, I don't care! That man may have deserved everything you dished out, but he was my guest, and . . . and I wanted to throw him out. I'd appreciate it if you'd remember that the next time."

She didn't wait for any further words or actions. Instead, she stormed up the stairs and slammed the bedroom door behind her.

Well, hell and tarnation. Don't that beat all.

Chapter 8

Wind whipped through the trees and beat against the windows, like an outcast begging to come inside. Elizabeth lay on her side, curled up tightly in the massive old bed, and clutched her pillow for comfort. She looked through the window, watching dark clouds break apart and scatter across the sky as the storm ebbed once again. Moonlight raced across the floor, over the foot of her bed and slid under the door leading to the hall. It lit the room just enough that she could tell no one occupied the space but her. But still she sensed she wasn't alone.

She'd tossed and turned for hours, listening and watching for the spirit that haunted her home. It didn't speak, though, or make its appearance known, except for the rhythmic sighs of the floorboards, as if someone was pacing back and forth, back and forth. There was no luminous apparition, no foggy mist in the shape of a human to let her know it kept her company, only the occasional flutter of the dust ruffle on the bed, the tinkling of a hanging crystal on a lamp, the rapid, not-quite-frightened beat of her heart.

Time ticked by on the clock downstairs. She could hear its incessant *tick-tock, tick-tock* echoing through the walls, keeping time with her heart.

She closed her eyes and tried to sleep.

Tick-tock.

Tick-tock.

She woke with a start. Cool air circled her pillow, and something gentle, like a lover's fingers, brushed over her hair. A tinge of fear shivered through her body. Was the ghost beside her? Was it touching her? She hadn't been afraid earlier, not when the rooms were filled with light. Not when her ghostly companion was harassing Matt.

But now, in the darkness, she felt so very alone, and so very vulnerable.

Her muscles tensed. "Please," she whispered with a quiver of fright in her voice, "don't hurt me."

The fingers stilled at her temple, then slowly drew away.

Elizabeth rose, balancing herself on her elbows, and searched the room. The new white lace panels fringing the window parted and she knew the invisible occupant of the hotel was once again standing there.

"Why do you look outside?" she asked, her voice low and trembling. It seemed insane, talking to the unseen thing, yet she felt compelled, as if something strong and powerful was willing her into a conversation.

But no one responded. The curtains didn't move. Nothing stirred at all except the fright rushing through her veins.

"Is there someone out there you want to see?"

The curtains dropped back into place, rippling slightly until they stilled, hanging lifeless once again. She could easily imagine someone at the window turning abruptly, staring at her, trying to think of a response to her question.

But no one spoke.

Cool air moved around her again. The icy fingers touched her face. She reached out, wondering if there was anyone or anything there to touch. But only the freezing air surrounded her, swirling faster and faster, and in an instant the caress ended.

Light footsteps crept up the stairs. A moment later Elizabeth heard a soft, plaintive cry.

It was the loneliest sound Elizabeth had ever heard, and she had to follow.

She pushed out of bed and ran up the stairs to the attic room, where she knew she would find him. *Him?* Yes, she was certain now of that fact. Only a man would stroke her hair so gently, caress her cheek like a lover, softly, tenderly; it was the touch of a man who wanted something he couldn't have.

Amanda.

The tender sigh filled the room—a man's voice, unbearably sad—and tears fell unbidden from Elizabeth's eyes.

She crossed the room and leaned against the wall next to the window. She didn't look outside, just continued to stare at the emptiness beside her, the lonely spot in front of the dingy pane of glass she knew was occupied by the spirit of a man.

"Why do you call her name?" Elizabeth asked.

But she heard only a sigh, and once again a ring of fog clouded the window.

"Is there any way I can help?"

No response.

"Who are you?" she implored. "Please, tell me."

The air stirred. The dust-filled curtains shifted, and Elizabeth wondered if he was going to appear. The thought frightened her, yet talking to an invisible man frightened her even more. How many more sleepless nights would she spend wondering if he watched her, wondering if he would hurt her? How many more restless nights would she spend listening to him roam the halls and the rooms, crying in the darkness, laughing behind her back? She had to make him stop.

But how?

"Please, let me be your friend," she said. "Let me help you."

I don't want any friends, his voice boomed, loud and angry. The walls reverberated with the sound. *Go away!*

"I'm not about to leave," Elizabeth barked back, just as she would with any other man who told her what to do. "I'm not going to run away, either. This is my home. *You're* the intruder, and I'm not about to sit around and let you scare the hell out of me or my friends whenever the mood strikes you."

I haven't frightened you! The windowpane shuddered at his booming voice.

"No?"

No! Frightened people snivel or cower in a corner.

Elizabeth laughed softly. "Maybe I haven't sniveled or cowered, but I am afraid. I've never encountered a ghost before." She took a deep breath. "Of course, it would take a whole lot more than your crazy antics to scare me away."

Maybe I'll try harder.

Elizabeth smiled, remembering the events earlier in the evening. "You didn't have to try very hard to frighten Matt Winchester."

He's a coward. A ghostly laugh echoed through the room. Elizabeth could sense him stalk across the floor and stop suddenly. An old parasol lifted into the air, twirling around and around while tattered silk and lace fluttered about its metal frame.

Again Elizabeth felt the prickly sensation of fear on her skin. Why didn't he show himself? she wondered. But did she really want him to?

Suddenly, the parasol sailed across the room and slapped against a wall, falling, bent and broken, to the floor. *Matt Winchester's a buzzard,* the voice boomed again. *A thieving, lying bird of prey who's got nothing on his mind but pecking away at your bones and eating your heart. He's just like every Winchester who's ever walked the streets of Sapphire.*

Elizabeth fought the urge to laugh again. "I take it you don't like him?"

I won't be happy until every Winchester is dead or gone from this town.

"Why?" she asked. "What do you have against the Winchesters?"

One of them buried me alive, he said matter-of-factly. *And I won't rest until I get revenge.*

"I don't believe you." Elizabeth cried out. Jon couldn't be a murderer. Not even Matt. It wasn't possible.

It's true, whether you choose to believe or not. Now, go away. She heard defeat in his voice. *If you have no trust, you cannot help. So, please—just leave.*

"And you'll continue to haunt this place. You'll

laugh and cry and make my life miserable?"

I will continue to do as I have always done, he said, his voice fading to a whisper. *I'll try to drive you away. I'll make your life hell, just as mine has been. Now, go.*

Dishes rattled in the kitchen. Stairs creaked. Crying rang out from the attic. And Elizabeth jumped at every sound as night moved closer to morning. If she wasn't frightened, why were her nerves on edge? Lack of sleep? Tension? Or the startling realization that she was sharing her home with a disagreeable spirit, a being that was living up to its threat of making her life a living hell?

She pounded her fist into her pillow, buried her head deep into its softness, and tried to sleep.

A loud scraping noise made her crack open an eye just in time to see her nightstand slide across the floor.

Elizabeth wrapped the pillow around her head and tried to drown out the noise.

Lights flicked off and on.

She squeezed her eyes tighter.

Something tickled her nose, but when she opened her eyes, nothing was there. She closed her eyes again and dozed.

Bzzzzz.

It tickled her nose again. A fly? she wondered. Elizabeth swatted thin air.

Bzzzzz.

Her eyes popped open.

Bzzzzz.

No fly. No bee. No sleep!

Deep laughter filled her room. *Fooled you, didn't I?*

"Go away."

I believe I said the same thing to you, yet you're still here.

"Yes, but I have nowhere else to go."

Maybe. But at least you have the option. He sighed deeply. *I have no choice. I cannot leave.*

Elizabeth heard light footsteps across the floor, then all was quiet. *I cannot leave,* he'd said, and once more she wondered what she could possibly do to help.

The loud, incessant knocking woke Elizabeth from a deep, sound sleep.

"Go away."

She buried her head deeper beneath the comforter.

Knock. Knock.

Groaning, Elizabeth peered out from under the blanket and peeked at the clock. Seven forty-five. "Oh, heavens!" She never slept that late.

She pushed out of bed and wrapped up tightly in her robe. "This had better not be another trick," she muttered, as she crept downstairs.

Knock. Knock. Knock.

"I'm coming. I'm coming." She padded across the floor and pulled open the door. No one was there, only the most glorious blue-skied day she'd seen in years. Snow sparkled on rooftops and on the ground, and for the first time, she didn't seem to mind the cold, or the fact that her companion had tricked her once again. This place must be growing on me, she thought.

But when she turned around, her mood shifted from good to not too thrilled. Picture frames hung helter-skelter on the walls in the parlor. Furniture had been pushed to the center of the room and stacked like a pyramid. And high above the melee was a red satin bra, draped casually over the brass rungs of the chandelier.

Elizabeth shook her head and headed for the kitchen and coffee. Good, strong coffee.

She pushed through the swinging door, half expecting to find the kitchen flooded or gutted by fire, but this morning she was lucky. "Thank you," she whispered to anything that might be within earshot.

Still half asleep, she filled a mug with yesterday's coffee and popped it into the microwave she'd purchased on a trip into town. It wouldn't taste great, but it would be fast—and she needed a jolt of something strong to get her going. She crossed the room, pulled open the refrigerator door and a dozen eggs crashed to the floor. She closed the door again and leaned against it, eyes closed, and wondered what could possibly happen next.

With another deep sigh and a halfhearted laugh, Elizabeth began the nearly impossible task of cleaning raw eggs from the hardwood floor.

She was just taking a sip of coffee when footsteps sounded behind her. "Oh, please!" Her exasperation exploded in a huff. "Must you bother me this morning?"

"I don't have to, but I'm going to do it anyway."

She spun around. It wasn't the ghost this time. Jon was standing behind her, arms folded across his chest. "I couldn't miss the mess in the parlor. Matt didn't hurt you, did he?"

"Do you really care?"

He reached out and touched her cheek. Dark circles pooled under her reddened, tired eyes, and he felt the need to gather her into his arms and comfort her. "I care. I was an ass last night. You have every right to hate me."

"I don't hate you. I don't dislike you, either. The problem is, you don't trust me. Maybe you have reason. The more time I spend with Matt, the more I realize why he's so despised. I don't want to be his partner, Jon. I don't want anything to do with him."

He drew her into his arms, holding her close, his hand smoothing the long, silky lengths of her hair. "You didn't answer my question, Elizabeth. Did he hurt you?"

She shook her head. "No. He didn't make that mess, either." She pulled away and ran her fingers through her hair. "I drank too much last night. I was mad at Matt, and I was even madder at you. I just started throwing things."

Jon couldn't help but smile. Her explanation sounded fabricated, but he hated to think about what might have really caused the mess. Had the ghost been playing tricks? If so, did she know the ghost existed? Unfortunately, he couldn't ask. People had thought he was crazy once. He didn't want to go through that again.

"Y'know, I hear a punching bag does wonders for aggression."

"Are you volunteering?"

"If I can withstand a two-by-four, I think I can

stand up to whatever you feel like dishing out."

She laughed. "No, I don't want to hit you. I just want to go upstairs and get cleaned up."

"Good. I'll straighten up the parlor, and when you come down, I'm taking you out of here."

"Why?"

"For starters, we need to talk. Second, you've been cooped up in this place too long, and you need a change of scenery."

"Where do you plan on taking me?"

He smoothed his fingers over her cheek and looked deep into her sparkling amber eyes.

"Have you been to heaven lately?"

An eagle soared across the blue horizon, its wings spread wide as it circled the snow-covered meadow. On the ground, a cottontail peeked out from under a sheltering shrub and cautiously hopped out into the open. Its winter-white fur blended with the snow, a perfect camouflage, except for its telltell shadow.

Jon stood a short distance from the place where Elizabeth sat, and he pointed toward the eagle. It was hovering now, watching, waiting. Suddenly it swooped toward the ground, talons extended, and the rabbit ran, snaking out a zigzag pattern across the snow, dodging the raptor's claws at the very last second and diving into its hole.

Not one heartbeat was skipped as the eagle climbed back into the sky, coming to rest on the top branch of a naked birch. It tucked its wings into its sides and sat there, stately and serene, the master of its surroundings, with its head erect, and alert.

They'd driven nearly half an hour on unplowed and rugged roads and hiked for another fifteen minutes to reach the spot where she sat on a blanket Jon had spread out over a fallen log. Before her, a narrow stream of water could be seen in the center of the ice- and snow-blanketed river, and the sun beat down, slowly melting away the cover of winter. All was quiet except the trickle of water, the call of a bird somewhere far away, and the lightness of her breathing.

"It's beautiful," Elizabeth said, watching Jon as he knelt down to touch animal prints in the new-fallen snow. "I think I could take up permanent residence here."

"It's a little primitive," he said, looking at her over his shoulder.

"Try bedding down in mud with a three-thousand square foot house collapsed on top of you." She laughed. "After living in not much more than a coffin with only spiders and dirt to keep me company for three days, nothing bothers me."

Jon stood slowly and moved toward her, stroking away a wisp of hair the light breeze has blown across her cheek. "Feel like talking about it now?" he asked.

"I never feel good talking about it. I talked about it with a psychiatrist till I was blue in the face."

"I know all about psychiatrists," Jon said, surprising her. But he didn't elaborate. Instead, he swung a leg over the log, clasped her shoulders gently to turn her around, and pulled her comfortably into the warmth of his chest. He wrapped her in his embrace and rested his chin on her shoulder, his cheek against her cheek. "Psychiatrists give you a box of Kleenex and ask you questions. Rarely do they give you any answers."

Jon's words brought back memories of a cold, unsympathetic voice that didn't believe. "And they tell you your imagination's run wild," Elizabeth said.

Jon laughed. "Mine said the same thing." He pulled off his gloves and dropped them into her lap. Slowly he released the top few buttons on her coat and pulled it down around her arms. She didn't even feel the cool air through the light sweater she wore underneath her jacket; all she felt were his hands, his fingers, as they brushed her hair to one side and gently, warmly kneaded the muscles of her neck, her shoulders, and her spine. "You're tense as hell, Ellie," he said, continuing the gentle rhythm. "Close your eyes and relax."

It was easy to follow his directions. It was easy to give her body over to the tenderness of his touch. And he called her "Ellie." He'd called her that once before and she'd lashed out at him, but this time she didn't mind. She'd always been "Elizabeth" or "Liz." Never "Ellie." She liked it, though. It sounded more like an endearment than a name.

"What did they tell you was in your imagination?" he asked, his voice little more than a whisper in her ear.

No one had believed her before, but for some reason she felt Jon would believe. He might even understand. "They said I was only hearing voices. They said when you're in pain or under stress you dream up companions, someone to keep you company. But I wasn't dreaming."

In slow, circular motions his fingers caressed the tops of her arms as he drew the coat around her again. But his fingers didn't leave, moving casually over the curve of her throat, her ears, to her temples, and again he began to massage, very slowly, very gently. "Who did you talk to when you were in pain?" he asked.

And she answered without fear of his response. "God. I'd prayed to Him when the roof caved in and while my house and my bed slid down the hill. I prayed to Him when the center beam of the house hit my chest, when the plaster fell on me, and the shingles. I prayed even harder when the rain started falling and the mud slid over me. All day, all night, when I wasn't screaming for help, I prayed. And then I lost my voice and I couldn't scream any longer. I thought I heard voices. I thought someone might have come looking for me. But I was all alone, until He came and kept me company. I hadn't been much of a believer before that, but it didn't seem to matter. I made so many promises before they found me, so many promises while I prayed. And then He told me I'd be safe, and not to worry, and He stayed with me for three days and three nights, until the rescuers came."

The gentle massaging over her temples ceased, and for one moment Elizabeth was afraid he might not have believed her, until she leaned forward and tilted her head to look into smiling eyes. He pulled her back, wrapping her once more in his embrace. "I'm glad He was there with you," he said. "I'm glad you weren't alone, or afraid."

She put her hands over his and watched the eagle swoop down once more from its perch, then soar high above in the sky.

"I always imagined if God wanted to visit you, He'd do it in a place like this," Elizabeth said. "Do you think heaven looks this way?"

"I wouldn't be surprised."

He pulled on his gloves and rose from the log, standing just a short way from her, looking down at the stream, at the blue sky overhead. Elizabeth watched his profile as he talked about the mountains, the valleys, and the animals he studied. Slowly he turned, looking into her face with those sapphire eyes that rivaled the most beautiful gems. "I've always liked coming out here alone," he said. "Never found anyone I wanted to share it with—" The gems caught fire, blazing in the intensity of his stare. "Until you."

Elizabeth could barely breathe. "Me?"

"Yes. You." He didn't walk toward her. He didn't try to kiss her, but Elizabeth felt something powerful building up behind his strong countenance, and she knew when that kiss finally came, it would probably curl her toes and even her hair.

He reached for her then, and she took his hand. "Come on. I want to show you something." They hiked at least another five minutes through knee-deep snow. Trees grew dense, their heavy, snow-laden boughs blocking most of the sun. Finally Jon stopped, leaned against a tree, and pulled Elizabeth's back against his chest. He wrapped his arms around her, and even through the heavy lamb's wool of his coat she could feel the rapid beat of his heart.

"Look up there, just under the ridge," he said,

pointing to an outcropping of rock. "The den I was watching is behind all that snow. I used to watch the cubs play around that log where we were sitting and catch fish in the stream."

Elizabeth could see it so vividly—the mother, her babies—and now only one remained. "What about the second cub?" she asked. "Can she live on her own?"

She felt the shrug of Jon's shoulders. "I don't know. It's been nearly three weeks and there hasn't been any trace of her. It's possible the poacher butchered her, too, maybe dumped the remains somewhere else."

"Does it happen often?"

"Too often."

"Matt says you're a little fanatical when it comes to the animals around here."

Jon laughed cynically. "He does, does he?"

Elizabeth nodded. "He says the people in town get tired of your environmentalist stance."

"I don't consider myself a fanatic. Matt might; there might be a few others in town who feel that way, too; but most of the population sides with me. Hunting's one thing, poaching's another. Get a permit, hunt your limit, dress down the animal, and haul your meat away. That's fine with me. Senseless butchering doesn't fit into that picture, though."

Elizabeth turned around in the warmth of his arms and looked into his eyes. "Have you always felt this way?"

"My grandfather and I used to hike all over these hills together. He'd tell me Indian legends and tales about the mountain men. He was a walking book of knowledge and a big-time environmentalist. I thought he walked on water and would have believed anything he put into my head."

"Must have been nice to have someone care for you that way."

"Oh, we had our problems. I rebelled a time or two, and I'm sure I wasn't an easy kid to raise. Matt's not the only one I punched. In fact, one time I even smacked his dad."

Elizabeth laughed. "You're joking, of course?"

"No. My uncle and Matt dragged me along on a hunting trip once, stuck a rifle in my hands, and made me get a deer in my sight. I was eight years old and scared to death, but Matt's dad wrapped his arms around me, held my finger to that trigger, and made me pull. He stood over me while I skinned it, carved out the meat, then took my picture holding the antlers. It was a five-pointer. I had tears in my eyes, and when he laughed at me, I took a swing. After that, I never went hunting again."

Jon sighed deeply, and Elizabeth could feel the heavy rise and fall of his chest even through his coat and hers. "I thought Matt's dad was totally responsible for the poaching that had been going on around here, but it continued even after he left. I figured Matt had known about it, but I didn't think he'd get caught up in anything illegal on his own. I've changed my mind over the years, although I can't prove a thing."

Jon released his hold on her, knelt down, and dug his fingers into the snow. "Y'know, I didn't bring you out here to talk about Matt or poaching."

"Did you have something else in mind?"

That lopsided grin spread across his face as he gathered snow in his hands. A ball formed in his palm, and it was growing bigger and bigger with each speck of snow he added. "Ever had a snow fight, Ellie?"

She shook her head slowly, not quite certain she liked the turn of the conversation.

"Well, there's always a first time."

He didn't move quickly; he waited and waited as his grin spread wider across his face. She watched his hands, his eyes, and suddenly she ducked, and the snowball narrowly missed as it flew by her and hit a tree.

She scraped snow into the palm of her glove and threw it back, hitting her target smack in the chest. It was his face she'd been aiming for, wanting to wipe away that grin she was growing to love.

He grabbed another handful at the same time Elizabeth scooped hers, but he was moving back, further, further, winding up for the pitch, and he threw, smacking her in the shoulder, as Elizabeth's miserable excuse for a snowball disintegrated in midair.

And then he charged. He grabbed hold of her shoulders, twisted, and pulled her down with him in the snow, rolling over slowly until he pinned her to the ground.

She inhaled deep and hard, trying to catch her breath, knowing the difficulty she was having wasn't from exertion but from having his body so close against hers, so intimate, even through layer upon layer of fabric.

"God, you're pretty, Ellie," he said.

The laughter had left his eyes, replaced with

warmth and longing. He gently caressed her lips with gloved fingers, drawing them slowly across her cheek and jaw. He lowered his head.

And a pinecone fell from the tree.

Chapter 9

Elizabeth sat in front of the mirror and traced the invisible trail Jon had left on her cheek and over her lips when he caressed her skin. Of course, that pinecone had interrupted everything when it had dropped on his head. They'd been so close, so very, very close.

Finally.

He'd cussed. Boy, had he cussed, using many of the words Elizabeth had used herself before that fateful day last year when she gave it up. It was another promise she'd made, and so far, so good. But not Jon. He lay on his back in the snow and stared at the bright blue sky, asking what he'd done to deserve such a steady stream of bad luck.

He was angry, and the kiss had been forgotten, until he dropped her off at her door. He put his hands on her cheeks, looked into her eyes with those bright blue sapphires of his, and asked her to dinner. And he'd promised her something special, something to remember.

What she wanted to remember was a kiss, not a near-missed one. And she had the feeling it was all going to happen.

Soon.

After dabbing perfume behind her ears and on her wrists, Elizabeth threw caution to the wind and swiped a trace behind each knee and self-consciously looked around the room before applying a tad in the very center of her belly button. It was one of the most sinful things she'd ever done, and she loved the feeling.

Until she heard the faint snicker.

Her head snapped around in time to see a wavering shadow, like a mirage on the pavement on a hot summer day. Her lip quivered. She clutched the edges of her robe and pulled them tightly together across her chest, her fingers wringing the silky cloth.

He's here, she thought. The ghost. The one who calls for Amanda.

She turned away from the nearly transparent vision. It's nothing to be afraid of, she told herself again and again, yet she kept her eyes trained to the mirror, searching the room. She applied a light touch of black mascara to her lashes and a faint trace of blush across her cheeks, but behind the makeup she looked deathly pale. The flush of color she'd experienced while thinking of Jon had disappeared, replaced by fear of the unknown.

She brushed her hair. The long bristles smoothed through the tresses that hung unfettered over one shoulder and curled below her waist. No braid tonight. Jon would like it this way—maybe he'd like it any way she wore it. And then she remembered. The invisible being now in her room had touched her hair, too.

"What is it you intend to accomplish with all this primping?"

Oh, God! She closed her eyes, afraid to open them, fearing the dark silhouette which had just appeared behind her shoulder.

"Open your eyes, Elizabeth. I will not harm you."

Something touched her shoulder. Fingers? A hand?

It stroked her hair, and she could feel it lifting one end of the heavy mass of hair. She tensed and pulled air deep into her lungs. What would the spirit do next?

"Please. Go away," she begged, her voice quivering.

"I've told you before: I have nowhere else to go. Please. Don't be frightened."

Slowly she opened her eyes, hoping the vision would be gone.

She saw him in the mirror, no longer a transparent thing but something real, with substance and depth. She studied his face, his form, while her breathing calmed, and he stood perfectly still, as if he wanted her to take her time and get to know him before he spoke or moved again.

He was clean-shaven except for the droopy mustache trimmed evenly over his upper lip and hanging down at the corners of his mouth. It looked like the tips had just been waxed and curled. His face was slender, his cheeks a bit hollow, and dark blond hair had been parted slightly off center and slicked back behind his ears. It waved over the collar of the black coat that hung nearly to his knees. He wore a stiff-collared white shirt buttoned tightly around his neck and a black string tie. His fitted black vest was adorned with a silver chain that looped from a button at his chest and disappeared behind the front of his coat. She half expected him to pull a watch out of his pocket and stare at the time, maybe wish her good day, like a proper Western gentleman, and disappear.

But he didn't.

Elizabeth twisted around in her seat, but the man who stood behind her still didn't move, not a muscle, not a twitch, even when she stared at the trousers that hung trim and well fit over his legs, all the way down to the toe of his spit-polished black boots.

"I bought these things to get married in," the man told her.

Her frightened eyes shot back up to his face. This was the man who cried at night, who called out for Amanda. The man who'd asked for help. But who is he? she wondered.

"I know your next question," he said. " 'Who am I?' you want to ask, but you're too afraid to speak." He tucked one hand in the pocket of his trousers and wandered pensively toward the fireplace. He turned toward her and leaned against the marble. "Just sit quietly," he said. "Try to calm yourself, and I'll attempt to explain."

Elizabeth could see him quite plainly now. She could hear the timbre of his voice, no longer a haunting echo that reverberated through the hotel. She could see the sparkling blue depths of his eyes that gazed at her with humor and warmth and sadness. But she didn't want to believe he was real, or standing in her room looking at her, talking to her.

Maybe she belonged on that psychiatrist's couch again. But she hadn't imagined what had happened a year ago; she wasn't imagining this now. She closed her eyes tightly and wished him away. She didn't want to live with a ghost; she didn't want him spying on her, scaring her, or spending his nights pacing her room. She just wanted him out of her hotel, out of her life.

Opening one eye just a crack, she prayed he'd be gone. Unfortunately, her prayer went unanswered. Her visitor leaned against the fireplace with a wide, insufferable grin on his face.

"I'm the late, great Alexander Stewart, at your service, Elizabeth." His grand and glorious bow made her smile. His name, though, struck a cord of fear within her.

She frowned, and her lip began to quiver again. "I don't want you here, Mr. Stewart. I know about you."

He laughed. The walls shook. "I know you've heard stories about me, but they're lies. All lies." He paced the room, his hands behind his back, his head tilted down, and finally returned to the fireplace. When he looked at her again, she saw fire in his bright blue eyes. "Contrary to popular belief, I wasn't a thief." His voice grew louder. "I wasn't a murderer, either, or a blasted scoundrel. And I didn't leave my intended standing at the altar."

"But you didn't marry her."

"No." He looked down, and just as Elizabeth envisioned, he pulled a watch from his pocket, popped open the cover, and stared at the time. Or was he looking at something else inside? He closed the watch again and pushed it back into the small pocket of his vest. "No, I didn't marry Amanda."

"You ran away," Elizabeth blurted, angry that he could have done such a thing.

"I didn't run—"

The grandfather clock struck the hour, interrupting his words. "Maybe the stories I've heard haven't been true, Mr. Stewart."

"Of course they're not true! I've just told you that."

"I know. But please, could we talk some other time? I'm expecting someone. I need to get ready."

Oh, Lord! She wanted to know more about Alexander Stewart, but Jon was probably on his way right now. She couldn't tell him to wait. She couldn't tell him she had a ghostly visitor she needed to talk with. Oh, Lord! As much as she wanted to talk to her present companion, she wanted to be with Jon even more. But how could she tell a ghost to leave? Be straightforward, Elizabeth. Don't let him get the upper hand—not the way you gave it to Matt Winchester.

"Could you please leave, Alexander?" she asked, with as much authority as she could muster, under the circumstances.

He folded his arms across his chest and didn't move.

She expelled a frustrated breath. Her fear seemed to be leaving—but not her companion.

There wasn't time to argue; she had to get ready.

Crossing the room, she stopped in front of the antique cabinet where she'd hung her clothes. "Look, I've got to get dressed. Could you leave—this room at least? Maybe we could discuss all this tomorrow."

"Very well."

She turned and he was gone, but his quick acquiescence unnerved her. "Thank you," she said to the empty space where he'd been just a second before. Had he really been there? she wondered. It all seemed so unreal. She wanted to believe, yet at the back of her mind, once again, were the psychiatrist's words about stress and loneliness.

No, it had to be real, but she would never admit it to anyone.

Sighing deeply, she pushed blouse after blouse aside until she settled on a red linen jumpsuit to wear under the white wool Eisenhower jacket with gold military buttons that she'd found in a thrift store on Sunset. The outfit went perfectly with her red leather boots, the ones Jon liked, the ones that weren't worth diddly when it came to walking outside in the snow. What did it matter, though? Jon Winchester looked like he could lift her in the palm of his hand and carry her across the ice. She halfway hoped that he would.

She slipped out of her robe and hung it on the peg just inside the cabinet door and slid her legs into the jumpsuit, pulling it up slowly over red silk tap pants that she found much more comfortable than bikinis or briefs.

"Nice birthmark."

Elizabeth slapped her hand over the strawberry-colored crescent moon peaking over the red lace of her bra. She turned around, one hand gripping the waist of her jumpsuit to her stomach, the other attempting to cover her breasts. Alexander Stewart had reappeared, looking just as healthy and real as any warm-blooded American male.

"I thought you'd left," Elizabeth stammered.

"You thought wrong. I've been here all along. Actually, I've watched you for weeks. You should dress more warmly, you know. Personally, I prefer ruffled flannel nightgowns to those flimsy bits of silk you wear."

That did it. She gritted her teeth and forgot all about covering her birthmark or any other part of her anatomy. Instead, she tried shooing him out of her room with a pointed finger. "Out! Now!"

Instead, Alex swooped to the top of his favorite marble mantel and stretched out, carefree and smirking. "There's not a thing you can do to me, Elizabeth." He shrugged. "And, thunder and tarnation, there's not a thing I can do to you, even if I wanted to—which I don't. So you might as well continue dressing."

"I don't think that's such a good idea, Mr. Stewart," Elizabeth said, with more calm than she felt. "Personally, I'd prefer it if you left."

"Even if I followed your suggestion and disappeared, I'd probably stick around and let you wonder if I was still here watching. Haven't had company in too long a time. Don't rightly think I'm gonna disappear now."

Elizabeth blew out her frustration and shrugged into her jumpsuit, turning her back to the apparition on top of her fireplace. This couldn't really be happening, she told herself. A ghost was one thing, but a ghost watching her dress was another.

"I suppose you plan on wearing those red boots, too?"

"What difference does it make to you?"

"Not much. But that fellow you're gussying up

for was taking a mighty keen interest in those boots. Taking a mighty keen interest in other things, too. I don't think it's such a good idea, you getting yourself all worked up over him."

"Why not?"

"I told you before. He's a Winchester."

"Yeah, and I wish you were just a figment of my imagination." She sat on the edge of the bed and yanked on her boots, trying her best to ignore the man in her room. But she couldn't. His glaring eyes beat against her back. She jerked around. "What do you want? Why are you bugging me?"

"Bugging? I'm not quite sure I know that word."

"It means annoying," she blurted out. "You're driving me crazy."

He nodded. "Yep, just as I intended. As for what do I want from you, well, I want you to help me get out of this place."

"And how do you propose I do that?"

"I don't have a clue. I've been trying for one hundred years and haven't yet been successful. But this time I know it's going to work. You're the one I've been waiting for. I've felt it for days now."

"Felt what?"

Elizabeth jumped at the knock on the downstairs door, and Alex swooped from the mantel and stood right smack in front of her. Again she noticed his eyes . . . startling blue, and they seemed to burn into hers. "You'll help me, won't you?"

The knock sounded again. Elizabeth tore her gaze away. Part of her wanted to run down to that door and throw herself into Jon's arms and ask him for protection. But she felt no real threat from Alexander Stewart. No, she felt something else entirely: compassion. She knew what it felt like to be trapped, with no way out.

She nodded. "If I can help, I will."

"Thank you."

A tear falling from his eye wasn't any more possible than his being a ghost, but she thought for sure she'd seen water pooling in the corners of his eyes and a drop sliding down his cheek.

She reached out to touch him but realized the foolishness of that move. "We'll talk about this when I get home tonight. I promise. Is that good enough?"

He nodded slowly and faded from view.

Oh, Lord! she inwardly sighed. *I haven't helped anyone in a good long time, and I've got the crazy feeling this isn't the place to begin.*

Elizabeth looked like a million bucks, Jon thought, when she opened the door. Damn, he liked red, and he might have told her so if she hadn't slammed the door behind her. "Are you ready to go?" she asked, a bit out of breath.

"Are you in a hurry?"

"I'm starving. Can't wait to eat." She latched onto his arm and pulled him halfway down the stairs. "Where's your truck?" she asked, stopping suddenly when they reached the street.

"At home. Another storm's coming in. Thought we should stick around town."

"Okay, fine. Anywhere but my place. I've been there too much lately and really need to get away."

She put one red hooker boot on the icy pavement and slipped, falling backward right into his waiting arms. The moment couldn't have been better, he decided. He lifted her slowly and easily, turning her toward him. He held her tight . . . very, very tight . . . and with a gloved finger tilted her face so he could see the warmth in her amber eyes.

"You're very beautiful, Ellie." He didn't waste time listening for a response. He lowered his head and captured her lips—soft, full, gentle. His imagination had drummed up many thoughts of what this kiss would be like, but his fantasies were nowhere close to the real thing. There was power and desire in her touch—and this wasn't even a full-blown kiss. This one was tender and only a prelude of what was to come.

Slowly, he moved away, but his gaze stayed on her face, on the eyelids that had closed, on the ebony lashes that rested against porcelain skin, on the tinge of red on her nose and cheeks. "Cold?" he asked.

"No," she whispered. Her eyes opened, and he saw the depths of the passion he'd just tasted, along with the slow, lovely smile that touched her lips. "I haven't been cold since you entered my life."

He felt her hands slide up his chest and wrap around his neck, her gloved fingers weaving through his hair. She pulled him down, closer, closer, and returned the kiss. Lightly, tenderly. Slowly, oh so slowly, and he could feel the heavy beat of his heart drumming rapidly in his chest.

A snowflake hit his cheek. And another. And another. Hesitantly, he pulled away. "Still hungry?" he asked.

"Yes." She nodded. "Starved, but not for food." That deep, throaty lilt returned to her voice, and

Jon had half a mind to pick her up right then and there and carry her off to his turret, lay her down on that chaise, and do a whole hell of a lot more with her body than sculpt its form.

"That kind of sustenance," he managed to croak out, "will have to wait till you've put something a little more substantial inside you."

The smile on her face widened to a grin. Had he said something funny? He didn't think so, yet she continued to smile, and her amber eyes turned to burning embers.

Snow began to fall more heavily as they stood at the edge of the street, the white flakes dropping like confetti into Elizabeth's hair. God, how he wanted her—more and more with each passing moment. What had begun as a desire to capture her beauty in bronze had now become a raging desire to capture her heart and soul and make them part of his.

"Come on," he finally said, slipping an arm around her waist and holding her steady as he led her across the road. "I asked Libby to prepare something special."

Jon pushed open the door of the Tin Cup Cafe and guided Elizabeth inside. He watched her eyes glow even brighter when she saw the "Welcome" sign hanging above the kitchen's aluminum counter and half the population of Sapphire gathered inside the cafe.

Leaning over, Jon whispered in her ear. "I was mean and insufferable when you arrived a few weeks ago. I've been that way a time or two since. But you deserve more than that, Ellie. You deserve the friendship of everyone in this town."

He squeezed her fingers as the gathering of people moved in close. He felt hers tighten, too, and she looked at him and smiled. "I'll thank you for this later," she said, and his imagination kicked into gear once again, wondering what *later* would bring.

Harry was the first to greet her, wrapping her in a heartfelt bear hug. Andy came next, shaking her hand and introducing her to the entire Andrews clan—his wife, his seven kids, and his elderly mother and father. Libby took Elizabeth's coat and gloves, her husband, Jack, placed a glass of wine in her hand, and people laughed and smiled as one after another they made their way toward Elizabeth.

When the introductions subsided, Jon cleared his throat, and standing at the far end of the room, which seemed nearly a million miles from Elizabeth at the other, he raised his mug of beer. "To Elizabeth Fitzgerald," he began, "the prettiest newcomer to ever set foot in Sapphire. May you find peace, prosperity, and contentment in our community."

Jon watched her lips move, saying a silent thank-you. "May you find everything your heart desires here, too, Elizabeth, and a home you'll never want to leave."

Applause reverberated against the walls, and someone turned on a stereo. Music filled the room, something slow and soulful, and Jon crossed the floor. He took Elizabeth's hands and placed them on his shoulders, wrapping his around her waist. He moved in close, closer, feeling her fingers glide over his neck, and he didn't even care if the entire room was watching.

"This feels so good, I think I could dance all night," Jon said, moving easily with the music. "How about you?"

"As long as you're the one holding me."

And he pulled her even closer, planning on being that way for a good long while.

Others joined them on the dance floor, but as far as Jon was concerned, they were the only two in the room. He held her tightly, soaking up her warmth and spirit and her generous smile.

A heavy hand slapped down on his back. "Mind if I cut in, Mayor?" Jon hesitantly released Elizabeth to Harry, who wasted no time at all taking his place.

Some of the warmth left her body when Jon stepped away. She turned her head and followed him with her eyes. He joined Andy and Jack and a few other men whose names she couldn't quite remember, but he turned his gaze toward her and smiled.

Oh, his smile warmed her so. And his kiss. She wished she was back in the middle of the road, reliving that first moment their lips had touched. Fire had shot through her. Her toes had tingled, her stomach had quivered, and those lips that had seemed so unremarkable at first didn't seem that way any longer. They were firm and warm and . . . and she couldn't wait to kiss them again.

Harry lumbered around the floor, smiling at her every time he stepped on the toe of her boot. "Not much of a dancer, am I?"

"It's the company that matters, not the quality of your dancing."

Harry laughed, twirled her around a time or two, and stepped on her toes three more times.

"Jon took me out to Schoolmarm Gulch today," she said, when Harry slowed down a little and became more conscious of his feet.

"Yeah, he told me while we were setting up for this little get-together." She felt Harry's hand tighten around hers, and she could see anger in the frowning set of his eyes. "Good thing you didn't go yesterday."

"Why?"

"I found the cub. She must have come back looking for her mom, or the den. She'd been killed, just like the others."

Elizabeth felt her throat tighten. "We didn't see anything. We thought she might still be alive."

"Guess last night's snow covered up the spot where we found her." He stepped on Elizabeth's toes again, the pain not as noticeable as the hurt she felt inside for the cub. "I've been in this business a long time," he said, "but I still can't get used to the slaughter."

"Can't you get more help?"

"I've asked, but it's a big country and there's a lot of poaching. I'm too well known around here to go undercover, and that's about the only way we can catch illegal hunters."

"Mind if I cut back in?" Jon interrupted, sliding a hand around Elizabeth's arm. "You two are looking a little too serious."

"Only if you promise not to step on her toes." Harry laughed. "I've done enough of that already."

He nodded and smiled. "Thanks for the dance, Elizabeth."

"Thank you, Harry."

"Harry looked a little serious," Jon said, when he pulled her close to his chest.

"He told me about the cub."

A touch of sorrow filled his face, but only for a moment, and then he masked it with a smile. "Hell of a thing to talk about when you're dancing. What do you say we change the subject?"

"Any ideas?"

"What are you going to do if the hotel doesn't succeed?"

"It will. I know you don't want it to . . ."

He stilled her protests with a gentle finger over her lips. "Pretend I want it to succeed just as much as you. Okay?"

Elizabeth smiled. The stubborn man she was beginning to really, really like was trying his hardest to see her side of things, and she knew it couldn't be easy. "I don't know what I'll do if things don't work out," she said. "I've got money to fix up the place and to tide me over for a year or two. But if things don't work out, I'll have to go somewhere else. There's no other work in Sapphire, and I don't think people around here are interested in hiring me for fashion photography."

Jon's hand slid into the hair at the nape of her neck. "There's a big market for wildlife photography."

"I know my way around a camera, Jon." She laughed. "But I'd be useless out in the wild."

"I wouldn't let you go alone. I could show you places few people have ever been. I know where wild horses graze, where eagles nest and grizzlies fish." He leaned over and softly kissed the hollow beneath her ear. "I'll take you to all those places," he whispered.

"You trust me, then?" she asked.

He lifted his head and their eyes met. "I should have trusted you all along."

Yes, he should have, but she wasn't about to argue the point. He trusted her, that's all that mattered now. She rested her head against his shoulder as they danced, happy to be in Jon's arms. Around and around they turned, circling the room time and time again as the evening passed by. They drank wine, ate potluck, and danced some more.

The cafe door opened and Matt stepped inside, bringing the cold and the snow with him. Most people looked his direction and turned away, but not Elizabeth. Jon didn't look away, either, especially when Francesca Lyon walked in right behind Matt.

Elizabeth looked up. What could Jon possibly be thinking? He'd said Francesca was an old friend; surely it must hurt to see her with Matt. "Jon," she said, touching his cheek and turning him to face her. "Are you okay?"

"Yeah," he said through gritted teeth. "She was asking me about Matt when we were together the other night." He smiled slowly. "Guess she solved her boyfriend problem."

"Are you upset?" Elizabeth asked.

"What you really mean is, am I jealous. Right?"

"Well—"

"I told you before, Ellie. Francesca's a friend—nothing more." He pulled her to his chest, his hand pressing against her back, holding her close. He leaned over and rested his cheek against hers. "I'm only interested in you. No one else."

Those were the words she wanted to hear, and she totally forgot about Matt and Francesca.

Hours passed, the dancing continued, and Francesca and Matt departed without saying a word. They nibbled on pies and cakes and cookies, and Harry and Andy poured beer and wine. They line-danced, stood in small groups, and talked about inconsequential things, and as the evening drew to a close, Elizabeth watched Jon sitting in a corner with two children on each knee, telling some of the yarns his grandfather had told him long, long ago.

"That man's a real catch for the right woman," Libby said, sidling up close to Elizabeth. "It's about time he settled down, got married, and had a few youngsters of his own."

"Are you sure that's what he wants out of life?" Elizabeth asked.

"It's what most men want. Some just don't see it quite as clearly as others."

"Guess I've never seen that life too clearly for myself, either."

"Well, dear, most of the townspeople don't have blinders on. We placed bets earlier tonight on when we'll be holding the wedding reception." Libby squeezed Elizabeth's fingers. "I bet late April, and I sure don't like to lose."

Elizabeth laughed. A husband? A family? She'd never considered either. But she tucked the thought away. It was something she might consider later.

The evening wore to a close just a little before midnight. Elizabeth insisted on staying behind to help Libby and Jack deal with the mess, but Libby wouldn't hear of such nonsense. "It can wait till tomorrow," she said, and locked the mayor and guest of honor out in the cold.

Snow fell lightly as Elizabeth and Jon stepped out from under the covered boardwalk and onto the street. "Nice night for dancing," he said, taking Elizabeth into his arms right smack in the middle of the road.

Pressing his hands low on her back, he pulled her hips close and danced slow and easy, with her cheek resting on his shoulder. He felt so good, so right, so near.

"Come home with me," he whispered softly into her ear.

Elizabeth didn't want to waste time going home—his or hers. She wanted him here and now. But that wasn't any good. They'd freeze in spite of the heat he was generating in her body. Maybe they could just run across the street and into the hotel, to her room, to . . .

Oh, Lord. She couldn't take him there, not with Alexander in residence. Not when Alexander liked to watch. Why hadn't she just given in and gone immediately to Dalton House?

She made the mistake of looking over Jon's shoulder at the old Victorian, and high up in her bedroom window, she saw the curtains flutter and noticed a slender-faced figure peering through the glass.

"I take it you don't like my suggestion," Jon said, his slow, easy movements coming to a halt.

"I liked the suggestion a lot." She kissed him quickly and drew away. "It's just that something's come up." She glanced up at the empty window, at the fluttering curtains, then looked back at Jon. She was so torn. But she'd promised she'd talk to Alexander tonight. Oh, Lord! Why had she made that promise not to break promises?

She pulled away slowly. "I need to go. I made a promise to someone, Jon. If I don't go home now . . ."

He crossed his arms and grinned. "Suit yourself."

"Oh, heavens! If I wanted to suit myself, I'd go home with you. But—I can't."

His grin widened, and he quieted her words with a kiss. "I have some business to take care of tomorrow, but why don't we get together after? Four o'clock. My place."

Her eyes widened. "I usually prefer a little more spontaneity."

"I was thinking an early dinner—not sex." He laughed. "Although we could take our chances and see how things progress."

The man was totally infuriating, but he felt so good, and that made up for a multitude of sins. Pressing her hands against his chest, she slid them slowly to his neck and wove her fingers into his hair. "Four o'clock. Your place." She kissed him, slow and easy. "Who's cooking?" she purred. "You or me?"

"Hopefully we'll do it together."

Chapter 10

"You're home early."

The voice came from the top of the stairs right after Elizabeth stepped into the foyer and closed the door. She raised her eyes and there he was—Alexander Stewart, looking just as he had on his infamous wedding day.

She slipped off her coat and hung it on the rack by the door, then tucked her gloves into the pockets. Brushing the light sprinkling of snow from her hair, she inched her way up the stairs.

"When I saw you smooching up with that big oaf, I thought for sure you were gonna back out on your promise."

Elizabeth laughed. She'd never wanted to back out on a promise so much in her life, but she had tomorrow at four o'clock to look forward to. Spending the evening talking with Alexander Stewart didn't seem like a total imposition.

Besides, she wanted to know more. She'd been fascinated by the few things Jon had told her; hearing Alexander's side of the story promised to be just another highlight to a perfect evening.

"For your information, I turned down a wonderful invitation from that 'big oaf' to spend time with you."

"I've watched him ogle you. I can well imagine what kind of invite you got from him—probably didn't have anything at all to do with a buggy ride after church, either."

"Things have changed in a hundred years."

"And not for the better!"

Elizabeth laughed as he walked at her side, his hands behind his back, until they reached her bedroom door. "I'm going to change first. Maybe climb into bed and get comfortable."

"Sounds good to me."

Elizabeth stepped into her bedroom and stopped short when Alexander followed. "What are you doing?"

"Following. I do it quite well, especially when no one can see me."

Elizabeth folded her arms across her chest and stared him down. "Let's get something straight right this moment, Mr. Stewart. This room is off-limits while I'm dressing. I don't want you anywhere around, visible or invisible. Have I made myself clear?"

"Perfectly."

Alex disappeared, and Elizabeth shut the door.

With Alex out of the way, at least for the moment—she hoped—she stripped out of her clothing and slipped into a red satin and lace negligee. Eric had told her several times to buy thermal underwear and flannel nightgowns to fight the cold Montana winter, but no way was she going to be bound up tight when she slept. Besides, she liked the feel of satin and lace, and if she was going to be bound up tight, it would be with a man, not with too many layers of nightwear.

She slid under the covers and drew them to her chin. Closing her eyes, she thought of Jon's kiss and how it had been more than worth the weeks of frustrating wait. And she thought of the fragrance he wore. What was it? Obsession? Maybe something as masculine and old-fashioned as Old Spice? The fragrance had been on his skin when he'd kissed her, it was in every room where he'd worked in the hotel, and it was so fresh and vivid in her memory that with her eyes closed, she felt he was near.

"He'll hurt you, you know."

The sudden, unexpected intrusion made Elizabeth's fingers tighten on the sheet. "Who?"

"Jonathan Winchester."

Elizabeth smiled and shook her head. No, Jon would never hurt her. They'd shared something new and special today. They'd talked, they'd held each other, they'd kissed, and she sensed that each new day would bring something even more special. No, Jon would never hurt her.

Elizabeth pulled the covers close to her chin and scooted up into the pillows. Slowly, a frown crossed her face as she looked at the door and back to the man standing at the edge of her bed. She hadn't heard him come in. She hadn't seen him walk across the room. He'd just appeared—from nowhere. "What are you doing here, anyway? I thought I told you to stay out."

"You told me to stay out while you were dressing and since you failed to let me know when you'd finished, I came in to check for myself."

"When?"

"When what?"

"When did you come in? Was I dressed?"

"Well, not completely."

"What are you? Some kind of pervert?"

"I'm a ghost!" he bellowed. "And a long time ago I was a man with the same kinds of desires that Winchester fellow has. Only difference is . . ." Alex looked away. She could see the heavy rise and fall of his chest, his anger raging through his body. He turned toward her again, the calm, reflective side of him returning once more. "I can't do anything about those desires, either. I have needs and wants. I can feel sad and lonely and happy. And I can feel terribly, terribly frustrated."

"I'm sorry."

"Don't be!" he barked, and then his voice calmed. "Talking to you, looking at you, dressed, undressed, gives me the only comfort I've known in . . ." His words trailed away. He seemed to be thinking about something in the past. "It's been a lot of years since I've had anyone to talk to."

"Then talk, Alex. I want to listen. I want to know everything."

The grin returned to his face. "Mind if I have a seat?"

He might bark, he might bellow, but, Elizabeth thought, at least he's polite. "Be my guest," she said.

He floated in a light, fluid motion from her bedside to the high, solid mahogany footboard. He sat down and leaned forward, his elbows on his knees, his chin resting on the backs of his folded hands. He proceeded to study her with those bright blue eyes of his, and that slight, off-kilter smile.

"You sure do wear some peculiar get-ups."

"What does that have to do with you?"

"Nothing at all. I'm just making conversation till you get used to my company."

"You're a ghost. I don't think I'll ever get used to you."

"You got used to that big lug Jonathan Winchester."

"He's flesh and blood."

All traces of good humor left his voice. "He's a Winchester, and all Winchesters are bad news. Stay away from them."

"If you wanted me to stay away, why have you allowed Jon in the house? You kicked Matt out. Why haven't you done the same to Jon?"

"Matt Winchester's nothing more than snail slime. He touched you—"

"Jon's touched me, too."

"It's not the same!" Alex bellowed. "Look, I don't want to talk about that big lout. I want to talk about me."

Elizabeth smiled. "Okay, why don't you tell me why you deserted Amanda?"

His frown deepened. "So, you believe the rumors? You think I ran away? You think I'm a murderer?" He no longer sat hunched over and relaxed at the edge of the bed. His back had stiffened, his quirky smile had disappeared. "Don't believe everything you hear, Elizabeth. The words you've heard are false. They're lies. All of them nothing but lies!" His protests reverberated through the room like thunder.

He bolted away, his form changing from a man

to a streak of lightning as he circled the room, knocking over everything in his path. The down comforter flew from the bed, the sheets billowed upward like stormclouds, and Elizabeth gripped them even more tightly to keep them from blowing away. Her hair whipped around her face, stinging her eyes, slapping her cheeks.

She didn't like what was happening. Alexander's anger was out of control and she had no idea what he might do next. But she wasn't going to let him intimidate or frighten her. No way! She pushed out of bed, stood like a drill sergeant in the middle of the room and yelled "Stop! *Now!*"

In less than a heartbeat the turmoil ended. Picture frames lay on the floor amid broken shards of glass. The blanket hung over the statue of marble lovers. The sheet had wound tightly around a bedpost. And Alexander Stewart sat cross-legged against the headboard, a silly-assed grin again plastered on his face. "I don't like to be angered," he announced.

"And I don't appreciate your tantrums, or your attempts at humor."

"I'd apologize, but . . ." He shrugged. "I'm a ghost. I do what I'm supposed to do."

"And what's that?" Elizabeth asked.

"I annoy the hell out of people." He winked, and Elizabeth forced herself not to smile.

"Care to join me?" Alex pointed to a spot at the other end of the bed. Elizabeth's eyes narrowed as she studied his smirking face. Did she dare climb up on the mattress?

"I don't bite, Elizabeth."

"I wouldn't put it past you."

His expression softened. "Trust me. Please."

"Well . . ." She started to move but stopped when he disappeared in a flash. In half a second he stood behind her, draping the comforter over her shoulders.

"It's too cold to be standing around half naked. Tarnation, woman! You're in Montana, and it's winter! If you don't dress a little more appropriately, you're going to end up in bed with pneumonia."

"I'm perfectly healthy, but thanks for your concern," she said, while Alex floated back to the place he'd claimed on her bed. Slowly, she stood on the footstool and climbed onto the mattress that was nearly four feet off the floor. She sat cross-legged, facing Alex, with the blanket wrapped loosely about her shoulders and over her legs. Settled down and comfortable, she waited for him to speak, but he didn't. Instead, he stared at her face, at the chaotic disarray of her hair, and then she noticed he was twiddling his thumbs.

"Do I bore you?" she asked.

Alex shook his head. "It's a bad habit," he answered, as his thumbs continued their circling motion. "Have you ever thought what it would be like to live alone for a hundred years, rarely having anyone to talk to? Have you wondered what it would be like to have no friends, no acquaintances?"

"I'd be lonely."

"You'd be desolate. You'd long for your family, your loved ones. You'd savor every conversation. You'd hate everyone who scorned you. You'd want to sink into oblivion because kind words are never spoken about you, and all you ever hear is lies. You'd shut your mind away from everything. And," his voice softened, "you'd wish you were dead."

"But—" Elizabeth frowned. "You *are* dead."

"I suppose." He shrugged. "But I'm still here. I never got the benefit of finding out what heaven's all about. Never even got to give hell a try, either, although I've sworn for one hundred years that this hotel is a damn sight worse than Hades could ever think of being."

Elizabeth listened to his words. His sadness was overpowering. She'd promised earlier to help him, but she didn't have a clue where to begin. "What happened, Alex? Why are you here? Why did you leave Amanda?"

Anger returned to his face, and Elizabeth feared another hurricane was brewing inside her ghostly companion. "Leave her?" Alex shook his head. "You believe that hogwash? I loved Amanda."

"But Jon told me the story, he told me how you left her standing at the altar. That doesn't sound like love to me."

"What do you know?" Alexander vaulted from the bed and paced the floor, back and forth, back and forth, his hands clenched tightly behind his back. Elizabeth waited for his frustration to ebb. Finally, he began muttering as if she weren't even present. "I never loved any woman until Amanda. There were other women at one time. I'm a man, after all. But once I met Amanda, I didn't want anyone else."

Alex stopped at the end of the bed. "See this?" he said, pointing to the little finger of his left hand.

A thin gold band rested just below his knuckle. "I'd planned on putting that on Amanda's finger, but I never got the chance."

His hands began to shake, and he shoved them into his pockets. "It was my wedding day," he began. "I had a room here in Phoebe's boardinghouse. Upstairs." He looked toward the ceiling, and Elizabeth knew he was talking about that room where she'd heard the crying, the desolation. "I'd just finished dressing, and I'd put Amanda's ring on my finger so I wouldn't have to dig it out of my pocket when I got to the church. I remember looking out my window and seeing her walking down the street. She looked so pretty in her wedding dress, her long blond hair hanging in ringlets over her shoulder. Every time I looked at Amanda she took my breath away."

Alex took his hands out of his pockets and pulled a shiny silver watch from his vest. With his head tilted down, he opened the cover and stared at the inside for nearly a minute, then held it out for Elizabeth to see. "I loved her. I never loved anyone but Amanda."

Elizabeth looked at the black and white photo. It wasn't faded with age, as she'd expected, but looked as if it had just been placed inside the watch. A delicate face with a loving smile peered up at her. "She's pretty."

"Beautiful." Alex snapped the watch cover closed and returned it to the place it had been for one hundred years.

"The doctor was holding Amanda's arm as they went into the church," Alex said. "Her father passed away suddenly, just a few weeks before the wedding, and the doctor was his friend. Amanda had asked him to give her away, and we'd invited the entire town. I remember it all so vividly. The streets were empty. Everyone was in the church waiting, and it was time for me to go."

Again he stopped his story and went to the window, pulling aside the curtains and looking down on the darkened town. "Something hard and heavy hit me on the back of the head. I remember the pain, and feeling sick to my stomach."

Alex turned around and gazed directly into Elizabeth's eyes. Tears streaked her cheeks. She couldn't keep them from falling, not when she heard his anguished words, not when she felt his pain. "I'm so sorry, Alex." She wiped them away, thinking of the man standing at that window upstairs, longing for the moment he would say "I do." And then losing everything.

"Do you know who hit you?" she asked.

He nodded. "Yes, I know." Bitterness took away the hurt in his eyes. "I didn't die from the crack on my head. No, my killer was much more cruel than that. I remember waking up with bile rising in my throat. The back of my head felt like someone had driven an ax through my skull, and when I opened my eyes, I was surrounded by darkness. Then something heavy fell on my legs and chest. I couldn't move. I couldn't see much of anything, either, but I could hear a shovel digging into dirt. And then I felt it falling down on me, a few grains of soil hitting my chin and my face. I could see a little light glinting off the shovel. And then I saw his face. He was smiling." Alex stared straight across the room, and when he turned again to face

Elizabeth, she saw his pain and fear. "I opened my mouth to scream at him, and he tossed another shovelful of dirt right into my face, into my mouth. I tried spitting it out, but I couldn't. It was coming down faster and faster, and I could hear him laughing. I tried to breathe, but I couldn't. I tried to move, but . . ."

Alex turned away again, and Elizabeth climbed from the bed. She went to his side to give him solace. She knew that fear of being buried alive. If the rain hadn't been falling so heavily, she, too, might have suffocated with a mouth full of dirt and debris. But the rain had washed it away. Alex hadn't been so fortunate.

She reached out slowly to put a comforting hand on his arm, but even though he looked solid and real, her hand sliced right through.

He looked down at her and smiled. "You can't touch me, Elizabeth. No one can touch me." He put his hand over his heart. "I can feel your sympathy inside, though. It's been a long time since anyone's cared enough to cry for me."

Alex went to the window. He parted the lace curtains and stared out. "That last minute, before my life faded away, I thought about Amanda, about how much I loved her. I swore I'd be with her again, and I swore revenge against the man who'd taken me away from her."

"Who was it?" Elizabeth whispered, but deep inside she knew the answer—at least part, of it.

"A Winchester, of course." He laughed. "Luke Winchester, the thieving, lying bastard who buried me alive, tarnished my reputation, and worst of all, stole my Amanda."

Alex looked straight into Elizabeth's eyes, and she shuddered at what she saw. Hatred had changed the bright blue pools into dark, fathomless pits. "Living here for one hundred years has been a miserable existence. But I won't leave, and I won't be happy until my good name's restored and every last Winchester is dead and buried, or run out of this town."

Elizabeth didn't see him leave her side, but she felt the icy *whoosh* of air blow through the room and heard the thunder of his anger. Suddenly, all was quiet.

And then it began again, high above, in the attic. The lonely, plaintive cry reached through her chest and gripped her heart.

She didn't bother grabbing her robe or shoving her feet into slippers; there wasn't time. Alex needed her. She ran from the room, the blanket dragging on the floor behind her. She rushed into Alexander's attic and even though she couldn't see him, she felt his presence.

Cold air stirred about her and the curtains ruffled. She could hear an occasional creak of a floorboard. He was pacing. Back and forth. Back and forth.

Elizabeth sat down on top of an ancient leather trunk and waited for his frustration and anger to ebb, listening, watching, somehow knowing it wasn't yet time to speak.

"Leave me. Please," he begged.

"I'm not leaving, Alex. I'm staying put right here until you're ready to talk."

Seconds passed. Minutes. All was silent, and Elizabeth continued to wait. Finally, the curtains parted and the shadow of a man appeared, leaning against the wall. "She married Luke Winchester three weeks later," he said, the hazy vision slowly turning into a man. "I've never blamed her for hating me, and I've never blamed her for getting married. But I never understood how she could fall in love with that murderer and marry him so quickly after my disappearance."

"She must have had a reason," Elizabeth said. Maybe Amanda hadn't loved Alexander enough, she thought. Maybe she'd been so hurt she married the first man to walk into her life. The possibilities were endless.

"Luke Winchester owned one of the saloons in town," Alex said. "He was a gambler, a ladies' man. He talked big and he had hopes of one day being the richest man in town. He wasn't the kind of man Amanda would have fallen in love with."

"It's called rebound, Alex. Someone hurts you, you reach out to the first person to come along, whether that person is right for you or not."

"He was all wrong for Amanda. But she was just what he needed. With me out of the picture, Luke Winchester stepped in, put a ring on her finger, and suddenly all the riches he'd ever wanted were in his control."

"That must have been what he'd planned all along."

Alex nodded his agreement and turned back to the window. "I would have given him everything. All I wanted was Amanda."

Elizabeth contemplated his words. *I would have given him everything.* They didn't make sense, but she was too tired to think about them now. She put her fingers to her mouth to stifle a yawn.

"You're tired. Go to bed, Elizabeth, we'll talk again tomorrow."

"There's too much I want to know. Too much I need to know if I'm going to help you."

Alex smiled and she felt the light touch of his fingers wrapping around her hand. "Come. I'll take you downstairs."

Again she yawned. Her eyelids had grown heavy, and she allowed him to pull her to her feet. She turned her hand over to weave her fingers through his, but when she squeezed, she felt only her own fingers touching her palm. Looking down, she saw just the transparent outline of his fingers interlocked with hers, and she looked back into his face with even more questions in her eyes. Why, she wondered, could she feel his touch, and yet she couldn't touch him in return?

As if reading her mind, he answered her question: "I'm dead, Elizabeth, but I have powers I don't even begin to understand. I can move furniture. I can twiddle my thumbs. I can speak and fly around this hotel, and I can touch you and make you feel me when I do. But I feel nothing in return, only the pain in my heart, and anger, and the longing to be with Amanda again."

Once more he squeezed her fingers. "Tomorrow we'll talk more. Now, though, you should get some sleep."

Elizabeth allowed him to lead her down the stairs and into her bedroom. She climbed into bed, and Alex removed the sheet from the bedpost, smoothing it over the top of her, along with the comforter. There were so many questions she wanted to ask, so many things that made no sense. Tomorrow, though, she would ask her questions and learn the answers. And tomorrow she would try to help, try to find a way to release Alex from the bonds holding him here on earth.

Sitting on the end of the bed, Alex watched Elizabeth sleep. Her lips parted slightly. She breathed deeply, and her eyes fluttered beneath the nearly transparent skin of her eyelids.

He'd sat on Amanda's bed the night her father had died. All he'd wanted to do was console her, to hold her in his arms and let her weep. Her tears had made him ache, increasing his own grief. He'd loved the man nearly as much as Amanda had.

Alex sighed, thinking back to the day Jedediah Dalton had taken him in. The richest man in town had shown up at his parents' funeral, paying homage to them and all the others who'd died of influenza. Alex was thirteen at the time, nearly a man. But Alex was just what Jed Dalton wanted—a son—and Jedediah took him under his wing. Alex protested, he was stubborn and proud. He'd told Mr. Dalton he'd rather work at the Dalton copper smelter, or hire on as a cowboy at one of the ranches, rather than become a pampered brat. But Mr. Dalton didn't want that, and Mr. Dalton had always gotten what he wanted.

Figures came easy, Alex remembered. Mr. Dalton pored over his ledgers and accounts with Alex at his side. He took him to meetings with the state's other copper kings, and when Alex was old enough, he sent him to New York to get a taste of big-city life. New York might have been fine for

Mr. Dalton's wife and daughter, but not for Alex. He made it only as far as Saint Louis. That was big city enough for him. And once he got his fill, he worked his way back to Montana and told Mr. Dalton he didn't plan to leave ever again.

Ten years later Mr. Dalton had sent for his daughter. Alexander was twenty-nine, Amanda had just turned nineteen, and Mr. Dalton felt it was time for her to marry. He wanted her union to be with the young man he'd fostered and nurtured, the young man who would take his place at the head of the Dalton empire when he died. He'd already signed everything over to Alex. The deeds were in a vault at the bank, because Mr. Dalton didn't believe in waiting until the last minute to make plans for the future.

Alex had protested again, but he knew Mr. Dalton wouldn't change his mind. "What's done is done," Jedediah said. "I'll announce my plans at your wedding."

Wedding. That word had frightened the hell out of Alex. He liked freedom; he liked the ladies. He wasn't ready to settle down. But that was before.

Alex smiled when he remembered the day Amanda had stepped off the train in Helena, her ruffled, lacy pink-and-white–striped parasol extended over a jaunty little hat to keep the sun off her peaches-and-cream skin. "Pretty" didn't even come close to describing her. They ate dinner and spent the night in the governor's mansion, then caught a train early the next morning for Drummond. He'd left his horses and wagon at the livery, and once he had the rig ready to go and Amanda's trunks loaded, they began the last leg of their trip.

On a hill overlooking Sapphire, he proposed to the woman he'd met just the day before. He would have done it whether Mr. Dalton had wanted him to or not. She was the sweetest little thing he'd ever met, and he had no intention of letting her out of his sight—not that day, not ever. Amanda didn't hesitate a moment when he popped the question. She slapped his face and told him to take her home.

It took an entire year to woo her. He bought flowers and candy and sarsaparilla. He escorted her to church. He even tried his hand at breaking wild broncs, catching the biggest fish, and lassoing the biggest and meanest bull—all to impress Amanda. And he'd failed miserably at each of those things.

But somehow, he didn't fail at making her fall in love.

When he proposed the second time, she was sitting in a swing on the porch at Dalton House, and he was down on bended knee in front of her, pledging his love and devotion. She rewarded him with their very first kiss, and Alex thought for sure he'd died and gone to heaven.

But waiting was hell. Immediately after their engagement, he moved to Phoebe Carruthers' boardinghouse. He didn't trust himself being too close to Amanda. If she could wait till their wedding night to catch another glimpse of heaven, so could he.

Six months later Mr. Dalton was dead. After the funeral, after the mourners and well-wishers had left the mansion, Alex had carried Amanda to her room. She'd pulled him into her arms, comforting him just as he'd comforted her. And they made love, hesitantly at first, then sweetly, then passionately. Alex found heaven again that night, with archangels and cherubs and harps, and he'd remembered and relived that night again and again—for one hundred very long years.

His thoughts returned to Elizabeth, slumbering peacefully while he waited out the night. In the morning he would tell her about the deeds. He'd tell her that he was the rightful owner of Dalton House, of the town of Sapphire, and of most all the property a person could see when they stood in the turret room of the mansion. He'd persuade her to find those old records and when she did, he'd ask her to take them to the authorities and have all the Winchesters evicted from the town. It was his right as owner. It was his right as a man who'd been wronged. It was his revenge—and he thought, it might be the only way he could end his cursed existence and once again lie in Amanda's arms.

Chapter 11

Elizabeth tossed and turned, finally burrowing deep into the feathered pillow, but she couldn't return to sleep. Thoughts of Jon came to her, and thoughts of Alex, all too vivid and real to give her any peace.

How could Alex go on? she wondered, year after year, tortured by his past, his memories. She wanted so much to help him, to think of a way to get him out of the bonds that held him within the hotel. But if those bonds could be broken only by wreaking vengeance on the Winchesters, one very big hurdle stood in the way—Jon.

She touched her lips, remembering the kisses they'd shared. She wanted more, and more after that. She thought about Libby's bet and laughed that someone would be foolish enough to wager money on the date when two people who had never even mentioned the word "love" to each other would marry. What had Libby said? April? That wasn't the least bit plausible.

She wasn't in love.

Or was she?

When she couldn't sleep any longer, she went to

the kitchen at four A.M. and baked up a frenzy while drinking cup after cup of strong coffee—anything to keep her going strong.

Alex kept her company, watching her bake two of her "best this side of New York" cheesecakes—one for Libby, one for Jon. A dozen and a half huckleberry muffins found their way into plastic bags, some for the cafe, some for her freezer. Jon would like them with his mug of strong morning coffee.

She cracked eggs, whipped up an omelet for breakfast, and kneaded dough for fresh warm bread to take with her to Jon's. And while she fussed around the kitchen, Alex told her the rest of his tales about the day Jedediah Dalton had taken him in, the day he met Amanda, and all the things in between.

At eight she filled the clawfoot tub upstairs with hot water and bubbles, gave Alex explicit orders to stay out, and soaked for nearly an hour. She thought of last night's kisses, the dancing, and Jon pulling her hips close to his. He'd wanted her, of that she'd had no doubt.

She'd wanted him, too, but her promise to Alex had been in their way. At four o'clock, though, nothing would keep them apart.

At nine she was lacing her combat boots over Levi's when she heard the knock downstairs.

"It's that big lug," Alex informed her, as he zipped into her room. "You want me to get rid of him? It's not four o'clock yet."

Elizabeth grinned. "No, Alex. I don't want you to get rid of him, and I don't want you doing anything to hurt, maim, or annoy him."

"There's no fun in that."

Shaking her head, Elizabeth brushed past Alex and ran down the stairs.

She threw open the door. "Good morning."

"I couldn't wait till four," Jon pronounced, his lopsided smile warm and wonderful and the best thing she'd seen all morning. "Keep me company today."

"But you said you have business to take care of."

"Won't take more than a couple of hours. I'll drop you off at the mall in Helena, if you'd like, then we can have a late lunch."

Well, Elizabeth thought, riding in a pickup over icy roads sounded a whole lot better than sitting inside a haunted hotel waiting for four o'clock to arrive. "Think we could hit a few antique shops, too?" she asked, slipping into her parka and grabbing her purse.

"I take it your answer's yes?"

She stood on tiptoe and quickly kissed his lips. "Would you have settled for any other answer?"

He shook his head slowly. "One no from you in a twenty-four-hour period is enough. Anything more and I might get angry." He wrapped his arm around her shoulder and closed the door behind them as they headed for his truck.

While Jon drove they talked about her brother, his new wife, and about a few of Eric's entrepreneurial disasters. He tried everything, and succeeded at little, but he had a good heart and he'd been a loving brother. Of course, he had a bad habit of disappearing for weeks at a time, which he never explained and which annoyed and worried his sister. Eric always laughed it off when Elizabeth expressed her concerns, saying not to worry, he could take care of himself.

They talked about Jon's parents, Thomas Jr. and Joanna, about their environmentalist activities, which had come to such a screeching halt, and about Thomas—Jon's grandfather—and how Luke Winchester had deserted him when he was sixteen.

"Luke married a French actress not too long after Amanda died," Jon told her. "She didn't care much for her stepson or the mansion they lived in. My grandfather said she used to flounce around in feathers and flimsy silk and make demand after demand on the servants. She had a poodle she adored, and nine months to the day after she married Luke she had a brand new son to devote all her attention to. Living with her and Luke was absolute hell, my grandfather used to say."

If only you knew the entire story about your great grandfather, Elizabeth wanted to say. But she'd promised Alex not to divulge his presence or any of his secrets until they could prove his innocence and hopefully find the records.

"I don't know how long they were married before Luke had Winchester Place built," Jon continued, "but Thomas was sixteen when they moved out of Dalton House. He wasn't invited to go along, of course, but he didn't seem to mind. That big old mansion I live in was deeded over to my grandfather along with a hundred acres of land and enough money so he could live comfortably."

"The more I hear about Luke Winchester, the more I despise him."

"Everyone has to have a black sheep in the family, I suppose."

Luke Winchester, though, was blacker than black, and somehow she had to prove it.

"I wish there were some way I could learn more about Luke and Phoebe, even Alexander Stewart," Elizabeth said, as they neared Helena. Her curiosity grew moment by moment. She sensed a need to know everything possible about the history of the town and a few of its earlier citizens. Whether she could help Alex once she learned more, she didn't know.

"There's a history museum in Helena," Jon said. "I don't know how much information you'll find, but I could drop you off while I'm at my meeting, if you want to check it out."

The thought of digging through old records excited her. She'd always been fascinated by antiques and old clothes. She'd collected tintypes and old diaries and had had a wonderful collection before everything had been destroyed. But she'd had no real connection with any of the things she'd accumulated.

She might not be a Dalton or a Winchester or a Stewart, but she was caught up in their lives. They seemed real because Alex and Jon brought them to life. And she couldn't wait to learn more.

Elizabeth pored over old newspaper accounts, checking every reference on Luke Winchester, Alexander Stewart, Phoebe Carruthers, and Amanda Dalton. She flipped through page after page, reading article upon article, mostly short, cryptic gossip about births, weddings, and the latest fashions being sported around town.

After 1897 there were no references at all to Alexander Stewart, but prior to that there was a full account of how he'd masterminded the devastating robbery of the Bank of Sapphire. Accounts claimed he'd had an accomplice, a mysterious man in black who'd been seen skulking around the bank earlier that morning. But no proof had ever been found. Speculation ran rampant that Alexander had gone back to Saint Louis, where, rumor had it, his mistress lived. Of course, every lead in that direction had fizzled. The only thing chronicled were theories about his misdeeds . . . only lies, those dreaded lies Alex hated so much. But lies or not, Alexander Stewart's name had been slandered. And Elizabeth vowed to learn the truth.

Looking at her watch, Elizabeth realized she'd killed over an hour checking out just the references on Alex. She expected Jon in another hour, so she pushed on with her search.

Hastily she plowed through the few articles about Amanda. So little was written about the woman Alex loved. Scant mention had been made of her acquaintance with Alexander Stewart, and only a paragraph had been wedged into the society column about her marriage to Luke Winchester. The words claimed her to be the luckiest woman in Sapphire, catching the handsome and eligible bachelor. Months later she took a European tour with Luke and when they returned, Amanda stepped off the train carrying their new bundle of joy—Thomas, who'd been born in Paris in the summer of 1898.

In article after article, Elizabeth found very little that intrigued her until she read Amanda's obituary in 1904, followed several months later by the front page story of Luke Winchester's marriage to stage actress Claudette, the French beauty who'd stolen the grieving widower's heart and made him smile, something people had rarely seen since his first wife's death.

Elizabeth carefully read each line of the article, including the guest list, but she learned nothing new. There had to be something somewhere in all the references that could help her in her search to prove Alexander's innocence.

Finally, on the next-to-last page, she found a tongue-in-cheek article about the wedding with a caricature of Luke and Claudette in their finery with a scowling hag standing in the background. The inscription underneath read, "Did the Widow Carruthers expect to be the next woman to walk down the aisle with the dashing Luke Winchester?"

"Well, look who's here."

Elizabeth jumped at the sound of Matt Winchester's voice. "Hello, Matt," she said, tilting her head up from the ledgers. "What are you doing here?"

"I was in town getting a few sticks of dynamite to clear stumps off a piece of property. Figured I might as well stop here at the same time and check out some old land records. Of course, none of that's nearly as interesting as bumping into you."

He lifted the edge of the paper Elizabeth had been browsing through and frowned at what he saw. "Checking up on my family history, huh?"

"Not your family in particular. Just intriguing things about the town."

"If you're looking for anything special about Sapphire, maybe I can help."

"I don't really know what I'm looking for," she lied.

He sat down at the table beside her and put a hand on the back of her chair, his fingers lightly brushing against her arm, a feeling she disliked intensely. "Why don't you have lunch with me? I know a nice, quiet little place where we can have a drink or two."

"Thanks, but—"

"Francesca and I didn't get a chance to welcome you properly last night. Why don't you let me welcome you now?"

"I don't think so," she said bluntly. "I'm here with Jon. In fact, he should be back any minute now."

"In other words, you'd like me to leave?"

Elizabeth only smiled, surprised he'd figured that out all on his own.

"You will tell him hello for me, won't you?"

"Of course," she lied.

Relief flooded through Elizabeth when he started to get up, but he hesitated, leaning closer to her instead. "Tell you what, Liz," he said, putting a hand on top of hers. "If you want to know more about Sapphire and its leading citizens, I've got photo albums dating back to the wedding of my great-grandparents. Why don't you come by this evening? Have dinner with me. I'll pull out the pictures and you can browse as long as you want."

Dinner with Matt? The idea nauseated her, especially after their last get-together. But the newspaper accounts were getting her nowhere. There were no photos, and the articles were all innuendo. Somewhere there had to be information that would give her a clue about how to help Alex. "I'm afraid I don't have time for dinner. Maybe you could just drop the albums by the hotel one day."

He laughed. "Sorry, Liz. I don't trust valuables like that out of my sight. Have a drink with me, at least. Surely you can take half an hour, maybe an hour out of your busy schedule."

She didn't want to devote even five minutes to Matt, but if he had information that might help, she had to go. "I'm awfully busy, but I suppose I could stop by sometime."

"This evening, then," he stated. "Seven o'clock. Since you don't have time for dinner, you can have a few drinks."

Drinks? And pictures that might help Alex? She had to take a chance. "All right," she said. "I can't stay long, though."

"Yes, Liz. You mentioned that before."

He pushed up from the table and glanced quickly at his watch. "I've got a client to meet right now, but I'll look forward to tonight." He blew Elizabeth one of his infernal kisses and disappeared around the corner—fortunately, before Jon arrived.

"Interesting reading?" This time Jon's voice startled her.

"It's always fun reading old newspapers," she answered, wondering if Jon had seen her with Matt. "Unfortunately," she continued, "the information I was looking for is rather sparse."

Setting his Stetson on the table and pulling out a chair, Jon sat down across from Elizabeth. His brow furrowed and he looked like a man with a lot on his mind.

"How'd your meeting go?" she asked.

"Meeting was fine."

His eyes leveled with hers. "What did Matt want?"

Was that jealousy she heard in his voice, or anger? "Nothing much. He was here looking up old land records."

Jon laughed. "Is *that* what he told you?"

Elizabeth nodded. "Why? You don't believe him?"

"I believe very little he says."

"Do you believe me?"

"I told you I did," but his gaze had turned away and he concentrated on the table and her notes rather than looking her straight in the eye. It didn't seem like a very good sign of faith.

"You took a lot of notes," he said. "Find anything worthwhile?"

"A few things." She decided not to worry about Jon's suspicions and thought about her notes instead. The one piece of information that captured her interest was the cartoon and its caption, and she wondered about Phoebe and her relationship with Luke. She rested her elbows on the table and looked across at Jon. "Did your grandfather tell you much about Phoebe Carruthers, other than what you told me before?"

"A little. Nothing favorable, though."

"Do you think she was in love with Luke Winchester?"

The lopsided grin she was learning to love brightened Jon's face and eyes. "That was a hundred years ago, Ellie. What does it matter now?"

"It'll add a little more spice to the stories I'll tell my guests."

"You're incorrigible, you know."

She laughed. "I just might surprise you with a story or two someday. I'll even feed you cheesecake while you listen."

"Why don't you tell me a story or two over lunch?"

"Any particular story you have in mind?"

"You," he said, reaching across the table to caress her fingers. "I want to know every little detail."

Every little detail? She could think of hundreds of things to say, she only hoped her plans for tonight with Matt wouldn't leak into their conversation.

Elizabeth forgot all about Alex while they ate lunch. They talked about frivolous things like football and baseball, favorite movies, and music. They talked about travel, and politics, and what they would do in the spring. Afterward, they stopped at an antique store and Elizabeth bought two Tiffany lamps, and nearly two dozen hand-crocheted doilies that would look good as new once she bleached and blocked them. She found a set of bentwood and cane chairs in excellent condition, and although they were probably made in the early 1900s instead of the nineteenth century, she knew they'd be perfect on either side of the mahogany tea table she'd already begun to refinish.

They laughed and held hands; they even stole kisses; and Elizabeth leaned her head against Jon's shoulder as he drove the winding road home.

The sun had gone down by the time they arrived

in Sapphire. Together they unloaded Elizabeth's purchases from the truck, and she sensed Alexander's presence as she and Jon moved about the downstairs rooms. He didn't appear, though, and he made no noise, but she felt him staring over her shoulder as they stood hand-in-hand in the doorway.

"Had enough of me for the day?" Jon asked, cupping her face in his hands.

She shook her head and kissed him, waiting till his eyes were closed so she could try to shoo Alex away.

But it didn't work. Her friend might be invisible, but she knew he was hovering about, and she had the distinct feeling Alex was getting a little steamed over the kiss she and Jon were sharing.

"Why don't you come over later? We can grill some steaks, play some slow music." He kissed her ear, the curve of her neck, the hollow at the base of her throat, and she wanted to walk out the door with him right then and there.

But she'd already accepted Matt's invitation, and instead of a wonderful evening in Jon's arms, she was going to spend too many minutes fending off—what was it Alex called Matt?—snail slime.

She wove her fingers through Jon's hair and softly, tenderly, kissed his neck, moving her lips toward his ear. "I didn't sleep well last night, Jon. Would you mind terribly if we got together tomorrow?"

"Tomorrow's too far away. Tell you what. I'll bring dinner here. After we eat, you can stretch out on the couch, and I'll massage your shoulders."

Oh, Lord! It sounded so good—but she couldn't. Not tonight.

"It sounds lovely, but we've been together all day and—and I'm really tired."

"I could tell funny stories. Make you laugh." He tucked his chin into her neck and kissed her ear. "There are a whole lot of things I could do tonight to keep you awake."

"I'm sure there are, but . . ."

Jon backed away. "You're playing hell with my self-confidence, Ellie."

"I've had a wonderful day. I just want to be alone tonight. That's all."

He studied her eyes. Did he know her well enough to sense she wasn't being truthful?

"Does this have anything to do with your visit with Matt today?"

"Of course not!"

He shook his head. "I don't believe you. Tell me the truth."

"If I tell you the truth, you'll get mad. You'll say you can't trust me. You'll say I've been stringing you along and that I'm involved with Matt, and—"

Jon grabbed her shoulders. "I *told* you I trusted you. Dammit, why can't you trust me enough to give me an honest answer?"

His eyes burned into hers, and she was afraid of his anger. Afraid that they'd built up a relationship and this one evening with Matt would ruin everything. She was afraid she might lose him.

She couldn't tell him everything. But she could at least tell him the truth about her plans for the night.

"Matt has some photo albums I want to look at."

"Hell, Ellie, if that's all it is, I'll go over there myself and get them."

"He won't let them out of his house. I already asked."

"This is insane. I thought we were going to have a nice evening together, and now you tell me you'd rather spend time at Matt's, looking at some blasted photo albums."

"There's more to it than that."

"What?"

"I can't explain."

His fingers tightened on her arms. "Don't go, Ellie."

"I have to."

"Why? Is he holding something over you? Something to do with your brother? Your partnership?"

"It's nothing like that." She tried to twist away, but Jon pulled her even closer. "Let me go. *Please.*"

"Give me one good reason."

She pushed against him, and this time he released her. "I don't need to give you a reason, Jon. I appreciate your concern, but this is *my* life, not yours."

"I'm asking you one more time, Ellie. *Don't go.*"

"You're not asking at all. You're telling. And you know what, Jon? I'm really tired of you and Matt and every other man telling me what to do."

She opened the door and let in the cold, but the chill had already spread through her body—especially her heart. "Go home, Jon."

"I know you don't want to listen, but he's dangerous, Ellie."

"Please, Jon. Just leave."

He sighed deeply, grabbed hold of the brim of

his Stetson, and pulled it low over his eyes. "I'll be home if you need me."

"I don't need you," she lied.

He looked at her one more time with imploring eyes, but Elizabeth turned away. She had to go. She *had* to.

For Alex.

She heard Jon's bootsteps on the stairs and on the icy pavement.

And off in the distance, thunder rumbled through the darkened sky.

Chapter 12

"He's right, you know. You have no business going to that buzzard's home."

"Leave me alone. Please," Elizabeth snapped back when Alex appeared just inches from her nose.

"You're a woman, and whether you like it or not, you need a man to take care of you."

"In your day, maybe. Not today."

"Things like that don't ever change." Alex paced the length of the foyer, and Elizabeth leaned against the door, watching him.

"He may be a Winchester," she said softly, "but Matt's not a murderer."

Alex stopped suddenly and stared at her. "Do you know that for sure?"

"He's egotistical, self-centered, and a bore, but he's *not* a murderer. I doubt he's even a thief. So if you'll excuse me, I've got a date to look at photographs—in an effort to help you, I might add." She brushed past Alex and headed up the stairs.

"Mind if I follow?"

Elizabeth rolled her eyes. "What if I said no?"

Alex laughed. "I'd follow anyway."

"You know what they say about out of sight, out of mind?"

"Yes, I've heard that saying a time or two."

"Well, unfortunately, it doesn't apply with you." Elizabeth walked straight to her closet and searched for something to wear; it didn't matter what. She was more than positive Matt wouldn't approve of anything she put on. And she didn't care, either.

"How about this?" she asked, turning around and holding a strapless red sheath dress up to her body for Alexander's perusal.

"Hell and tarnation, Elizabeth! He'll have that thing off of you in half a second flat."

Elizabeth laughed. "I didn't think you'd approve." She returned it to its hanger, then motioned for Alex to turn around. "Don't worry. I'm not going to wear anything sexy or dangerous. But I would appreciate it if you'd turn around while I get dressed, and stay visible so I know you're not watching."

"You're going to deny me the one little thrill I have in this existence of mine?"

Elizabeth nodded and motioned again with her finger for Alex to turn around. She busied herself searching through her closet, and when she turned around again, Alex stood at the window, staring down at the town.

"It hasn't changed much in a hundred years, has it?" she asked.

Alex shrugged. "Hardly ever see a horse on the street anymore. Not many people go into church on Sunday morning, either. I remember when that cafe across the road used to be the saloon owned by Luke Winchester. And I remember when women used to dress up all pretty in frills."

"Did Phoebe Carruthers dress up in frills?"

Alex snorted a laugh. "Of course not. Black. Nothing but black. The respected widow wouldn't do anything wrong, unless she was behind closed doors."

Elizabeth slid a red knit dress over her head and smoothed the clinging fabric over her curves. "Did she do anything with Luke Winchester behind closed doors?"

"Before, during and after he married my Amanda."

"Tell me what you know about their relationship."

"Can I turn around yet?"

Elizabeth walked toward the window. "How's this?"

Alexander's eyes roamed from the neck-covering collar, over the long sleeves, and down the slim fitting dress that stopped just below her calves. He nodded his approval and swooped to his favorite place on the mantel, stretching out across its expanse.

"That big oaf who's been hanging around here would have liked you in that dress."

"I'd rather not talk about him."

"He loves you, you know."

"He's a Winchester."

"I suppose, but hell and tarnation, he sure doesn't act like one."

Elizabeth sat at the dresser and mirror Jon had found in the attic and carried down especially for her room and picked up the mother-of-pearl brush he said had once belonged to his grandmother. She slid it through the end of her braid and remembered him saying a pretty brush like that deserved beautiful, silky hair like hers.

Ripping a tissue out of a box, she dabbed it at her eyes.

"Maybe you shouldn't help me, Elizabeth. Maybe you should make up with him," Alex said.

Elizabeth shook her head. "I promised I'd help you, Alex. And Jon is just being a pigheaded fool. He has no reason to be jealous."

"He's more than jealous. He's worried about you getting close to that scavenger."

"Why are you sticking up for Jon?"

"Haven't rightly figured that out yet."

Elizabeth twisted around in her chair and looked at Alex, still stretched out on the mantel. As much as she wanted to think and talk about Jon, she needed to learn more from Alex. "I believe you were going to tell me about Phoebe and Luke."

"Well, let's see," Alex began. "Phoebe had her sights set on Luke long before that husband of hers kicked the bucket. I had a hunch they were spending evenings together when the mister was out of town. Got easier for them when Carruthers passed on. Of course, no one in town knew the real truth. It was all speculation, mind you, and far be it from me to spread gossip."

"Why was it such a secret after Phoebe's husband died?"

"One year of mourning. It was expected, and Phoebe wanted respect more than anything. Luke came here a lot during that year, when Phoebe wasn't entertaining other guests. He wined her and dined her, and Phoebe had a tendency to get a little tipsy. I was alive then, and living here. I saw it all, except what went on behind closed doors."

"Do you think he loved her?"

"Luke Winchester never loved anyone," Alex fumed. He swept down from the mantel, all casualness forgotten. He prowled the circumference of the room. "My theory's always been that he was using Phoebe."

"For what reason?"

"An alibi. He wasn't at the church when that robbery happened. Neither was Phoebe. I think he planned the holdup for a long, long time, and he was just waiting for the right moment."

"Did anyone ever ask them where they were when the robbery occurred?"

"That you'll have to find out. If you'll remember correctly, I was dead—buried six feet underground. First thing I remember after Luke tossed down those shovelfuls of dirt was trying to get my bearings, trying to get a clue about what had happened. Took quite a while to figure out I was dead. Took me even longer to figure out how to move, or go from room to room."

Elizabeth swiped a tear from her cheek. She hated to think of all the pain Alex had endured. "You must have been frightened."

"Yes, but that's old news. When I realized I couldn't get out of the house, I started searching rooms, looking for some other way out. First people I saw were Luke and Phoebe, going at it in this very room. Found out later it was his wedding night. He'd married my Amanda. Made her think he loved her, consummated the marriage, then left her alone. He and Phoebe were laughing about it. '*One day soon this entire town will be mine,*' Luke told her." Alex held his hands up in front of his face and studied them. "I tried to strangle him, but I couldn't."

"Why? You can move furniture. You can touch my hair and I can feel you." Elizabeth hesitated a moment. "Not that it would have been right, but why couldn't you strangle him?"

Alex shrugged. "I don't know."

Elizabeth grabbed her favorite red boots from the closet and sat down on the footstool next to the bed. Alex sat at her side and watched her pull the tight-fitting leather onto her legs.

"Did I ever tell you that you have mighty fine legs?" His cheerful laughter resounded through the room and lifted Elizabeth's spirits. "I used to love those days when the wind kicked up," he said. "I'd be walking down Main Street and a gust would catch the hem of a pretty lady's skirt and swirl it way up above her knees. Of course, I quit wanting to look at other women the minute I set my sights on Amanda." Alex looked into Elizabeth's eyes and shook his head. "She sure had the prettiest legs I ever saw."

He sighed and went back to the window. "She didn't deserve the treatment she got from Luke. She deserved a husband who loved her. I would have killed Luke if I could. I tried putting my hands around his neck, but he never realized I was there. Back then I couldn't even blow a speck of dust across the room."

He paced again, his restlessness unnerving. He slumped into a chair near the fireplace and looked into Elizabeth's eyes. "I was in this room the night Amanda died. Luke had brought a bottle of wine to celebrate. I think I hated him more for that than for murdering me. I have to get revenge, Elizabeth."

"And I want to help. But I don't want to hurt anyone—not Matt, and definitely not Jon."

"I wish there were another way, but there isn't. I swore I'd never leave as long as a Winchester walked the streets of Sapphire."

"Can't you just take back your vow? You died a hundred years ago, Alex. Could it really matter so much now?"

"It matters to me. I've always been an honest man, I've always kept my word, and I won't go back on it now. You have to help me, Elizabeth. You have to."

Oh, Lord! She didn't want to go to Matt's. She wanted to be in Jon's arms. She wanted to forget Alex's revenge, Jon's anger, Matt's photographs, and her promise to help. But she couldn't forget any of those things.

Alex needed her, and she prayed Jon would want her again when all this insanity was over. As for Matt, she had to be pleasant. If she wasn't, he might not show her those photos; he might not share his knowledge.

She pushed through the gate in the white rail fence and trudged up the crushed granite path bordered by winter-bare shrubs that led to Matt's antebellum-style home.

The massive mansion with round white columns looked as cold and unwelcoming as Matt. She thought about turning around and running to the other end of town to spend the evening with Jon. That's where she wanted to be, but instead, she put a boot on the first of a dozen marble stairs and kept on climbing until she reached the wide double doors.

Hesitantly she knocked, hoping Matt had forgotten, but one of the doors opened just as her knuckles hit the wood the second time, as if the man who ushered her in had been standing in wait. "Good evening, Ms. Fitzgerald. Please come in. Mr. Winchester's expecting you in the dining room."

"Thank you," she said.

Formal. Too, too formal.

The man took her coat and gloves and Elizabeth followed the stately gentleman with a heavy British accent through the entry and down a long, dimly lit hallway. When they neared the end, he left her standing at the entrance to a room where a blazing fire burned in a massive white marble hearth, and off to one side she saw Matt filling crystal stemware with dark red wine.

"You're late," he said, handing her a glass when she was close. "I expected you at seven."

"It's barely ten after. Surely a few minutes isn't a crime."

He sipped his wine. "This time you're forgiven," he said, smiling indulgently before he took another taste and studied her over the rim.

All the fear Jon had tried to instill in her came rushing in when she looked into Matt's obsidian eyes. Had Amanda seen obsidian eyes just like Matt's when she'd looked at Luke? Did she fear him whenever he came near? Oh, Amanda . . . why did you marry him? Elizabeth wondered.

Elizabeth brushed her fingers over tables and along the backs of chairs as she circled the room, wanting to stay out of range of Matt's hands and his eyes. "You've done quite well for yourself," she said, knowing she needed to make some type of conversation.

"Real estate's lucrative; so's the outfitting business. Of course, I owe most of this to my great-grandfather. He invested well."

"So well he needed two homes in town?" she asked.

"He lived in Dalton House with his first wife, and built Winchester Place for his second. This one's bigger, grander. It suited their needs and tastes."

He poured more wine into Elizabeth's glass before she could refuse. "Why all the questions?" he asked.

"A little gossip to spread to paying guests, that's all."

"Not much gossip where the Winchesters are concerned. My great-grandfather was a rich and powerful man in this town, as were my grandfather and my father."

"What about Thomas? He was Luke's son, too?"

Matt took another drink of his wine. "He invested wisely. I believe that's about the only thing Thomas and my great-grandfather saw eye-to-eye on. But that isn't something people will want to know, and it's not something I'm all that interested in discussing."

"You knew why I came tonight. I wanted to talk about history, to look at your photo albums."

"I knew," he said, moving closer, much too close. "Of course, some plans are easily changed." Slowly, he tilted his head and kissed her.

Elizabeth backed away until she hit a wall and couldn't move any further. He'd cornered her like a frightened animal. And he was smiling. "You're very beautiful, Liz."

"So I've been told." She avoided another kiss by taking a sip of wine.

"Perhaps I could look at those albums now?" she asked.

"Actually, I decided we needed a little dinner to go along with the drinks. I had my cook prepare something light. It's in the study." He set down the bottle of wine and took her arm, leading her easily across the room and down another darkened hall. She wanted to pull away, she wanted to run, but she had to see those pictures.

They passed through double doors and into a massive room paneled in knotty pine, darkened with age to a rich whiskey color. It was like stepping into a high-ceilinged hunting lodge. The heads of bear, buffalo, bighorn sheep, deer, antelope, and elk lined the walls, dozens of brown eyes staring emotionlessly across the room. Bearskin rugs had been tossed here and there on the parquet floor, and many pieces of furniture appeared to have been made out of twisted antlers. Elizabeth realized her home might have a ghost creeping around, but she felt the souls of many more beings haunted this room.

"Most of these trophies belonged to my great-grandfather. He rather liked having them hang around so he could enjoy his conquests. What do you think?" Matt asked.

"It's not exactly my taste in decorating, but it's your home, Matt, not mine."

"I take it you share my cousin's feelings about hunting."

"Senseless killing has never set well with me. But I'm not here to judge you."

"That's right. You're not. We've never had much opportunity to talk. I hope we'll become better acquainted tonight."

Elizabeth disagreed. "We had a chance not too long ago when you had dinner at my place. As I recall, you ran out."

Matt snorted a laugh. "I prefer not to dredge up the past." He pulled out a chair for Elizabeth at a small, intimate table in front of the fireplace, then sat across from her. "The present is much more interesting." He poured more wine and held his glass in toast. "To tonight. To us."

Elizabeth smiled indulgently and took another sip of her wine. He'd offered a similar toast the last time they were together, and she liked it even less tonight. "Tell me more about Luke," she said, moving her fork about in the food on her plate.

Eyes narrowing, Matt tasted the shrimp salad and lightly wiped his mouth with a black linen napkin. "Your interest staggers me, Liz."

"It's all part of an advertising scheme. Surely you must understand the need to have something provocative to draw people in."

"I understand advertising perfectly. Unfortunately, I can't honestly think of anything significant that happened in that hotel."

"It's amazing what you can do with even the smallest hint of history," she said, digging far more than she probably should. "It's like photographing a black sheath dress. There's nothing attractive about the dress all by itself, but put it on the perfect model, add just the right accessories, find the perfect background, and you'll have women dying to buy the thing. It's all very simple."

Matt leaned back and sipped at his wine, the food on his plate all but ignored. "Surely Jon is able to give you a history lesson on Sapphire. He lived most of his life with a man who thought and talked about nothing but the past."

"We've talked briefly about it, but there's more than one side to a story. Please, tell me about Luke."

"He didn't need window dressing to spruce up his character," Matt said as he drank his wine. "He loved life and made a habit of taking what he wanted."

"Legally?" Elizabeth interrupted.

Matt grinned. "Of course." But Elizabeth could easily see the lie in his eyes.

"Luke came to Sapphire quite a few years after Jedediah Dalton built the town. He'd been a gambler most of his life and in those days, settling down in a town inhabited mostly by men meant there were plenty of opportunities for card games and dice. He found himself a table at the saloon and within a few weeks the owner was dead and Luke bought the place."

"Is there any possibility he had a hand in the owner's death?"

"He died in bed with one of the ladies of ill repute who worked for him." Eyes narrowed, Matt leaned forward and poured more wine into Elizabeth's glass. "Why all the questions, Liz? Do you think tainting my great-grandfather's memory will bring even more guests to your hotel?"

Elizabeth sipped at the wine. "Colorful characters are much more interesting. Besides, Luke is past history. Knowing what he did or didn't do a hundred years ago won't affect anything that's going on in your life or mine today."

Matt studied her as he tilted his glass and drank the wine. "Luke Winchester was an industrious man who wanted to be rich, and fate played him a few lucky hands. He owned the saloon and was in the right place at the right time when Jed Dalton's daughter got jilted at the altar. Marrying her put everything that had belonged to the Daltons into Luke's hands. Fortunately, he became a very, very rich man."

"Did he love Amanda?"

That grin returned to Matt's face. "What do you think, Elizabeth?"

"I have nothing to base a judgment on."

"Maybe something you read today triggered these questions. Those old papers were full of gossip. Come on. Tell me? What did you read that intrigued you so much?"

"It was a cartoon, actually, of Luke's second wedding. He was smiling at the actress he was marrying, and Phoebe Carruthers was standing in the background, scowling. I thought there might have been something going on between Luke and Phoebe."

"Phoebe Carruthers was a homely, loved-starved

old widow who wouldn't have known what to do with a man if she'd had one."

Elizabeth laughed. "You sound so sure about that. How can you possibly know?"

"Jon's grandfather wasn't the only one who told stories. Mine did, too. Luke Winchester never gave Phoebe Carruthers the time of day. Apparently she wrote some scathing diaries detailing every sordid day and night she and Luke supposedly spent together. But no one ever saw those diaries, and they've never been found. Personally, I think the lady was mad, and so lonely she dreamed up romantic fairy tales."

Diaries. Elizabeth tucked that thought away, along with the bar owner's death. She'd have to ask Jon if he knew anything about them; she'd have to ask Alex. Surely if Phoebe had left behind a record of her life, somebody would know its whereabouts. If she could find the diary, perhaps she'd learn more about what had happened in the days before the robbery and Alexander's murder.

"What about the pictures? Are there any of Phoebe?"

Shaking his head, Matt pushed away from the table. "They're family photos. I don't think anyone ever considered including Phoebe, but we can take a look."

He pulled out Elizabeth's chair and handed her a refilled glass of wine. Heaven forbid, she was going to end up drunk if he continually plied her with alcohol. Of course, she could always stop, but having the wineglass in hand or at her mouth kept his lips from hers. The strategy had repercussions, but it worked.

Sitting on the bearskin rug in front of the fire

seemed terribly uncomfortable and just one step closer to ending up in Matt's arms. But that's where he'd led her, and he sank down beside her with several large photo albums in hand.

"This one," he said, "dates back to the late eighteen hundreds." He opened the cover and Elizabeth was instantly transported back in time. "That's Luke and Amanda's wedding day," Matt said, putting his finger under the photo of a man who could have been Matt's double: tall, dark, handsome. He stood with one hand tucked between the buttons of his coat, like a Western Napoleon, his other hand rested on the shoulder of a petite young woman sitting in a stiff-backed wooden chair. Her face was somber, her eyes staring straight into the camera with no expression at all, her lips pressed together, her hands folded in the lap of a dark, high-necked dress. She didn't look at all like a bride, and she didn't look happy.

She looked nothing like the photo of the beautiful, contented woman Alexander carried in his watch.

Luke flipped through page after page, photos mostly of the dashing Luke—in the bar, on the stairs of Dalton House, sitting in a spiffy black buggy. Elizabeth studied his face, looking for something she liked, but all she could see was the face of the man who had stood above Alex, shoveling dirt over his mouth and eyes and nose.

"These were taken in Europe," Matt stated, turning page after page to reveal photos of Luke standing along the banks of the Seine, in front of the Eiffel Tower and the Louvre. Occasionally Elizabeth saw a picture of Amanda. Standing alone, she glimpsed a smile; with Luke, the expressionless face returned. Poor Amanda . . . she must have been so unhappy.

"One of the articles I read said Amanda and Luke had a child while they were in Europe."

"Yes, that's true. They didn't waste much time after their wedding day. They spent a little over nine months wandering around England and France and Italy. Luke bought a lot of furniture while they were overseas and had it shipped home. From what I've been told, Amanda was ill most of the trip and spent the biggest part of her time resting. Thomas, their son—that's Jon's grandfather—was born in Paris. He was two months old when they sailed home."

Elizabeth wondered what Luke did those few months while Amanda rested in Paris. Had he met the actress who would eventually become his wife? And what of Amanda? Had she been lonely and ill? Had Luke abandoned her while he'd roamed the streets and cafes, just as he'd abandoned her on their wedding night?

Amanda had been so pretty. Alex hadn't exaggerated. Elizabeth wished she could slip one or two of the photos out of the album and take them to Alex, but it seemed impossible the way Matt huddled over her. But . . .

Downing the remainder of her wine, Elizabeth looked at her glass. "This wine is delicious, Matt. Would you mind getting me some more?"

It worked. Matt climbed up from the bearskin rug and while he went back to the table, Elizabeth slid two of the prettiest pictures out of the album and flipped the pages. Unfortunately, she had nowhere to hide the photos. Her dress already revealed too much, there were no pockets, and Matt was walking back.

Quickly she unfolded her long body from the floor, cupping the pictures close to her side with her left hand.

"Surely you're not leaving."

Elizabeth took the glass of wine Matt held out to her. "Of course not. It's just that I haven't found sitting on the floor all that comfortable since I was about eighteen." She gracefully sat in one of the atrocious elkhorn chairs placed at the edge of the rug.

"Are you afraid of me, Elizabeth?" Matt asked.

Elizabeth shook her head. "What makes you ask that?"

"You've been jittery ever since you arrived."

"Maybe I've just had too little to eat today and too much wine to drink. Really, I'm not the least bit frightened of you. Please, show me the rest of the photos."

While Matt pulled a matching chair close to Elizabeth's and retrieved the albums from the floor, Elizabeth gently slipped the photos down her leg and under the protective cover of her boot.

The pictures Matt showed her seemed to skip several years, then took on a whole new character when a woman decked out in feathers and frills showed up in every one. It could be no one else but Claudette, Luke's French actress wife.

A few pages later they stood before the house Elizabeth was now in, a baby pram in front of them, with Luke holding a bundle in his arms. Year after year she watched the child grow in those pictures, a child with coal black hair, just like his father's.

Matt turned the last page of the second photo album and closed the cover. "Seen enough for one evening?" he asked.

Elizabeth felt the alcohol swishing around in her head, and her senses seemed to dim, but one thing that was clear was her recollection of what she *hadn't* seen in any of the pictures they'd looked at: Amanda and Luke's first son, Thomas. And she remembered the story Jon had told, of Luke shunning his first child. The pictures made it obvious.

"Do you know why Luke neglected Thomas?" Elizabeth asked.

Matt shrugged. "I've never given it any thought, and I never asked. But Thomas was a recluse; my grandfather, on the other hand, was dapper and debonair, and he had a flair for the ladies, just like his dad. You can understand how a man would be partial to a son who was more like himself."

"No, I can't."

"But it happens, Liz. All the time." He rose from his chair and stood behind her, his fingers working their way under her hair to her neck. She felt his hands tightening over her shoulders, his thumbs massaging the muscles on either side of her spine. She wanted to fight the natural instinct to lower her head and let his fingers work miracles on the tenseness in her body, but she couldn't. The wine had confused her thoughts.

"Does that feel good?" he asked. His voice was low and whispery near her ear.

She nodded, finding herself unable to utter any words.

"Just relax, Liz."

She felt hypnotized—by his voice, by the wine, by the heat in the room.

His fingers swirled around her neck, over her chest. Lower. Lower.

He touched her breast. She felt a slight tingle, but nothing magic, nothing wonderful.

Suddenly the realization of what was happening hit her smack in the face. She jerked out of his grasp, her eyes flaring as she sprang from the chair. She wobbled. Her head spun. But she still had control of her mind. "I didn't come here for that."

Matt's eyebrows raised. "No? You're not going to tell me you came just to drink my wine and look at my pictures, are you?"

Elizabeth nodded. "I came *just* for the photos, and I've seen all I needed to."

Matt stepped closer and put a hand on her arm, but Elizabeth twisted away. "I need to go."

Matt laughed, shaking his head. "Go where? Back to that run-down old hotel? Back to being lonely?"

"I'm not lonely."

"But you are," he said, moving closer, so close she could feel his warm breath against her cheek. "I can end your loneliness."

Elizabeth shook her head. "I don't think so. Besides, it's getting late." She dodged around him, but he grabbed her arm and whipped her into his embrace.

"It's not that late, Liz. I'd like you to stay." His fingers tightly gripped her arms, and he pulled her hard against his chest, his head slanting down, his mouth moving toward her.

Elizabeth turned her head, felt his warm, wet lips on her cheek, and somehow found the power to pull away. "Touch me again and I'll scream."

"These walls are very thick."

Without giving it a thought, she smacked her wineglass against the hearth and held the broken glass toward his face. "Is your skin thick, too?"

Chapter 13

"Not thick enough!"

Jon stood just inside the doors to the study. The walls reverberated from the sound of his voice, and the floors shivered as he stormed across the room and grabbed Matt by the collar.

"What the hell do you think you're doing?"

Matt wrenched Jon's fingers from his shirt and backed away. "Having drinks with the little lady."

"That's not what it looked like to me."

"If it looked like anything else, you were letting your jealous imagination run wild," Matt said, downing the rest of his wine. He turned away and filled the glass again.

Jon took several deep breaths as he looked toward Elizabeth. Tears flowed from her eyes. The hand holding the broken glass shook at her side. In one long step he was next to her, the glass crashed to the floor, and he pulled her into his arms.

He held her for what seemed an eternity, her cheek against his chest. He felt her heart beating fast and hard in time with his. When it finally slowed, he drew away slightly and cupped her cheeks, looking gently into her eyes. "Did he hurt you?"

She shook her head. "Take me out of here. Please."

Gathering her close to his side, he gave Matt one last look. "Touch her again, do anything to her again, and I'll put my fist right through that pretty face of yours."

Matt swallowed more wine and laughed. "I'm not afraid of you."

"You should be," Jon said calmly, drawing Elizabeth across the room. When they reached the door, he looked back at Matt again. "I broke your nose when I was ten. I'm three times as big and three times as powerful now."

Matt raised his glass. "We'll see who's the most powerful."

"Is that a challenge? Would you like to go outside right now?"

"All in good time, cousin. All in good time."

Jon felt Elizabeth tugging on his coat. "Please, Jon. Let's just go."

He was angry—at himself for letting Elizabeth go to Matt's in the first place and for not punching Matt out when he'd first walked into the room. He wanted to grab Matt and hang him on the wall like all the other trophies, but he heard the plea in Elizabeth's voice and saw it in her eyes.

He didn't want to run from a battle that needed to be fought, but he wanted to hold Elizabeth more. He wanted to comfort her, to kiss away her tears, and hold her and make her forget all that had happened tonight—not only Matt's attack, but his own cruel and senseless words.

Wrapping a hand gently around her waist, he led her down the long hallway, helped her into her coat, and took her outside, into the softly falling snow.

When they reached the hotel she started to turn, but he pulled her even closer to his side and looked down into her tired, worried eyes. "Come home with me, Ellie." He touched her cheeks and smoothed away the stains of tears. "I'm sorry about tonight. I was too damn jealous. I shouldn't have gotten so angry, and I never should have let you out of my sight."

She put a finger to his lips. "Just kiss me, Jon. Make me forget about everything that happened. Please."

Right there in the middle of town, in the middle of the road, he lifted her like a babe in his arms and lowered his lips to hers. She tasted like wine and tears, and she felt soft and oh so right in his arms.

He kissed her in front of the hotel and in front of the church. He kissed her as he pushed through the gates of Dalton House and all the way up the meandering steps that led to the porch.

He came up for air just long enough to open and close the door, and he carried her up the winding staircase to the third floor, to his room, to his bed.

"If you want me to stop," he said, his chest rapidly expanding and falling as he uttered the words, "say so now."

"Don't stop, Jon. Please, don't ever stop."

He stood her on the floor just long enough to push her coat from her arms, then shrugged out of his. He laid her gently on a bed of pillows and goosedown, and her amber eyes burned intensely into his as he stripped his shirt out of his jeans and came close to ripping off the buttons as he tossed it aside.

Elizabeth held her hands out to him, beckoning him to come to her. Instead, he pulled her up to kneel before him on the bed.

"God, you're beautiful," he said, and slowly, ever so slowly, his fingers brushed over her shoulders and found the catch of her zipper. And even more slowly he slid it open.

Elizabeth could feel the cold of the room against the bare skin of her back, then the overpowering warmth of his fingers as they skimmed over her flesh. He gathered the red knit fabric in his hands and pulled it away from her neck, from her shoulders, then slid his hands over the fabric all the way to her wrists, never once removing his gaze from hers. He tugged on the cuffs and pulled the knitted sleeves away, and the top of the dress lay limp at her sides.

His smile sent heat rushing through her breasts. They tingled, hot and flaming, when his sapphire eyes lowered to the satin and lace of her bra.

He wanted her, needed her, with a passion he'd never known. Placing one knee on the bed, he lowered her into the pillows, kissing her sweetness again.

He felt the creamy softness of her skin, afraid for just one moment that the roughness of his fingers and palms would scratch her delicate flesh. But she only moaned when he touched her, sighing deeply, weaving her fingers tightly into his hair and pulling him closer, closer.

He had to taste more of her, all of her. He straddled her legs and knelt before her. Slowly he lowered his head and trailed kisses from her mouth, along the curve of her throat, and over the porcelain skin that flared out soft and full where red satin and lace hid her beauty. He tasted her through the fabric, nipped at her lightly with his teeth, and captured her mouth again when he heard her moan with want.

He rolled over, taking Elizabeth with him. He pulled at the hem of her dress, dragging it to her thighs as she sat up and straddled his hips.

And, oh Lord, he wanted her more.

He lifted the dress, higher, higher, until he'd pulled it over her head and dropped it to the floor.

He lay there and watched her, capturing a memory of perfection.

He reached up again, released the hook between her breasts, and let his fingers slide easily over her curves to the straps, drawing them down until the bra fell away. He cupped her breasts in his hands and just as he'd always expected, they fit perfectly.

Again he rolled over, and as he moved from the bed, he slipped his fingers under the last remaining piece of satin and red lace, caressing her legs as he pulled her panties away. He stood, looking down at the vision he'd pictured over and over, the Rubenesque beauty he'd sketched from memory, from imagination. She wasn't on the chaise in his turret, but she was in an even better place—on his bed, and she lay on her side watching him, that look of wonder and innocence in her eyes, and wanton red hooker boots clinging to her calves and encasing her feet.

God, how he wanted her.

"I've dreamed of you, Ellie."

"Stop dreaming. Please, stop dreaming."

Somehow, in just a matter of seconds, he pulled away his boots, his socks, and the Levi's and shorts that were way too confining, and he crawled back onto the bed and wrapped her in his arms.

Her lips were hot when he kissed her, and she was wet and oh so ready when he touched her. He couldn't wait another moment, his need and want were stronger than his will to wait.

And he entered her and felt he'd just gone to heaven.

Elizabeth raised her hips, her fingers digging into the muscles of his back. Oh, how she wanted him and needed him. He felt so right inside her, so perfect.

They moved together slowly, rhythmically, in a dance as old as time, but new and magical to them.

Each touch, each stroke, each whispered word sent her higher and higher.

Each cry, each sigh, each beat of her heart sent him beyond the realm of thought.

The enchantment captured them.

His fingers wound tightly in her hair.

Her boots dug deep into his thighs.

He was hers.

She was his.

And a million fireworks exploded and scattered, raining down slowly, softly, a flicker here, a flicker there, till only smoke and heat remained.

Her breathing calmed.

His heartbeat slowed.

And they lay together, waiting to strike the match that would send them soaring again.

"Are you cold?" he asked, tucking the comforter more tightly around her neck, taking the opportunity to run his hand over her blanket-covered breasts.

"A little, but that's no reflection on the efforts you've made to warm me. It's just plain old cold in this room."

"I'll have that taken care of in a few moments."

Jon bounded from bed and Elizabeth watched the stark naked titan stroll across the room. With each move he made, a muscle flexed. Two hundred and sixty pounds of muscle, if she remembered correctly. They'd discussed his size sometime during the night when intimacy had turned to reflection, and that had turned to laughter.

He'd pulled off her hooker boots. Hooker boots! Yes, that's what he'd called them. She'd smacked him for laughing at her taste in clothing, and he, in turn, smoothed his hands over her body and told her he hoped her style would never change.

She watched him now as he fed kindling into the flame, piece after piece, until it caught hold and the room filled with warmth and light. His body glistened, every inch of him, and he slipped back under the covers and pulled her close.

Elizabeth rested her head against his chest and yawned.

"Long night?" he asked.

"Not long enough." She yawned again. "But there's always the morning."

He softly kissed her hair, and Elizabeth closed her eyes and slept.

A thread of morning light inched between the curtains and raced across the bed. Elizabeth stretched and reached out to hold Jon again. But the bed was empty and the place where he'd slept was cold.

She sat up, pulling the blankets with her, but she didn't need their warmth. The fire blazed and crackled on the hearth, and Jon sat silently in a chair, legs crossed, and watched her.

"Good morning," he said.

"I thought you'd gone."

He shook his head slowly. "You'd have to do a lot more than snore to run me off."

"I don't snore."

He grinned and nodded. "Afraid so, Ellie. Hooker boots and snoring . . . best combination I've ever found in a woman."

He sat a little straighter in the chair and uncrossed his legs. He was still naked. Still splendid.

"Care to join me?" he asked.

Elizabeth pulled the blanket with her as she climbed out of bed, and then she saw Jon shake his head.

"You don't need the blanket, Ellie. It's warm enough here without it."

She felt an instant quiver shoot from her heart, through her stomach, and between her legs. Her breasts burned again. How could he do that to her, she wondered, with just a look, with only his words?

Her fingers slipped away from the comforter and

it dropped to the floor, puddling thick and deep around her legs. She stepped over it and walked slowly across the enormous room, the heat of Jon's gaze rushing through every speck of her body, every place he looked.

She stood before him in the light of the fire. He could see the rise and fall of her breasts, could almost hear the rapid beat of her heart. Her porcelain skin glistened, and he could feel her raging heat when his fingers were still inches away.

He touched her and the warmth spread through his chest, his stomach, his groin. He was hotter now, the flames leaping on the hearth cold compared to the blaze that stepped between his widespread legs.

She placed a soft hand on his heart, branding him for all eternity, and her fingers slid downward, over his stomach, as she knelt before him. She looked up momentarily and smiled, then she lowered her head and caressed him with her mouth. Oh, God! All he'd wanted her to do was sit with him by the fire, but her idea was so, so much better.

He rested his head against the back of the chair and tried to control his breathing as she swirled him with her tongue, and kissed him, and tasted him.

And when he could stand the torture no longer, he slid his hands around her and laid her down on the carpet before the fire.

Once more, and once again, he made love to her.

Elizabeth curled up in the big chair by the fire, wrapped warmly in the blanket Jon had draped around her before he'd gone downstairs for coffee and something to curb the growl in her stomach.

He'd slipped into his Levi's before he'd left her, and she rather missed watching the beauty of his hard naked body as he walked from the room. But she'd see it again; of that she was certain.

Soon. Very soon.

She watched the flames playing leapfrog across the logs and for the first time noticed the large pad of paper lying just to the side of the fireplace tools, a charcoal pencil resting on top. Leaning over, she picked up the pad and opened the cover.

Her own face looked back at her. The drawing was rough, the details not very well defined, but she could tell it was definitely her. She turned another page and saw herself again: a little bit more this time—head and chest, with her braid curling across the bottom of the sheet.

Page after page she flipped through, and page after page she saw her face and her form, clothed and unclothed. She couldn't help but smile, in spite of the mistakes he'd made. Her hips couldn't possibly be that small or her breasts that large. Her smile wasn't quite that wide, and her eyes didn't sparkle quite that brightly.

But at least he had the red hooker boots right.

She turned one more page and saw herself again, lying in the middle of Jon's bed with only a sheet draped across her hip. She slept peacefully, her eyes closed in slumber. And at the bottom he'd written, *Ellie, my love.*

A tear rolled down Elizabeth's cheek.

"Now you know what I do in my spare time."

She looked up at the man who stood in the doorway with a tray in his hands and coffee steaming out of two big mugs. "You're good, Jon. Really good. You could make money at this," she said, and glancing around the room, added, "*if* you needed more money."

"You really think I might have some talent?"

"I know so. I know tons of artists in Los Angeles and Hollywood who can't hold a candle to you."

Jon took the sketch pad from her hands and substituted it with a cup of coffee. "Want to see more?"

Elizabeth sipped at her coffee and nodded.

"Come on," he said, taking hold of her fingers and drawing her up from the chair.

She followed behind him, still wrapped only in a blanket. He led her out of the bedroom and down the hallway to the far end of the house. He opened an arched door and mounted a narrow spiral staircase.

"Where are we going?"

"My favorite room in the house."

"I thought we just left your favorite room."

"I have favorite rooms for different things. I used to use my bedroom only for sleeping. That wasn't very high on my list of things to do until you crawled into my bed."

Elizabeth's heart skipped a beat, and the next one reverberated in her ears. Lord, the man walking up the stairs in front of her made her body do a lot of strange and wonderful things.

The stairway was dark, and suddenly Elizabeth saw light ahead. They stepped into a round, stone-walled room with many long, narrow windows. And she remembered. "I've watched the lights in this room at night. All night."

"That's when I do my best work." He set the tray on his workbench and picked up the second mug of coffee. "Take a look around."

While Elizabeth roamed the room, Jon sat on a stool in front of the window where he'd sat many nights and watched the lights in the hotel. But this morning he watched Elizabeth up close, realizing all the mistakes he'd made when he'd sketched the pictures and molded the clay. Her cheekbones were a little higher, a little more well defined. Her shoulders more broad, her breasts fuller. He turned his hands over to look at his palms, and he smiled. Yes, they were made for each other.

"Is this the chaise in those pictures?" Elizabeth asked, and Jon could hear the lilt of laughter in her deep, sexy voice.

"The one and only. Care to give it a try?"

"Sounds tempting, but . . ." She walked across the room, her grace making her look as if she were floating. She caressed her fingers over the clay figures of a bear and two cubs, frolicking together in a grass- and wildflower-strewn meadow. Head still bent, she looked up at him through long black lashes, the smile on her face hidden behind a touch of sadness. "Are these the ones?"

Jon nodded. "There's a whole sketch pad full of them. An entire summer of watching and studying and learning their habits."

Elizabeth picked up the pad and thumbed through a few pages. "Do you do this for all your work?"

"Not always. Only when something catches my interest."

"Like me?"

"Like you."

She smiled, and Jon realized his sketches hadn't caught the true depth of her emotion. He'd have to begin again and fill another entire pad.

She picked up one of the muffins Jon had placed on the tray and nibbled at it as she roamed further around the room. The blanket slipped slightly from her shoulder as she reached for a bronze on one of the shelves. Again he saw his mistake: he'd drawn a well-defined shoulder, square, pronounced, the bones too prominent. Her shoulders were rounder and smoother, like the hips he'd held when they'd made love.

"You do bronzes, too?"

Jon nodded again. "The clay's only for making the molds. The bronze is the finished product."

"You sell them?"

"Does it seem that hard to believe?"

"No, but you never mentioned it. Why?"

"It's a secret."

"Is there something special I have to do to make you divulge the information?" she asked, and slowly, ever so slowly, she glided across the floor and stood right between his legs. The blanket draped her like a stole, just off her shoulders and gathered together with one hand below the soft, full creaminess of her breasts. He had a strong desire to pull the blanket away, but she offered her lips in exchange, softly, tenderly.

"There's something special, all right. In fact, I think you've already figured it out. But I need you to do it again—just to be sure."

She stepped back slightly, her fingers tracing a

straight line over his skin, from his lips to the buckle of his belt. "Am I on the right track?"

He smiled.

She let the blanket slide away.

Chapter 14

What a grand and glorious day, Elizabeth thought, as she set foot on the street in front of Dalton House. The sun shone high in the bright blue sky, and the temperature must have been at least a degree over freezing because water dripped from the icicles hanging off the eaves of every building lining the road. To top all that, she'd fallen in love, and what could be better than that?

Yes, it was definitely a grand and glorious day, but Elizabeth knew she had hell to pay for having had a grand and glorious night.

"Where in tarnation have you been?" Alex bellowed, the moment she stepped through the hotel door. Elizabeth grinned and Alex turned away, pacing the hardwood floor, his hands clasped tightly behind his back. "No, don't answer that. I saw you and that big oaf out in the street last night. I imagine everyone in town knows what the two of you were up to."

"They can guess. *You* can guess," Elizabeth said with a devilish smile, "but it's all personal and private, and I'm not telling a soul."

He stomped back and forth, back and forth, making a point of letting every one of his footsteps be heard.

Elizabeth sat down on the stairs and waited for his anger to subside. She'd already learned it could be a slow process, but nothing, she promised herself, was going to spoil the day.

Finally, Alex stopped smack in front of Elizabeth and crossed his arms over his chest. "I warned you about those Winchesters. They take sweet young things like you and spoil them."

"The same way you spoiled Amanda?"

Alexander's jaw tightened. "It's not the same thing. We were engaged."

"Do you regret what you did?" she asked, already knowing the answer but wanting to prove a point.

"I don't regret anything I did. I loved her."

"It wasn't all that many hours ago that you told me I should go to Jon. In fact, you said he loved me."

"That was a lack of judgment on my part. He's a Winchester."

"There's only one Winchester in this town who deserves your revenge."

Alex stopped short in his pacing and stood over Elizabeth, glaring down with fire in his eyes. "Did that buzzard hurt you?"

Elizabeth shook her head. "Jon came to the rescue."

"See? It's just as I said. You need a man around to take care of you."

"Even if that man's a Winchester?"

Alex threw his hands in the air. "I don't want to hear any more talk about that big oaf. I'd rather know if you learned anything new last night—anything that might help me get out of here."

"Possibly."

"Well, spill it, woman!"

Elizabeth laughed. It didn't seem right to tease, but Alex had tortured her with his antics from the moment she'd moved into the hotel, and it seemed only fair to give him a taste of what it felt like to be toyed with. "You've waited a hundred years; I think you can give me time to take a bath."

"Thunder and tarnation!"

Alex disappeared and less than a second later the chandelier began to sway. *Ten minutes,* an invisible Alexander barked. *That's all you've got. If you're not out of the tub, I'm coming in to talk.*

"Twenty?"

Fifteen! Not a minute more.

Elizabeth sat cross-legged in the middle of her bed, her hair wrapped in a towel, her body bundled in a white terrycloth robe she'd bought at the Beverly Hills Hotel, the frivolous place she'd checked into the moment she'd checked out of the hospital. She'd squandered nearly a year's worth of savings pampering herself after the earthquake. It was decadent, reckless, and fun. She'd met dozens of other misplaced and unfortunate people, and it was one of the best weeks she'd spent in her life. But it wasn't nearly so decadent, reckless, and fun as last night.

"You're grinning like the Cheshire cat," Alex muttered from the top of the mantel, where he lounged. "Makes me think that personal and private stuff that went on last night is something I should pop that big galoot in the jaw for."

"You do, and I cease all efforts to get you out of this place."

Alex frowned. "You wouldn't back out on a promise."

No, she wouldn't, but Alex didn't have to know that. "Want to give it a try and find out?"

Elizabeth could hear the resignation in Alexander's sigh. "I'd rather know what you found out last night."

"What I found out isn't nearly as important as what I found." Elizabeth reached into her pocket and pulled out the two pictures of Amanda she'd snatched from Matt's valuable collection. "These are for you," she said, smiling as she held out her open palm.

Alex floated down from his place above the hearth and sat on the footboard. With hesitant fingers, he touched the photos, then took them from Elizabeth's hand one by one. Elizabeth's heart lurched when she saw the tear slide down Alexander's cheek. What was he feeling? Happiness? Sorrow? Pain?

"She's beautiful, Alex. I can see why you loved her."

"She was everything to me. She was my life, and . . ." He slowly left the bed, roaming aimlessly across the room as he looked at the pictures of his beloved. "I wanted to grow old with her, Ellie. I wanted to have babies with her. I wanted to hold her and love her all night long, every night." He sighed deeply. "Forever."

Alex disappeared through the wall in a flash of fiery light, and the pictures of Amanda floated gently to the floor like falling autumn leaves.

Elizabeth walked to where the photos had fallen, picked them up, and took another long look. In one, sadness filled Amanda's eyes, and loneliness. In the other, peace and contentment shone in her smile as she looked down at her hands—hands that wove gently together over her belly. Elizabeth's throat tightened. Why hadn't she realized when she'd pulled the photos from the album that Amanda was pregnant in these pictures—pregnant with Luke Winchester's child?

Tucking the photos back into her pocket, she went into the hallway and up the stairs to Alexander's attic room. He stood at the window and watched the house at the end of the street. Amanda's house. The home where he should have raised his children and loved his wife.

Forever.

Elizabeth balanced the pictures on top of a dusty dresser. Later she'd clean this room from top to bottom, spread pretty white doilies around, and make it more of a home instead of a tomb. It was the least she could do for Alex, since there might never be a way to help him leave.

She walked to the window and touched his arm, realizing once again the foolishness of her action. She couldn't touch him; he couldn't feel her warmth; but did any of that really matter?

"I wish there were some way I could comfort you, Alex. I wish I could hug you and let you know how sorry I am for everything that's happened to you."

He looked at her then, tears—that seemed impossible—fresh on his cheeks. "Maybe I could just . . . no, never mind."

"Just what, Alex?"

"Could you hug me for just a little while?"

"I don't know how."

"Just pretend. Please?"

Elizabeth smiled, and Alex wrapped his arms around her, resting his head on her shoulder. She felt his sobs, she heard his cries. Slowly she reached out, putting her arms about him and pretended he was real, that he had substance and form, two things he wanted, two things he could never have.

"Thank you," he said, when his tears had subsided. He walked away, across the room, and sat on the edge of an old and dusty steamer trunk.

Elizabeth followed him and sat at his side. "I wish you could feel what's in my heart when you cry."

"I haven't felt anything but anger in a very long time. But just now, when I held you, I let my imagination wander and remembered what it was like to be held and to hold someone back. I remembered the warmth and the heartbeats and the whisper of a sigh against my cheek. And I remembered the feel of tears falling from Amanda's eyes to mine."

Alex wove his fingers through Elizabeth's. "I remember holding her hand as we sat on the porch in the moonlight, the softness of her kiss, and the sweet taste of her mouth. Even if you can't help me get out of here, Ellie, at least you've helped me remember those things."

"I *will* get you out of here, Alex. And somehow, I'll get you back into Amanda's arms again."

He took a deep breath and a wicked grin replaced the sadness. "So maybe now you'll tell me what else you found out from those lily-livered buzzards."

"*One* lily-livered buzzard," Elizabeth corrected, holding her index finger in front of his face. "One lily-livered buzzard who appears to know a lot more than he wants to admit. But he *did* mention two things last night that I found rather interesting."

"Such as?"

"What do you know about the saloon owner who died shortly after Luke went to work for him?"

"Tim Drummond?" Alex asked, his eyes narrowing as if he couldn't understand what a saloon owner had to do with Amanda.

"Matt didn't give me a name, just a story."

"Don't know that Winchester fellow's story, but the one I heard was that old man Drummond was having a gay old time with sweet little Rosie, the nicest strumpet to work the town of Sapphire in close to a decade."

Elizabeth's eyebrows rose. "You knew her well, did you?"

"I knew a lot of women well before Amanda came into my life, but quit interrupting me or I'll never finish this tale." Alex grinned and tossed Elizabeth a wink. "Seems somebody heard Rosie scream late one night, and they found Drummond lying like a whale on top of her. Man must have weighed close to three hundred pounds, even had a special chair to sit in 'cause nothing else would hold him. Crushed Rosie's ribs when he up and died on her. Put her out of commission for better than a month, which sure upset a lot of men in town."

"You included?"

"Suffice it to say, I was a pretty enterprising fellow until Amanda came along. Funny thing, though. Drummond never was one to spend time with the ladies—his or anyone else's. Didn't seem quite right for him to expire in the throes of passion."

"Did anyone think he might have been murdered?"

"Murdered?"

"It's just a wild hunch, Alex. Was there an investigation of any kind?"

"I don't rightly know. The sheriff and I weren't the best of friends since he had a tendency to associate with the likes of Luke Winchester, which didn't set too well with me. In fact, the two of them got awfully chummy right after Luke came to town. Seemed to be even better friends after Luke became owner of the saloon. If you ask me, Drummond's death was awfully suspicious. But, where's the proof?"

Elizabeth shrugged. "I doubt there is any—not on Drummond's death, not on Phoebe's romantic escapades. Definitely not on your murder. I doubt there's any documentation anywhere that's going to help us out."

Alex laughed. "I doubt Luke Winchester kept a diary of his actions, either."

Diary! How could she have forgotten about that? "Matt made another comment, too," Elizabeth said, "something about Phoebe keeping a diary. Do you remember seeing her writing in anything? Maybe she knew what Luke was up to."

"The woman looked like Medusa and acted like a shrew. I stayed far away from her except when Luke Winchester was around."

"Why?"

"Because they talked about Amanda. They might have laughed at her behind her back and said wicked things, but it was the closest connection I had with her."

"Well, if Phoebe *did* keep a diary, maybe it's hidden around here somewhere."

"You think I haven't looked? I've combed every square inch of this place for something that might get me out of here, but I've found nothing."

"Have you pulled boards from the walls?"

"No."

"Have you looked up the chimney, or for hidden panels?"

"No. But maybe we should look now rather than you going off like a madwoman, hollerin' at me for things I should have done but didn't."

Elizabeth's laughter was interrupted by a loud knock at the door below. Alex disappeared in a flash and returned before she made a move. "It's that big galoot who kept you out all night. You've got to get rid of him so we can find that diary."

Elizabeth shook her head. She might be more than willing to help Alexander, but she wasn't about to lose Jon in the process. "He can help us look."

"You mean, you plan on telling him about me?"

"He could help, Alex."

"Absolutely not! I don't want him helping, and I don't want him knowing I'm here."

"Then keep out of sight and let me deal with it."

Alex seemed to think about it. "I'll stay out of sight, but I won't be far away." In half a heartbeat he disappeared.

Elizabeth heard boots on the stairs. Jon's boots, the sound of his unmistakable gait as he came closer and closer.

Suddenly he appeared in the doorway, his shoulders nearly touching the jambs, his head bent so he could enter the room. Oh, Lord, but he looked good.

"You sure wear some of the oddest get-ups, Ellie," he said, moving in close. "Is this a look I should get used to?" He wrapped one arm around her waist and pulled her against him, then tugged one end of the towel she wore about her head.

"It's a fresh-out-of-the-shower look."

"Then I approve," he said, dropping the towel to the floor. "On one condition."

"Which is?"

"That you let me step out of the shower with you before you get into this outfit."

"I think that could be arranged."

Slowly he let his hands drift to her bottom and a flood of last night's memories hit her. She couldn't think of too many places that he hadn't touched, that he hadn't kissed, and she wished with all her heart that she was back at Dalton House once again.

He lowered his head and tenderly kissed her cheek, her ear, trailing kisses down to the soft hollow at the base of her neck. She could hardly breathe from the intensity of the desire he was raising. He felt so good, so right, and she wanted him again.

Right this very moment.

"Is this the personal and private stuff you wouldn't talk about?"

Jon didn't stop. Jon didn't hear, thank heavens, but Elizabeth's eyes popped open and she saw Alex standing in the doorway, shaking his head and clicking his tongue. She couldn't think of a more unpleasant and unwelcome sight. How could she possibly have forgotten about Alex the moment Jon had stepped into the room? It was easy, she told herself: Jon took up nearly every spare inch of her heart, her mind, and her soul, and there was very little left over for a ghost.

Jon eased away, weaving his fingers through damp strands of hair, trailing them tenderly over her terrycloth-covered breasts, which seemed to be heaving more heavily than they should. She had to back away. He was too hot, too passionate, and in the same room as Alex. That would never work at all.

"I got to thinking about something Matt told me last night," she said in a rush, pushing out of Jon's arms and backing a good two feet away. "It's been bothering me all morning."

"I honestly can't see anything important coming out of Matt's mouth," Jon said, moving close again and taking the ties of her robe into his fingers.

"He told me Phoebe Carruthers kept a diary."

"Phoebe Carruthers has been dead at least eighty years." He moved his fingers from the tie to the knot at her waist.

She stepped back another foot and bumped into the steamer trunk. "Yes, I realize she's been dead eighty years, but you know how interested I am in history, and, well . . ."

He yanked on the tie and pulled her hard against his chest. He looked down at her with that lopsided grin. "Well, what?"

"Well," she said, zigzagging her index finger in and out of the buttons running down his shirt. "I thought you could help me look for Phoebe's diary today, instead of tearing down wallpaper and stripping wood."

"Hunting for missing diaries doesn't fall within our regular payment plan for my handyman services. You're going to have to pay a little extra."

Elizabeth smiled. "Can I pay you tonight?"

He tilted his head down and whispered in her ear, "I charge double for diary hunting."

"Only double?" Elizabeth asked, as he nibbled ever so nicely on her ear. "I was thinking triple was a little more appropriate."

"You think I'm worth it?"

"Oh, Jon . . . you're worth that and a whole lot more."

Jon sat down on the edge of Elizabeth's bed and watched the crazy woman walk over every square inch of floor, testing for loose boards. Not one thing in half a dozen rooms had escaped her scrutiny in her quest to find the secret hiding place where Phoebe Carruthers might have stashed a diary. "I don't think it exists, Ellie," he said, wishing they could move on to more creative endeavors, like going back to Dalton House, collecting at least part of his fee for services rendered, and adding a new room to his list of favorite places.

"It does exist," she insisted, looking at Jon in annoyance, "and in case you haven't figured it out by now, when I get an idea into my head, I don't let it drop until I'm successful."

"Yeah, I figured that out a while back."

A board creaked. Elizabeth looked up at Jon and grinned. "Success—I think." She lifted her foot, then pressed it down again into the floor, adding a little more weight.

It creaked again.

"Try this one," she said, standing back to give Jon room to perform the services she was going to pay him quite nicely for.

He pushed off the bed, claw hammer in hand, and knelt down by her legs.

"You're sure?" he asked, using his vantage point to slowly gaze at the long length of calf and knee and thigh, before he moved further up her anatomy and caught a glimpse of her eyes.

She nodded, but her smile was mixed with hesitance. "We've torn up about two dozen. What's one more ripped-up board?"

"That's my girl." He winked and watched her grit her teeth as he wedged the claw into a minuscule crack between two boards. She had so much hope in her eyes, so much need, as if finding the diary meant the difference between life and death. He wanted to tell her to give up, to get back to the job of restoring the hotel rather than tearing it down board by board, but he couldn't do anything but help her out when he saw the look in her amber eyes.

Sometime in the middle of the night, when he'd lain awake and looked at her, he realized he'd do anything to make her happy.

"Relax, Ellie," he said. "I think this is definitely going to be your lucky board."

He wrenched the hammer in the crack.

The wood crackled and the board popped out of the floor and into the air.

Jon lost his balance and tumbled back onto Elizabeth's legs.

She stumbled and smacked into the lovers' statue, grabbing on to marble body parts to keep her balance.

But the statue toppled, taking Elizabeth down with it.

The sculpture cracked, and bits and pieces of pink and white faux marble scattered about the room.

Jon pushed himself up from the floor and offered a hand to Elizabeth. "Well, so much for your valuable piece of art."

"I hated the thing anyway. I should have let you haul it off to the dump weeks ago."

"I'll get rid of it now and we can get back to our treasure hunt."

"Why? It's useless," Elizabeth said, defeat ringing out in her voice, as she began picking up scraps of plaster. "I'm sure Phoebe's diary is just another rumor."

"You can give up if you want, but I've got a nice, fat salary coming to me tonight, and I plan to earn every ounce of it." Jon grinned at Elizabeth's gloomy face as he began to tilt the intact portion of the statue back up on its base.

"Okay, I won't give up, but . . ."

Jon saw a distinct frown furrow Elizabeth's brow. "What's wrong?"

"There's a hole in the bottom."

Jon laid the statue back on its side and together they inspected the bottom.

"It's hollow," she said, looking at Jon, smiling hopefully. "Do you think maybe we got lucky?"

"Stick your hand inside and find out."

Slowly she wedged her hand and arm through the hole. "There's something there. I can just barely feel it," she said. "There. I've got it." She pulled her arm out, and in her hand was a book bound in dark leather, its pages yellowed with age.

She looked at Jon and grinned. "I told you that was the right board. And to think you wanted to haul this thing off to the dump!"

Elizabeth sat on the edge of the bed, gently opened the cover of the book, and Jon saw tears welling in her eyes. What on earth could possess her to cry over a diary? he wondered.

"Listen to this," Elizabeth said. " 'The diary of Phoebe Carruthers, a madwoman, or so I've been told.' "

Jon couldn't help but laugh. "A madwoman? Is that what she considered herself?"

"It's what she's written." Elizabeth turned to a spot somewhere in the middle of the book. " 'He thinks I don't know what's going on, but I do.' " she read. " 'He thinks I'm mad, but I'm not. I'm in love, and I'd do anything to have him love me in return.' "

Elizabeth looked at Jon and smiled. "I think we're in for a night of enjoyable reading."

"Enjoyable reading? What about my triple payment for services rendered?" he teased, moving in close and kissing the hollow below her ear. "Why don't you save the reading for tomorrow?"

Elizabeth looked at the thickness of the book and then at Jon. "It shouldn't take much more than an hour to read. You don't mind waiting, do you?"

He laughed. "Mind? I'll just tack a bonus onto that payment you owe me."

She crooked a finger under his belt and tugged him a little closer. "Bonuses have always been a specialty of mine," she teased.

Jon sucked in a deep breath. That one simple touch of her finger sent ripples of desire through every part of his anatomy. "You're sure that reading can't wait?"

"Positive," she whispered, tugging once again. "But I'll definitely make the wait worth your while."

He looked at her face, her eyes, the slightest tip of her tongue wetting her lips, and the finger tucked under his belt. "Is that a promise, Ellie?"

She nodded slowly. "I always keep my promises."

Oh, hell. If he could just wait till later, he knew he was in for a night neither of them would ever forget. And the only way he'd wait till later was to get away now, find something to occupy his time. Maybe he'd go home and sketch the way she looked right this moment—a seductive temptress. On second thought, if he attempted to draw that beguiling smile, he'd spend his waiting time in agony.

Maybe he'd just go to the cafe, eat pie, drink coffee, and build up his strength and stamina for the night ahead.

Reluctantly backing away, he looked at his watch. "Two hours? My place?"

A devilish grin covered her beautiful face, reaffirming once again that he'd never liked angels. "Do you have a particular room in mind?"

He quickly calculated the number of rooms in Dalton House and smiled. "Every single one, Ellie. Should take a while, but I can't think of any reason to rush."

Chapter 15

Two hours? Waiting that amount of time to be with Elizabeth again would seem more like an eternity, Jon thought, as he stepped out of the hotel. He could have stayed with her, of course. But she wanted to read, she wanted to learn more about crazy old Phoebe Carruthers, and reading was the furthest thing from his mind. Jon didn't mind doing a little research tonight, but the only thing he wanted to study and explore were all the intricacies of Elizabeth Fitzgerald's mind and body and soul.

He'd fallen in love. It didn't seem possible when he'd started out with nothing more than shallow thoughts of stripping her out of her clothes and sketching and then sculpting that Rubenesque body of hers. And Lord, her body was more beautiful than he'd ever dreamed . . . soft and sweet and flawless. But it was all the extra things that had made his passions soar. It was the way she fought back when they didn't agree, the way she flew through life, taking advantage of every minute as if the next might not exist. It was the way she smelled of cinnamon and sugar when he arrived in the mornings, and the cuteness of her nose when it was covered with flour or soot.

She was everything he wanted and needed, and two hours apart was going to be a hell of a long time.

Coffee and pie didn't seem like a viable alternative to making love, but for now he'd have to make do.

Trudging across the street, he gave just a moment's notice to the unfamiliar olive drab pickup parked out front and entered the warmth of the cafe, stopping short when he stepped through the door. Sitting by the window were Matt, Floyd, and a stranger, deep in conversation while eating pie and drinking coffee or beer.

"Hello, Jon," Matt called out, as Jon hung up his coat and hat. "I'd invite you to join us, but I think we had enough of each other's company last night."

Jon studied the contemptible grin on Matt's face, wishing he'd rearranged his cousin's mouth and nose when he'd had the chance last night. He hadn't used his fists in nearly twenty years, but remembering last night made him itch for a fight, made him wish he'd just gone home and suffered through his wait with pleasant thoughts. Now all his thoughts centered on how Matt could have hurt Elizabeth last night, and the realization that if Matt tried anything again—if anyone tried to hurt her—he didn't know if he could hold back.

Jon walked across the room, stopping for just a moment beside Matt's table. He casually checked out the stranger with long black hair, noting something vaguely familiar about him, and studied the map spread out on the table between them. "Planning a trip?"

Matt shrugged. "That's always a possibility."

Jon couldn't make out the details on the small section of map, but it looked like a part of the range not too far from Schoolmarm Gulch, and he had a horrible feeling Matt and his friends weren't discussing a leisurely vacation.

Libby pushed through the kitchen door carrying three plates laden with gravy and potatoes and steak and slid them on the table. Her timing couldn't have been more perfect; it allowed Jon to leave Matt's side and escape to the kitchen.

"Mind if I use your phone?" he asked Jack, who was flipping hamburger patties on the grill.

"Not a problem," Jack said casually, as if customers used it all the time.

Jon punched the buttons on the wall phone, waiting patiently for the ring, less patiently for an answer. By the tenth ring, he was ready to hang up when he heard the familiar voice.

"I think something's going to happen tonight," he said. "Matt, Floyd, and some stranger are in the cafe right now."

A frown crossed his face as he listened to the voice on the other end.

"If you know, how come you're not doing anything?" he asked, raising his voice, then calming down when he remembered he wasn't alone.

He leaned a shoulder against the wall, watched Libby walk into the room and halfheartedly returned her smile while words droned on in his ear.

"Yeah, I'll trust you. Seems to be the thing I do best lately."

Libby's foot was tapping madly on the floor by the time Jon hung up. "Now that you've made that call, why don't you call Elizabeth and let her know her brother's here, once again being an obnoxious bore."

"What are you talking about?" Jon asked.

"Oh, I forgot. You were out of town the first time Eric Fitzgerald gifted us with his presence. A real pain in the butt. Elizabeth says I must have had him mixed up with someone else, but I'll never forget the way he strutted in here, told us his name, then proceeded to complain about the food, the town, and the hotel. He was bad enough on his own, but he's even worse around Matt and Floyd."

Jon frowned at Libby's words, then peered through the window of the kitchen door and checked out the stranger who'd seemed rather familiar. Instantly he knew why—the same high cheekbones, and coal black hair nearly as long as Elizabeth's but not quite as bright. He had a gold ring in his ear and a smug look on his face as he conversed with Matt and Floyd.

"I just left Elizabeth," Jon said. "She didn't mention anything about Eric coming to visit."

"I don't think she knows, so if you won't call her, I will."

Jon captured Libby's hand before she grabbed the phone. "Let me talk to him first, get him to go over and see her. She doesn't want to believe he's involved with Matt, and I don't want her to see them here together."

"She'll find out sooner or later," Libby added. "Matt's going to get arrested one of these days, and his friends are bound to end up with him. How do you think she'll feel if her brother ends up in jail?"

Jon shook his head, but he knew perfectly well how she'd feel. She'd talked so much about Eric. She loved him in spite of his irresponsibility, in spite of his wandering ways. She'd love him even if he ended up in jail, but seeing him there would hurt her terribly. And Jon had sworn before that he'd never let anyone hurt her again.

"He might not listen, but I sure as hell want to give it a try," Jon said, squeezing Libby's fingers. "Could you bring me a beer? Might make this a little easier."

A moment later he pushed through the door, grabbed a chair from an empty table, and set it down between Matt and Eric. "I just found out you're Elizabeth's brother," Jon said, straddling the chair and offering his hand to Eric. "I'm Jon Winchester."

"Matt already filled me in," Eric said, leaning back, sipping at a beer. "Hear you've been keeping my sister company."

The man had an attitude, all right, one Jon didn't particularly like. "We're good friends. I'm surprised she didn't tell me you were in Sapphire."

"If you're such good friends, you already know I don't keep Elizabeth apprised of all my comings and goings." He leaned forward, staring directly at Jon. "This is a business trip, not a social one. There's no need for her to even know I'm here."

Jon clinched his fists, making every attempt to control his anger. "You prefer Matt and Floyd to your sister?"

Eric grinned. "I don't see where that's any of your business."

"I couldn't agree more," Matt added.

Libby pushed between Jon and Eric, shoving the beer Jon had requested right into his hand. She was frowning at him, her head shaking, and Jon knew she was warning him to back off. He probably should, too. He had the feeling that Eric Fitzgerald didn't care about anyone but himself and that any efforts Jon made to change him would be useless.

Jon downed a good quarter of his beer. Useless or not, he had to make another attempt to sway Eric from Matt. Eric might not be worth the trouble, but for Elizabeth's sake, he had to try. "While Matt was filling you in about me and Elizabeth, did he happen to mention that she'd had to fend him off with a broken wineglass last night?"

An instant spark of fury blazed in Eric's eyes and Jon hoped the words he'd just spoken would sink into Eric's head and make him see what kind of man he was dealing with.

Eric glanced past Jon to Matt. "Is that true?"

Matt shrugged. "A slight misunderstanding. The Lone Ranger here came in and saved the day, though."

Jon gripped Matt's collar just as he'd done the night before, and his chair went skittering across the floor as he dragged Matt out of his seat.

Eric grabbed Jon's arm, yanking him away from Matt, who slinked back into his chair, his fingers massaging the skin at his neck. "If he says it was a misunderstanding, it was a misunderstanding," Eric said, his face just inches from Jon's.

Jon twisted out of Eric's grasp. "You'll listen to him rather than your sister?"

Eric chuckled. "Elizabeth's not easy to get along

with. Just ask any of her old acquaintances in L.A."

This time Jon grabbed Eric's shirt and moved in close, almost eye-to-eye with him. Maybe he was overreacting, but he didn't like this man and he didn't like the way he spoke about Elizabeth. "I know what your sister's like," Jon said through gritted teeth. "So does everyone in Sapphire. We also know that if it came to making a choice between believing her or Matt, Matt would lose."

Eric laughed, twisting halfway out of Jon's grasp. Their height was nearly the same, but Jon outweighed Eric by a good forty pounds of muscle, muscle he could very easily exert right now.

But Eric twisted again, doubled his fist, and connected with Jon's chin.

Jon stumbled back a few feet, taken by surprise by Eric's strength. The blow didn't stop him, though. In just a matter of seconds, Jon's knuckles smashed into Eric's jaw, knocking him into the table.

Beer bottles and plates crashed to the floor. Floyd rushed to get out of the fray; Matt shoved out of his chair and casually leaned against the wall to watch.

Eric regained his footing. Jon tightened his fist for another swing . . . and the cafe door burst open.

"What's going on in here?" Elizabeth yelled. She ran across the room, grabbing Eric's arm just as Jack restrained Jon.

Tugging out of Jack's grasp, Jon slowly rubbed his chin. "I've just had the pleasure of meeting your brother," he said sarcastically, and suffered Elizabeth's glaring frown.

"Who provoked the fight?" she asked, her eyes blazing.

"*He* did," Eric stated, jerking away from his sister.

"I didn't like the company he was keeping," Jon told her. He hated the anger in her eyes, the way she directed it right at him. But Eric's companions weren't the real reason for the fight . . . it stemmed mostly from Eric's treatment of his sister. It didn't appear to matter to Eric that she'd raised him, sent him to college, and catered to his every whim. Eric Fitzgerald was no damn good; but Jon couldn't hurt Elizabeth by telling her so.

Elizabeth sank down in a chair and Jon watched tears well in the corners of her eyes as she looked from Eric to Jon and on to Libby and Jack. "Thanks for calling me, Lib," she said.

"I'm sorry I had to, hon." Libby grabbed her husband's arm and drew him out of the room, as if she knew they'd done all they could for now.

"Floyd and I are going to my place," Matt said, slapping Eric on the shoulder. "Join us when you get through here."

"Shouldn't take long," Eric tossed back, then leaned down, grabbed an unbroken beer bottle from the floor, and drank the remains.

Elizabeth looked dazed by all that had happened, and Jon touched her shoulder, wanting to talk, needing to explain, but she shrugged away and didn't look even once in his eyes. Instead she looked at her brother, who was lightly rubbing the knuckles of his right hand. "Why didn't you tell me you were coming to Sapphire?" she asked him.

"I've been busy."

"With Matt and Floyd?"

"I told you a long time ago that Matt was my friend. We had some business to take care of and then I planned to stop by." Eric put a hand on Elizabeth's shoulder and Jon could see her tense, but she didn't push him away, not the way she had when he had touched her.

"Do you have any idea what those two friends of yours are like?"

"I've never questioned you about your friends," Eric said, glaring at Jon. "I haven't always approved of them, either."

A tear fell down Elizabeth's cheek, and Eric gently brushed it away, surprising Jon by his tenderness. "I haven't meant to hurt you," Eric whispered. "I had every intention of visiting you before going home."

"I don't even care about that anymore," she said, grabbing his hand and holding it tightly. "Please, Eric. I don't trust Matt or Floyd. Stay away from them—please."

Eric grinned. "We have a partnership with Matt, remember?" All the love he'd shown a moment before had disappeared.

"I don't have a partnership with him any longer," Elizabeth said. "You'd be wise to forget all about your agreement, too. Besides, it isn't anything legal or binding."

"You might go back on your word, but I won't."

"Please, Eric," she implored, but he only laughed.

"I'm not a seventeen-year-old kid anymore. You can't tell me how to run my life."

"No," Elizabeth said, wiping away her tears.

"You're twenty-six and I always hoped you'd become a little more responsible, but you haven't. I'm not going to beg you. I'm just going to ask you one more time. Go back to the hotel with me. Forget about your friendship with Matt."

Eric shook his head. "Sorry, sis. A deal's a deal, and what I've got going with Matt is something I aim to follow through on." He crossed the room, grabbed his coat, and headed out the door.

Elizabeth rushed after him but stopped in the doorway. She didn't move for the longest time. Then she slowly turned around and looked at Jon.

"Are you happy now? You wanted to know if he was involved with Matt. Well, I think you just got your answer." She didn't say anything more, just walked out of the cafe.

Rushing after her, Jon caught her arm and stopped her in the middle of the road. He tilted her face toward him. "I'm sorry you had to see what happened in there. I'm sorry about your brother."

"But you're not sorry you hit him, are you?"

"He had it coming."

"So you settled it with your fists." She twisted away. "Seems to be the way you handle all your problems. You've been close to hitting Matt every time I've seen you together."

"I should have punched him last night for what he did to you. I should have hit him tonight, too."

"I don't think it has anything to do with me. I think it all goes back to the day you shot that deer. You can't forget. You just want to get even."

"You think that's what all this is about?" Jon asked, taking hold of her shoulders and keeping her from turning to walk away. "What about what he did to you?"

"I had things well under control."

"Yeah, right. Would you really have stuck that glass into his neck? Could you have pushed it deep enough into his skin to make him stop? What if he'd grabbed you? What if he'd wrestled the glass out of your hand?"

"Stop it, Jon."

"I won't stop. Your brother just might get himself thrown in jail if he keeps on hanging around with Matt and Floyd. I was trying to talk some sense into him."

"I don't like Matt, I don't like Floyd, and I don't want Eric running around with them. But you don't have proof they're doing anything wrong, and neither does anyone else."

"That could change at any time."

Elizabeth looked away. "Eric's never been in trouble before. He's not the type."

"I got a real good look at his character tonight."

"That wasn't my brother in that room," she fired back. "I don't know what's going on, but Eric's never acted like that before."

"Maybe you just never saw this side of him. Maybe he's always put on too good a show."

She jerked away and Jon realized he'd said too much. "He's my brother, but that doesn't seem to make any difference to you." She laughed. "Why would it, though? You've got a vendetta against your own cousin. I sometimes have the feeling you're looking for a fight. You're bigger than everyone else, and if you can't intimidate them with your size, you just use your fists."

"Your brother deserved it."

"Guilt by association, right?" she asked. "My brother doesn't deserve to be on your enemy list any more than I did, but you've put him there. I guess that means you might as well put me back on that list, too."

"I told you I was sorry. I told you I trusted you."

"Yeah, so you did. But I had to prove I was innocent. What if you hadn't seen me with that glass to Matt's neck? Would I still be trying to make you believe in me?"

Jon shook his head. No amount of words would calm her, would make her understand that everything he'd done today was for her.

"If you'll take your hands off me, Jon, I'd like to go home now."

"Don't go, Ellie," he asked softly, but her eyes glared into his.

Slowly he released his grip, and without hesitating a moment, she walked up the hotel steps and through the door.

There was nothing more he could do now, nothing more he could say. But Jon swore as he watched that door close that he wasn't about to let her walk out of his life for good.

Chapter 16

Elizabeth rocked back and forth while Alex paced her bedroom floor. It had taken her ten minutes to stop crying and nearly half an hour of pacing along with Alex to calm her anger. The problem was she didn't know who she was mad at—Jon, her brother, or herself.

Eric was irresponsible and his association with Matt just proved it even more. Jon had a temper, just like most artists she'd ever known. Being big and powerful on top of that just made him all the more passionate. She leaned her head against the high-backed wooden chair and closed her eyes. Lord, but she loved his passion. There was nothing meek or timid about him and he stood up to her at every turn. Other men had never tried.

Thinking about him made her smile for the first time in an hour. She'd been so wrong to yell, to take her frustrations out on the man who'd attempted to tell her he was only trying to help. Knowing Jon, that's what he was doing. Helping.

He'd helped her again and again. He sculpted and gave all the money to wildlife charities. He organized work crews to take care of things in town, bounced children on his knees, and told them stories of long, long ago.

Jon Winchester was, by far, the best man she'd ever known, and she loved him with all her heart.

"You going to sit there all night mooning away over that big galoot or are you going to finish reading that diary?"

Alex was standing right in front of her when she opened her eyes. "I'm sorry, Alex. I forgot." Libby's phone call had interrupted her not even halfway through the revealing details of Phoebe's diary. She'd run to the cafe, seen Jon smash her brother in the face, and exploded. Oh, she was still angry about the fight; she was still angry about her brother showing up in town without saying a word, and she was more than angry with herself for losing her temper.

But right now she had to finish that diary. She could deal with all the other problems when she was through. The most important thing at the moment was taking care of Alex.

She picked up the diary he'd set beside her chair and once again began to read.

Elizabeth turned over the last page and set Phoebe's journal in her lap, folding her hands over the top. "Everything we need to prove your innocence and Luke's guilt is right inside here," she said to Alex.

"But will anyone believe it?" Alex asked. He'd been leaning over her shoulder, listening to every word she read, adding his own truths to Phoebe's.

"She was a madwoman," Alex stated. "She said

so herself. Why would anyone believe an ounce of that drivel?"

"Because it's the only proof we've got."

"It proves only that Luke killed me. It doesn't say anything about me being the rightful owner of all the Dalton assets. That's important." He prowled the room for a moment, then knelt down before her. "Once you prove that Jedediah deeded everything to me, the Winchesters will lose everything. They'll be out on the street with nothing, and I'll have my revenge."

"I don't really think that would happen, Alex. Not a hundred years after the fact. Not when too many generations of Winchesters have lived on Dalton property, invested the money, and built a completely different empire from the one that existed all those years ago."

"It has to happen. They need to suffer."

Elizabeth put her elbows on her knees and rested her chin on her folded hands. "Is that what you really want? Do you think two men who had nothing at all to do with your death should suffer for the sins of their great-grandfather?"

"Of course I do!" Alex thundered. "You'd want it, too."

She shook her head. "I don't care all that much about what happens to Matt, but I care very much about Jon. I was under the impression you were starting to like him, too."

"Liking him and getting out of here and back to Amanda are two different things. I swore I'd get rid of the Winchesters, and I will."

"Will getting revenge take away your pain? You

don't even know if getting revenge will get you out of here."

Alexander's shoulders drooped as if all the fight had been knocked out of him. He paced the floor again, back and forth, back and forth, and finally he stopped. "Take the diary to Jon. Read it to him, and tell him about me. Maybe he can help us."

She sat up straight in the chair and frowned, wondering what had brought on this sudden change. "He'll think I've lost my mind if I tell him I've been communicating with a ghost."

"He won't."

"Why?"

"He's known about me since he was a boy. He knows I'm here now."

Elizabeth sat motionless, trying to fathom the words Alex had just uttered. Was he telling the truth? Surely she would have sensed it if Jon had known about Alex. "Why hasn't he said something to me about you?"

"Because a long time ago he told people about me and no one believed him. Because he's never seen me, and he's not even sure I exist. I think he halfway believes he's crazy."

"You think that's funny, don't you?"

Alex nodded. "I'm a ghost. I'm supposed to scare people, or at least make them think they've gone plumb loco."

Elizabeth frowned. "And the fact that he's a Winchester made it ten times as enjoyable?"

Alex shook his head. "Some twenty-odd years ago that big oaf was my best friend. He came here every day. We'd play games, we'd talk. He'd sit up in the attic for hours at a time and draw pictures while I watched. I managed to forget he was a Winchester, but when he told those other men about me I was afraid this place would be overrun by people trying to exorcise me. I didn't want to leave this place—not till I knew I could be with Amanda. So I didn't talk when he asked me to. They laughed at him and that lily-livered buzzard who wasn't much older than him at the time said he was crazy."

"Didn't you feel sorry for him?" Elizabeth asked.

Alex nodded. "I hated what was happening to him, but I had to think of myself first. Maybe I was wrong, but I can't change any of that now. Your Jon's a good man. I still find it hard to believe he's a Winchester."

The grandfather clock struck.

Once.

Twice.

Six more times.

Elizabeth bolted out of the chair she'd been sitting in for too many hours. "It's eight o'clock! I'm supposed to be at Jon's."

"Two hours ago you told me you never wanted to see him again. Let's see, what were the exact words you used—"

"I lied. As for the words I used, I'd appreciate it very much if you never told a soul. I was angry."

"So, do you plan on lollygagging around here all night, or are you going to get down the street and apologize?"

Elizabeth laughed. "I don't know if a mere apology will get me back in his good graces. I was pretty mean."

"Thunder and tarnation, woman! Apologizing

doesn't have to be done with words alone. Now, you'd best get moving."

Elizabeth rushed down a flight of stairs to the entry. She pushed the diary into her coat pocket and slipped into the sleeves. "I'll be home—" Her words trailed off as she looked at Alex. "I won't make any promises about when I'll be home," she said. "Apologizing might take a while, but when I get back, I hope to have a plan that will get you out of here."

It didn't take more than a moment for Elizabeth's combat boots to hit the road, and she ran for the first time in years. Icy air stung her cheeks and burned her lungs, but none of that mattered. She had to get to Jon. She had to beg forgiveness, and she had to say she loved him.

There were few lights on in the buildings lining the street, but a small bit of moonlight squeezing through a hole in the clouds lit her way. Even the lights that usually shone in Jon's turret room were darkened—and that frightened her. Had he gone away? Had she lost her chance to say she was sorry?

She pushed through the iron gates and rushed up the steps. She knocked. And waited.

She rang the bell. And waited.

Finally, she turned the knob and entered the unlocked house. Every room downstairs was dark, silent, and empty. She ran upstairs to the second floor and into Jon's bedroom, hoping against hope that maybe he'd just gone to bed. But that big old mattress was just as empty as the rooms downstairs, the covers just as mussed as they'd left them that morning.

Could he be in his studio? In the dark?

She ran down the hall, her boots thudding against the creakless boards. She climbed the narrow stairs, around and around, until she reached the top of the house and the circular room where he practiced his craft and put all his emotions into works of art. Yet even surrounded by beauty, the room felt lifeless without his presence.

Where can he be? she wondered, as she walked around the room, peering out the tall, narrow windows. She saw a thread of light beaming through the storm shutters in a building behind the house and felt her heart beat a staccato rhythm against her chest.

She left the room, running down the stairs, step after step, and exited the house through the kitchen door. The building was at least a hundred yards from the porch and appeared to have once been the stables or carriage house. Slowly, she pushed on the thick oak door, opening it just a crack so she could peer inside.

What she saw took her breath away.

Jon stood silhouetted before the open doors of a furnace, the flames leaping high inside. He was pouring molten metal, and the yellowish-brown liquid flowed easily from the long-handled crucible into the mold she'd seen before in his studio—the first mold he'd made of her face and shoulders.

She leaned against the doorjamb and watched him at work, doing the thing he'd described to her at one point during their long night together. His chest was bare, his hands and forearms covered in thick insulated gloves. Sweat glistened on his flexed muscles, and Elizabeth wished she had her camera so she could capture this moment, where bronze flowing from the vessel looked like an extension of his bronzed and beautiful skin.

She sighed deeply and Jon's eyes fluttered up through long blond lashes and looked at her. His jaw hardened, and he looked back at his work once again.

When the last of the metal flowed from the crucible, Jon set it aside, closed the door on the furnace, and removed the gloves. He looked at her again, and the flames she'd seen leaping in the kiln now sparked in his sapphire eyes.

He stalked toward her, his deep, penetrating stare never once leaving her, not for a moment. She swallowed hard. Was he angry? Was he going to tell her to leave and never come back again?

He stood in front of Elizabeth, his chest heaving in time with hers.

She looked up.

He looked down.

Elizabeth swallowed again.

"I didn't expect to see you again," he said.

"I promised I'd be here. I may get angry and say stupid things, but I always keep my promises."

She hoped that he'd smile, but he didn't.

"If you've come for an apology, you're not going to get one."

"It's my turn to say I'm sorry," she said. "Not yours."

He gently brushed wisps of hair from her cheek. "Just saying you're sorry's a damned poor attempt at making up."

"I thought of a few other ways, too," she said softly, pressing her hands to his chest and sliding them upward to wrap around his neck. "I only hope you'll give me the chance to try."

"One chance. That's all you get, so you'd better make it good." He swept her into his arms. He smelled of fire and smoke and felt slick and hot, and she buried her face into the cords of his neck and kissed him.

He carried her outside through the cold winter chill. He carried her into his home and up the wide circular staircase. He carried her into his bedroom and stood her on the floor, and without saying a word, peeled off her coat, her gloves, the red knit shirt she'd been wearing all day long as they'd searched the house. He snapped loose the hook of her bra and pulled it away, freeing her breasts.

She fought for every breath as he watched her, studied her, and touched her skin with only the power of his unwavering stare.

He lifted her again and carried her to the bed. His fingers easily released the laces of her boots and slipped them from her feet. Her socks followed. Her jeans. The tap pants she loved to wear.

And then he stared at her again.

His chest rose and fell. He kicked off his boots and shoved off his Levi's.

He was hard with need and want.

And Elizabeth wanted him.

She opened her arms, and he bent just low enough for her to wrap her hands around his neck, her legs about his waist, and he lifted her once more, carrying her to the bathroom. He opened the shower door, turned on the water until it pulsated fast and warm from the nozzle, and he stepped inside.

His mouth covered hers with passion and possession. She felt his hands gripping her bottom and her legs, his fingers just beginning to explore. She felt the cold, wet tiles at her back. She felt him hot and hard against her legs.

And she cried out when he entered her with one swift and easy stroke.

Jon threw his head back and the warm water slipped over him and between them. She combed her fingers into his hair and drew his face to her, kissing him with a hunger she'd never known existed. She didn't care at all about the roughness of the grout between the tiles as it scraped against her back; all she cared about was the rhythmical beat as Jon moved within her, higher, deeper, harder, stronger. He seemed out of control, lusting to possess everything he could touch, everything he could reach.

Again and again Elizabeth moaned with need and screamed with pleasure, wanting him to stop, wanting him to go on and on. And slowly the heavy beat of his movements turned into a soft, lilting rhythm of tenderness and care. He turned her from the wall and into the warmth of the water, holding her tight, tighter, until his tempo built again.

Again he kissed her, his mouth wild and hot. Beneath her fingers she could feel the muscles of his shoulders, his neck, and his back tighten. She felt her own muscles grabbing hold, not wanting to let go of him now or ever as he filled her completely, and together, mind, body, and soul, they skyrocketed into the heavens.

For the longest time, Jon rested his cheek on her

shoulder. The rapid rise and fall of his chest slowed, and finally he tilted his head and whispered into her ear, "Damn fine way of apologizing."

Elizabeth smiled. "I haven't done a thing yet."

"All in good time, my love. All in good time."

And he picked up the soap and began another erotic adventure with her body.

Morning came and went, and when afternoon rolled around, they stirred from sleep and crept downstairs, filling a tray with crackers and salami and cheese, the only worthwhile things they could find in Jon's kitchen other than beer and coffee.

He told her the housekeepers came just once a week, and since his grandfather had passed away he'd made a point of eating most of his meals at Libby and Jack's. They were old friends and good company. Jack didn't talk much, but Libby had always kept him entertained.

They ate in the middle of Jon's massive down-filled mattress, talking and laughing about nothing important, both of them staying far away from the subject of her brother and his association with Matt and Floyd.

An hour later, an empty tray sat at the end of Jon's bed, and Elizabeth sat to one side, wrapped in the same blanket she'd worn the day before.

She studied Jon's form as he stretched out on his side with only a sheet draped over his hips, and once again she wanted him. She wondered if that need would ever subside. They hadn't talked about a lifetime together. They hadn't talked about marriage or children or even living together. They'd made love, not so plain, not so simple, and they'd done it again and again.

She leaned over and kissed his nose, stroking away a lock of hair that had fallen across his forehead. It seemed the best way to begin a discussion she'd dreaded all morning long, a discussion that had haunted dreams that should have been peaceful after a night of so much love.

"Something's wrong, isn't it?" Jon asked, and she wondered how he could tell. Did her face give away her secrets, her fears?

She grabbed a pillow and tucked it close to her stomach. Jump in with both feet, she told herself. Get it out in the open just as fast and as easily as you can. She'd never hesitated telling people things in the past, but this wasn't your normal, everyday topic of conversation.

"I've seen the ghost," she finally blurted out. "I've talked to him. I know all about him."

Jon didn't move, not a finger, not an eyelash, not a heartbeat.

"He told me you've seen him, too."

He rolled onto his back and crossed his hands behind his head, staring straight up at the ceiling.

"I didn't believe it at first," she went on, when Jon refused to speak. "I thought it was the house making noises. But it's not."

Suddenly, Jon's silence made her doubt her sanity. "Please, Jon. Tell me you've seen him, too."

"I've never seen him," Jon said. "I've heard him. I've talked to him. Years ago I thought I was crazy; so did half the people in this town. That's why I know so much about psychiatrists. The teacher, the principal, my uncle—they all insisted I see one."

"No one believed I talked to God, either. But I knew I wasn't crazy then; I know you and I aren't crazy now," Elizabeth stated. "He didn't appear to me at first, but he talked to me and I could sense it when he came near. And just a few days ago he let me see him."

Jon rolled onto his side, his head propped up on his fist. "I always wondered what he'd look like if he appeared. I imagined he'd be a shadow, or translucent."

"He looks like any other flesh-and-blood man. I've even seen him cry."

"Cry?" Jon shook his head. "Why would he cry?"

"He's been accused of murder. He misses the woman he loves."

Elizabeth was surprised to see the questioning frown appear on Jon's face. "You don't know who he is, do you?" she asked.

"I don't have a clue. He never appeared to me; he never told me his name."

"It's Alexander Stewart," she told him. "He didn't desert Amanda—he was murdered."

Moving into Jon's arms when he sat up in bed, she related the entire story, just as Alexander had told it, leaving out nothing. They talked about what had happened when Jon was a child. They talked about Alexander's loneliness, the friends he wanted, the help he needed.

"I take it you believe him?"

Elizabeth nodded. "Every word. And I've got the proof now, too."

"What? That diary?"

Elizabeth climbed from the bed and retrieved the

journal from her coat pocket. Getting comfortable once again in Jon's arms, she flipped through the pages and stopped somewhere close to the beginning. "Listen to this.

" 'I've at last found a man to love. Herbert must never know, although I don't know why he should mind, as he has dalliances of his own.' " Elizabeth looked up from the book. "Herbert was Phoebe's husband."

"So I gathered," Jon quipped.

Elizabeth looked down at the pages again. " 'Luke Winchester arrived in town just two days ago and I had the extreme good fortune to accidentally bump into him as I walked out of the mercantile. He helped me with my parcels, and I invited him into the parlor for tea. He's a gambler and made no attempt to keep that piece of information a secret. Herbert would find that scandalous. Maybe that's why I found Mr. Winchester so exciting. What a stroke of luck it was for me that Herbert had gone out of town. I expected him back but thought it was time I gambled a bit myself. Life is so very boring with Herbert, and I found nothing the least bit boring about Mr. Winchester. He was worth the price I would have paid had I lost.' "

"Guess those stories my grandfather told about Phoebe Carruthers and her dalliances were true." Jon laughed. "Of course, I doubt he knew anything about her fling with his dad."

"He knew his father wasn't exactly a pillar of society, and he knew his mother didn't love him. I imagine she didn't have any idea what he was like when she married him, but she must have figured it out pretty fast, because she didn't look happy in her honeymoon pictures."

"Read some more," Jon said, pulling her back against his chest.

Elizabeth flipped through a few more pages and continued to read. " 'Tim Drummond died tonight and Luke now owns the saloon. Luke and I toasted his prosperity with a bottle of Tim's finest champagne, and then we made love. Herbert has never made me feel like Luke does. I doubt Herbert even knows that a woman can get excited in bed. Luke told me he could treat me special every night if it wasn't for Herbert. I laughed, of course, and told him that unfortunately, Herbert was in the finest of health. Luke laughed, too. "No one expected Tim Drummond to die, either," Luke told me. "If you want something badly enough, you take it—one way or another." He made love to me again after that, and when he left, I found the vial of powder next to my bed. I believe it's arsenic.' "

Jon laughed and Elizabeth tilted her head around and frowned. "You find this funny?"

"I knew there were some black sheep in my family, but I figured the worst ones were still living. Now I'm finding out that my great-grandfather debauched Phoebe Carruthers, killed a man so he could stake claim to the saloon, and it appears he's going to be partially responsible for Herbert Carruthers' death. Nice man, huh?"

"I wish this diary didn't show your family in such a bad light, but it does. I hate the thought of having to divulge this information to anyone other than you, but I promised Alex I'd help him and I just can't think of any way other than clearing his name."

Jon kissed her, and the feel of his arm around her shoulders brought back some of the warmth that had left her while she was reading the chilling revelations in Phoebe's diaries.

"Read some more, Ellie. Don't worry about smearing the Winchester name. Matt's done that already, and being related to him and his dad isn't something I've ever been proud of."

"If it makes you feel any better, you're nothing like Matt. The only trait the two of you share is a name."

"Maybe I'll change it one of these days." He laughed, and Elizabeth lifted the book and began to read again.

" 'Luke said it's only proper to mourn for a year. Of course, if I'd realized his visitations would become less frequent during my mourning period, I never would have poured that powder into Herbert's tea. Luke did, however, send me a lovely bottle of champagne wrapped in a plain brown box tied with black ribbon. I hated drinking it alone, but it was the only thing I could do to ease the pain of not having Luke beside me.' "

Elizabeth thumbed through pages that were little more than the ravings of a woman who'd felt she'd been spurned. " 'My lawyers tell me Herbert had made some unsound investments,' " Elizabeth continued. " 'I have nothing more than this house now, and I've considered turning it into a boardinghouse or perhaps a hotel. I've taken the first step by inviting that nice young man Alexander Stewart to board in the attic room until his wedding. The money he gives me each week will barely pay for food, but it's a beginning. Sheriff Ralston has expressed an interest in calling on me, though, and the husbands of both Mrs. Wyatt and Mrs. Vernon have tilted their hats and smiled quite nicely as I've passed them on the street. It was so very easy to keep my encounters with Luke Winchester a secret. I do believe I might be able to do the same with a few other gentlemen in town. I understand a woman can turn a handsome profit, given the right set of circumstances. Perhaps I might make Luke jealous, and perhaps I might enjoy myself in the bargain.' "

"Don't stop now," Jon said, when Elizabeth put the book in her lap. "Phoebe's become rather interesting."

"I find her sad and pathetic."

"Why? She doesn't seem much more redeeming than Luke."

"She was lonely and gullible. She fell in love . . ."

"Did she?" Jon interrupted, raising an eyebrow. "Or did Luke give her a taste of something new, something she wanted more and more of?"

"I don't know. Maybe it's both, although I don't know what she could possibly have seen in him."

"Maybe the same thing women see in Matt," Jon threw in.

Elizabeth laughed. "What? Charm? Looks?"

"Maybe Matt's the reincarnation of our great-grandfather."

"That's not funny, Jon. I don't care for Matt, but Luke was sick. He killed for the sake of money and property. If he wanted something, he took whatever means necessary to get it."

"As I said, Matt's just like Luke. Of course—" Jon frowned, apparently thinking about the similarities. "I doubt he'd ever resort to murder."

"No one believed Luke was capable of murder, either," Elizabeth said, turning more pages before she continued to read. " 'There was a party at the church tonight. Everyone was there, even Luke. He smiled at the congregation, he kissed babies, and he danced with the elderly ladies. He even danced with Amanda Dalton, and I could tell Mr. Stewart was not the least bit pleased that his intended was in the arms of another man. I wasn't pleased, either. Luke ignored me the entire evening, walking past me as if I didn't exist. But he came to my home later that night with two bottles of chilled champagne. I slapped his face for ignoring me, and he slapped me back for having the nerve to want to be seen in public with a man while I was still in mourning. His slaps rarely hurt, and he usually makes up for them in bed. But tonight he drank the champagne straight from the bottle and he talked about Amanda Dalton and how life wasn't fair. Luke wants to be more than just the owner of a saloon. He wants respect. And he wants to marry the richest woman in town. "But there will always be room for you in my life," he told me. I drank the rest of that first bottle of champagne and Luke opened the second.' "

Elizabeth skimmed through paragraph after paragraph, then began again. " 'Luke comes every night now, long after Mr. Stewart's in bed. He brings champagne and I fall asleep in his arms.

And every morning when I wake, I take his boots downstairs and clean away the dirt as I make his coffee.' "

Elizabeth sat up and Jon massaged her shoulders, somehow sensing the tension building inside her as she skimmed more lines. " 'I believe Luke is digging a tunnel. I confronted him with my concerns, but he only laughed and asked how he could possibly do that when I'm asleep in his arms every night—all night. But my head is so dizzy every morning that I feel an illness is coming on, and I believe I sleep so soundly that I would not know if Luke was with me or not.' "

Elizabeth turned another page. " 'The bank was robbed today and Elmer Jones was killed. Alexander Stewart disappeared, along with all his belongings, and Amanda Dalton was left standing at the altar. The only incident that bothers me is the latter, for I fear Luke will leave me. Of course, when he comes the next time with his bottle of champagne, I will tell him my secret. Yesterday I found the tunnel to the bank, and tonight the hole in the basement was filled in. I believe Luke might have killed Mr. Stewart and buried him downstairs. I believe he might have killed the bank clerk, too, after he conspired with him to rob the bank. It is only a hunch, but I have seen them talking many times outside of business hours. I have no proof, of course, but my plan is to tell Luke that I saw him murder Mr. Stewart, and that I'll promise to keep it all a secret if he agrees to marry me. It's a gamble, but once again the stakes are worth the risk.

" 'Luke's marrying Amanda today. He threatened to tell the sheriff about Herbert and the arsenic if I say anything about the tunnel or Mr. Stewart. We did reach a compromise, though. I won't tell a soul, and he won't tell a soul, as long as he comes to my bed.' "

Elizabeth shut the book and leaned back into Jon's chest. "What do you think?"

"That Phoebe Carruthers was totally insane."

Elizabeth sighed. "Then you don't believe what she's written?"

Jon wrapped his arms tightly around her and rested his cheek against hers. "I believe every word. I also think Luke was just as demented as Phoebe."

"Now that you know everything, how do you feel about helping Alex?" she asked.

"You mean, a ghost who's sworn vengeance against me and my family?"

Elizabeth slowly nodded.

Jon rose from the bed and walked across the room. "I don't know if there's anything either one of us can do," he said. "That diary might prove Luke was a murderer, it might clear Alexander's name; but no one's going to run Matt and me out of town because of it."

"What else is there?"

"I don't know, but we'll figure something out," he said, parting the curtains just as she'd seen Alex do time and time again.

The afternoon sunlight poured through the window and shone on blond hair Jon had combed away from his face with his fingers. It had fallen into an off-center part and curled slightly behind his ears and over his neck.

He was deep in thought as he looked out the

window, his slow breathing making a circle of fog appear on the glass. He leaned a shoulder against the wall and continued to look out at the town, just as she'd seen Alex do time and time again.

And suddenly it all became clear.

Their movements were the same.

Their hair.

Their walk.

That slightly off-kilter smile, and that lopsided grin.

Jon might be six-foot-six while Alex couldn't be much more than five-eleven, but . . .

No, she told herself. Her thoughts were crazy, and she laughed.

Jon turned around and smiled at her with eyes that curled her toes and warmed her heart.

Sapphire eyes—just like Alexander's bright blue ones.

Chapter 17

A quiver of excitement raced through Elizabeth's body. She climbed off the bed and ran to Jon, reaching up and cupping his face between her hands. "Smile again."

He laughed, but he smiled, too.

And she knew.

"You're not related to Luke Winchester," she stated.

"It's not something I'm proud of, but he *was* my great-grandfather."

Elizabeth shook her head. "No, Jon. You look like Alex. The same hair, the same walk, the same eyes."

"You're seeing something you *want* to see."

"Luke Winchester had black hair. Yours is blond. Alexander's is blond."

"Family traits have a strange way of changing in a hundred years."

"What about your grandfather? What did he look like?"

"Old," Jon stated flatly.

"Not always. Surely there must be some pictures around here from when he was young."

Jon shoved his fingers through his hair. "I've never been much of one to look at old photo albums. There might be one or two downstairs, or—" He smiled slowly. "My grandfather kept a lot of things just as they were when he was young. I seem to remember a picture of him on the dresser in his mother's room."

"Show me."

They slid into jeans. Elizabeth rummaged through the pile of clothing Jon had tossed on the floor the night before, found her red knit shirt, and pulled it over her head. Grasping her fingers, Jon led her to the second floor, to a part of Dalton House where she'd never been. They walked along the landing that looked out onto stained glass windows rising from floor to ceiling in the foyer and passed three doorways leading to bedrooms decorated in pastel florals with lots of ribbons and ruffles and lace. "My grandfather said his mother had once dreamed of filling all of these rooms with children," Jon said.

"I imagine if Alexander had lived, there would have been half a dozen rambunctious kids running around this place."

"You really think he was Thomas's father, don't you?" Jon asked, his fingers tightening around hers.

She nodded. "You're so much like Alex. You have to be related, and then his threat of revenge won't apply to you."

"That threat doesn't worry me."

"It doesn't matter now, anyway."

Jon stepped into the grandest bedroom on the floor. A mahogany bookcase with rosebuds carved in the upper corners was centered on one wall, surrounded by richly framed oil-painted florals in the softest pastels. A four-poster was draped in heavy Venetian lace and swagged with pink satin ribbons and bows, as were the windows and a dainty vanity table with an oval mirror mounted on the wall above it.

Everything was beautiful, but what caught Elizabeth's eyes was the ornate silver picture frame on top of the vanity. She pulled her hand free of Jon's and crossed the room. Picking up the frame, she studied the picture. "It's Alexander," she said. "I can't believe she kept a photo of him out in the open like this, especially after she married Luke."

"I doubt it was around when Amanda was alive," Jon said. "It's probably something Thomas put there later, probably a picture of him, not Alexander." Jon took the frame from Elizabeth's hands, slipped the picture out from behind the glass, and turned it over. " 'Thomas Winchester, age twenty-nine,' " Jon read. "See? It's my grandfather."

"Alexander was twenty-nine when he died." Elizabeth looked into Jon's eyes, the same eyes she saw in the picture, the same eyes she saw when she looked at Alex. "Alex is your grandfather, Jon. Not Luke."

He laughed. "You're pretty sure about this, aren't you?"

"I'm positive."

Jon shook his head. "Well, I just lost a murderer as a relative and gained a ghost." He leaned against the wall and folded his arms over his chest. "Hell of a day, isn't it?"

What could she say? In her mind, Jon was inheriting the better part of the past, but everything he'd known as his family history had suddenly changed.

"I wonder what else is in here?" he said, putting the frame back on the dresser and pulling open one of the vanity drawers.

"Are you sure you want to look now? Wouldn't you like to talk about what you've just found out?"

Jon cupped her cheeks in his hands and leaned over, kissing her softly. His hands trailed from her face, through her hair, then tightly wrapped around her back. He held her close, his kissing turning from soft to passionate, and as he lifted her toes from the floor, her spirits soared.

She sensed relief in his kiss, in his caress, and she saw the smile on his face when her feet once again touched the floor. "It's a hell of a day, Ellie," he said. "I can do whatever I want to Matt and not have to feel the least bit guilty about it."

"Y'know, Jon. I'm beginning to think a vengeful streak runs in your family."

"Makes us rather interesting, don't you think?"

"Just as long as you never turn it against me."

He kissed her forehead. "Not a chance. Personally, I prefer you taking your anger out on me. You have a damn fine way of apologizing, and I'm giving serious thought to picking fights with you every single day."

"You're incorrigible."

"And you're the best thing that's ever come into my life."

Elizabeth thought for sure he was going to kiss her again, but instead, he smiled with those sapphire eyes and she just stood back and admired the man she loved as he rummaged through the vanity drawer.

"Well, what do we have here?" he said, withdrawing a small heart-shaped box decorated in ribbons and lace. Elizabeth remembered Alexander's story of how the first time he'd seen Amanda she was dressed in pink and carried a ruffled and lacy parasol of pink-and-white stripes. Elizabeth could see Amanda vividly, gliding around this room, putting keepsakes in that box, or sitting on the front porch, being plied with Alexander's protestations of love. They'd missed so much together, but at least their love had had a chance to live on—in Thomas, in Thomas, Jr., and now in Jon.

He lifted the lid of the box and sorted through buttons and hair ribbons until his fingers slipped around a thin gold chain. A heart dangled from the bottom, and Jon carefully opened the front. A small picture of a man had been wedged into one side, and Elizabeth knew instinctively that it was Alexander she looked at this time, not Thomas. His clothing was from an earlier period, his hair parted slightly off-center and curled behind his ears. And his mustache was waxed and curled at the ends—just as Alex appeared today. On the other side of the locket the gold had been inscribed *Alex loves Amanda.*

A tear slid down Elizabeth's cheek. She wrapped her arms around Jon's neck and rested her head against his chest. "We have to tell Alex about Thomas, about everything."

"I'd rather show him," Jon said.

"That's impossible."

"Nothing's impossible. We just have to figure out a way to get him here."

Jon saw the curtains flutter in the attic room as he and Elizabeth neared the hotel. He saw a face in the window, too—his great-grandfather's face—and he couldn't help but smile.

His pace quickened, and he barreled up the stairs and through the front door, pulling Elizabeth with him. "Come on. He's upstairs. I saw him."

Elizabeth tugged on his hand. "He could be down here by now, too, Jon."

You've told him, I see. The voice thundered through the parlor, and for the first time Jon realized he didn't remember it solely as the sound of a ghost. Instead he remembered his grandfather. The two voices had the same lilt, even when angry. Funny, how he'd never noticed it before.

A cool breeze circled like a slow tornado in the middle of the room. When it stopped, Jon heard crystals tinkle against each other, and when he looked up, the chandelier hung a bit off-kilter.

"Yes, she's told me," Jon finally answered. "She's read the diary to me, too, and we've talked about the property, your death, and how much you loved Amanda."

The chandelier wobbled and Jon heard a thud on the floor just a few feet in front of him.

Has she told you about my vow of revenge?

"Yes, she's told me about that, too."

And you've come anyway?

Jon could sense Alexander's pacing, could hear the creak of floorboards with every footstep.

"You've had many opportunities to harm me. I'm not afraid."

Winchesters are lying, thieving, lily-livered buzzards, Alexander bellowed. His pacing stopped and his voice softened. *You're not a typical Winchester. If you were, you wouldn't be here now.*

"I'm here, Alex. And one way or another, we're going to get you out."

Alexander slowly began to materialize. His face, his hair, his shoulders, his chest, and his legs. Jon thought for sure if he reached out he could touch his great-grandfather, but Elizabeth had already warned him it wouldn't work. They'd also made a pact not to reveal the truth to Alex. They wanted to take him to the home that should have been his, take him to Amanda's room and let him see the photo of his son. They wanted him to see the truth, not hear it, and let it sink in slowly.

"How do you propose to get me out of here?" Alex asked, when he'd fully materialized.

Jon clutched the back of a chair as he looked at his ancestor and saw the similarities. He watched him walk and smile; he listened to him talk and laugh.

"I've tried everything," Alex continued, "but I can't go beyond the outside walls."

"Have you concentrated really hard?" Elizabeth asked. "Remember, you told me it took you nearly a year to figure out how to move from room to room and even longer to speak. Maybe you just haven't tried hard enough."

"I've tried hard enough. I've tried again and again. Do you want to see what happens?" he bellowed. "Watch. I'll show you." Alex sucked in a deep breath and squinted. "Keep watching." He marched through the parlor and the entry and smacked face first into the door, bouncing away as if it were rubber.

He turned around with his arms folded across his chest, a stance Jon knew very well. "It doesn't work," Alex stated.

"Try again," Jon said.

Alex glared at him. "You want to try it? You think it's fun, looking like a silly-assed fool bumping into doors? Well, I don't. I've done it in private and now I've done it once for you. That's enough!"

Alex walked over to the chesterfield and slunk down into the cushions. "Got any other idiotic notions you'd like me to try?"

Jon crossed to the chair in front of Alexander. He sat down and leaned forward, resting his elbows on his knees. Slowly he began to twiddle his thumbs.

"Am I boring you?" Alex asked, staring down at Jon's hands.

"Bad habit," Jon quipped. He hadn't twiddled his thumbs since he was a kid, but suddenly it seemed the thing to do. "My grandfather used to twiddle his thumbs. You would have liked him."

"I doubt it. Just another Winchester."

"He came here looking for me once. I was upset about shooting a deer."

"I remember."

"Do you?"

Alex nodded slowly. "You were crying," Alex said. "I tried to comfort you as best I could, but nothing worked. You wouldn't listen to me. Then the old man came, your grandfather, I suppose. He told you what was done was done and you couldn't change history. He said you'd learned a great deal from what happened, that hunting would never make you happy, not like it does some men. He said there was nothing wrong with that, and that you should turn your energy in other directions."

"You listened that closely?" Jon asked, smiling across the coffee table that separated him from Alex.

"I would have said the same thing to my own son—if I'd ever had one." Alex sighed. "I might have liked your grandfather if he hadn't been a Winchester."

"You would have liked him," Jon stated.

"He gave you a stick of wood and a knife that day," Alex said. "Told you when he was upset he liked to carve. Said he wasn't much good at it, but it made him feel better. He kissed you on the forehead and left. Next time I saw him was when you tried telling the town about me. I had the feeling he believed, but not that other buzzard."

"My grandfather told me it never hurt to have friends and loved ones, invisible or otherwise. He even told me that when he was little, not too long after his mother died, he'd go to her room and wish she'd come back. Once or twice he thought he heard her speaking to him. No one believed him, either. He stayed out of her room after that because he didn't want anyone to think he was crazy."

"Did he ever go back?" Alex asked.

"I moved him into her room a few weeks before he died. He never said whether he talked with her, but he seemed more comfortable there; happier, too."

Elizabeth put her hands on Jon's shoulders. He could feel her fingers tightening, kneading away the tension that had formed in his muscles. "We want to take you to her room, Alex," Elizabeth said.

Alex looked at Elizabeth, to Jon, and then to the door. "I can't go."

Elizabeth walked around the chair and stood close to Alex. "You have to," she said, reaching out to him. "Hold my hand." Jon watched the way Alex touched Elizabeth's fingers, tentatively at first, as if he was unsure what she planned to do. "I'm going to walk out of here, and you're going to go with me."

"Hell, might as well give it a try."

Alex rose from the davenport and followed Elizabeth across the room. She opened the door and smiled at Alex. "Hold on tight." Jon watched Alexander grip Elizabeth's fingers as she walked through the doorway and saw Alex stop abruptly when he hit the threshold, and not of his own accord.

He jerked his hand from Elizabeth's. "It won't work."

"It *has* to," Elizabeth cried.

"Let me try," Jon said.

"You're a Winchester! It definitely won't work with a Winchester."

"Is that why you never touched me? Is that why you never appeared to me? Because I'm a Winchester?"

"Seemed a good reason at the time."

"What about now?"

"You're still a Winchester."

Jon grinned and held out his hand. "I'm Amanda's great grandson. Surely that accounts for something."

"Ah, thunder and tarnation! I should have stayed invisible."

Alex stuck his hand out to grip Jon's.

And the two hands merged and became one.

Alex jerked away.

Jon felt a tremor of weakness shoot through his body.

"Oh, Lord!" Elizabeth cried out. "This could work."

"No!" Alex thundered. "I'm not doing that again. It didn't feel right."

"How the hell do you think I felt?" Jon bellowed. He could still feel the pain of a million needles jabbing at his skin, could feel the heat inside his hand.

"Stop it, you two! Stop it right now." Elizabeth stepped close to Jon and lifted the hand Alex had touched.

"Does it hurt now?" she asked.

He shook his head and she looked at Alex. "Did you really feel something, Alex?"

"What? You think I'd make a commotion if it felt good?"

Elizabeth grinned. "Did you hear what you said, Alex? You felt something. You haven't felt anything in a hundred years."

Alex frowned as he looked from Elizabeth to Jon, then back again to Elizabeth.

"If you want out of here, you've got to try it again," she said. "Both of you."

She didn't know what she was saying, Jon thought. She didn't have a clue how painful that brief experience had been.

Jon walked away. He went to the picture window and looked out at the light snow falling and at Dalton House, the place where Alex should have lived a good, long life. But he hadn't. He'd been stuck in this godforsaken Victorian with no way out.

He turned and looked at Alexander—his great-grandfather, a man who'd known pain for a hundred years. Surely, Jon thought, he could endure a little—for Alexander's sake.

"She's right, Alex," Jon finally said. "We have to do this if we're going to get you out of here."

Jon held out his hand again, and slowly, Alex took hold.

Jon closed his eyes to the agony. "Come closer, Alex." Jon felt the heat racing up his arm, through his chest, his legs. He felt as if he'd slipped and fallen into the furnace in his foundry, the pain was so intense. He fought to breathe. His chest heaved, and he forced the torture from his mind.

Jon opened his eyes and saw the tears flowing down Elizabeth's cheeks. "Don't cry." He managed to laugh. "This is only a temporary condition."

Elizabeth slipped her fingers into his and they felt like ice against his skin.

"You're burning up, Jon. You can't do this."

"You'd be amazed at the things I can do, Ellie."

"I've sampled some of them. I want a chance to try others, too," she said. "Please, Jon, don't do this. We can think of some other way."

It's hotter than Hades in here! Quit your jabbering and let's see if this works.

"Did you hear that?" Jon asked Elizabeth, and she shook her head. "Well, our friend Alex is raising a ruckus inside my body. I can hear everything he's saying perfectly clear. Come on, let's see if we can walk out of here."

Elizabeth opened the door, and Jon easily walked out onto the porch. "We're outside, Alex," Jon said.

Well, thunder and tarnation, don't this beat all? I can see everything plain as day, just like I'm looking through your eyes. Come on, boy, I've got more things to see before you're through with me.

Jon smiled, and Elizabeth frowned. "Are you all right?"

"For the moment." Jon gripped the railing as they walked down the stairs, then wrapped his arm around Elizabeth's shoulder for support when they reached the street. Thank God they didn't have to contend with wind and heavy snow as they made their way toward Dalton House, Jon thought, and thank God none of their friends were roaming about. He'd have a hell of a time explaining the awkwardness of his walk, or the heat burning his skin if someone shook his hand.

Slowly, Jon mounted the steps leading to his home and Elizabeth rushed ahead of him, opening the door so he wouldn't have to exert what little energy remained in his body.

He walked through the entry and turned around slowly.

Well, I'll be! I'd almost forgot how pretty this place is. Always loved those stained glass windows. Your great-great-grandfather had them shipped here all the way from England. And that chandelier up there—Jon could hear Alex whistle inside his head and the shrillness of it sent pains shooting through his skull. But he refused to tell him to stop. For the first time in a hundred years Alex was halfway free.

"Tell me about the chandelier, Alex," Jon said. "Is there something special about it?"

Jedediah took Amanda and his wife on a European tour when Amanda was just about five. They were in some castle in Austria and Amanda couldn't take her eyes off the chandelier. She said it was the prettiest thing she'd ever seen. Well, Mr. Dalton was a very rich man, and he loved Amanda something fierce. He made a downright fool of himself bargaining for that thing. Paid a damn sight more than it was worth and shipped it home. I remember the way Amanda stopped to look at it every time she came through this room. Her eyes sparkled prettier than those crystals.

"Is he talking to you, Jon?" Elizabeth asked.

Jon put his finger to his lips. "I'll tell you later." He hated to keep Elizabeth in the dark, but he didn't want to interrupt Alex. When he was calm like that, when he was reflective, the pain lessened, and Jon rather enjoyed listening to his great-grandfather talk. It was like listening to his grandfather's stories all over again.

With Elizabeth's hand on his arm, Jon slowly crossed the floor and put a foot on the marble staircase. Each step up the stairs took effort, and halfway up, Jon grasped the banister to help pull himself up. "Remind me to install an elevator in this place one of these days," he managed to joke.

He heard Elizabeth's weak laugh.

I carried Amanda up these stairs once, Alex said. *It was the night of her father's funeral.*

Jon felt Alexander's sadness, not only in his body, but in his heart. He'd only heard stories about his ancestors; suddenly they seemed real, like they were there in Dalton House right now.

When they entered Amanda's room, Jon sat in one of the dainty Chippendale chairs before the fireplace, hoping and praying it would support his weight.

I remember this room. Amanda and I talked here about the family we wanted to raise. We talked about going to Europe on our honeymoon and buying chandeliers for each of our children.

Jon's throat tightened at the emotion in Alexander's words. What, he wondered, would happen when they showed Alex the picture of Thomas, when they let him know he and Amanda had fathered a child?

I like chandeliers. They always remind me of Amanda. Jon heard and felt Alexander sigh deeply. *She must have hated me something awful when I disappeared.*

Jon watched Elizabeth open the box he'd taken from the drawer and placed on top of the vanity. She pulled the locket from inside and lifted the frame with Thomas's photo, too. She walked toward him, holding the picture frame to her breasts. "Do you remember this locket, Alex?" she asked, holding it before Jon's eyes.

That was my wedding present to Amanda. I gave it to her the night before I died.

Jon repeated Alexander's words so Elizabeth could hear, then he took the frame and looked closely at the picture of Thomas. "This was my grandfather when he was a young man," Jon said.

He has Amanda's smile.

"It might be her smile, Alex, but what about his eyes, his hair? Look closely." Jon popped open the locket and held the small picture of Alex next to the larger one of Thomas.

There was too much silence for too long a time, and suddenly Jon could feel the pain intensify, could feel sorrow ripping through his body.

That's my son, Alex cried.

Jon felt Alexander's tears, his sobs, and slowly, he experienced his joy.

"Elizabeth and I realized it just this afternoon," Jon said.

Jon felt the pain again.

How she must have hated me. I gave her a child, and then I left.

"You had no control over what happened, Alex," Jon told him, trying to ease his sorrow. "Luke had everything planned. He needed someone to take the fall for the bank robbery and the murder, and he wanted to marry Amanda. By getting rid of you, he covered both bases."

None of that matters!

Alex raged inside Jon's body, and Jon could feel every tormented movement and thought. Jon's heart beat rapidly. The pain intensified, and the locket slipped from his fingers to the floor as he clutched his chest.

Elizabeth dropped the box and grabbed Jon's arms. "We've got to get you out of here."

"I don't know if I can stand."

"You've got to. Please, Jon."

He tried to move, but Alexander's anger took away all his strength. "I can't, Ellie."

Elizabeth grabbed Jon's arms and pulled, budging him only an inch in the chair. "You're hurting him, Alex!" she yelled. She shook Jon's shoulders as if Alex could feel it, too. "Stop it. Please. I don't know what's going on, Alex, but if you don't stop, you're going to kill him."

Tears flooded her eyes and spilled down her cheeks. "He's your great-grandson, Alex. Please. Don't hurt him."

Jon felt the rage slowly subside, and somehow he pushed up from the chair and willed himself to remain standing. "Let's get out of here, Ellie."

Elizabeth swept the locket into the box. She held it with one hand and Jon with the other, leading him carefully down the stairs and back into the street. He thought they'd never reach the hotel, thought he'd die before they got inside, and the moment he crossed the threshold, he felt Alex rip from his body. His fingers and toes numbed. His legs cramped, but he made it to the sofa before he collapsed.

He had no idea how much time had elapsed before he opened his eyes. Elizabeth knelt before him with her head resting in his lap. She seemed to sense him stirring and looked up. Damn, but she had the prettiest smile he'd ever seen. "I could sure use a beer if you've got one."

Her smile deepened. "Don't move."

As if he could, Jon thought. He felt like he'd been on a ten-day drinking binge and run over by a semi as he lay passed out in the street.

His strength was just barely returning when Elizabeth popped open the tab and set the can on the table in front of him, but it didn't take more than a moment to realize he needed her a hell of a lot more than he needed the beer. He wrapped one big hand around her neck, weaving his fingers through her hair, and pulled her close. His mouth covered hers with every spare ounce of power and passion in his body. Hell, everything had been drained from him when Alex had inhabited his insides, but now that Alex was out of his body, he felt he was slowly getting everything back tenfold.

Again his heart beat rapidly against his ribs, but it wasn't pain he experienced this time, it was longing and desire, and he wanted to lift Elizabeth into his arms and carry her back to his bed.

She seemed to sense his need and drew away, taking his fingers and pulling him with her from the sofa. "Do you think you can make it up the stairs?" she whispered.

"Upstairs, downstairs, doesn't really matter, Ellie," he teased, and felt another surge of power flow through his veins. He swept her up in his arms and didn't give her time to protest. Instead, he covered her mouth with his lips and took the stairs two at a time. He pushed through the bedroom door and closed it behind them. "Is that door going to keep Alex out?" he asked, as he laid Elizabeth down on the bed.

"Alex goes where he wants when he wants. But he took Amanda's box and said he wanted to be alone. I don't think he'll bother us, not for a good long time."

Jon smiled slowly and lowered his body over hers. "Mind if *I* bother you for a good long time?"

Elizabeth shook her head as her fingers wove through his hair. "You're no bother, Jon. No bother at all."

Chapter 18

Alex stood outside the bedroom door and listened, trying to recapture a memory. He had lain with Amanda behind closed doors once, and he'd loved her. Oh, how he'd loved her. She had skin softer than rose petals and as pearly white as freshly skimmed cream. She tasted sweeter than molasses, and . . . and he'd gotten her with child and left her. God knows what she'd suffered.

Amanda had deserved so much more. She'd wanted a house full of children, she'd told him, as they'd lain together beneath covers of pink satin and white lace. Twelve children, she'd said, and begun ticking off names she'd already picked. Thomas would be first, of course, since that was her mother's maiden name. Each child would be pampered and spoiled, and she didn't care a fig if Alexander had other ideas on how to raise their children. At the time Alex figured if that's what Amanda wanted, spoiling them sounded like a right nice idea.

But he'd never even had the chance to hold his son, let alone spoil him.

Oh, how Amanda must have hated him for leaving her.

He floated down the stairwell, leaving his great-grandson and Elizabeth alone. They didn't deserve prying eyes or listening ears—not from him, not from anyone.

He sat on the chesterfield and twiddled his thumbs, thinking about the old man who'd visited Jon in the hotel all those years ago. *Thomas . . . his child.* Alex wished he had talked to the man, wished he had touched him. He'd been so near to his son, yet so far away.

A tear trickled slowly down his cheek.

Life hadn't been fair.

Not to Amanda.

Not to Thomas.

Not to Alex.

He wiped the tear away and roamed aimlessly around the empty room. He swept Amanda's heart-shaped box from the table and carried it to the foot of the steps, sat down, and took off the cover. She'd worn pink ribbons in her hair the day they'd met, and he touched them now, wishing he could feel their smoothness. Instead, he tried to remember how they'd felt, how Amanda's hair had felt, all soft and shiny and blond. He brought the ribbon to his nose and pretended he could smell the sweet fragrance she'd always worn. But he couldn't feel. Couldn't smell.

Couldn't do a damn thing but want her!

He crushed the ribbon in his fist and closed his eyes. Don't hate me, Amanda. Please, don't hate me, he prayed silently.

Opening his eyes, he dropped the ribbon into the

box and thumbed through the rest of the contents, taking out the golden locket, the one he'd given to her the night before he died, and he looked inside it once more. "Alex loves Amanda," it read. The sentiment hadn't faded with age, not from the locket, not from his heart.

The box fell from his lap. His concentration centered on the past, not on the present, and his power to hold something solid in anything but his fingers had diminished. After he wiped away another tear, he leaned over and picked up the box, wanting to keep Amanda's belongings clean and safe for as long as possible. They were the only things he had to remember her by, except his memories, and the pictures Elizabeth had given him.

He dropped a pearl-studded hat pin into the box and watched it slide to the edge. It seemed an odd thing to happen when he knew he was holding it level. Suddenly he realized the bottom of the box had shifted and one side was higher than the other. He plucked at the insides, using all his concentration to finally pull the fabric-coated bottom out of the box.

Wedged inside was a piece of paper, and Alex thought his hands would shake off his arms in his nervousness to pull it out. He placed the box on the table and carefully unfolded the sheet of pink stationery. It was Amanda's writing. He'd know the dainty swirls anywhere.

My dearest Alexander,

It's been so long since you went away, but I see

your face every waking and sleeping moment.

The people in town have said so many horrible things about you, but I don't believe a word. Luke has tried to convince me it's true, but I refuse to listen to anything he says. I don't know why I married him. I did it so suddenly while grieving for you that I did not think of the consequences. Now I realize the wagging tongues of the people in town would have been easier to accept than the presence of a man I loathe.

We have a son now. No, not Luke's child, but yours, my dearest. He is happy and chubby and looks just as I imagine you must have looked as an infant. I've named him Thomas, as I told you I would. I hope you will see him one day. I know you will love him just as I do.

Luke knows the truth, of course. I told him before our marriage, and he knows no other child will be his because I will not allow him to touch me. I have given him a home and money and power. He does not need me, too. That, my dearest, was for you and you alone.

You're in my heart, the place where you'll always be. I've locked your memory away, for I fear Luke would try to steal it from me if he could.

I know whatever took you away from me was beyond your control. You loved me. That sweet thought and our son are what keep me alive and happy.

Someday you'll come back for me. I don't know when, I don't know how, yet I know you'll return. And I'll give you my love all over again.

Amanda

Alex swooped from the stairs to the top of the ceiling. He caught hold of a brass rung on the chandelier and swung carefree and happy like a circus performer, then shot up the stairwell and stood once again before Elizabeth's door.

He put his hand up to knock. Thunder and tarnation! They were having their own kind of fun, and once upon a time he'd known how to be polite and leave people alone. There was time enough to tell them his news.

Amanda had never stopped loving him.

If he had to stay on earth another hundred years, so be it.

Amanda had never stopped loving him.

Her letter was enough to sustain him through anything and everything. He clasped the piece of pink stationery to his heart and floated up to his attic room, to his window, and to thoughts of the woman he loved.

Jon leaned against the kitchen counter and watched Elizabeth expertly crack eggs with her left hand while sautéing onions and bell peppers with her right. And to think he'd once told her he was incredibly talented with his hands. Hers, he decided, could do many things at once, too. Wonderful things, the least of which was fix him a breakfast fit for a king. He much preferred the wonderful things she'd done to him in her bedroom, in his bedroom, in his studio. Lord knows what they could do for each other when he took her back to Schoolmarm Gulch in the spring and made love to her in a blanket of flowers.

"Penny for your thoughts?" she said, tilting her

head toward him as she blew a wisp of hair from her cheek.

"Mind if I offer my thoughts instead?" Alex interrupted, appearing literally out of nowhere. He sat on the counter next to Jon with his arms folded across his chest and grinned, first at Jon, then at Elizabeth. "It appears you don't mind, so here's the plan for today."

Alex jumped down and circled the room, his hands folded behind his back. "First off, I want out of here. One hundred years is long enough."

"We're trying to think of a way, Alex," Elizabeth said.

"You've been upstairs making love," Alex fired back, "and I've been moping around feeling sorry for myself. We haven't been thinking about getting me out of here, but that's over now." He stopped next to Elizabeth and leaned over the skillet. He pretended to inhale. "I want to smell food again. I have the feeling God might make that an option in heaven."

He climbed back on the counter again. "While you two were indisposed last night, I found a letter from Amanda stuck in the bottom of that jewelry box. She said she loved me. Said she'd never stop, and said she knew I'd come back for her someday. Well, I aim to do what she wants."

"So, what's your plan?" Jon asked.

Alex shrugged. "That's your assignment. Figure something out, and the sooner you do it, the better. You have to prove my innocence, and I need revenge."

"Why don't we just concentrate on the innocence

part?" Elizabeth asked. "I told you before, revenge won't get you anything."

"I beg to differ with you," Alex snapped back. "Luke Winchester took away my life, he hurt Amanda, he hurt my son. Luke Winchester's no longer around to suffer for what he did, but Matt Winchester is, and from him I'll seek revenge."

Jon laughed and eased some of the tension in the room. "Thank God I'm not a Winchester any longer."

"I'm mighty happy about that myself," Alex said. He draped an arm around Jon's shoulders, and Jon jumped at the instant shock of a thousand needles prickling his skin.

"Tarnation!" Alex bellowed. "I don't want to climb inside you again, I just want to touch my own flesh and blood."

"Maybe that's the problem," Elizabeth said. "He *is* your own flesh and blood, he's part of you and you're part of him. If you touch him, you become him."

"I think she's right," Jon said. "So for now, let's just *pretend* you want to show some grandfatherly affection, okay?"

Alexander's laughter bounced off the walls. "Grandfather, huh? Has a nice sound to it, although I would have preferred hearing *Pa* or *Dad* once or twice." Alex waved the thoughts away. "Doesn't matter anymore. What matters now is finding that evidence. So, what do we have so far? Phoebe's diary?"

"Which, more than likely, no one will believe," Elizabeth stated.

"Amanda's note?" Jon asked.

"Personal and private," Alex declared. "It says Thomas was my son, but any fool can look at the pictures and figure that out."

"So we have nothing," Elizabeth said.

Alex shrugged. "What about this?" He reached into his inside coat pocket and withdrew an envelope. "I'd almost forgotten about it." He took a piece of paper from inside. "Jedediah Dalton gave this to me the day he signed the property over. It was a copy of what he planned to say at the wedding, and he figured I might be too caught up in the excitement to hear his words. He wanted to make sure I knew how he felt."

"Why didn't you show it to me before?" Elizabeth asked.

"It's one of those personal and private things I didn't want to share. Guess maybe I should have."

Alex slowly unfolded the stationery and began to read.

Alexander,

You are my partner, my friend, and the son I always wanted. The greatest treasure I could give you, for all you have meant to me, is my daughter's love. But that she has given to you freely.

Now I have only one thing left to give, and I do so just as willingly. All that I own is yours—my home, my businesses, my wealth. Share them, as you will your love, with my daughter, your children, and your children's children.

And be happy.

Your servant,
Jedediah Dalton

"Do you think this is enough proof?" Alex asked.

Jon felt a tightness in his throat for the pain, the loss, and the truth of what that piece of paper meant. He sought out words to say to Alex, taking a deep breath and exhaling slowly. "That note won't do us any good at all," he said finally.

"And why not?" Alex fired back.

"Because the moment it leaves your hands, it will disappear. We see it only because you want us to, just the way we see you."

"We need tangible evidence," Elizabeth stressed.

"I died with it in my pocket," Alex said. "That means I must have been buried with it."

"You don't want us to dig up your body, do you?" Elizabeth asked incredulously.

"Hell, no! But I don't see any other choice."

Jon shook his head.

Elizabeth turned the fire off under the skillet. "Suddenly," she said, "this omelet doesn't look so appetizing."

"Are you sure this is the right spot?" Jon asked, as he tossed another shovelful of dirt out of the four-foot hole he'd dug.

"Of course I'm sure," Alex bellowed, as he paced back and forth. "Just keep digging."

They were at the far end of the basement, a dark, cobweb-strewn place no one in his right mind would venture to unless he had a perfectly good reason. At least the dirt was easy to dig, Jon thought, as he shoveled another load, and another.

He hit something hard and closed his eyes, fearing he'd hit bone. As much as he wanted to uncover that letter Alex had carried in his vest, he didn't want to find the body.

"What was that?" Elizabeth asked, leaning over to look into the pit.

Jon moved the lantern closer to the spot where his shovel was stuck into a good eight inches of dirt. "I don't know." He knelt down and began to dig more cautiously with his fingers, moving out only a handful of dirt at a time.

Something white came into view, and he swallowed deeply. He moved a few more scoops of dirt, then dusted a thin layer away with gloved fingers.

He closed his eyes and leaned back against the edge of the hole.

"What's wrong, Jon?" Elizabeth called down.

He looked up into two pairs of worried eyes. "I found it," he whispered. He turned his gaze downward again, and the empty eye sockets in Alexander's skull stared back.

"Want some help?" Elizabeth asked.

He shook his head. "No, thanks. It's bad enough that one of us has to do this. Maybe it would be better if you didn't look down. You either, Alex."

"You're damn right I won't look down. I've got a hell of a lot of memories about that dirt, and none of them are pleasant. No need dredging them up now."

Jon went back to work, bit by bit tossing dirt into a bucket and handing it out to Elizabeth to dump. Slowly, he uncovered more. Tattered shreds of fabric, rotting leather shoes, a tarnished belt buckle, and a few coins that had fallen from where a pants pocket once had been.

"Have you found it yet?" Alex called out.

"Not yet."

"Well, hurry up. I'm not particularly fond of this place."

Jon dug around the edges of the skeleton looking for something, anything, but he knew his search was useless. What could he tell Alex? That it had been too long? That there was nothing here but bones? Hell, he had no choice in the matter; he had to tell him the truth.

Standing up, Jon easily looked over the top of the hole. He smiled weakly when he saw Elizabeth. A deep sadness furrowed her brow, and he realized she knew.

Jon looked across the basement to the place where Alexander paced back and forth, back and forth, twirling something on his finger.

The ring.

Amanda's wedding ring.

Jon knelt back down and blew dust and dirt from the delicate fingerbones that lay haphazardly at the body's side. Luke Winchester hadn't laid Alex gently to rest in the bottom of the hole before shoveling in dirt. He'd dumped him, and Jon felt the sting of tears in his eyes for the treatment Alex hadn't deserved, for the experiences—the wife, the son, the other children—Alex had missed.

At least the ring wasn't missing. At least Luke hadn't robbed Alex of that, too. Maybe it was that ring that had kept Alex and Amanda tied together forever.

Jon climbed up to the basement floor and Alex was immediately at his side. "Do you have it?" he asked.

Jon shook his head. "Most everything's disintegrated. I'm sorry."

Alex just stood there and stared at him, the corners of his mouth turned down in disbelief. "I thought this was my chance. I thought . . . hell, what does it matter, anyway? I was getting used to sticking around this place. Maybe you can take me out for a stroll once in a while, when you're in need of a little pain."

"Stop it, Alex," Elizabeth yelled. "Stop it right now. We *will* get you out. We *will* prove your innocence."

"How?" Alex thundered. "Do you think Luke Winchester left anything behind saying he killed me?"

"Maybe not, but . . ."

"But what?" Jon asked when he saw the look of intense concentration on Elizabeth's face.

"Matt told me that Luke Winchester liked trophies, reminders of his conquests, and that half the animal heads hanging at Winchester Place had belonged to him. Maybe Luke kept all the property deeds when he robbed the bank, especially the one saying Alex was the rightful owner to the Dalton estate. Luke would have gloated over that victory."

"And how do you propose we find something like that? Break into Matt's home and search for it?"

Elizabeth nodded.

"I don't think so, Ellie," Jon said, shaking his head.

"Do you have a better plan?" she asked.

"No, but . . ."

"But nothing," Elizabeth tossed back. "I'll go alone if you don't want to help me."

"It's dangerous. It's insane. Hell, Ellie, I'll go, but you're not going with me."

"You're not going *without* me."

Jon smoothed dirt from her cheek. She looked pretty, and he couldn't imagine doing anything ever again without her. "You can go, but only if you do what I tell you to."

"Would I ever do anything else?" she asked.

"Always."

He shook his head, grabbed the blanket he'd brought down to the basement, and lowered himself once again into the hole. Carefully he covered Alex's body and stood silently for a moment, his hands folded in prayer. No one had said a prayer when he was buried, but Jon vowed that when all this was over, when Alex was reunited with Amanda, he and Elizabeth would give him a proper burial.

Suddenly he realized he'd said "when all this was over," and for the first time he truly believed they'd find a way to help.

"Are you about ready to get out of here, Alex?" Jon called out.

"For one hundred years," Alex yelled back. "Can't you hurry it up?"

That's what he liked to hear. He would miss the cantankerous old guy, but he'd have a lot of memories to hold on to.

Jon gripped the edge of the hole to pull himself out, but the ground caved away from around his fingers and he fell, slamming backward against the wall.

Dirt crumbled away, layer upon layer, and slowly, wood slats appeared where a solid wall of soil once had been.

Jon looked over the edge of the hole at Elizabeth and Alex. "I think I've discovered Luke's tunnel."

"Made a convenient grave, didn't it?" Alex said, his laughter filling the basement. "I might have had a chance to struggle and get free if he hadn't already had this thing dug."

"It supposedly leads into the bank," Elizabeth said. "Want to check it out?"

"Personally, I'd rather break into Matt's house before we break into the bank. My chances of conviction might not be as high that way."

Jon set the lantern on the basement floor and crawled out of the hole. Elizabeth put her hands on his cheeks when he finally stood before her. She brushed away dirt and mud from his nose and chin, and then she kissed him. "Maybe they'll give us adjoining cells," she said.

Jon laughed. "I'm the mayor. Maybe I could talk the judge into a single."

Alex cleared his throat. "If you don't mind, do you think you could give my situation a moment's thought instead of jabbering on and on about prison accommodations? I've got a woman waiting somewhere for me, and I'd sure like to get to her before another century passes."

Chapter 19

"How do you propose we get Matt out of the house?" Elizabeth asked, turning away from the window that looked out across the park next door and down to the end of the street. They'd taken turns watching. In the late afternoon Jon had seen Matt go into Winchester Place, and together and separately they'd waited for him to exit, hoping some business or other engagement would draw him away from the house. But the man wasn't co-operating.

Just as Alex had said earlier, it seemed useless, Elizabeth thought. Surely there must be some better plan. Of course, from the looks of her companions, she was the only one who cared.

Alex sat on one end of the chesterfield, twiddling his thumbs, and Jon sat at the other, leaning back with his fingers wrapped behind his neck. His eyes looked closed, but she knew they weren't. They watched her, and she felt the same shiver she'd felt that first day. This time, though, it wasn't a fear of the unknown that sent that tremor through her body, it was anticipation of what was yet to come.

Slowly he rose and walked toward her, slid his

fingers into the hair at her temples, tilted her face, and kissed her. "Maybe it's time we asked someone else to help us out," he said, his hands still cupping her face.

"And who do you know besides me who's willing to break into a man's house to help a ghost?"

"I don't want someone else to break in," Jon said, laughing softly. "We need someone to get him out."

"I could have done that hours ago if I'd wanted to put my body on the line. All it would have taken is a phone call, a dinner invitation, and a seductive dress."

"You're never going near him again, Ellie," Jon said, turning her in his arms and holding her tight so they could watch Matt's house together. "I don't even like the idea of you going into that house with me."

He rested his chin in her hair and he felt so right, so good. She'd never liked being on the receiving end of orders, but she didn't seem to mind when they came from Jon. After all, he wanted to protect her. And Lord, it felt nice to be protected.

Right now, though, she wanted this whole thing to end so she could go on with her life, so Alexander could go on to another stage of his. She didn't want protection to be necessary any longer.

"I do know someone who wouldn't mind spending time with Matt," Jon said.

Surprised at his words, Elizabeth tilted her head to look into his eyes. "Who'd be crazy enough to want that?"

"Francesca."

"Francesca? Your friend with boyfriend problems? The one who's been seeing Matt?"

Jon laughed. "I get the sense you don't like her?"

"Why shouldn't I like her? I don't know a thing about her."

"You're jealous."

"That's impossible. You said she's just a friend, and I believe you. Of course, what kind of friend would want to help us break into someone's house?"

"An undercover agent for fish and wildlife."

Elizabeth twisted around to see the laughter in Jon's eyes. Undercover agent? Francesca? That flame-haired beauty? The woman Elizabeth had despised the moment they met?

"Speaking of Francesca, it looks like help's just arrived," Jon said, and Elizabeth turned back to the window.

She saw the same olive-drab truck she'd seen parked in front of the cafe last night. She saw her brother climb out in army fatigues, and petite, pretty Francesca climbed out right behind, dressed in the same type of camouflage attire.

Tears welled in the corners of Elizabeth's eyes. "He's going to get arrested tonight, isn't he?" she asked. She didn't mention her brother's name; she knew Jon understood.

"More than likely. There's nothing we can do about it now, though," he said, pulling her more tightly into his arms.

Matt came out of the house as she watched, a rifle tucked under his arm. He shook hands with Francesca and Eric; they talked for several minutes, then climbed into the truck and drove out of town.

She should have been happy Matt had gone.

They could go to Winchester Place, hopefully find the missing deeds, and perhaps solve all of Alexander's problems. But she wasn't happy.

Unfortunately, she didn't have time to weep.

The dark of night and the lightly falling snow gave Jon and Elizabeth the cover they needed as they headed down the street to Winchester Place.

"That's the butler's room," Jon said, pointing to a lighted window on the second floor. They stood still for a moment at the edge of Matt's property and watched a darkened silhouette moving about in the room, finally shutting off the light.

Elizabeth sighed with relief and Jon clutched her hand as they soundlessly made their way to the back of the house.

Jon had once told Elizabeth there was no need to lock doors when you lived in Sapphire because the crime rate was pretty close to zero. Of course, he hadn't been counting what they were doing right now when he'd thrown out that figure. She'd laughed at the notion of leaving a door unlocked anywhere, but tonight she rather liked the idea as Jon turned a knob at the rear of the mansion, and they easily walked inside.

"Where should we begin?" Elizabeth whispered.

"It's a big place, but I keep thinking about those trophies you mentioned. My guess is we start in the drawing room."

Jon held a flashlight out and shined the thin beam down at the floor. He reached behind him and captured Elizabeth's hand. "Don't go anywhere without me."

She squeezed his fingers in answer, trying to make as little noise as possible.

When they reached the drawing room, her stomach cramped, partly in fear, partly in remembrance of the way Matt had touched her and the way she'd broken that glass and held it to his neck. She loathed the man, and with any luck, they'd bring his little game to an end tonight.

Sadly, her brother was going to be caught in the trap, too.

They went from table to table, carefully sifting through drawers so nothing would look out of place. They lifted carpets and bearskin rugs and checked for hidden doorways leading to a basement, but they found nothing.

"Let's try another room," Jon said, pulling Elizabeth after him.

"Wait." Elizabeth tugged on his hand to make him stop.

"Why? We've looked at everything."

"We must have knocked into that moose head. It's crooked. Just give me a second to straighten it." Elizabeth twisted the oak mounting and heard a groan. She swallowed hard and looked at the animal whose glass eyes stared aimlessly across the room. She twisted the mounting a little more to the left and heard the same groan. She watched the gun cabinet slide along the wall.

"I can't believe he's stupid enough to put the control behind a moose head," she said. "It's so obvious, that's the first place anyone would look."

"*We* almost overlooked it," Jon whispered, then held a finger to his lips to silence anything else she might say.

Smiling with some degree of victory, he took her fingers and led her through the passage.

They descended a narrow staircase, the beam from the flashlight the only thing keeping them from walking in total darkness. They reached the floor and Jon shone the light across the walls.

Hundreds of eyes stared back at them. Bald eagles sat with talons wrapped tightly around fake tree branches that protruded from the plaster. A bobcat poised on the edge of a boulder, and a California condor perched on a tree branch above it. "He's made this place into a gallery," Jon stated.

"More like a mausoleum, if you ask me," Elizabeth said. She stepped back, away from the displays, and tripped. She fell to the floor, feeling fur beneath her.

"Are you okay?" Jon asked, giving her a hand and pulling her up.

"I think so." She looked sadly at the head of a grizzly she'd tripped over, its fur flat against the floor, its legs and paws spread out with the claws extended. What other horrors would she find, she wondered, if all the lights were on?

Jon pulled her away from the bearskin. "Let's see if we can find what we came for and get out of here."

He managed to locate a desk and pulled on the drawer. "It's locked." He tugged harder. "Maybe this is where Matt's records are hidden. Nothing else is locked around here." He pulled out his jackknife and wedged it against the catch, jimmying it around until he heard a click. Slowly he pulled and the drawer slid open.

He rummaged around inside, careful not to displace the contents, and took out a ledger. Opening the book on top of the desk, Jon shone the flashlight onto the paper. "Look at this, Ellie. Dates, names of hunters, amounts paid, and what animals they wanted to kill. Not one legal hunt listed here, and a lot of protected species. There's enough here to hang him."

"What about my brother?" she asked, quickly scanning the list of names.

"I don't see it. But that doesn't mean his name's not listed. We can deal with that later, though. Maybe I can work something out with Francesca."

She had to let it go at that. They were in another man's home illegally. They had broken into a drawer and were stealing someone else's possessions. They didn't have time to deal with her fears.

"What about the deeds?" Elizabeth asked, hoping that would be the evidence they needed to unravel all the loose edges of the hundred-year-old crime.

Jon rummaged through the rest of the drawers. "I think this is all we're going to find."

Somehow Elizabeth managed to smile, although her heart wasn't in it, and she followed Jon up the stairs and back into the drawing room. They went to the moose head and Jon twisted it, just as Elizabeth had. Slowly the gun cabinet slid back into place.

Jon kissed her nose and gripped her fingers. "Come on, Ellie. Let's get out of here."

They took the same path out of the house that they'd taken coming in, quietly opened and closed the back door, and headed outside. The snow was falling harder now, covering up all traces of their tracks. With the ledger safely tucked under Jon's jacket, they walked quickly up the street, trying not to draw any attention.

Elizabeth was closing the hotel door behind them when she saw the lights of the olive-drab truck heading toward Winchester Place.

"I wonder why they're back so soon?" Elizabeth said, leaning heavily against the door. She took several slow, easy breaths of relief while Jon looked through the window.

"It's only Matt. Doesn't make sense that he'd come back alone."

Elizabeth began to worry, but Jon stilled her fears with a kiss. "Everything's going to be all right," he said, cupping her face in his hands. "Francesca knows what she's doing."

Jon slid his fingers behind her head and wove them through her hair. "Do you like the life of an undercover operative?"

She caressed his cheek and put one hand over his heart. Even through the lamb's wool coat and the journal still tucked underneath, she could feel the heavy rise and fall of his chest and knew, deep inside, he didn't like that life any more than she did. "I'll leave the intrigue to the Francescas of the world. Personally, I'd prefer operating an inn, cooking elegant meals, and having you pay me nightly visits."

Jon's smile disappeared, replaced by a mixture of relief, fear, and lust. He leaned down and kissed her long and hard, his fingers tightening in her hair.

"We're not doing anything stupid like that again, Ellie," he stated, whispering the words in her ear.

"If something had happened to you—"

"Nothing's going to happen to me," she interrupted. "I've already had my brush with death."

"Is that a promise?" Jon asked.

"It's a promise."

Alex cleared his throat. "Excuse me. I've been worried, too. Does that matter to either of you?"

"Don't worry, Alex," Jon said. "We found something to help you get your revenge."

Alex looked annoyed. "I wasn't worried about that. Thunder and tarnation! I was worried about the two of you tangling with that lily-livered buzzard."

Elizabeth leaned into Jon's chest and laughed.

"What we found is going to put that lily-livered buzzard behind bars, but it's not the information we wanted to find," Jon said, shrugging out of his coat. He carried the ledger to the chesterfield and leaned over to inspect the records. Alex did the same.

Close together like that, Elizabeth could see the resemblance. Although more than half a foot and probably a hundred pounds separated them in size, it was easy to see the family traits: the blond hair, the strong jaw and cleft chin, and the thumbs that twiddled when they were deep in thought.

She hung up her coat and joined them, sitting on the floor at Jon's side.

"Did you find my brother's name?"

Jon nodded, and she swallowed hard, wishing the truth didn't hurt so much. "Anyone else?" she asked, biting back her tears.

"No locals. A state senator from somewhere back East who I've seen mentioned in the papers a time or two. He's paid big money to get what he wanted, and he'll probably pay big money to make his bail and pay the fines once he's been tried. Looks like he was with Matt and his dad on that last trip to Florida, too. Hunting alligator isn't illegal anymore, but I don't know the limit or season, and it shows here that they made a haul."

"How does this help me?" Alex asked.

"It puts Matt in prison for a while," Jon told him, as he flipped through more pages.

"But what about the deed? Everything rightly belongs to you."

"We couldn't find the records," Elizabeth said. "Just the outfitting ledger."

"I've already got more than I need," Jon said. "Thomas took care of that, so the deeds don't matter all that much."

"It's not right, though," Alex said. "I don't want that Winchester to have anything that rightly belongs to you."

Alex sighed deeply and floated up from the sofa and across the room. He stood at the window and parted the curtains, looking down the road to Dalton House. "Do you think there might be enough evidence in those ledgers?" he whispered. "I'm getting awfully tired of this existence."

"I think you're the only one who can decide if it's enough," Elizabeth said. "You wanted revenge. You swore you wouldn't rest until all the Winchesters were out of town. With the information we have, we can get rid of Matt. We can smear his name and make it so he won't come back to Sapphire once he gets out of jail, and we can set the record straight about what happened a hundred years ago."

Elizabeth walked across the room and rested a shoulder against the wall next to Alex. "The property's not important to Jon. Is it all that important to you?"

He tilted his head to look at her, and that slow grin she'd come to love crossed his face. He shook his head. "No. All that matters is Amanda."

"Then I say we have a quick celebration before Francesca shows up for that ledger and I have to face watching my brother get hauled off to jail. Once that's done, we can take you back to Dalton House and see if we can send you on your way."

"You think it's going to be that easy?" Alex asked.

"I hope so." She smiled at Alex and at Jon. "Right now, I want to celebrate. I've got wine and bread and cheesecake. I know you can't eat or drink, Alex, but you don't mind sharing one more evening of fun with us, do you?"

Alex grinned. "Only if you'll let me swing from the chandelier."

"To Alexander Stewart." Jon raised his glass of wine, and his sapphire eyes sparkled, brightening the room even more than the crystal chandelier overhead. "May your days on earth be few."

Alexander's laughter thundered through the room. "A right nice sentiment, grandson. But now it's my turn." He raised his empty glass and added his own cheer. "To Jon and Ellie. May you have as much happiness in your lifetime as . . . as Amanda and I would have had in ours."

Music echoed through the room, and Jon took Elizabeth into his arms, waltzing her around and around while Alex swung once on the chandelier then swooped to the mantel to stretch out and watch.

"Think you're going to be able to let him go?" Jon asked, whispering in her ear.

Elizabeth rested her head on Jon's chest, feeling his warmth and the slow, steady rhythm of his heart. "It's not going to be easy."

Jon's arms tightened and his dance steps shortened. They whirled together beneath a calm, steady chandelier, his hands caressing her back, hers caressing his neck. Their legs moved together as one, slow and close. And he tilted his head and kissed her, even slower, even closer.

"Mind if I cut in?" Alex interrupted. "You've had the pleasure of the lady's company all night, and if you're lucky, you'll have it for the rest of your life. If you don't mind, I'd like at least a minute."

Jon brushed her lips one more time and released her into Alexander's open arms. But Alex didn't touch her. Not yet. He moved back a foot and offered her a most gracious and gentlemanly bow. Elizabeth smiled in return and curtsied, pretending she wore one of those frilly pink ruffled dresses that Amanda had liked to wear.

Alex moved closer then, and she felt his strange, weightless touch as he took her hand in his, placing his other lightly at her waist. "It's been a while. Forgive me if I step on your toes."

"I'm sure I won't feel a thing." She laughed and allowed Alex to lead her around the room. She was positive he could lift her high into the air if he wanted to, but instead he held her at arm's length and smiled as he waltzed.

"Amanda and I waltzed at our engagement party. Maybe we'll get another chance."

He spoke with so much hope it nearly brought tears to her eyes. "When you're together again," she said, "tell her about tonight, about Jon, and me. And tell her we loved you."

"Right after I kiss her and hold her and tell her how much I love her."

She looked over Alexander's shoulder, catching glimpses of Jon as they circled around and around. He was smiling at her, the same smile she'd seen on Alexander's face, and she realized even when Alexander was gone, she'd still have a part of him in her life—forever.

Jon swept her back into his arms just a moment later. "God, you're pretty," he said, and lowered his lips to hers as if they hadn't kissed or touched in ages. It was the sweetest, tenderest kiss she could ever remember.

It stopped all too suddenly when the sound of a million firing guns exploded. The chandelier crashed, and sent shattering glass spraying out in all directions. Jon dived over Elizabeth, pushing her to the floor and wrapping his arms about her to protect her body from splinters and shards.

"What's happening?" she screamed, as another blast exploded.

But she didn't hear another word.

Not from Jon.

Not from Alex.

And once again a house collapsed upon her.

Chapter 20

"Wake up, Jon—wake up," Alex yelled. "You've got to get out of here."

Jon heard Alexander's voice, but it sounded far away, or like something from a dream. Sharp pain ricocheted through his shoulders, his back, his head. So much pain he just wanted to keep his eyes closed and go back to sleep until it ended.

"The place is on fire, Jon. Please—get up."

Jon felt someone tugging on his arm, but he pulled away. He just wanted to sleep and pretend the pain didn't exist.

"Hell and tarnation, boy! Think about Elizabeth. You've got to get her out of here."

Elizabeth? What about Elizabeth? Had he really heard her name? Was she in trouble?

He tried to move, but something heavy lay across his back. "I'll help you." Was that Alex talking again? "You've got to push, son. I can't budge it all by myself."

"Jon?" He heard the faint sound of Elizabeth's voice, so quiet, so very, very quiet.

"Jon? Please, help me."

He forced his eyes to open and saw ebony hair and porcelain skin.

And blood.

"Ellie!" he screamed.

"That's what I've been trying to tell you," Alex yelled again. "She's hurt. You've got to get her out of here."

Jon shoved his fists against the floor and pushed, hoping what little strength he had in his body would be enough to lift the oppressive weight bearing down on him.

"Keep pushing, Jon. Keep pushing."

Hell of a time for Alex to become a cheering squad, Jon thought, as another burst of energy rushed through him. He pushed against the floor again, straightening his arms with the strength of all his muscles, and the heavy weight shifted and fell away.

Lighter debris tumbled down around him, bits of plaster, shards of crystal, and he wrapped himself around Elizabeth once more to keep her safe.

"Jon?" Her voice sounded weak and it frightened him.

"I'm here, Ellie," he answered, praying at the same time that she'd be safe, that he could get her out of the hotel and somehow stop her bleeding. "I'm going to get you out of here."

"I think I'm okay," she said, amid raspy breaths. "Nothing hurts. I just couldn't breathe."

He moved away just enough to see her face illuminated by flashes of fire. "You're bleeding."

"But I feel fine," she whispered.

Jon sucked in a deep breath of relief. The smoke and fire burned his lungs, and suddenly he was more than aware of what was going on around them.

He pushed against the floor with all the strength of his shoulders, back, and legs, sending splintered wood and glass flying about him. "Let's get out of here, Ellie."

He managed to rise just to his knees, and through the smoke he saw timbers lying horizontally, vertically, diagonally. He heard beams squeak and moan as if they were just barely holding the top floors of the house in place.

Suddenly, flames leaped about the entry, blocking that exit.

They jumped closer.

Closer.

And it was too damn hot.

"Can you crawl, Ellie?"

Somehow she managed to laugh. "Really fast, I think—if you can just find a way out of here."

"I've already found a way," Alex called to them.

Jon could see Alexander's face filled with worry and fear and excitement. "Lead the way, Alex. We'll be right behind." Jon pulled Elizabeth against him. "I can't hold your hand, Ellie," he screamed over the roar of fire and the crash of wood and plaster. "You're just going to have to stay close and keep your eyes on me."

"There's too much debris. We're never going to get through."

"Like hell! We're not getting stuck in here. Just stay close and I'll clear a path." He took one more look into her amber eyes and smiled. "I love you, Ellie; I'm not about to let anything happen to you."

Flames sprang up on his left and he began to

crawl, shouldering through timber and plasterboard, clearing the way for Elizabeth, holding things steady for her when he thought for sure they might collapse.

"Where are we going?" Jon yelled to the figure floating easily up ahead.

"The kitchen door," Alex hollered. "There's no fire there."

"Thank God," Jon heard Elizabeth whisper.

"Thunder and tarnation!"

"What now?" Jon screamed.

"The fire's moving into the kitchen. You've got to move faster."

Jon prayed, and pushed, and then he heard Elizabeth muttering at the top of her lungs as if she was chewing someone out. "This isn't fair, you know. I got crushed under a house a year ago. It's not supposed to happen twice. I promised I'd change. I promised I'd be a better person, and I've tried, I've really, really tried."

"Who are you talking to?" Jon asked, as he burrowed through a space so narrow a rat would have had trouble squeezing through. He arched up so Elizabeth could get to the next reasonably clear spot and she answered back when she was directly beneath him.

"I'm talking to God, if you really want to know. Guess He enjoyed last year's conversation so much, He dreamed up a reason to have another. Remind me to say my prayers more often, okay?"

"Quit gabbing, you two," Alex thundered. "We've got a slight change of plans."

"What now?" Jon yelled.

"The kitchen walls and the door are on fire. We've got to get to the basement."

"We'll be trapped if we go down there," Jon yelled.

"Not if you take the tunnel to the bank. Might be the only good thing Luke Winchester ever did in his godforsaken life."

Jon managed to laugh as he pressed on through. He had no idea where they were or how much farther they had to go, but the smoke was entering his lungs. It was getting more and more difficult to breathe, but somehow he began to crawl faster.

He thought he heard voices outside, yelling, screaming, and he thought he felt drops of water raining down from above.

He heard Elizabeth's coughs right behind him. *Oh, Lord. Help me get her out,* he prayed silently. *Fast.*

Please.

He recognized the black-and-white linoleum tiles and knew they were in the kitchen. He crawled over a door that had fallen. It was the door to the basement. If he'd had time, he would have said a prayer of thanks, but flames spread across the floor, coming closer, closer, and he forgot everything but getting Elizabeth out.

He could feel the heat. He began to cough, and his lungs burned.

The timbers lying over the entrance to the basement had to be moved before they could go anywhere, and Elizabeth crawled up alongside him and began to push and shove.

They cleared the opening just as flames begin to lick at the heels of Jon's boots. "Hold my hand while you go down," he instructed Ellie. He crawled over the hole to get out of the fire's path, and as soon as she was out of harm's way, he followed her quickly down the steps.

Her fingers were icy cold in spite of the intense heat of the fire, and he wished he could drag them over his face to cool the burn, but there wasn't time.

There wasn't time for anything except to run when another explosion rocked the remains of the house.

Jon jumped into Alexander's grave and lifted Elizabeth down after him. He ripped the slats from the entrance to the tunnel and turned around. "Come on, Alex." He held out a hand to his great-grandfather as he started into the tunnel.

"I can't go."

"What the hell do you mean, you can't go? I'm not about to leave you behind."

"I'm dead. This stuff can't hurt me. Besides, you need all your strength to get out of here."

"The hotel's gone, Alex," Jon shouted. "There's no place left to haunt, and once these walls totally collapse, you just might disappear completely. Where will you be then? Heaven? Hell? Or stuck in limbo somewhere?"

"Doesn't matter. You're the only ones who matter to me now," Alex cried. "Please. Go."

Jon looked back at Elizabeth, and tears and dirt stained her face. "Start moving down that tunnel. Don't worry about spiders or webs or darkness or anything. Just get to the end of the tunnel and get out of here before the fire barrels in after us."

"What about you?"

"I'll be right behind you." He kissed her quickly and shoved her away, then he pulled himself out of Alexander's grave and stood before the man he refused to leave.

"I'm not going without you."

"Stubborn fool!"

"Damn right. Something I must have inherited from you. Now, step inside and let's get going before that fire gets down here."

"It's going to hurt."

"Burning alive doesn't sound like a great alternative."

"I wouldn't know. I never experienced it." Alexander laughed, and Jon frowned.

"Okay. Okay. But we can't go yet," Alex said.

"Why not?"

"Just give me one second, that's all I need."

Alex disappeared in a flash of light, and it seemed an eternity before he returned.

"Hold these, will you?" Alex asked, shoving a collection of stuff into Jon's arms.

Jon looked down at the ledger, the locket, the photos of Amanda and a piece of pink stationery.

"Edges are a bit singed in the ledger, but it's fine other than that. And I couldn't leave without the things I need the most."

"No, I guess you couldn't."

"So, are you ready?"

Jon nodded, and an instant later Alex merged into Jon's body. Jon felt the needles. He felt the weakness in his muscles. He felt the hot flow of blood surging through every vein.

And he heard Elizabeth scream.

Hell and tarnation, boy! Let's get out of here.

Jon shoved the ledger into the waistband of his jeans and the remainder of Alexander's belongings in his pocket. He jumped back into the grave, stumbled, then pushed his hands against the cold, dank earth, using the walls to support his body. He moved slowly, concentrating all his efforts on the end of the tunnel, and on finding Elizabeth.

He shoved the pain from his mind.

He thought about kisses.

He thought about soft thighs.

He thought about red hooker boots.

"Ouch! You stepped on my foot."

"Ellie?" Jon whispered, reaching out and touching her face in the dark.

"Who else did you expect down here?" she answered back with laughter in her voice.

"I told you to get out."

"And you said you'd follow, but you didn't."

"But you screamed," Jon yelled. "What happened?"

"I kicked something. Feels like a metal box."

"You had me scared half to death!"

Elizabeth laughed in spite of the mess they were in. "I didn't scream because I stubbed my toe. I just needed some way to make you hurry, and I figured that would work. Now, give me your hand and let's get out of here."

By the time they reached the end of the tunnel, he had wrapped his arm around Elizabeth for extra support, needing her strength in order to walk.

I told you I shouldn't go with you, Alex bellowed inside Jon's head.

"You're here and you're staying put," Jon bellowed back, right before he and Elizabeth hit the dead end.

"We can't go any further," she said.

"It's going to take a whole lot more than a dirt wall to keep us down here," Jon roared, and pounded his fists in front of him, against the dirt at his sides. Somehow, he seemed to forget all the pain, all the weakness.

All he could think of was Elizabeth and getting her out of this makeshift grave.

Hit the wall above you.

Thank God Alex was with him. Thank God Alex was thinking clearly when his own head felt like it was being crushed in a vise.

He raised his hands above him until his fingers felt something solid and hard, something that felt exactly like wood.

He stretched upward and pushed. Nothing. He pushed again, but it was too high and he couldn't get any leverage.

He grabbed Elizabeth around the waist. "What are you doing?" she asked.

"I'm going to lift you up, and you're going to get that opening cleared."

"You can't lift me, Jon. You don't have the strength."

"The hell I can't!" He took a deep breath, then one more, and attempted to lift, but he couldn't get her high enough. Instead, he knelt down. "Don't argue, just get on my shoulders."

There was so much pain shooting through his body he couldn't even feel the extra weight on his shoulders. Somehow he stood, straightening his legs. "Are you close enough, Ellie? Can you push on the door?"

"I'm pushing. I'm pushing," she called down to him, and there was no doubt in his mind that she was using all her strength. He could feel the muscles of her legs tightening around his neck and shoulders with each push.

"It's open!" she screamed.

When Jon felt her weight lift from his shoulders, he knew she'd gotten out of the tunnel and he stretched up, wrapped his fingers around the edge of the hole, and slowly pulled himself to freedom.

There was no light in the basement, but they could feel heavy crates stacked everywhere. They pushed and climbed and stumbled, somehow making it to the other end, where they found and climbed a flight of stairs.

The door at the top was locked, but it didn't put a damper in their escape efforts. Jon just shoved his shoulder through, splintering the wood down the center. He slammed into the door again and busted a hole big enough to climb through.

The metal front door leading to the outside was another story. It was locked, and it was solid.

Jon heard the crash and jerked around, fear screaming through his body that another explosion had occurred, one that might hurt Elizabeth.

But she was fine, she was safe, and she stood before a shattered window, the metal box raised in her hands and a grin on her face. "You're the mayor," she said, shrugging. "They might not understand if you were the one who broke it."

He kissed her then. He kissed her with pain and fever and passion. She tasted like dirt and smoke and ashes, and he figured it was a taste he'd love for the rest of his life.

You two ever going to get out of here?

Jon kicked the remnants of glass out of the window with his boot and stepped out onto the street. He reached back for Elizabeth, pulling her to safety and into his embrace.

Suddenly he pushed her to arm's length. "You've got blood all over you." He ran his fingers through her hair, over her scalp. "Did you hit your head?"

"I'm fine, Jon." She touched cool fingers to his brow. "But you've got a huge gash on your forehead. It's your blood, Jon—not mine."

"Ah, hell, a little blood never hurt anyone," he said, pulling her back into his arms when she began to shiver.

"If I'd known we were going to end up out in the cold, I would have worn something warmer to our party," she said, somehow managing to laugh.

He tilted her chin and looked into her eyes. "God, you're beautiful."

A tear rolled down her face, and she rested her head against his chest and began to cry.

Jon wrapped one hand around her back and smoothed her hair with the other. He looked down the street to the area where friends and neighbors were standing, hosing down what remained of the old hotel. Flames leapt high through the wooden structure, lighting the faces of Harry and Andy, who stood with Libby and Jack, their heads hanging in sorrow.

"Come on. I think we need to calm the fears of a few people," Jon said, allowing his arm to drape over her shoulder for support as they walked toward the crowd. Now that they were safe, now that the adrenaline had quit pumping through his veins, the pain and weakness returned.

Harry looked up first, and a slow grin spread across his soot-blackened face. He nudged Andy, then ran toward Elizabeth and Jon. "You don't look too good," Harry blubbered, trying to squeeze a little laughter into his words.

"We look alive, don't we?" Jon asked.

"Yeah," Harry said, sliding another arm around Jon for support.

Jon pulled Elizabeth closer. "We're all alive—somewhat," he added, winking at her. "That's all that matters at the moment."

Andy and Jack threw blankets around Elizabeth and Jon's shoulders, and Libby gave them cups of fresh strong coffee.

"Let's get you two into the cafe," Harry said, trying to steer Jon across the street.

Jon pulled away, took a sip of coffee, and felt a little more strength building inside. He had no intention of going anywhere. He sensed Matt was outside somewhere, and he planned to confront him.

"Where's Matt?" he asked, somehow sensing his former cousin was responsible for the explosion.

"Mourning," Andy stated, then laughed. "His own demise, that is." He pointed to a spot past the burning hotel where the old Sapphire fire engine and half a dozen trucks were parked. "Would you believe that lady he was with at Elizabeth's welcome party is an undercover warden? Hell of a shock to me. Even more of a shock to Harry. Anyway, she saw Matt running away from the hotel when the place blew up. She has him handcuffed to the steering wheel of her pickup. I get the feeling she doesn't care too much for your cousin."

"He's not my cousin," Jon stated, realizing how good the words sounded.

"What do you mean, he's not your cousin?" Libby asked.

Jon just smiled. "I'll explain later." He wove his fingers through Elizabeth's and they walked together down the road. He had more strength now. He didn't know why, he just did. Maybe anger had washed away the pain.

He was just a few yards from the truck when he saw Matt's white-toothed smile. "Well, I see you made it out of there."

Jon raised a fist, but Elizabeth grabbed hold of his arm and held him back.

Slowly, Jon lowered his hand and pulled the ledger from under his belt. "Is this what you were trying to destroy?" Jon asked.

Matt only laughed.

"How did you know?" Elizabeth asked. "We left everything just as we found it."

"The moose head tilts to the right. Tonight it tilted to the left." Matt chuckled. "Next time you break into someone's place, you've got to be more careful."

"Is he giving you trouble?"

Elizabeth turned at the sound. Blue-eyed, flame-haired, much-too-beautiful-to-be-real Francesca walked up to them. Her hair was pulled back into a ponytail and she was wearing camouflage, yet she looked like she'd just stepped off the cover of

Vogue. Heavens! She was absolutely beautiful, even dressed like a man, but Elizabeth couldn't work up the energy to despise her any longer.

"Sorry I didn't get here sooner," Francesca said. "I had to find another vehicle when Matt took off with the truck we went out in. I thought he might be up to something and I couldn't risk letting him get away. Had to leave my partner behind to deal with all the others, which I don't usually like doing."

"Partner?" Jon asked.

Francesca smiled. "It's not something I announce to the world. It's usually a way of throwing the people we're after off track. It worked like a charm this time around, especially with Matt. It appears he's going to have a few attempted murder charges to fight in addition to arson, not to mention poaching. And we got three of his friends at the same time. One's a senator."

Elizabeth clutched Jon's arm. "My brother was out there, too," she said to Francesca. "He probably doesn't deserve any special favors, but . . ."

"What kind of favors were you hoping for?"

Elizabeth and Jon jerked around at the sound of Eric's voice. He had a blue bruise on his jaw and a grin on his face.

"I'd like you to meet my partner," Francesca said, as Eric stopped at her side.

"Partner?" Jon could feel the rage welling up inside Elizabeth. He felt her muscles tense. "You could have told me," she hollered. "I've been worried sick that you were going to get arrested and thrown in jail for the rest of your miserable life."

Eric laughed. "Sorry, Elizabeth. It was all part of the plan."

"Was making Jon suspect me part of the plan, too?"

Eric looked at Francesca and shrugged.

"That was my idea, Elizabeth," Francesca said. "We couldn't let Matt suspect anything."

"What about hitting me in the cafe?" Jon asked, looking directly at Eric.

"All part of the plan." Eric laughed as he slapped Jon on the back. "No hard feelings, I hope?"

Jon shook his head and grinned as he watched Eric massage his jaw. "Maybe you'll think twice before you pick on someone bigger than you."

"I rarely run into anyone bigger than me. You were a definite surprise. So, how's your chin?"

Jon rubbed a thumb over the spot where Eric's fist had connected with his face. "Can't feel a thing. What about your knuckles?"

"Never slammed them into steel before, but that swing sure made Matt a believer in my sincerity."

"Then I guess it was all worth it," Jon said, glancing at Matt, who was still handcuffed to the truck. He slowly pulled the ledger out from under his belt and handed it over to Eric. "You might be able to forgo some of your undercover operations once you take a look at the information in here."

Eric flipped open the ledger and ran a finger down one column and smiled. "Looks like entertaining reading." A moment later, Eric and Francesca were thumbing through the pages, completing forgetting Jon and Elizabeth existed.

Jon drew Elizabeth close, and for the first time

since they'd walked out of the bank, looked at the gray steel container she clutched in her fingers. "Is that what you stubbed your toe on?"

Her anger from a few moments before seemed to subside. "Yes, and it's getting heavy," she said.

Jon took it out of her hands, shoved his thumb under the latch until it loosened, and popped open the lid. "Interesting." He smiled down at Elizabeth. "Seems we have some property deeds here from the late 1800s."

Thunder and tarnation! I might get a little more revenge before I'm through!

Jon laughed at Alex's words, then turned to Matt, who'd been uncommonly quiet during the exchange of the past few minutes. "Let's see now," he said. "You're going to prison for poaching, arson, attempted murder, and God knows what else. That should put you out of commission for a few years. And when you come back, you're going to find out you have nothing much to come back to." Jon patted the box. "Inside here is all I need to make you leave Sapphire permanently."

"What are you talking about?" Matt hissed. For once his cocky smile was wiped from his face.

"I don't want to spoil your surprise by telling you too soon. I'll have my lawyer talk to yours. Until then . . ."

Jon looked at Elizabeth. "I know you don't like this vengeful streak running through me, and I know you don't like me using my fists, but I swear I'll give up fighting for good if you'll just give me one more opportunity."

She shook her head and folded her arms across her chest. "I'm not crazy about the idea, but do what you feel is right." In spite of what he knew she was thinking, she flashed him the prettiest smile he'd seen in his entire life.

He raised a fist and drove it toward Matt's face. Suddenly he stopped just half an inch from Matt's nose and shook his head. "You know what, Matt? You're not good enough to have your face reshaped by my hands."

Hell! You could at least kick dirt on him, or something, Alex mumbled. *But I suppose I would have done the same thing, too, even if he is a lily-livered buzzard.*

"Picture him behind bars for most of his life," Jon suggested to Alex, as he turned away from Matt. "It's not nearly what he deserves, but I'm afraid that's about the best our justice system will dish out."

Jon wrapped his arm once more around Elizabeth's waist. "I'm proud of you," she said, kissing him softly.

"I would have hit him if he hadn't been handcuffed, but that would have put me at his level. I don't plan on ever stooping that low."

He hitched Elizabeth a little closer to his chest. "Ready to go home, Ellie?"

"Home?" she asked. He watched her turn toward the burning embers of the old hotel. "For the second time in a year, I don't have a home to go to."

"You couldn't be more wrong, Ellie," Jon said, leaning over and kissing her tenderly. "You have a home. With me."

Chapter 21

"What do we do now?" Jon asked. He sat in a chair in Amanda's bedroom, elbows balanced on his knees, and twiddled his thumbs.

"I haven't a clue," Elizabeth answered. She prowled around the room, the same thing she'd done for the past hour, hoping, she'd told him, that some clue might magically pop out of the woodwork. "Alexander's gotten his revenge, and we can prove his innocence. You'll recover all the property. It seems something should just happen."

Jon stopped twiddling and rested his head in his hands.

"Are you in pain again?" Elizabeth asked.

"Just tired," he answered, afraid to tell her his true thoughts and concerns. The pain had dissipated somewhat, but he seemed to have less control over his thoughts. His imagination was conjuring all sorts of things foreign to him, like the streets of Sapphire teeming with horses and buggies, men carrying pistols and women in long dresses. He remembered the taste of sarsaparilla, the scent of bay rum, and the lemon verbena that Mrs. Lee at the drygoods store used to wear. One vision almost filled his mind entirely—a pretty woman with golden curls and a pink-and-white–striped parasol just stepping off a train.

Jon put his head in his hands as too many visions that weren't his own flitted through his mind. Visions that frightened and worried him.

Rising from the chair, he strolled across the room and wrapped his arms around Elizabeth, pulling her close, wanting to remember her softness, her scent. He lowered his mouth and covered hers, needing to know her taste, the touch of her lips, the feel of his heart when it beat out of control, and the erotic emotions that coursed through him when her breasts pressed against his chest.

He needed his own memories, not Alexander's.

He thought of the love he had for Elizabeth, the hunger to be near her forever and ever. Suddenly that passion that overwhelmed him when he thought of Elizabeth and held her in his arms pushed aside all those other remembrances, things only Alex should know.

He eased away from Elizabeth, looking into her amber eyes. "I love you," he whispered, and the pain began to flow back again. He struggled to breathe and Elizabeth looked frightened. Tears fell from her eyes.

"What's happening?" she cried.

"He's not doing it on purpose," Jon said, finding it difficult to speak, "but I think Alex is taking over my mind and body. All my thoughts are jumbled. One moment I'm thinking of you; the next, all I can think of is Amanda."

Jon tore his fingers from Elizabeth's arms and pressed his palms to his temple, trying to still the ache bouncing around in his head. Somehow he had to stop the torture. He had to get Alex out. Now.

If only Amanda were here, he thought. If only . . .

He stumbled toward the vanity. "I think I know how to help Alex," he said. "My grandfather told me he'd talked to Amanda. Maybe she's here somewhere."

Like a madman, he sorted through the photos of Amanda, the locket, her ribbons, her letter. He touched everything Alex had taken from the hotel, and then he began to talk to Alex, who'd been quiet far too long.

"She was awfully pretty, wasn't she?" Jon asked, touching one of the photos.

Prettiest thing I ever saw.

Alex had to remember more. He had to want to leave. He had to call out for Amanda.

Jon lifted the locket and popped open the front. "Remember the night you gave her this?" he asked, looking at the inscription and the photo inside.

It was the last time I kissed her. I've always remembered that moment.

"One hundred years is a long time to remember a kiss," Jon said.

I would never forget anything that reminded me of Amanda.

"Do you think she remembered it, too?"

A lilting feminine voice filled the room. *I remembered.*

Did you hear that? It's Amanda.

"I heard her, Alex."

Elizabeth slipped her hand into Jon's. Her fingers felt cold against the burning heat of his skin. The pain soared, taking away all his strength and energy.

"Talk to her, Alex," Jon said.

I can't. She won't hear me.

"Then tell me, and I'll repeat the words."

Jon waited, and he smiled when Alex finally spoke. "Don't worry, Alex. I won't get the words wrong."

He waited again and slowly he recited the words. "This would have been my wedding vow to you, Amanda, had I been at your side." Jon took a deep breath and clutched at Elizabeth's arm. Slowly he began again when Alex continued. "It comes a hundred years too late, but I still mean every word." Jon swallowed and listened. "Amanda," he repeated after Alex, "you are my life, my soul. Wherever you go, I will go with you. To be at your side forever is all that I ask, in this life and in the next." Jon closed his eyes. He could feel Alexander's tears, his mixture of happiness and loss. "I'll love you, my darling, forever."

The curtains fluttered. A light, cool breeze wafted through the room. It touched Jon's face in a soft caress, then backed away, whirling gently about. It took on color and form, a mouth, a nose, blue eyes, and blond ringlets. Like an angel she appeared in a flowing white gown with a halo of pink rosebuds and ribbons about her crown.

She smiled at Elizabeth and at Jon, then reached out a dainty hand. "Come to me, Alexander. I've waited so long for you to return."

Alex swooped out of Jon's body and sent him reeling backward against the wall. Elizabeth rushed to Jon's side and knelt down, and together they watched the reunion.

Alex caressed Amanda's cheek and tenderly tilted her face toward him. And he kissed her with one hundred years of longing, and with a vow never to leave again.

Amanda led him toward the window, but he stopped, pulling back, and Jon feared Alex might be changing his mind. But he looked at Amanda and smiled. "Just a few last things to take care of, and then I'm yours forever."

He floated toward Elizabeth and cupped her cheek. "Thank you for everything. The hugs, the love, the dance." Elizabeth had tears streaming down her face and Alex brushed one away. "Don't cry for me now."

"I'm not. I'm crying for me, because I don't want to lose you."

He put his hand over her heart. "I'll always be here."

And he turned to Jon, cupping his cheek. "They don't make Winchesters any finer than you," he said.

"Who's a Winchester? My name's Stewart now." Jon felt tears welling up in his eyes and his throat tightened, a lump the size of Montana stuck inside. "I've got a few headstones to have recarved, and I thought you might not mind if we buried you with Amanda." Jon forced a smile. "She's in between Jedediah and Thomas. Seems like a good place for you to be, too."

Alex nodded. "You're the best great-grandson a man could ever wish for and . . . I love you."

Alex drifted away, wiping tears from his eyes.

He slipped his hand into Amanda's. "I'm ready now."

The curtains fluttered again and the window opened gently, letting in a few errant flakes of snow.

"Wait!" Alex cried out. "Thunder and tarnation, I forgot one more thing."

Amanda smiled indulgently, as if she'd put up with Alexander's antics before—and loved him just the same.

Alex pulled the wedding ring from his little finger and slipped it onto Amanda's hand. "I've been waiting to do that for one hundred years. I love you, Amanda. I really do."

"I love you, too, Alexander. I've never stopped loving you."

Chapter 22

Nothing remained of the Sapphire Hotel but a marble mantel and charred timbers, twisted pipes, and crumbling brick chimneys. Here and there Jon and Elizabeth found bits and pieces of Tiffany lamps and shattered chandeliers, and all of it was coated with a sprinkling of powdery-white snow.

Elizabeth considered taking pictures for posterity, but it wasn't a sight she wanted to remember. She had recollections of good times inside with Jon and Alex—and not even Pulitzer Prize–winning photos could compare with her memories.

When the ashes cooled, Jon led the sheriff and coroner to Alexander's makeshift grave. Jon had slowly uncovered the skeleton, surprised to see the golden wedding band gone from Alex's little finger. He'd thought at first it might have been stolen, and then he realized Alex had put that ring on Amanda's finger right before they'd floated off to heaven—and it was probably on her finger now.

It seemed a crazy notion, but crazier things had occurred in Jon's lifetime.

The only thing that really made sense out of all

that had happened was falling in love with Elizabeth.

A week after Alexander's funeral—which most everyone in town attended so they could hear the real story of Alex's life and death—Jon watched Elizabeth cry as a bulldozer cleared away the hotel's remains, and not long after, he watched her smile when dark green sod was laid over the leveled ground.

The people of Sapphire banded together the first days of spring and built a large white gazebo where the kitchen had been, and the pink and white marble mantel salvaged from the parlor became part of the foundation for the monument Jon would soon be carving. Alex had lived in the hotel for over one hundred years, and Jon and Elizabeth had every intention of his memory living there for one or two hundred years more.

They designed a statue of Alex that Jon would cast in bronze, but when he finished the sketch, they knew something was missing. It didn't take long before Amanda was added to the drawing, standing face to face, hand in hand with Alex, just as they'd have stood together on their wedding day.

It was the perfect addition to the park where a hotel had once stood.

On the last day of April, with the sun shining brightly and puffy white clouds painting the sky, Libby collected bets as nearly a hundred and one citizens of Sapphire filled the rented chairs lined up in rows before the gazebo draped in red and white ribbons and lace. She'd wagered with everyone that Jon and Elizabeth would be married in

April—and Libby prided herself on always being right.

Jon stood at the edge of the gazebo's steps, decked out in a specially tailored black tux, with Harry at his side, and when the twelve-piece orchestra Elizabeth had hired from Helena played the Wedding March, all eyes turned to see the bride on the arm of her brother, walking up the red-carpeted path through the newly dedicated Alexander and Amanda Stewart Memorial Garden.

Jon's sapphire eyes glistened as he watched his bride glide toward him. God, she was the most beautiful creature he'd ever seen, and he loved her more and more with each passing day.

Elizabeth's amber eyes sparkled as she looked at Jon, big and powerful and full of passion. Her life had seemed so empty until he'd stepped into it and she knew that nothing, not even the collapse of another home, would ever, ever keep them apart.

He took her hand and they gazed into each other's eyes while repeating their vows. He slipped a ring on her finger. She slipped one on his. They smiled as he cupped her face in his big hands and she threaded her fingers through his hair. Slowly, ever so slowly, Jon lowered his head and tenderly kissed his wife, but it wasn't nearly enough.

He slid his hands from her face to her waist, lifted her from the ground and into his arms, and kissed her with a passion that had been building from the moment he'd seen her set foot on the icy streets of Sapphire.

"I love you, Mrs. Stewart," he whispered.

"I love you, too, Mr. Stewart," she answered.

They spent the next few hours slicing cake, posing for pictures, and dancing with one and all, and when the festivities were winding down, Jon took his bride's hand and stole her away from the crowd.

Together they walked to the end of town and up the steps to Dalton House. Jon lifted his bride, carrying her over the threshold, up the winding staircase, past Amanda's favorite chandelier and the stained glass windows imported from England.

"I really am capable of walking," Elizabeth said, as she planted kisses on her husband's neck.

"Humor me, okay? It's my wedding day, and I want everything to be perfect."

"It *is* perfect."

He slowed as he reached the arched doorway leading to his turret. "It's going to be even more perfect when I show you what's upstairs."

Elizabeth smiled. "What is it?"

"A surprise." He lifted her a little higher, a little closer in his arms, pushed through the doorway, and bounded up the stairs.

Setting her down in the middle of his studio, Jon leaned against his worktable and pointed a finger to a bright red box on the gold satin chaise. "That's my wedding present to you."

"But you've already gotten me a present," she said, moving toward him, weaving her fingers through his hair and kissing his cheek. "You're taking me to Europe, remember? And you're going to buy crystal chandeliers for all those bedrooms upstairs—the ones we talked about filling with kids. You haven't forgotten, have you?"

"I haven't forgotten a thing. But this is something special—something, well, a little more intimate than crystal chandeliers."

Elizabeth grinned and slowly traced a finger across his lips. "But I haven't gotten you a gift."

"That present's for me, too. It's something I've wanted for a good long time now."

"I suppose you'd like me to open it then?"

He didn't say a word; he only nodded.

Still in her wedding gown, Elizabeth looked like an angel floating across his turret floor. But she wasn't an angel; he'd known that from the beginning, and that was why he liked her so very, very much.

He watched her slide the gold ribbon and bow from the box and lift the lid. She drew tissue paper away from the middle, studied the contents, then looked up and smiled. "Would you like me to try my present on now, or later?"

"Now."

She crooked her index finger and beckoned him toward her. "Mind helping me change?"

Shaking his head, Jon walked toward his wife, and when she turned her back to him, he carefully, with somewhat shaky fingers, made a slow descent down the length of her dress, unhooking what seemed like a hundred minuscule pearl buttons.

Elizabeth held her hair over her head and he kissed a trail along the curve of her spine while his fingers slipped the gown over her shoulders and down her arms. He turned her around, fighting for breath as he admired the radiance of her porcelain skin lit by the late afternoon sun. "God, you're beautiful, Ellie."

He kissed her forehead, her eyes, her temples,

and her lips, tasting her sweetness as he loosened the clasp of her bra and let it fall away. He captured her breasts in his hands, kneading their softness, tasting their warmth as he moved lower and lower.

He heard her gentle sighs, the deepness of her breathing as his fingers smoothed across her stomach and over her hips.

Lifting her, he laid her on the chaise, beginning another slow trail of kisses over her feverish flesh until he reached her thigh high stockings. Slipping a finger under the top, he slowly slid one stocking and shoe from her longer than long leg and did the same with the other. There was only one barrier left, and he capturing the elastic of her white satin tap pants and drew them over her hips and thighs and knees and tossed them somewhere behind him. He stood above her, swallowing hard, trying to keep a grip on his body until she was wearing her present, until he'd gotten his gift in return.

"Could we just dispense with the present for now?" she asked, holding her hands out, begging him to join her on the chaise.

He shook his head, giving serious thought to abandoning his plan, but he'd thought about this moment far too long to stop now.

Taking her fingers, he helped her sit on the edge of the chaise. He knelt before her, pulling half the gift from the box. She was smiling when he slipped the first red hooker boot over her foot and helped her pull it to her knee. She was breathing nearly as hard as him by the time the second was securely in place.

And then he pulled a long length of sheer white

silk from the box. "I admired your boots the first time I saw them and thought I'd die when they went up in flames. I managed to find another perfect pair and I've been itching to sketch you in them for months," he said. "Indulge me? Just tonight?"

She smiled slowly and stretched out on the chaise as any good Reubens model would have done. She pulled the silk from Jon's fingers and draped it over her hip. "Will this do?" she asked seductively.

Jon took a deep breath. "Perfect."

Somehow, he managed to pick up a sketch pad and charcoal. Somehow, he managed to sit on his stool and find an empty page. Somehow, he managed to draw the outline of her body as she smiled and played with the silk at her hip.

"Ah, hell!" He threw the pad and charcoal in the air and stalked to the chaise. "What do I need a drawing for? I've got the real thing—right here, right now. And if you don't mind, I think I'd like to have you till the end of time."

Elizabeth drew the silk from her body and draped it around Jon's neck, pulling him close, so very, very close. "Suit yourself, my love. Suit yourself."